THE DOMINO MAN

Find out more about THE DOMINO MAN, and discover more of Stanley Salmons' sci-fi conspiracy novels—plus find an interactive quiz, author interview and message forum—at this Virtual Reality author room:
Inkflash.com/StanleySalmons

Stanley Salmons was born in Clapton, East London. He is internationally known for his work in the fields of biomedical engineering and muscle physiology, published in over two hundred papers and nine books. Although still actively contributing to the real world of research, he maintains a parallel existence as a fiction writer, in which he can draw from his broad scientific experience. He has written over forty short stories, which have appeared in anthologies and been serialised in magazines. This is his fourth novel.

stanleysalmons.com
inkflash.com/StanleySalmons

Also by Stanley Salmons:
THE MAN IN TWO BODIES
ALEXEI'S TREE AND OTHER STORIES
A BIT OF IRISH MIST
FOOTPRINTS IN THE ASH
NH_3

THE DOMINO MAN

Stanley Salmons

FINGERPRESS LTD
LONDON

The Domino Man

Copyright © Stanley Salmons, 2015
All rights reserved. Please respect the copyright of this work.

ISBN (pbk): 978-1-908824-64-6

Published by Fingerpress Ltd

Production Editor: Matt Stephens
Production Manager: Michelle Stephens
Copy Editor: Madeleine Horobin
Cover Designer: Jessica Bell

This novel is a work of fiction. Any resemblance to actual persons, living or dead, events or localities, is entirely coincidental.

```
www.fingerpress.co.uk
inkflash.com/Fingerpress
```

It is my great good fortune to have the love and encouragement of my wife Paula, and children Graham, Daniel, and Debby. Their critical feedback on earlier versions of the manuscript has been invaluable. My friends in the Liverpool-based writers' group Wordsmiths (formerly Rose Lane Writers) listened patiently and attentively to successive chapters and I am especially grateful to John Sayle, Neville Krasner, and Paul Dearden for their perceptive comments and suggestions.

THE DOMINO MAN

Glossary

Camo	Camouflage
Dead ground	Area, usually a depression, sheltered from gunfire
Enfilade	Gunfire directed along a line from end to end
Flashbang	Noise Flash Diversionary Device (NFDD) or "stun grenade"
IED	Improvised explosive device
Incoming	Incoming fire
Infil/exfil	Infiltration/exfiltration
LZ	Landing zone
OR	Other ranks
RPG	Rocket propelled grenade
SAF	Special Assignment Force (fictional Special Operations Force of the U.S. Army)
SAS	Special Air Service (Special Forces unit of the British army)
SEALS	United States Navy Sea, Air and Land Forces (Special Operations Force of the U.S. Navy)
tab	(Tactical Advance to Battle) March or jog with heavy equipment over difficult terrain
U.S.S.S.	United States Secret Service(man)

PART ONE

1

I stood at the window, gazing into the darkness, waiting for dawn. There was a crawling sensation in my stomach, a feeling I always got at times like this, a combination of excitement and apprehension. I'd been involved in hostage extractions before; we all had. We'd go in at night, a full platoon, well camo'd, a plan of the target area displayed on head-ups in the visors. We'd work quietly. If we encountered trouble we were equipped for it: multirifles fitted with ballistic and stun barrels, night sights, grenade launchers, flashbangs. Not this time. This mission was different. This one was off the scale.

I glanced behind me. A shaft of yellow light slanted from the slightly open door to the room where the aircrew were making their final preparations, or sleeping, I wasn't sure which. Gerry and Sef were sitting on a bench, Gerry supporting the camera on its tripod, Sef with his sound recording equipment next to him. They were wide awake. No one said anything.

I turned back to the window. There'd been a subtle change. Shapes were beginning to emerge from the blackness. Our transport materialized in shades of grey, looking far too large on that small airfield. The sun rose further, and the Roto-Fan's newly painted fuselage glowed first peach, then pink, then—within minutes—brilliant white. The words "CBC Outside Broadcast Unit" stood out in large black letters, hard as the long shadow that it cast across the apron. The hemmed-in feeling that came with darkness had gone; the landscape extended in every direction.

I heard movement and turned as the three aircrew emerged from their room. The pilot came over.

"Captain Forbes? We're all set."

I nodded. Sef and Gerry were already on their feet. We followed the crew out and climbed on board. The twin seats were arranged in well-spaced rows facing forward, civilian style. I chose a window where I could see the port engine pod without it obscuring my view. Sef and Gerry each took a window on the other side of the aisle. The crew chief handed me a lightweight wireless headset. He ignored the others.

One engine started, then the other, running up into a double whine and sending a wave of red dust to the limits of the airfield. The craft lifted, I saw the pod turning, and we began to accelerate. Ten minutes later we were cruising low over the sun-baked plateau that marks the western border of Chingala. We left it behind us and crossed into Ubindi. The terrain below was sparsely covered with dry grass, scrub, and a very few spindly trees. This was a dry and desolate landscape, devoid of habitation, devoid of wildlife. No villagers paused to look up at us; no herds of game stiffened then scattered with the rapidly approaching sound.

I looked to my right. Gerry was flicking the pages of an in-flight magazine he must have found in a seat pocket. Sef had dozed off. Looking at those two gave me a warm sense of fellowship. I'd chosen a good team—but then, I'd had plenty of choice. The SAF was so oversubscribed it could afford to be selective about who it signed up. One way and another we'd all earned our place.

Gerry Lucknow was from a farming family somewhere out in the mid-West. He came to the Force with an outstanding record in the regular U.S. Army. He had the sort of big, open countenance that invites friendship and we'd hit it off from the moment I joined the unit. Gerry was a big guy, six foot four and built to match. I once saw a squad loading up a transport, two to each crate of ammo, and then Gerry came out on his own, handling one like it was a box of cereal. He was pretty quiet for a man so obviously capable of creating mayhem, but if things did go pear-shaped there wasn't anyone I'd sooner have at my back.

Sefu Mwangi was from East Africa, and his face looked like it had been chiselled out of anthracite. Sef was picked from hundreds of foreign applicants. He was fluent in several Bantu languages, on top of which he was an engineering graduate and a first-class soldier. He might not have Gerry's strength but his endurance was unbelievable. After two goes at the assault course and a tab in between, the rest of us could hardly stand up. Sef would look like he could do it all over again. I was glad to have him with me on this trip; his language ability could be a big plus in this part of Africa.

Like Sef, I was one of the few non-U.S. nationals who'd made it into the Force. For me, it was a lucky break. Just a year ago I was with the 22 SAS. Then my Colonel assigned me to a joint op with the SAF. It was tough, very tough. I must have done okay because they asked me if I'd like to transfer permanently, at the rank of Captain.

I returned my gaze to the window. When the time came, Sef and Gerry would do what was necessary; meanwhile they'd switched off. That's what I ought to do, but I couldn't.

There's just one way to stay alive on a mission like this: you do your homework. You study every scrap of intelligence you can get. You memorize the layout, you learn about the opposition. You agree your primary strategy, discuss every possible scenario, and decide on alternative courses of action: if this, then that, if that, then this. Some of the time, maybe even most of the time, you'll get it right. Once in a while your luck runs out and something totally unexpected crops up. It can happen in an instant and get you killed, so you do your level best to see it doesn't.

That's what I didn't like about this operation. Here we were, going out to the camp of a secretive, highly mobile, rebel army. Until a few days ago we didn't even know their location. We still knew nothing of the layout and all we knew about the people was what they were capable of, and that was far from pleasant. We'd never met their leader—the man we were supposed to take out—but we'd seen some footage of him and a still of the hostage who needed to be rescued, and that was about it. It would be up to us, and me in particular, to respond to events as they unfolded.

There was an hour and twenty minutes ahead of us before we touched down. I decided to spend the time going over everything I knew—yet again.

Where to start?

The briefing?

2

"You sent for me, Colonel?"

"Come in Jim, have a seat."

He was my CO, so he could have called me Forbes or Captain Forbes but he called me Jim. There was nothing friendly about it. It was probably in a manual somewhere.

I sat down and watched him as his fingers moved and tapped the touch-screen that covered ninety percent of his desktop. Colonel Harken was in his forties, lean and fit. So far as I knew he never went out on missions; his battleground was Washington. He was probably the least popular person on the base, except perhaps for the Drill Sergeant, Bill Wicks; he didn't have many friends, either.

Harken gave the screen a final tap, switched it off, and looked up. His grey eyes were keen and penetrating, accentuated somehow by the short military stubble of his haircut.

"How many operations have you been on in the last year, Jim?"

"Three."

"All highly successful. No one else in the world could have brought those off—right? Even your old outfit."

I bristled a bit. I still felt a certain loyalty to The Regiment.

"Those guys are pretty good, Colonel."

"Oh, they're good, but they're chronically under-resourced. You heard about the latest round of defence budget cuts over there, I suppose?"

"Nothing new about that. It was one of the reasons I stayed on with the SAF. I was never too thrilled about going into battle with a wooden rifle."

"No regrets, Jim? About joining us?"

"It has its moments."

His lips quirked, very briefly.

"On the other hand, three assignments in one year—it's not exactly a heavy workload, is it?"

What's he driving at?

"We have to be operationally ready at all times, sir. That involves a lot of training and exercises. You know that more than anyone."

He leaned forward. "Yes, I do, Jim, but there are people out there who don't." He placed a hand flat on the desk screen. "What the bean counters in Washington see is a group of people who cost a lot to train, cost a lot to keep and equip, and don't do a hell of a lot for it."

I felt a slight flush of anger. None of us is idle and I resented the dig. My voice was dead level.

"We try to give good value, Colonel."

He looked at me sharply, trying to see whether the sarcasm was intentional, then evidently chose to ignore it.

"One of the problems," he continued, "is that nearly all these assignments are covert. By their very nature we can't crow about them. That's why, once in a while, it's good for us to take on something with a higher profile, something politically important, something," he stabbed a finger on the blank screen, "we can point to."

Here it comes.

"Jebediah Ngozi. Heard of him?"

"No, I don't think so."

"He's President of the People's Republic of Ubindi."

Ubindi, Ubindi… It was around the time I went to university—so that would make it 2035 or thereabouts. The UN had finally intervened in the big central African conflict and the settlement after the ceasefire involved some redrawing of borders. That created new states. Ubindi was one of them.

"Ngozi has a daughter, Suzanne." He opened a desk drawer, withdrew a print-out, and passed it across the desk.

I picked it up. I saw a woman in her mid- to late twenties. It was a handsome face. Skin the colour of dark honey shone on the high cheekbones, and the almond-shaped eyes seemed unusually pale. Her straight, dark hair hung to her shoulders. I assumed Ngozi was African; this face made me wonder who the mother was.

Harken pointed. "This young lady was snatched by rebel forces during a trip to the north of the country. The rebel leader's a man who calls himself General Ben Obadiah. Word is, he's keeping her as his personal sex slave."

"So Ngozi wants her back."

"Yes. He's a family man. He loves his daughter. It's driving him mad."

I held out the picture but he waved it away. "You can hang onto that."

I folded it and put it into a shirt pocket. "Why should we get involved?"

"Ngozi is a friend of the West and he's a vigorous opponent of the spread of Islamist fundamentalism in Africa. The U.S. government wants to help out. Problem is, it's still a sensitive region; no outsiders can have a military presence there, least of all a superpower. I've been asked if the SAF could do something quietly. I said yes. It's a good chance for us to demonstrate our usefulness to people in the right quarters."

"Okay," I said. "What's the strength of the opposition?"

"Obadiah calls it a liberation army. In reality it's an ill-disciplined, ragtag militia. They terrorise the local inhabitants into giving up food, possessions, even their children, to the cause. He coordinates the whole thing but he's smart enough not to keep all his followers in one place. We think the group with him numbers about a hundred."

"And we know where to find them?"

"You'll have to establish that when you're out there, but we have a contact."

"All right. What size force are we taking?"

Harken smiled thinly.

"I said *quietly*, Jim—we're not sending in an army. Choose two men. I'll brief the three of you tomorrow at 0800."

"Three?"

"Yes, you're going in as journalists."

*

As I walked back to my quarters my thoughts were interrupted by a lot of shouting coming from the assault course. It was the familiar sound of Bill Wicks putting a group of new recruits through their paces. I knew exactly what that felt like. When I transferred from the SAS I had to go through the induction process myself. So far as they were concerned I hadn't been fully trained. It pissed me off at first. Then I thought, what the hell? Typical army bureaucracy—it's the same everywhere. What's the harm, anyway? It'll be a bit of a lark.

It wasn't.

That assault course made everything I'd done before look easy. We went into it wearing armour and a full pack. Bill

Wicks would yell and curse at us all the way, and from time to time he'd loose off a burst of live ammo just to help things along. I'd be going arm over arm along a rope or trying to get under a net with my profile lower than an alligator's and I'd hear the rounds pass my ear. We'd finish the course, plastered with mud and sweat, and then Colonel Harken would turn up, looking cool in a spotless singlet and shorts. And he'd take us, still fully loaded, for a ten-mile run. Then he'd turn us over to Wicks for another go round the course while he went off to the officers' mess for a shower and a drink.

The guys out there probably think this is the worst part, but they've got a nasty surprise coming.

I remember how Harken had broken it to us at one of the morning sessions.

"In this line of work, there's a finite possibility that you'll get yourselves kidnapped and held hostage. It's vital you learn as much as you can about where you are, who's holding you, and why. Knowledge is survival. And we'd like you to come back because we've spent a lot of time and money training you."

Not because he thought we were worth saving or, God forbid, because he liked us. No, because we were expensive. That was the way he treated the men: like commodities, not people.

So we'd be taken to an unfamiliar town and shown the location on a map, and then driven round a whole maze of streets with a hood on. Then they'd show us the map again and ask us where we were. When we got the hang of that, they'd play us recordings of conversations from around the world, especially in trouble spots. We didn't have to learn the language but we had to be able to identify it and maybe pick up a local accent. And then they'd fly us out to some of those places, go through the hooded exercise again, and at the end we had to know not only where we were, but which country, sometimes which town. That was hard, very hard, and some of the guys couldn't hack it.

Like Perez. He flunked out at that point, and he was a damned good soldier. He went off to join the SEALS. For a quiet life, as he put it.

It was Harken who devised all these things.

"I want a bunch of men who can think with their brains and fight with their balls, not fight with their brains and think with their balls. Understood?"

So that's what those new recruits had ahead of them: classes on every sort of directed energy and ballistic weapon and explosive, climate, geography, comparative religion, lectures from experts on major terrorist and militant outfits. And in the afternoons, circuit training, or the assault course, and the tab with Harken for good measure.

And what you had at the end of many months was an elite fighting force. No wonder Harken wanted us to stay alive.

Then again, I had that same ambition.

3

Our contact in Africa would be a man called Justin Garvey. Garvey was the doyen of Africa correspondents, one of the few who'd managed to locate the rebel army and film an interview with General Benjamin Obadiah. The report he'd sent back to the BBC about four years earlier had been widely syndicated, and it made his reputation. Harken had a copy for us and we viewed it in the holovision projection room. On it Garvey was tall, slim, and tanned, with wavy brown hair. Back in his native England he could have been the captain of the village cricket team. Unfortunately he had the habit of talking out of the side of his mouth, and that made it look like he was sneering. Obadiah's face, on the other hand, was a permanent sneer. It was big and black and shiny, and he lifted his thick upper lip high as he spoke, which displayed a good set of teeth but wrinkled his flat nose. His chin carried a short black stubble that he probably thought was a beard. He preened and swaggered in front of the camera, obviously enjoying the attention. He was wearing a wide belt with a semiautomatic in the holster. I couldn't see the make because his well-filled khaki shirt bulged over the top of it.

Harken also handed over the picture of Ngozi's daughter Suzanne, and a set of stills he'd been sent. They showed villages burned to the ground, men, women and children maimed or slaughtered, and a final shot of a teenage girl pinned to a tree with a spear through her belly.

Gerry was almost speechless. "Obadiah's people—did—that?"

"So I understand. Now, we've had high level contact with the BBC and they're willing to set up a meet. One person only—that's you, Jim. You'll fly to Lusaka and await instructions."

"Does Garvey know the real reason for our visit?"

"No, and neither does the BBC. Everyone thinks you'll be making a film and that's how you'll play it. You'll be posing as a team from CBC." His mouth twitched. "You've got a weird sort of mid-Atlantic accent, Jim, so we thought you'd just about pass as a Canadian."

"Thanks."

"Okay," Gerry said. "So we just walk in, find the President's daughter, say to Obadiah, 'Excuse me but this young lady is coming with us' and walk out again."

Harken's expression was bleak.

"We anticipate that, in the course of filming, there could be some collateral damage."

"Like what?"

"Obadiah does all the thinking and planning for his so-called army. He doesn't tolerate lieutenants, sees them as a challenge to his authority. But he's engaged in guerilla warfare. He can't keep all his followers in one place: they'd be too vulnerable, and they wouldn't have the necessary mobility. So they're scattered around the country and each group has a local leader. No group will recognize the authority of the leader of another group, but they'll all accept orders from Obadiah. If he was taken out, there'd be a struggle for leadership that would fragment his followers. The whole operation would fall to bits."

"I see. So you'd like for me to shoot Mr. Obadiah between

the eyes. What with? A holovision camera?"

"Something like that. The CIA is working up something special for this mission."

"Will we have any other offensive capability?" I asked.

"No."

"Not even a knife?"

"Not even a knife."

"I see. Just the three of us, in a camp of maybe a hundred fully armed soldiers, and you want us to kill Obadiah and walk out with this girl?"

"That's about the size of it. Should be well within your capabilities."

*

The holovision camera was delivered in person by one of the CIA's technical gurus. It looked like a conventional broadcast quality camera. That was the general idea. As this gizmo was the only thing we'd have in the way of a weapon we paid plenty of attention when he gave us the guided tour. He started with the tripod.

"This leg houses your transmitter. You won't be able to send or receive messages; effectively it's an emergency beacon on a special channel. Activate it when you want to be evac'd. We're supplying a receiver for whoever will be waiting for the signal. They need to monitor that channel continuously. If they don't, you're out of luck, because no one else will receive the transmission."

"How do we activate it?" Sef asked.

"You have to hold down this toggle to slide the cover right back. Then press the button underneath. It's a combination, to prevent someone setting it off accidentally.

"The camera's been miniaturized to make room for the other features. Otherwise it's pretty standard, so you can take sequences and play them back for anyone who wants to see them. I'll leave you a manual; you'll need to know it backwards if you're going to look at all professional. The thing that doesn't come with a manual is the weapon."

We all craned forward.

"Basically it's a high-powered air rifle, firing 11-mm calibre lead balls. They're in a spring-loaded stack in this leg of the tripod. The compressed air is stored in a cylinder in the third leg. The plenum chamber and the firing mechanism are hidden in the camera behind these plates—they're riveted, in case anyone gets curious. Electronic sights with cross-wires, superimposed on the camera's viewfinder so it looks like you're filming."

I couldn't see any sort of barrel. "Where do the rounds come out?"

"Here." He pointed to what looked like the front element of the second lens. "This is a shutter. It opens a fraction of a second before it fires."

Gerry looked fascinated. "Where's the trigger?"

"The trigger is the same as the one you use for filming. Except when you want to fire, you press this recessed button first and hold it down."

Gerry glanced my way with a bemused expression on his face.

"Now listen. This thing has very limited penetration. It won't go through body armour, and it won't splinter ribs or thick bone. You'll have to go for the eyes—the bone at the back of the eye socket is thin enough for it to penetrate. Try and get a slight downward trajectory so the ball wrecks the brain stem. Swing through a small arc; that way you get both eyes. There won't be an exit wound; it hasn't got the energy. That's an advantage; less mess. Just remember: if your aim is slightly off, your target's likely to get up again."

"It's a bit basic, isn't it?" Sef said. "I thought you'd be giving us something, well, a bit more hi-tech, like a beam weapon."

He contemplated Sef for a moment, then answered testily:

"Beam weapons are for battlefield deployment: you need a large dish to get accurate collimation and you need a lot of power. There's no way we could have made something like that look like a camera. Look, we put a lot of thought into this. It may seem primitive but compressed air gives you a lot of firepower in a small space, it doesn't have to warm up, and it makes very little noise. All right?"

Sef nodded and so did we. And then we all went down to the firing range with our new toy.

I assigned the camera to Gerry because the target was tall and he'd get the best angle. Sef would be the sound recordist. I'd do the interviewing.

If we ever got that far.

4

I met Garvey at a bar in the western district of Lusaka. At first I did a double take: the man had aged. His face looked like a dried-out lake bed, the eyes red and rheumy. He was holding onto his glass as if it were a life raft. As I understood it, some of his reportage hadn't earned him friends and he had to keep a low profile. That would be hard for someone like him, an expert on Africa with a network of contacts that must have taken years to build. He wasn't really safe on this continent but if he went anywhere else he'd be starting from scratch.

We shook hands. I'd been warned not to use names. I pointed to the glass.

"Get you another?"

"Not here," he said. "We'll walk."

He led the way. Further down the road there was a street market, with plenty of noise and shouting. That seemed to suit him. It didn't suit me; I had to strain for every word.

"You're looking to film an interview, I gather."

"That's right."

"Obadiah is always on the move. Not many people get to see him, and he breaks camp immediately afterwards so they can't report his position. You'll have to work through a chain of intermediaries."

He passed me a slip of paper.

"There's only one name on this," I said.

"That's the first. I'll take you to him, then you're on your own. He'll direct you to the next, and so on. Probably three or four in all."

"How will they know who I am?"

"Look on the back of that note."

I turned it over. There was a message in a strange flowing script, presumably written by Garvey.

He must have read my expression. "No, it doesn't mean anything to you, but it will to them."

I pocketed the slip of paper. "Thanks."

"How many of you going?" Garvey asked.

"Just the cameraman and sound recordist. I'll do the interview."

"Good. They'll search you thoroughly when you go in. Don't take anything you don't want them to find."

"What, like a weapon, you mean?"

"Especially a weapon, or anything that even looks like a weapon. They're touchy and it doesn't take much to push them over the edge. That doesn't mean they'll shoot you or whack your head off with a machete, mind. They'll spare you that luxury. These people have a genius for inventing long-drawn-out and highly unpleasant ways of killing people."

"Thanks, I'm really looking forward to meeting them."

"And don't take anything of value. Expensive wrist watches, rings, bracelets, nice pens, anything like that. They'll kill you just to strip them off you." He gave a sardonic laugh. "They're not called the Liberation Army for nothing."

I smiled dutifully. These cheery comments were beginning to irritate me.

"Treat Obadiah with respect. And I hope you won't be so stupid as to ask questions of strategic importance, like how many men has he got, and who's arming them."

"Of course not. Just as a matter of interest, who is arming them?"

"Well, a lot of his followers defected from Ngozi and brought their kit with them. And there's more to it than weapons. Don't underestimate Obadiah. He's a damned good tactician and his people are well trained. Ngozi's army is a ragtag bunch by comparison."

I blinked. "That's interesting," I said slowly. "The briefing they gave me had it the other way around."

"Oh yes?" He gave a short, hollow laugh. "Obadiah whips the arse off them every time they meet. Then he walks away with a lot of their expensive toys. I imagine it pisses off Ngozi no end."

"So who's arming Ngozi?"

"Who do you think?"

"The U.S?"

"Of course. He's pro-Western, anti-Islamic Alliance, and in the grand tradition of your glorious country, he's also a despot, so what better candidate to support?"

"Canada's not the United States," I reminded him. I was anxious to maintain my identity as a CBC newsman.

"Oh yeah, I forgot."

I shot a glance at him, wondering if the sarcasm meant he'd penetrated my cover. Then one of the street traders came out from behind her stall, jabbering excitedly at me and thrusting some sort of foul-smelling fruit under my nose. Garvey waved a hand and said something and she shrugged and melted away.

As we walked on he said, "Don't you know anything about African politics?"

"Not as much as you do. I thought Ubindi was a democracy."

"If you can call it a democracy where people are too

scared to mount any effective opposition. Obadiah was one who tried. They clapped him in jail. He managed to escape and got his rebel army together. He aims to overthrow Ngozi's regime."

"Would he be any better?"

"It's an open question. Meanwhile Jebediah Ngozi stays in power courtesy of the U.S. of A. Of course, there aren't any Americans on the ground—the official stance is non-interventionist. Unofficially, they make sure he's well equipped." He laughed again. "And since Ngozi's weapons usually end up in Obadiah's hands you could say the U.S. is arming him, too."

"Jesus."

He leaned in. "Don't worry—you'll be safe enough with Obadiah. Just tread carefully. If you don't he'll feed what's left of you to the crocodiles."

*

We found the guy sitting on an up-ended packing case, an elderly African with iron-grey hair and a beard to match. He stood when he saw us approaching. Garvey went up and said something quickly to him and walked straight on, leaving me standing there, bewildered. The man crooked a finger and I followed him out of the market. He was tall and terribly thin, and the skin seemed to have shrunk in on him, so that the veins on his arms and legs stood out in wriggly black cords. It didn't look like he could make it to the next intersection but he led on at a good pace and in that heat it was all I could do to keep up. I couldn't even clear the dust that kept blowing across the street into my eyes for fear I'd lose him.

We halted at a garage. A much younger man was fiddling around inside the hood of a battered car. There was a strong smell of biofuel; evidently hydrogen technology hadn't penetrated here. The old guy said something and the mechanic looked me up and down. I dug in my pocket and produced Garvey's note. He wiped his hands on an oily rag, took the piece of paper and read it slowly. Then he returned it to me and pointed to an open-backed truck. I climbed into the passenger seat, he started the engine, and we lurched into the street. I turned to give the old guy a wave but he'd gone.

We left the town behind, following unmade roads across a flat plain that consisted mostly of grassland punctuated by the odd clump of acacias and an occasional small farm. We were driving with the windows open, so my face was constantly battered by an oven-hot breeze, laced with a cloud of our own dust each time we braked or changed direction. After an hour my tongue was sticking to the roof of my mouth. I tapped him on the arm and made a drinking movement with my hand. He drew the vehicle to a halt and went round to the back, returning with a large plastic jerry can. The water was warm and smelled of rubber and plastic, but I took a good swig and handed it back to him, nodding gratefully. We passed it back and forth a few times, then he screwed the cap back on and placed the can behind the seats. We set off again.

Ten minutes later we pulled into a primitive village, little more than a collection of round, thatched huts. We got out and I followed him over to one of the huts, from which a muscular guy was already emerging, stooping to clear the low doorway. The two of them embarked on a long conversation, glancing in my direction from time to time.

No way could Garvey communicate with places as remote

as this. What he'd done was inject me into one point in a network. Obadiah must have detachments of his army across the border, and this bush telegraph was the way they kept in touch.

My driver beckoned and the three of us headed for one of the larger huts, where there was a table and chairs. A woman came in and, after a brief exchange, returned carrying a plate with some sort of dense bread and a selection of strange looking fruits. She set it on the table and gestured to a chair. Although I was hungry I felt guilty about taking their food, but she pushed the plate towards me so I accepted what was on offer and washed it down with a hot infusion, which may have been tea.

Then I heard the sound of an engine starting up and a clash of gears. I looked up sharply. My driver was no longer with us.

I was at the door in a few strides. The open-backed truck had gone. I gesticulated to the muscular young man but he just shook his head and pointed at the chair. I sat down reluctantly and fidgeted.

Twenty minutes later I heard the engine again and jumped up. The truck had returned with a new passenger. He walked quickly over to the hut, acknowledged everyone, took a chair at the table, and waved me over.

He was older and paler-skinned than the others, and he wore wire-rimmed spectacles that gave him a studious look. It turned out that he had a little English.

"Newsman?" he said.

"Yes." I pointed to the CBC News logo sewn above the top pocket of my safari shirt: white letters on a black ribbon—another little present from our friends in the CIA.

"You go fly?" he asked, cruising an open hand through

the air. "In 'copter?"

"Yes," I said. "That's right."

It was a RotoFan, but if he knew the word "helicopter" it was good enough.

He put a piece of paper on the table and stabbed a finger at it. On the paper, written in pencil, was a set of coordinates. As I reached for it he grasped my hand. I looked at him and he slowly lifted a finger to his lips.

I nodded and he relinquished his grip.

We got up from the table and I saw my driver jerk his head towards the door.

Before we left, he took a can of biofuel from the back of the truck and emptied it into the tank. I had a fairly large bill in the local currency so I shook it at him, pointing at the can. He protested mildly but I shook it insistently and he accepted it. Then we climbed in and headed back the way we'd come.

At last I had the coordinates of Obadiah's camp in my pocket.

I'd succeeded. I should have felt elated. I didn't. Something didn't smell right.

5

The Rotofan's engines droned. Parched scenery stretched monotonously into the distance and unwound slowly below. I wondered why anyone would want to fight over such a godforsaken land. We'd been flying into Ubindi for the best part of an hour and I had yet to see any sign of life. The conditions must be too poor for farming.

I looked across the aisle. Both Sef and Gerry were asleep. That wasn't surprising; there was nothing in the unchanging vista beyond the windows to keep them awake.

I got up and strolled to the front of the craft. I'd get a better view of the land from the cockpit.

The crew chief was on a rear-facing bulkhead seat outside the cockpit.

"Where are you going?"

"I think I'll ride up front for a while."

"Negative."

I thought I must have misheard him.

"What did you say?"

"Sorry, it's not allowed on this category of flight."

I shrugged and returned to my seat. I'd never heard that one before.

I scoured my mind for anything more about the mission, but I'd exhausted what I knew and I sank into a doze. When I abruptly opened my eyes I realized it was because I'd become aware of a change in the background noise of the engines. I sat up and looked along the fuselage. The turbofans had turned almost to the vertical and we'd slowed to something near a hover. The pilot's voice sounded in my earbud.

"Captain, you receiving?"

"I hear you."

"Okay, according to the coordinates you gave me, the encampment should be right ahead of us. There's something down there all right. This valley runs north and south and I'm on one flank. I'm going to traverse it so you can take a look. They've probably heard us by now, so if anyone's interested I hope they'll see the paint job and won't take pot shots."

"My contact should have warned them."

"Sorry, but I don't find that very reassuring. After the traverse I'll move in closer and we'll put down. Be ready. I'm not hanging about."

"Understood," I said.

The turbofans rotated slightly and gave us a little forward motion. I was looking at a broad-bottomed valley with the same parched red soil and stunted vegetation as everywhere else. The sun was still fairly low and there was a hard shadow alongside every tree, bush, and rock. A couple of k's to the north there was a whole pattern of shadows, all the same size. The tents of Obadiah's army were low and camouflaged, but they were still obvious in this light. At the edge of the camp there was a larger, rectangular structure, also canvas-covered. There was no perimeter fence; it was the sort of installation that could be picked up at a moment's notice. Out to the right the ground rose in a ridge that travelled the length of the valley, dipped, then rose again into a high wall of mountains. We finished the traverse and swung towards the encampment in an arc.

The crew chief opened the door of the RotoFan before we'd even touched the ground. Gerry jumped down and I passed him the video camera on its tripod. Sef was next, with his little case for the mike, headphones, and sound level recorder. I jumped and the RotoFan took off and peeled away to the south, leaving us standing in a cloud of red dust.

There were some shouts from the compound, two hundred metres away. They sounded excited. I hoped they weren't too excited.

Sef breathed, "Here we go," and we walked over, all smiles.

They were waiting for us, assault rifles at the ready.

And they didn't look friendly.

6

Garvey wasn't wrong about the searching. Two of them did it while the others looked on, their weapons still cocked. They took their sweet time. Our smiles were beginning to get a bit fixed by the time they decided we weren't carrying anything worthwhile. Then one them pointed to the camera.

I held my breath.

The technicians at the CIA had done a good job; the camera would pass a superficial inspection. The one thing you couldn't disguise was its weight. Gerry was carrying it like a toy, but we certainly didn't want these chaps to heft it.

Gerry handed it over, but I noticed he kept one leg of the tripod in contact with the ground. He opened panels and pointed out the features, distracting the soldier's attention so that he didn't actually handle it. The guy was obviously out of his depth, and reluctant to admit it. After a few moments he waved it away angrily. He shouted something, and a passing soldier came over. He was just a youngster, maybe twelve years old. I'd seen kids that age on previous trips to Africa. You'd enter a village and they'd jostle around you, clamouring for food or money. Not this one. It was like all the lights had gone out for him. He regarded us without curiosity, his eyes dead. I noticed he didn't have any boots. An old, but well-oiled Heckler and Koch G36 assault rifle hung from one narrow shoulder.

The one who'd searched us barked some instructions and

the kid started to walk off to our right. The soldier gestured brusquely for us to follow him.

The tents we'd seen from the air were to our left. They were little more than canvas sheets, propped up by a couple of stakes and pegged to the ground. They wouldn't stand a high wind but they'd probably keep the rain off—not that there was any at this time of year. I tried to count them but they weren't arranged in lines—no doubt to make them harder to spot from the air. I estimated there were about twenty. They probably slept at least four, so that would make a minimum of eighty personnel. There were a few milling around, mainly on this side of the camp. Where the rest were was anyone's guess.

The boy soldier seemed to be heading for the big tent we'd seen from the air. It was rectangular, with vertical sides and a pitched roof. It was probably where they kept food, supplies and ammo, and their comms station. I would have expected them to place it in the middle, where it could be more strongly defended; it seemed strange to put it on the eastern fringe of the camp, where it was vulnerable to an attack force coming through the mountains, over the ridge, and across the valley. Maybe they had more to fear from pilfering within the camp.

Obadiah was waiting for us outside the tent. He was almost as tall as Gerry, but a lot thicker around the middle. Even so, he'd lost weight since Garvey's holovid report was made. He sported a bunch of campaign ribbons on his safari jacket and wore reflective dark glasses. Would that be a problem?

The kid said something to him and he scowled and waved him away. I decided to take the initiative.

"General Obadiah," I said, walking over with my hand

extended. "CBC Broadcast Unit. It's a real honour to meet you."

He barely touched my fingers, but the scowl had lessened somewhat.

"We don't want to waste your time, sir," I said, with great deference. "Where would you like to conduct the interview?"

"We can talk here."

The voice fairly exploded out of him.

"Very good, sir. Ted, would you like to set up the camera? And Brian, get some sound levels. Make it quick, the General's a busy man."

We'd agreed not to use our real names.

Gerry set up the tripod and adjusted the zoom and focus on the camera, and Sef had the headphones on and held out a microphone while he twiddled knobs on the recorder at his waist. I'd studied Garvey's programme carefully and started with the same kind of innocuous questions. He loosened up and became more expansive, especially about his desire to liberate the country from the oppressive dictatorship of Jebediah Ngozi. He spoke of poverty, of lack of opportunity. His people had the military advantage, he said, because they knew what they were fighting for. His English was heavily accented but surprisingly good, and from a newsman's point of view the interview was going well. What I needed to do was to find out where he was keeping Ngozi's daughter, but it was like treading on eggshells. I steered an indirect course.

"Still, you haven't done any real harm to Ngozi yet, have you?" I asked innocently.

Would he rise to it and show off his new acquisition? Gerry was busily filming and Sef was holding out the mike.

He didn't take the bait.

"Dese t'ings take time. We growin' stronger ever' day.

Dat's enough for me."

Time to try another tack. "Right, then, General. Now I understand you're a family man. Our viewers would certainly like to see something of that. Could we maybe have some shots of you with your wife and children?" I turned to Sef and said, clearly enough for Obadiah to overhear, "We won't need sound for this, Brian, we can just do a voice-over."

"Okay," Sef said, turning a switch.

Obadiah beamed. "My children not here. We leave dem where dey safe. We go to my wife."

Wife! He would call her that!

My pulse quickened. This was it: time to show off his new acquisition. He'd tell her to put a smile on and keep her mouth shut and face the camera.

He led the way down the eastern side of the camp in a rolling swagger, talking loudly all the way. We stopped at a tent, which looked the same as all the others. He gestured at it, still talking. He was in full flood.

"Dis is my tent," he said. "You see, I live jus' de same as ever'one else heah."

"Oh," I remarked, "just look at the democratic way the General leads his men." Then to Gerry: "Can you do a tight frame on this?"

Gerry's eyes met mine. It was the agreed code.

"Sure," he said, setting up the tripod. He had a quick look through the viewfinder and said, "General, I wonder if you'd mind removing the glasses? We have a lot of reflections from this angle."

Obadiah swept off the glasses and continued to spout. Gerry adjusted the tripod and put his eye to the viewfinder again. I felt a pang of guilt. I'd assigned Gerry to the camera because of his height, but in doing so I'd made him the executioner. On the other hand I could imagine him thinking about those stills, the lives ruined, the burnt villages, the children killed, maimed, or abused, and somehow it wouldn't be so hard to pull the trigger…

There was a curious thudding sound and simultaneously Obadiah's booming soundtrack came to a halt. I got a glimpse of black eye sockets as his head jerked back, and then he dropped to the ground, as if he'd disappeared into his own boots.

This whole thing was going to be easier than I thought. We'd knocked off Obadiah; now we just had to grab Suzanne and make our exit.

At that moment, the tent flap was thrown back and a woman appeared.

It wasn't Suzanne.

7

She was heavily built, and her face was dark and lined. She looked at us, then she saw the crumpled body of Obadiah.

"What have you done to ma man?" she demanded. She raised her voice, bordering on panic. "What have you done to ma man?"

And she opened her mouth to scream.

It never came. Instead there was that curious thudding noise again and she dropped. I looked at Gerry. He grimaced and gave a helpless shrug.

"She'd have brought the whole camp over here."

I heaved a sigh. "I guess you're right. Let's get these two inside. Shit. There weren't supposed to be any other women."

We dragged them into the tent. I could see now what the CIA man meant about this weapon not leaving a mess. Normally a couple of head shots like that would have scattered blood and brains everywhere. I took Obadiah's semiautomatic. It was an FN Herstal Five-seven, and it looked like a recent U.S. Army variant. I quickly dropped the magazine into my palm, checked it was full, and slammed it back. The indicator pin was protruding, which meant there was a round in the chamber. I stuffed it into my trouser belt, under the cover of my travelling vest. Then I came out of the tent, closed the tent flap behind me and straightened up.

"This must have been his real wife," I said, "or one of

them. So where the fuck's he keeping Ngozi's daughter?"

"Not near here—that's for sure. His wife would give him grief."

Sef looked at me thoughtfully. "You know, when we were going over to that big tent, I'm sure I saw a soldier outside one of the small tents, off to the left."

"Guarding it? Could be. Okay, we'll go over there as a camera team. We'll say Obadiah's letting us film what we want. Don't do anything rash. I don't want to use this," I patted the semiautomatic, "unless I have to. Show us the way, Sef."

We set off, but I was still thinking about the woman. Some would write it off as "collateral damage". That's probably what Harken himself would say when I reported it. They could think what they liked. Killing an armed soldier was one thing; killing an innocent civilian was another. I was caning myself.

It wasn't Gerry's fault; it was yours. What made you think Obadiah would lead us straight to Suzanne? The man wants sympathetic treatment by the Western media so what's he going to do: show the whole world he's a kidnapper? Idiot!

Things could still work out, though. We had half the job done. Unfortunately it wasn't the most important half.

Sef half-turned to them, his hand at waist level, pointing. He was right; there was a tent down there with a soldier outside it. As we approached I recognized the man's weapon, an HK616 assault rifle, cross-slung and ready. It came up and we heard the safety click off.

He was as tall as Gerry and looked equally strong. He wore a dark green beret, which seemed to be one of the few consistent features of the local uniform. His deltoids, bulging out of a sleeveless camo vest, looked like they'd been hewn out of ebony.

I held up a hand. "It's okay," I said airily. "General Obadiah said we could film down here."

There wasn't the slightest flicker in his expression, and I realized he hadn't understood. I looked round at Sef, and jerked my head slightly in the guy's direction.

Sef tried a few words out on him. Something changed in his eyes.

"Contact," Sef said. "What do you want me to say?"

"Tell him General Obadiah wants his finest soldiers to appear in the programme we're doing. He specifically mentioned this guy. He's busy right now, otherwise he'd be here with us."

Sef translated. It seemed to take an awfully long time. When he finished the man didn't say anything and he didn't put the safety back on. We had to take a chance.

"Okay," I said to Gerry. "Set the tripod up, real slow. We don't want to hustle this guy."

I loosened my travelling vest a little so that I could get to the semiautomatic if I needed to.

Gerry seemed to be ready. Then he stole a quick glance left and right to see if anyone was around. It was a stupid thing to do. A murderous light entered the guard's eyes and he lifted the rifle. That was as far as he got. There was a thudding noise and he dropped.

I looked around. Actually Gerry had timed it well. There were guys on the other side of the camp but no one near enough to see or hear what had happened. The CIA technician had been right about that, too; the weapon was quiet.

I stepped up to the tent and opened the flap.

It was Suzanne all right—there was no mistaking the

smooth skin, high, sculpted cheekbones, almond eyes, straight black hair. Her burgundy trouser suit was a little dusty and creased. She looked startled, but only for a moment.

"It's okay," I said, to reassure her. "We're from your father. We've come to take you away."

She gave me a look that was empty of any sort of emotion. "Yeah," she sniffed.

Maybe I read too many fairy stories when I was a kid, but in my book the maiden you just saved from a fate worse than death doesn't say "Yeah". Arms round neck, big kiss, maybe, but not "yeah".

Make allowances. She's probably traumatized.

"Come on. Outside. Very quiet, now."

I extended a hand but she ignored it. I thought she'd yelp when she saw the guard, but she didn't so much as flinch. Sef had taken the automatic rifle, but she lunged forward, lifted the semiautomatic from the soldier's belt, and tucked it into her waistband. I hesitated for a moment but there was a look of determination on her face. The last thing we wanted right now was a loud argument, so I let it pass.

We dragged the guard inside the tent. At my suggestion Sef put the guy's beret and camo vest on and took a large knife off his belt. Like this he could be taken for one of the army escorting us through the camp, unless they got a close look. He cocked his head.

"Can I dump the sound equipment, Jim?"

"Sure. Leave it in there. We won't be needing it any more."

As he re-emerged I said, "We'll go back to the eastern side of the camp and keep going. There's a ridge about a klick beyond the perimeter. The dip on the other side is dead ground. We can make our way along it towards the landing site without being seen. Copy?"

They nodded.

I turned to the girl, "There's no fence. Do these people lay claymores?"

"Lay what?" she snapped.

"Claymores. Mines operated by a trip wire to secure an area."

"I wouldn't know."

"Okay, guys. Keep your eyes skinned for trip wires. Let's go."

We moved off. There weren't many soldiers on this side of the camp and it looked like we'd make it to the perimeter without encountering one.

We didn't.

The guy just came out of his tent, bang next to us, scratching his belly. He looked a little startled but he didn't go for his gun. I gritted my teeth and decided to walk on as if nothing had happened, hoping he wouldn't challenge us. I'd just passed him when I was aware of a movement at the edge of my vision. Almost simultaneously there was a volley of shots and a scream. I whirled, dropping to one knee and reaching for the semiautomatic.

Suzanne was standing there calmly holding the guard's semiautomatic pistol in her hand. She'd emptied half the clip into the man's crotch and he was writhing around on the ground, clutching himself and yelling blue murder.

I leapt up and snatched the pistol.

"You stupid bint!" I shouted. "What the hell did you do that for?"

"He tried to rape me," she said simply.

"Now we'll have the whole camp after us!"

"You can handle it."

I grabbed her arm and shoved her roughly towards the perimeter.

"Run!"

8

Gerry paused only to snatch the pistol from the wounded man's belt and we legged it full pelt out past the edge of the camp. Suzanne could run fast and she stayed ahead of us. If there were trip wires she'd hit them first. My blood was still boiling and I half hoped she would. There were shouts all over the camp and a few shots, and when I looked over my shoulder it was like we'd stirred up an ants' nest.

We ran fast, bent double to lessen the target. Gerry carried the heavy tripod tucked under one arm. Ahead of us I could see the ground rising to the ridge. It wasn't far now, but we'd be sitting ducks as we mounted the higher ground. I prayed that they were still too disorganized to grab rifles and start shooting.

Somewhere in the back of my mind I thought:

Reason we can do this is you, Bill Wicks, you bastard, for kindly putting us through the assault course with live rounds buzzing over our heads.

We hadn't hit any trip wires and we were well up the ridge when I heard more shooting and lines of red dust starting puffing up around us. It was hard to jink going uphill like this but we did what we could. I saw Suzanne apparently getting shorter, and realized she was already going down the other side of the ridge into the dip. Moments later Gerry, Sef, and I followed.

"Stop!" I shouted, and we hit the ground.

Suzanne paused, looking puzzled, and walked back to us. Again I grabbed her arm and dragged her down. She shook off my hand.

I was breathing hard. I swallowed and looked round at the others.

Gerry was hunched down on my right. Beyond him Sef was calmly examining the captured rifle.

"Gerry," I said. "Activate that beacon right away. We have to hold them off here. If we let them follow us into the ridge we're dead."

I saw Gerry press the combination of buttons. Then he looked at me.

"Hold them off? What with? One assault rifle and this pea shooter?"

He hefted the tripod to illustrate the point. He was right. The camera weapon was only lethal at close range. It might still be helpful up to about thirty metres but simply trying to fire it would leave him hopelessly exposed.

"Sef, I don't suppose there was another magazine for that HK?"

"No. I'll use it semi-auto."

"Good. Make every round count. Gerry, if they get closer we'll use the pistols." I jerked my head towards the camp. "Shall we take a look?"

We crawled forward on our stomachs until we could see what was going on. Fortunately the ridge was topped with scrubby grass, which would break up our outlines.

Inside the camp, soldiers were running in all directions. But at the perimeter, close to where we'd run out, twenty or thirty of them were coming our way, carrying automatic rifles. It was good in one sense: either they didn't have mortars or they'd decided not to use them. We'd have to slow them down, though.

Sef had the only weapon capable of any accuracy at this distance. Firing the pistols from here would be a complete waste of ammunition.

"Can you drop one, Sef?"

Sef extended the rifle through the grass. He sighted carefully and pulled the trigger. Then cursed.

"Fucking sight's off."

I believed him. I was considered a crack shot and Sef could trounce me on the range.

"High or low?" I asked.

"Hard to say. Low, I think."

"Aim high."

It didn't need me to tell him. There wasn't any point in trying to adjust the sight without a stable target, and those guys were closing the distance fast.

Sef fired again. And cursed again.

"Must have been high," he muttered.

The third shot took one of them in the chest and knocked him backwards. For a moment nothing happened. Then the others realized what was going on and threw themselves to the ground. They started to come forward more carefully: up, quick run, down, five metres at a time, not quite enough time to bring a weapon to bear. Garvey was right: whoever trained these guys knew what it was all about.

Sef fired again. He must have seen one go into cover and popped him as he came up again. Two down. There were plenty more and I could see another bunch coming out over the perimeter. Sef had got his eye in now and he was hitting one with every round. He'd move a few feet to the left or right between shots in case they'd spotted the muzzle flash.

Trouble was, he had nothing like enough ammo to take all of them out. And then I saw something that put a chill through me. The melée in the compound was sorting itself out. Someone had barked an order and everything had gone quiet. They started to deploy, and I knew they were using hand signals. The soldiers had split into two groups, one moving out to the left, near to where we'd entered the camp, the other out to the opposite side.

"Bugger that," I said to the others. "They're going to outflank us. If they get over the ridge above and below our position we'll be enfiladed from both ends. Where's that evac ship?"

Gerry gave me a grim look. He tapped the tripod.

"Jim, we don't even know if this thing sent the signal. Or if they picked it up—that line of mountains behind us could have blocked the transmission."

Something went zip and I felt a searing pain in my shoulder. I slammed myself down instinctively. A few more went over my head. I straightened up slowly.

At first I couldn't see Gerry. Then I realized why. He was lying on his back with his eyes open. I crawled forward and grasped his shoulders. His head flopped to one side and I closed my eyes when I saw the mess.

My gut constricted. I looked up.

Sef had swivelled to target the sniper. A moment later he fired.

"Got him!" he grunted. "Jeez, he must have been travelling fast to get right up there."

I checked out my shoulder. Blood was spreading into the sleeve of my shirt, but to judge from the length of the track it hadn't penetrated, just grazed through the skin over the deltoid. It hurt like hell anyway. I managed to unstick my throat.

"Sef," I croaked. "That sonofabitch got Gerry. Head shot. He's dead."

Sef didn't move. "Shit," he said. "Sorry. I just didn't see him."

"Not your fault."

He heaved a deep sigh. "If those bastards get in here," he said out of the corner of his mouth. "Keep three bullets for us."

I knew what he meant. A quick death would be a lot nicer than what those guys had in store for us.

Sef fired again and another man went down. He was near enough that we heard the cry. Near enough to toss a grenade? That was the worry—they seemed to be advancing on all sides. We heard a burst of gunfire and ducked as a stream of bullets whizzed overhead. Some more pecked into the ridge.

"Sef, give me a hand with Gerry. We have to change position."

I removed the pistol that was still in Gerry's belt and we dragged him further along, staying low behind the ridge. Suzanne followed us, also keeping low. Finally she seemed to have got the message.

I took another look, very carefully this time. The group aiming to outflank us to the left was moving fast, too fast. More shots came from the frontal assault. They were beginning to rake the ridge indiscriminately, giving themselves cover as they closed in. Sef held his nerve, firing one or two shots, then shifting quickly to a new position.

A sick wave of resignation swept over me. It was going to end up at close quarters after all. Well, I'd take a few with me.

I drew both pistols, thumbed back the hammer of the FN, and waited.

9

Sef fired again and moved low to dodge the answering hail of bullets. Then I thought I heard something. I laid a hand on Sef's arm and he looked round. I could see he'd heard it, too: a faint engine note, a characteristic double whine.

Moments later the white-painted RotoFan appeared between the mountains, turned and started to fly up the valley.

I sighed with relief.

"Thank Christ for that," Sef breathed.

We couldn't stand up but we waved furiously from the ground. It was low, low enough for us to feel the warm downdraught from the twin turbofans as it sailed right over us without stopping.

I looked over at Sef. "What the fuck's going on?"

He shrugged.

I pointed to the tripod, which was lying where Gerry had dropped it.

"Is that thing still sending?"

"Should be—it's like an emergency beacon."

"Well, it brought them here. They must know where we are."

"Hot LZ. They don't want to stop."

My stomach dropped. "I don't believe this."

The RotoFan continued up the valley and swung left in a wide arc. I looked over the top of the ridge to follow it.

I could see the engines rotate almost to vertical. What

were they playing at? They didn't seem to be leaving, but they were nowhere near us, or where we'd put down.

It hung there for a moment, then moved slowly towards the camp.

Suddenly the air was filled with the white pencil-streams of rockets. Fireballs expanded all over the camp and the ground rocked with the explosions. Before the echoes had finished bouncing off the mountain walls, another sound rose: the staccato drone of fast-firing cannon. The RotoFan continued its forward progress, unleashing a torrent of bullets, shells, and rockets, until the entire encampment was enveloped in a rising cloud of dust, flames, and smoke. An even larger explosion sent a great mushroom up from the vicinity of the big rectangular tent. They must have hit the ammunition store.

There was so much smoke I couldn't see the RotoFan any more, but moments later it appeared on the left and ran up fast towards the group who'd tried to outflank us. They were heading for cover but they didn't have a prayer. The fast-firing cannon droned and every last man went down. The RotoFan hovered.

I shoved both pistols back in my belt.

"Let's move," I shouted. "You," I said to Suzanne, "take this."

I thrust the tripod at her. She gave me a rebellious look, but she must have seen the expression on my face and took the tripod. She sagged a little with the unexpected weight but didn't make a murmur.

Sef and I lifted Gerry between us, his arms over our shoulders, and we started to hurry down the dip. It wasn't easy, with poor Gerry's feet trailing on the ground, and my shoulder stinging like fury, but you don't pay much attention to pain and fatigue when you're running for dear life.

We reached the RotoFan. The crew chief was in the open doorway. He helped us hoist Gerry aboard.

"This guy's dead!" he said.

"Of course he's fucking dead," I snapped.

I whipped the camera and tripod out of Suzanne's hands and passed them up. Then we shoved her roughly aboard, and Sef clambered in after her.

I took a last, quick look around and noticed now how cleverly the gunship had been disguised. With the covers retracted, the guns and rocket pods were in full view, still smoking.

Sef extended a hand, we gripped each other's forearms, and he hauled me up. The crew chief shouted something, and we took to the air.

While Sef strapped Suzanne into her seat, I crossed to a window and looked out. Smoke drifted across the entire area. From time to time there was a rising blush of red and orange as something else in the ammo dump exploded and sent a rippling column of smoke even higher. I glimpsed some figures running up the rise and dropping into the dip, presumably members of the frontal assault party who'd missed the carnage.

The crew chief touched me on the arm. He had a body bag in his other hand. Was it out of respect, or because he didn't like the blood seeping out of Gerry's shattered head and spreading onto his nice clean floor? We laid the bag down and manoeuvred the body into it. I closed Gerry's eyes before we zipped it up.

"You'd better get strapped in," the crew chief said.

Instead I jerked my head towards the cockpit. This time he just shrugged and led the way forward.

The cockpit was crammed with hi-tech paraphernalia: ground-hopping radar, electronic counter measures, target acquisition displays, the lot.

"Thanks," I said to the pilot. "Things were getting a little tight down there."

"So it appeared. Thought we'd join the party."

I pointed at the control panels. "You seem well enough equipped for it."

The pilot looked over his shoulder at me. He may have been smiling, but I couldn't see his eyes, because the combat visor was still down, and there was a mike close to his mouth.

"We didn't know anything about their surface-to-air offensive capability," he said. "Had to be ready in case they started shooting."

"Why didn't you tell me you were a gunship when we went in?"

"Sorry, buddy—orders. Someone thought you'd be more motivated if you didn't know."

Now I understood why I hadn't been allowed in here on the outward leg. I wondered who the "someone" was, but I was pretty sure they wouldn't tell me.

"Where we going now? Back to Chingala?"

"No, Kebe. The Ubindian International Airport. We'll be met there. They'll take the girl off your hands."

"Well that can't come quick enough."

"What's the matter, don't you like her?"

"She didn't exactly endear herself to us. Nearly getting us all killed was the turning point in our relationship. As it was we lost a man. A damned fine one, too."

The pilot looked round and ducked his head in acknowledgement. He spotted the pistols tucked into my belt.

"Where did you get the artillery?"

"They're kind of on permanent loan from Obadiah and some of his people."

"Well you'd better get rid of them in case anyone sees you. Officially this crate belongs to CBC and we'll be landing in the civilian part of the airport."

"Civilian part? Is there a military part, then?"

"Not exactly military. It's a cargo area. But it's high security, so you need special documentation to get in there. Which we don't have."

"What do we do with the camera?"

"Leave everything in the ship. When we get to Chingala we'll put it on a military flight back to the States."

"Okay. How long to landing at Kebe?"

"About an hour."

"We'll disembark there, too."

"No. You come back to Chingala with us. You'll be transported from there."

"Negative. I want to repatriate my dead friend. Kebe's the international airport—they'll have the right facilities. We can book a civilian flight back from there."

"Okay, suit yourself. When you're done making arrangements, the airport hotel is half decent. Give you a chance to clean up, have a drink and a meal, and a night's sleep."

"Thanks."

Back in the cabin Suzanne was sitting sullenly, her hands in her lap. She didn't even attempt eye contact with me as I passed. I felt a surge of anger. My buddy was lying back there in a body bag because of her, and she was acting like a truculent teenager. I wanted to slap her face.

Sef was sitting in the row behind her, quietly looking out of the window. I took the seat across the aisle from him. I wanted to talk, but it would wait until we'd put down and unloaded the girl.

The countryside floated by but I didn't see it. My mind was clouded with dark thoughts.

The conversation with Garvey had started it, a growing feeling that I'd been given only half the picture. It was stronger still on the way back to Lusaka after I'd met the contacts. They didn't seem like terrorists to me, more like members of a resistance movement. Now I'd repaid their trust and hospitality by killing the very man they were trying to protect. We'd taken out his wife, too. Nice going.

And what about this Rotofan? You might expect a door-gunner on an extraction flight, but this thing was equipped like an entire artillery division and they'd shot up the whole bloody camp. There were kids in there, like the one without any boots who took us to Obadiah, and maybe other women, too. What was it all for?

I glanced over at Suzanne. She was still staring stonily ahead. That was another enigma. I couldn't understand her attitude. Shooting that guy in the crotch alerted the entire camp. She must have known she was risking recapture. Didn't she care?

I tried to piece together exactly what happened when I pulled back the flap of the tent. At the time I was so relieved to find she was in there I didn't pay too much attention to anything else. Now I closed my eyes and replayed that moment…

She'd looked up from something—I was sure of it. She'd been reading.

A hostage who'd come in for some rough handling, sitting there in a nicely cut trouser suit, reading?

I had to have this whole thing wrong. She wasn't there against her will at all. Obadiah had posted the guard outside the tent, not to stop her escaping but to protect her from some of his dick-happy entourage—like the one she shot. Maybe she didn't get on with her father, and aligning herself with his hated rival was a way of getting back at him. She would expect Ngozi to set up a "rescue" and he had, and now she was on her way back to face the music. I was sorely tempted to ask her outright, but why should she say anything to me? In her eyes I was just an instrument of her father.

Well, if we'd been fed a load of crap about her being held against her will, what about the rest of it? We'd been shown pictures of villages, of people maimed, killed, and burned but we didn't actually see who did it. This wasn't an entirely stable country and there were other, smaller militias; maybe it was the work of one of those, and the blame was put on Obadiah. Maybe—this whole thing was full of "maybes"— he did have a vision for his country and he had attracted the loyal following he'd boasted about. Well one thing was certain: if he enjoyed that sort of popular support, we, and the SAF, had nothing whatsoever to be proud of.

The engines moved into a different key. We were on the approach to Kebe airport. Looking out of the window, I could see the control tower, the airport buildings, and the runways crisscrossing in front of them. Moments later the engine pods were close to vertical, the ground was rushing swiftly past, and we were heading across the runways to the landing pad. Off to my right I spotted an Airbus A400M. I didn't know those big cargo carriers were still flying. I hadn't seen one in years, but there was no mistaking that high tail and the four, eight-bladed turboprops. It was evidently parked in the secure area. As we swept by I caught a glimpse of tall wire fences, and pylons that no doubt carried high intensity lights and security cameras. There were a few camo uniforms moving about in front of the hangars.

The pilot came over the general comm and warned us to keep our seat belts fastened. Suzanne ignored him, of course; she unbuckled before we'd settled onto the pad. The chief opened the door.

A black limo was waiting there. She jumped down and walked over to it without a word or a backward glance.

10

I was all prepared for a long drawn-out legal wrangle over Gerry's repatriation. That was certainly the way it started, but I put a call through to Harken and he turned out to be surprisingly helpful. I wouldn't say he was prepared for it, but he knew what to do. He must have used some high level contacts, because suddenly all the barriers melted away. The next day Sef and I watched the plane take off with Gerry on board. The preparations were in hand for his reception stateside so there was nothing more we could do and no reason to stay on any longer. We booked a civilian flight home.

*

The day after we got back I gave Harken a full report. Initially I stuck to the facts.

"I'm sorry about Gerry," he said. "He was a damned fine soldier."

I gritted my teeth. "The best."

"It was a hard assignment, Jim, perhaps our trickiest operation yet. You acquitted yourselves well, all three of you. I'll have a word with Sef later. Is there anything else?"

"Colonel," I said, "I thought this operation was supposed to raise our profile with the administration."

"Yes, and no doubt it has."

"Have you seen this?"

I tossed a newspaper on the desk, open at an article with the headline "Ubindian army defeats terrorists". I let him read it—I knew it almost by heart. According to the official report, a crack Ubindian unit had ambushed the thousand-strong militia who called themselves the Liberation Army. There'd been a fierce battle and although the government troops were heavily outnumbered the terrorists had been routed. Their leader, the self-styled General Ben Obadiah, had been killed in the fighting. President Ngozi praised the valour of his soldiers.

For too long this band of thugs and murderers has been terrorizing the countryside, raping and killing and looting. We can all sleep more easily, now that this appalling evil has been removed from our midst.

There was no mention of his daughter.

Harken looked up, a half-smile on his face.

"So? It's normal for local forces to get the credit for what we do. In this case it's exactly what we wanted. The U.S. can't meddle openly in the affairs of a sovereign country, especially one of these central African states. This way we can keep our involvement out of it. Don't worry, the people who matter know very well who was resposible."

"I just don't think we had the full story on this one, Colonel."

The smile vanished. He held up a hand. "Let's take a walk."

He led the way out of his office and along the path that ran the length of the parade ground. We walked in silence.

Saplings had been planted on either side to provide a little shade. In fifty years' time it would be quite pleasant; right now I was a lot taller than they were, so the sun's heat reached me twice, directly on my head and reflected into my face from the magnacreted surface. Sweat began to dampen my armpits.

We reached the end of the parade ground and turned right to follow its perimeter. Here a series of narrower paths came off at regular intervals and disappeared between the long, brick-built accommodation blocks to our left. A group of guys jogged past us carrying full packs. I'd done it often enough in this heat myself, and I didn't envy them. As the synchronized tramp of their boots receded I became aware of the distant crack of rifles coming from the firing range.

I waited patiently for Harken to resume the conversation.

Quite suddenly he said, "What's on your mind?"

I drew a deep breath and gave him my interpretation of events in Ubindi. I wound up by saying, "We lost a good man out there, sir, and for what? To prop up an African dictator with pro-Western sympathies? Or does Ubindi have natural resources that we either want ourselves or don't want other people to get?"

His face set.

"Look, Captain, I shouldn't have to tell you the score. The Force couldn't function if everyone asked for 'whys' and 'wherefores'. You signed up for this. You swore an oath of allegiance, and you have to follow the chain of command. It was a tough mission, and you carried it out to the best of your ability. That's where your responsibility ends."

Harken was quite in order to deliver the rebuke, and I was half expecting it, but that didn't mean I was going to back off.

"I accept that, sir. But I want to be proud of the service,

and proud of what we do. And so far as this last operation is concerned, I'm not."

He was thoughtful. When he spoke again his tone was less harsh.

"You may be right, Jim, and you may be wrong—I'm not in a position to say. I do know this, though. The world's changing. There are different sorts of villains, and they're not always easy to identify. We have to rely on others, people who have the bigger picture, to make those decisions for us. Our job is to carry out their orders. You're intelligent and thoughtful, and those are good qualities. But I advise you to keep these doubts to yourself. Stick to soldiering. Otherwise you could be entering dangerous territory."

Was that a threat?

"We're trained to face danger, sir."

"Not this kind of danger, you're not."

He turned and walked back to his office. I was left standing there, wondering if maybe I'd gone too far.

*

A few days later Sef called me over.

"Here, Jim," he said. "Something to show you."

He was holding a newspaper. "I like to keep up on things back home," he said. "I've got an uncle sends me this regularly. *All Africa News*, English language edition."

I grinned at him. "And you're about to show me some gorgeous semi-naked black female on page three."

"No, I'm not—that sort of shit is for you sex-starved Westerners. Now stop fucking around and take a look at this."

He pointed to a single column article on an inside page.

ROTOFAN CRASH

A RotoFan aircraft crashed near Chingala's small Huanguele airport on Tuesday. Sources say that it was operated by a news media company. The airport spokesman said that contact was lost during approach. The pilot had not reported any problems. Observers on the ground claimed they heard a small explosion, then a very loud one, probably caused by ignition of the pressurized hydrogen fuel tanks. This has led to speculation that the craft was brought down by a surface-to-air missile fired by guerillas operating in the area. There were no survivors. Crash investigators are examining the wreckage.

I read the article and looked up at Sef, frowning.
"So…?"

"You're a bit slow today, aren't you, Jim?" he said. "I get this paper about a week after it comes out. Look at the date on that page."

I looked at the date and then up at him. My back had gone cold. "Are you saying…?"

"Yeah. If we'd followed the plan, we'd have been on that crate."

My eyes were still on Sef, but they were focused somewhere beyond him.

We only stayed behind at Kebe to see to Gerry. It seemed like the big guy was looking out for us, even after he was dead.

I swallowed hard. Then I looked back at the article and read it again. "That's not guerilla territory! Chingala's stable."

"Supposedly."

"What about electronic countermeasures? That ship was fully equipped."

"They must have turned them off. They were over the border by then. They probably thought it was safe."

"Pressurized hydrogen fuel tanks, my arse! That craft was still packed with munitions. 'A very loud explosion'—I should just about think it was."

"The crash investigators probably didn't pick up a piece bigger than a dime. Poor bastards."

I pinched my lip, thinking. "You know, Sef, there's something fishy about this whole thing. We do a nice discreet job, just like we're asked to, and then this gunship comes in like the bloody U.S. Cavalry and shoots the whole place to bits. If they're into wholesale destruction, why bother with our part of the operation at all?"

"They wanted the girl out."

"Yeah, all right. So why didn't Harken say something about the rest of it? Just to keep us motivated? I don't buy that."

"Maybe Harken didn't order up that part of the operation. It's not his style, that's for sure. He's all for the quiet approach. Precise, very clinical."

"Exactly. Well, whoever did order it up sure as hell didn't want anyone else to know about it. So they circulate this press release about the brave Ubindian army defeating Obadiah. And then they make sure there's no one around to say otherwise."

Sef blinked. "You're saying those guys in the RotoFan were killed deliberately?"

"Well, it'd be mighty convenient if the only eyewitnesses were blown to pieces, wouldn't it? Including us, don't forget—if Gerry hadn't been killed, the three of us would have been on board that death trap."

Sef passed a pink tongue over purple lips. "So what are they going to do when they find out we weren't on it?"

11

A week went by and the lapse of time seemed to put things into a new perspective. The conclusion was clear: we'd overreacted. There could have been an explosion on board—the craft was certainly carrying enough live material for that to happen. Or maybe there *were* a few guerillas operating in the area and they did bring it down. Even if Ngozi was behind it, he probably didn't have an international reach. It was too late, in any case: we'd come back now and gone through the debriefing, so what would be the point?

That Friday a bunch of us went out on a training exercise. It was very hot and humid, even for North Carolina, and it took a lot out of us. After we'd showered and cleaned ourselves up we got together in the kitchen for a brew. Sef began to talk about fishing.

"This is a great country," he said, "but you know, there's one thing I miss. Back home we used to go up to this deep, deep lake and drop a hook with some bait, way down, and man, you should see what we used to catch! I don't know what you call those fish here, but I can tell you they'd make your arm ache bringing them in. Good eating, too." He sighed. "That's what I miss."

Dave held his hands wide apart and said, "Big as this, eh, Sef?"

Sef's lips parted in a dazzling smile. "No, Dave, way bigger than that."

"Well," said Kit. "I don't know what y'all were catchin' out there, but catfish can come in pretty damn big."

Sef looked interested. "Not round here, though, eh?"

"Sure as hell round here. M'daddy used to take me up to Lake Bening, and that ain't more than 80 k's. There's a dam at one end and the water's real deep. You get some big, big fish swimming in that hole."

"Do you have a rod here, Kit?" I asked.

"Sure do. If you like you can use the rod, an' I'll give you some weights and a bunch o' hooks. You can pick up some bait on the way."

Sef rubbed his hands. "Right man, you're on!"

"I'll tell ya, Sef, it'll take more'n you to bring in one of those big ol' mothers."

Dave raised his eyes to the ceiling. "Here we go again."

Sef looked at me. "What do you say, Jim?"

"Sure, why not? Do me good to get some fresh air."

"If you call th'air in this goddam State fresh," Hermann moaned. "I'd say the air was fresher inside my dog's mouth."

Tomaso said, "I didn't know you had a dog, Hermann."

"I don't, but I used t' have. And if he licked your face you'd know 'xactly what I'm saying. 'Course, that's if he could bring himself to lick anything so ugly."

Tomaso rose obligingly to the challenge, and the two engaged in some light punching and wrestling. When things had settled down again, Sef and I arranged things with Kit. It was the weekend so I didn't think there'd be a problem setting it up for the following day. There wasn't.

*

The weather was just as hot, but a little less humid. Sef pulled his old burner into a station that still sold diesel-ethanol and filled the tank; then we set off. We bowled along with the windows down, and I felt a lightness of heart I hadn't experienced in a long while. Sef put the radio on and he tapped the wheel while I drummed on the dash. The miles flew by.

Then Sef said, "Jim?"

"Yes?"

"There's a big pickup about half a klick behind. He's been with us pretty much since we left the camp."

My good spirits evaporated. I manoeuvred the courtesy mirror so that I could see it. "You think he's following us?"

"Sure seems like it."

"Standard evasive manoeuvres, Sef. Get off the highway at the next exit."

"Okay, but I looked at the map before we came out and I'd say there's nothing on this stretch for at least twenty k's."

"Can you outrun him?"

He clicked his tongue. "If it's what I think it is, he's on hydrofuel with twin turbo-boosters. This crate's too old."

"You never worked in the motor pool, then?"

It was well known that guys who worked in the motor pool liked to hotrod old cars.

"No," he said. "I never did."

I bit my lip, watching the truck.

Sef glanced over at me. "Take a look in that cubby."

I opened the flap and whistled softly. Sef's shooter was lying in there. It was against regulations—I knew it, and he knew it. I lifted it out and looked at him.

"Just a precaution. After our little conversation last week."

I nodded. "Makes sense."

I turned the weapon over in my hands.

You don't see too many IMI Gauss pistols. The shells—low-velocity, laser-guided jobs—cost plenty. The theory goes, while the other side is letting fly with everything in sight, you put in one, well-placed round and finish the job. But they only get issued to people who can run up perfect scores on the shooting range, and who can hold the red dot steady when all hell's breaking loose. Sef ticked both those boxes.

I flicked on the electronics and two little lines of lights told me what I already suspected: it was fully charged and fully loaded. I slid the long barrel under my belt so I could get at the weapon easily, and took another look in the mirror. The pickup had started to close the distance.

It came up very fast, then stayed behind us, far too close. The mirror was full of the big bull bars on its front and I could hear the engine roaring. I laid a hand on the grip of the Gauss pistol but I had no reason to use it. Lots of drivers are stupid like that, hanging on your bumper just before they overtake. Sef pulled over slightly to make way for him.

He didn't overtake. The car lurched as the bull bars banged into the back of us and now the truck's engine was screaming and we were being pushed along in front of it.

The rest happened very quickly. Sef was struggling with the wheel, his leg straight as he stood on the footbrake. We were entering a long, left-hand bend and I knew we weren't going to make it. Within seconds we were smashing through the roadside fence and flying out over the embankment.

Instinctively I released my seatbelt, opened the door and jumped. I felt the shadow of the car pass over me, heard the crunch as it bounced, and then I hit the slope and kept rolling until something knocked all the sense out of me.

The first thing I saw was a tunnel, filled with coruscating light, which became larger, as if I were flying into it, and suddenly it expanded in every direction and I was looking at the leaves of trees against a blue sky overhead. I had no idea how long I'd been out. I turned my head and realized I was lying next to a tree. It must have broken my fall. Broken seemed to be the operative word: I could barely move. I lay there as if I had all the time in the world, testing out hands and feet, and moving my limbs a little at a time.

Two things jerked me into a state of awareness. The first was the smell of smoke. The second was a cough, not far away, and some voices.

I felt along my belt. Miraculously, the pistol was still there. I drew it out and rolled over. The grass was tall here. A picture flashed through my mind: crawling like an alligator under that damned net on the assault course. I did just that, placing the tree between me and the voices.

Thanks again, Bill Wicks, you bastard.

Then I carefully stood up behind the tree and peeked out.

The smoke was coming up the slope from somewhere down below. It wasn't wood smoke—it had that oily, black look you get from burning tyres. I just hoped to hell Sef had jumped clear. The air thinned for a moment and two men appeared. One was a black man with a receding hairline that gave him a curiously high forehead. The other was Caucasian and older, or at least prematurely grey. They were walking up the slope, presumably retracing the path the car had taken. They moved slowly and systematically and as they came I saw that each of them was fanning a pistol over the area on their side.

I didn't need to ask who they were looking for.

12

I did a quick calculation. About halfway between the two men and me was a bush, and at the rate they were moving they'd be lined up as they came level with it. That would be ideal. If I could make it to the bush, the far one couldn't fire without hitting the near one. I went forward, keeping low, and took up my new position.

From behind the bush I watched them coming up the slope. The breeze pushed another billow of smoke over them, and one started to cough. At that moment I stepped out to the right.

The black guy whirled as he saw me but I'd squeezed off a round before he could bring his pistol to bear. The shell struck him at the top of the chest and exploded, ripping him apart. Usefully, it also blew his head off. For a moment the body remained oddly upright on stiffened legs, fountaining blood. Then it folded.

I stepped back behind the bush as a shot rang out and a bullet buzzed over my head. I looked out between the branches.

The grey-haired one had dropped into a crouch, holding the pistol expertly in a two-handed grip. I thought I might find out more if I could disarm this one, but then he fired again and the bullet zipped uncomfortably close. I settled the laser spot quickly on his weapon and fired. I might just as well have aimed for the body. The shell exploded, raking his head and chest with shrapnel and it was all over.

I raced down the slope without pausing to examine the bodies. All I could think of was Sef.

The car was burning fiercely. It had hit a tree and the front end had folded. The rear had opened up like a flower so the tank must have ignited. That shouldn't happen, even with diesel-ethanol; one of those guys must have put a bullet into it. I tried to move in but the heat drove me back. I stood there, darting my head to one side and the other, trying to see inside. The flames had created their own updraught and rose in a column that swayed in the breeze coming up the hill. I caught a glimpse of a dark silhouette slumped over the wheel. Something the size of a grapefruit materialized in my chest and moved up into my throat. I could hardly breathe.

I took a few paces back and sat down hard on the grass. First Gerry, now Sef. I felt numb.

Minutes passed. I rose wearily to my feet and picked my way back up the slope. I carried out a quick search of the two bodies, but I didn't expect to find any I.D. and I didn't. The pistols were both Walther 159 Compacts. That didn't tell me anything either—there must be thousands of those things in circulation. At least it wasn't U.S. government issue, and that reinforced my conviction that these were hitmen with a contract. So who hired them? It seemed a long way away for Ngozi.

The police would have to sort this lot out; I had to focus on getting back to camp. I retrieved my cloudphone from a zipped pocket and spoke to it.

"Call base."

There was a long buzz. I spoke as soon as I heard the voice of the Colonel's aide-de-camp, Sergeant Bagley.

"Sa'rnt, this is Captain Forbes. It's an emergency. Put me through to the Colonel right away."

Moments later, I heard, "Harken."

"Colonel, Jim Forbes. We have a bit of a situation here. Two hostiles in a truck forced Sef and me off the road. Sef's been killed."

There was a short silence.

"Are you all right, Jim?"

"Yes, more or less. It was no accident, sir. The guys in the truck came out to finish us off."

"And…"

"Well, they're both dead, too."

"Jim…"

He had the "now-what-have-you-done?" tone of voice my teacher would use back at school when I got into trouble, which was often.

"Give me your coordinates," he said, in the same tired voice. I barked "GPS" at the phone, then "send coordinates".

There was a pause as Harken waited for the data to come up on his screen.

"All right," he said. "Now stay there and don't move. I'll come out to get you. No need to notify the police. I'll look after all that."

"Thank you, sir," I said, and the line went dead.

I stood there looking at the phone and a nasty feeling started to crawl up my spine.

I found a handy tree stump and sat down, staring at nothing. From time to time the breeze would change direction and a thin pall of smoke would settle all around me, then dissipate, leaving the smell in my nostrils. It barely registered.

Half an hour later I walked over to a tree that rose above the level of the highway. I climbed up to a horizontal branch from which I could watch the road and wait. Then I went over it yet again.

Whenever we left base we scribbled down where we were going in a log book—that was regulations, so they could contact us if something big came up. The book sat in Bagley's office, and Harken could look at it whenever he wanted to. He knew where we were going today.

Then there was the RotoFan. Who had access to our movements after the operation at Obadiah's camp? Harken.

Questions bounced back and forth in my head. Did he know we'd found out what happened to the RotoFan? Had Sef shown the newspaper article to him? Had I said too much at the debriefing?

It made little difference. Right now there was only one thing I could do: wait for him and play it by ear.

Another twenty minutes went by. Then I saw a camo SUV approaching. It looked like it was a car from the motor pool. As it began to slow down I strained to see who was in it. I could make out a driver but no one else. He was on his own. Was that good or bad?

I checked to make sure there wasn't another vehicle behind him before I climbed down. Keeping behind the tree, I drew the Gauss pistol out of my belt and looked at it for a moment. Against those two hoods it had been an excellent weapon. At close quarters it wouldn't be my first choice. It was unwieldy, and although the loss of laser guidance wasn't an issue, the risk from flying shrapnel was. I could have taken one of the Walthers, but the cops had to know those guys were armed.

I slipped the barrel into my left hand trouser pocket, jabbed it through the lining so that I could get the rest inside, and closed my left hand around the grip. One of my small accomplishments is that I can fire a pistol accurately with either hand. With the other hand I undid the cuff of my shirt. Then I tucked the left arm tight against my body, pretending it had been injured, and moved carefully up the slope.

Above me I heard the crunch of roadside gravel. Then a car door slammed.

Harken appeared at the top of the slope and started to come down. I hobbled up but inside I was coiled like a watch spring. He saw me.

"You all right? You need a hand?"

"No. I can manage."

"Where's the car?"

"Follow the smoke."

I didn't go down with him. The smoke had thinned out a lot, and I guessed the fire had died down. Things might be clearer down there, and it was as much as I could do to cope with my loss now.

When he came up again he said, "You're sure Sef was inside?"

That meant there was nothing left. I swallowed, and managed to answer, "Pretty sure."

He heaved a sigh. "What about the two you killed?"

"Over there, sir."

I pointed with my right hand and followed him to where they were lying, remembering to limp and hold my arm close. We came to the headless corpse first.

He stood there, looking down at it, hands on hips.

"You didn't leave much behind, did you?" he said. "Did it occur to you it might be an idea to disable him rather than blow his head off?"

"I was using Sef's Gauss pistol, sir. With one of those it's kind of all-or-nothing."

He grimaced, then walked over to the other body, looked

at the blood-spattered face, peered at the firearm.

"You ever see either of these men before?"

"Nope."

"All right, there's nothing more we can do here. Let's go."

I followed him up to the car. As we walked he said, over his shoulder:

"What happened to your arm?"

"I jumped out as the car went over the edge. Hit a tree."

"Anything broken?" He sounded very casual.

"No, I don't think so."

The SUV was standing on the verge, next to the splintered gap in the fence where we'd left the road. I checked the back seats before I got in, but I was right first time: he'd come on his own.

I watched him carefully as he got into the driver's seat. He didn't seem to be carrying, but he could have a firearm in a door pocket or the centre console.

He just engaged gear, did a three-point turn, and drove back. Nothing more was said until we arrived at base. Security waved us through the barriers and he parked the SUV in front of his office. Then he turned to me.

"Get some rest. We'll talk tomorrow, first thing."

13

I was awake half the night, my mind filled with pictures of Sef: Sef looking relaxed after a tab in full kit; Sef coolly picking off rebel soldiers with the borrowed HK616; Sef full of anticipation as we set out for a day's fishing; Sef a charred figure at the wheel of a burning car... Time and time again I went over the events of the previous day, asking myself what I could have done differently. There was only one conclusion. When that truck came up behind us I should have put a shell through their windscreen. If we'd been in a battle zone I wouldn't have hesitated, but this situation was different enough to make me hold back. And because of that my buddy was dead.

I got up as soon as daylight began to filter through the blinds and went for a long run. The exercise was good; the sweat poured off me, and when eventually I came back to my room the haunting images had receded. The ache remained.

After I'd showered I went to Colonel Harken's office. He didn't move from behind his desk, just waved me to a chair opposite.

"Okay, tell me what happened. In detail, this time."

It was a debriefing. He was my CO and he was entitled to ask for a full account, so I gave it to him. How much he knew already I couldn't say. He listened impassively, without interrupting.

The facts were straightforward enough; the self-recrimination couldn't be put into words. When I'd finished he continued to look at me, as if he were turning options over in his mind. Finally:

"This is a bad business, Jim."

Something flared up inside me. "You bet it's a bad business—"

He held up a hand. "What I mean is, this is not a good moment for you. Three people have died. You'll be arrested."

I grimaced. "I'm surprised the FBI isn't here already."

His lips twisted sardonically. "I called it in on an unidentifiable line. Said I just happened to be passing by and saw the smoke. No need to say more. On Monday I'll report that Sefu Mwangi, out on a weekend furlough, failed to report back to base, and the wheels will be set in motion. That will give us a head start. In the meantime, we'll get you out of the country. I've identified another foreign assignment for you."

I gasped. "The Feds'll go ballistic if they realize you shipped me out after what happened."

He shrugged. "The mission was already arranged. Timing was critical. A delay would have put people's lives in danger. No details, the rest is Top Secret."

"That makes it even worse for me, doesn't it? I leave the scene of the crime and then I leave the country. What happens when I get back?"

"Things will have calmed down by then. With luck they'll have some idea who those men were. They were clearly armed, and presumably the weapons had been fired?"

"At least one of them, yes."

"So you were acting in self defence. Whereas at the moment the heat is on. Everyone's excited, and you'll be treated as a potential murderer. On top of which, the Press will get hold of it and I don't want to see 'Special Forces officer kills two civilians' in the headlines."

My mind was whirling. On the one hand, I was aching to find out who was behind all this, so that I could tear his throat out. On the other hand, I knew I wouldn't get the chance. With Sef reported missing, the military would contact the civilian authorities. By that time they'd have found some human remains in the wreckage. They'd get the owner from the vehicle identification number—it was stamped in so many places it was bound to be readable somewhere. Then they'd want to know who killed those two men, so they'd come to the base and start asking questions. A whole bunch of guys knew I was going out there with Sef. I'd be thrown into jail. There'd be endless questions to answer, not just once but over and over again.

Getting me out of the country would avoid all that, at least for a while. Was that Harken's real motive? Or was it to make me an easier target, so I could be eliminated quietly over there?

Harken interrupted my thoughts. "You only just completed one mission, Jim, so I was going to give this assignment to Captain Daniels. Now you've got it. I'll brief you. Then I want you on a plane within twenty-four hours."

"Where to, sir?"

"Initially? Prague."

*

The target was a guy called Bogdan Zajc. He was a sex trafficker, with a difference. He led a small, well-armed group of criminals and outcasts, probably no more than a couple of dozen men. Their technique was to descend on an isolated village, massacre the adults and the small children, and put the rest of the youngsters—boys and girls, but mostly girls— into a pipeline that led to brothels in Russia and Eastern Europe and probably India. Before they shipped them off, Zajc and his followers gave them a free, and fairly prolonged, introduction to their new careers. The gang members weren't natural joiners, but apparently they enjoyed this part so much they were prepared to follow orders and operate as a team. The money that came through the pipeline in the opposite direction probably went directly into Zajc's pockets. The men would be allowed to loot the village and keep whatever they wanted.

There were certainly more discreet ways to run a trade in human lives, but this group seemed to revel in rape, murder and destruction. Ironically it was the very scale and audacity of their operations that made them so elusive. The first the authorities would know about it was when someone discovered a totally deserted village full of bodies. Sometimes it was burned down, but they didn't often bother. It always had a school: that way they could be assured there were enough youngsters to make it worth their while.

So far no one had come near to catching them. They were highly mobile, crossing borders and striking without warning. They never stayed in one place for long; as soon as they'd exhausted whatever food and drink there was in the village, they'd melt away.

Now, at last, the police had a lead.

*

Ahead of a mission I'd sometimes get a sense of foreboding: this would be the bad one, this would be my turn to come back on a stretcher or in a body bag. It wasn't unnatural for someone in a dangerous job and I suspected the others all experienced something of the sort from time to time. They'd never mention it, of course; it was foolish and superstitious and it simply wasn't healthy to let your thoughts run that way. In any case, the misgivings invariably turned out to be groundless.

I told myself all that, but as I packed my things the feelings weighed heavily on me and this time they were hard to dispel.

*

I arrived in Prague the next day. Because Harken had been so anxious to get me out of the country it would be several more days before the rest of the force could join me. Orders or no orders I wasn't going to make the same mistake I'd made in Ubindi. I had some time to assess the facts for myself, and that was precisely what I proposed to do. I started by making contact with the Czech police unit that had requested SAF assistance.

The unit specialized in people trafficking. They explained they'd picked up a seventeen-year-old Albanian girl who'd been captured by the gang about a year earlier and sold to a dealer in Prague. She wasn't the first they'd found, but usually they were too traumatized by the whole business to provide useful evidence. Luljeta was different: she'd made a mental note of everything that had happened and all the stages they'd passed through en route. She was a mine of information.

Her intelligence was so good, in fact, that the police could now post investigators to monitor crucial points on the route. They'd moved on the dealer in Prague, and under interrogation he'd revealed when he was expecting another consignment. When the transport came through they would intercept it and ask the kids what village they'd come from. What they needed was a highly trained squad who could fly in at a moment's notice and catch the gang while they were still in that village. No one knew where it would be, and they were reluctant to cross borders themselves, which was why they'd requested help from the SAF. Of course, they were hoping Zajc could be taken alive so he could stand trial in their country.

I wasn't quite satisfied yet; I wanted my information firsthand. I sought, and obtained, permission to interview the girl personally, in the presence of a psychiatrist and my own choice of interpreter. It was, I said, so that I could build a picture of the way the group operated.

The interpreter and I arrived together, and they led us to a comfortable room where Luljeta and her psychiatrist were waiting. The psychiatrist made the introductions and warned me, in good English, that if the girl was upset by my questions the interview was over.

We all sat down and I looked at the girl. She would have been pretty if her experiences hadn't etched themselves into her face, haunting it with deep hollows and shadows. Above all, there was a deadness about her eyes and a general lack of reaction that chilled me.

We weren't far into the conversation before I realized that not only was she genuine, but so, too, were all the stories about Zajc and his gang.

"When it first happened, did you hear any shooting?" I

asked.

The interpreter repeated the question and the girl shook her head.

That fitted with what we knew of their methods: these people worked quickly and quietly from house to house, drugging the children and using knives and silenced weapons on the adults. That way they never had to control large numbers of villagers.

She and her friends were herded into the school, which Zajc always referred to as "his school" because of the kind of tuition he and his followers were dealing in. There was a guard on the door and at least one in the room to make sure no one tried to get out of a window. They ate in the school hall and slept on the floor—when they were allowed to. She drew me a picture of a portable wooden contraption fitted with leather belts, that Zajc used to restrain the girls in various positions while he raped them.

"Can you describe Zajc for me?"

She said he was of medium height, thick set, with a dark complexion and a drooping moustache. No beard, although he wasn't clean shaven. She also mentioned that he wore a diamond stud in his left ear.

As for the journey to Prague, she said the gang were still in the village when she and the other youngsters were packed into a large delivery van with a guard and a couple of drivers. The van was white and the name of a company was painted on the side in red letters. She was even able to draw the logo that appeared underneath the name, although she only glimpsed all this before they climbed in.

I smiled reassuringly at the girl and said, through the interpreter, "This detail is very helpful. You have a remarkable memory."

The girl shrugged and muttered something. The interpreter relayed it to me. "It has always been this way. I see a picture. I tell you what is in it, that's all."

A photographic memory! This was quite a break.

The interview was over. There was no longer any doubt in my mind. Before this, the people I'd most wanted to get my hands on were the ones responsible for killing Sef. Now Zajc and his nasty friends had joined them.

A sense of purpose had taken over, and for the moment I put my premonitions on hold.

14

I decided to make our base at Sziminica, because it had a reasonably central location. It was a small airfield, which didn't matter a damn because a RotoFan can take off and land on a dime. All we needed were refuelling facilities and a little accommodation where we could wait, and it had both.

After a day or two, my team arrived: Dave, Hermann, Chuck, Kit, Gus, Eric, Tomaso, Reza, and Jason. I would miss Gerry and Sef, but what I did have were nine really good guys; ten, counting me. I didn't want a big force on the actual operation; I was relying on the element of surprise and it was hard to maintain it when you had people milling about all over the place. But Luljeta had given me a better idea of the size of Zajc's gang and I knew we'd need some help with the exfil if I was taking prisoners. So I requested a second team, which would move to a holding point during the operation, ready to come in when we gave the signal. Colonel Harken, working through his contacts at the Department of Defense, located a platoon of Navy SEALs who were just finishing a deployment in Italy and arranged for them to fly straight to Sziminica. The Officer in Charge was Lieutenant Glen Avery.

I didn't know Avery and I suspected the SEALs would be less than thrilled to be acting as backup to an SAF team instead of returning home. My guys raised some mild protests, too. Each of the Special Operations Forces liked to think it was superior to all the others; the rivalry encouraged identification with the unit, so although the senior officers didn't encourage it they didn't exactly discourage it either. I settled things down by pointing out it was the best we could do at short notice, and at least the SEALs wouldn't be involved in the primary action.

My doubts about Harken began to recede. There was a real mission on here. We were going to put an end to a grim racket that had cost a lot of lives and ruined a lot of others. It was something we could feel proud of. I was convinced we'd been doing someone's political dirty work in Ubindi. This was my chance to put things right.

*

In the event things moved more quickly than I expected. The SEALs were still on their way from Italy when I was contacted by the Czech police. They'd intercepted two vans answering the exact description Luljeta had provided. Each van was full of youngsters. They'd been taken from Raljevo, a village in Serbia.

I consulted hurriedly with the flight crew. They identified the village, which lay near the foot of a plateau. I pointed to a destination five k's short; we'd make the drop there. It was a compromise: speed was of the essence but I didn't want to alert the target to our arrival. Fortunately the scenery was mountainous and if we flew low along the valleys our engine noise wouldn't carry. I assembled my team and we took off right away. The pilot communicated with the incoming SEAL platoon and gave them the coordinates of the holding point. They'd have to fly there independently.

In the cabin the engine note settled to the usual monotonous drone. No one spoke. I looked along the length of the cabin. This was no CBC gunship in disguise; it was fitted out as a conventional military transport with a single long bench down each side. Dim, red illumination from above glowed in the black-streaked faces and accentuated the dark snaking camo patterns on the helmets and the shoulders of the full body armour. The short MX-90 multirifles formed a row of tiny green lights on either side of the cabin, each weapon fully charged.

Forty minutes later the flight crew called me forward. They'd reached the river I'd identified from the map; it would guide us in. I pointed to the ground. The pilot slowed the craft to a hover over a roughly level patch and we fast roped down. Then the RotoFan rose, turned, and headed back to the holding point. We set off before the sound of the engines had faded, striking a good pace.

The terrain wasn't hard and, even in full kit, walking alongside the river in the cool of the evening was pleasant, especially compared to what we were used to on the base. When I saw the flat-topped hill ahead of us I signalled a halt.

"Okay. The village is on the other side of that plateau. We should have a good view from up there. We'll survey the target, then decide a plan of attack. All right? Good. No noise. Let's go."

Night fell as we reached the plateau and moved cautiously forward. The village was below us. We lay on our stomachs, surveying it. It was larger than I'd expected—I suppose I should have guessed that from the number of kids they'd taken from the vans. I reached up to my helmet and pulled down the night vision binocs. Most of the village was in darkness. The big building would be the school; no lights on there, either. Then an open square, which was some sort of market place, with houses along one edge. The windows in those houses were illuminated, so it was fair to assume the gang members were inside. I listened carefully with the telemike but I couldn't hear anything. Then I zoomed the lenses, panned slowly up the street, and stopped. One of the houses had a satellite dish lashed to the chimney. Portable comms outfit? I scanned further up the street but I couldn't see any other dishes like that. I came back to the house. There was just one light on, and a guy was hanging around outside, glowing eerily in the intensified infrared, a multirifle slung casually over one shoulder. A sentry, for sure. That clinched it; it was almost certainly where we'd find Zajc. I lifted away the binocs.

The squad was right with me, waiting for instructions. I spoke softly.

"Okay, we'll move off together, then divide into two groups at the edge of town. Chuck, Kit, Reza, Hermann, you come with me. Primary target is the house in the street beyond the square. Chuck, you take out the sentry. Make it quiet. Kit, on my signal, toss a flashbang through the window. Reza, Hermann? The moment it detonates, you take the back door. Chuck and I will take the front. Kit, you stay outside in case anyone tries to escape. Dave, you go with Eric, Gus, Tomaso, and Jason and lie up in that alley at the end of the square. Wait there until you hear the grenade. The rest of Zajc's gang will hear it too and come running. Use your stun barrels—setting six, we don't want to kill them but we don't want them getting up too soon. Tie their hands and feet. Dave?"

"Sir."

"You have the beacon?"

"Yes, sir."

"Good, activate it as soon as you've immobilized them. We'll need the SEAL team to take over the prisoners while we clear the rest of the houses. All understood?"

I heard a low murmur of assent.

"Okay, let's do it."

And that's all I can remember.

15

The engine note changes as the pods rotate to near-vertical, slowing the Navy RotoFan to a hundred and fifty knots. Captain Glen Avery separates himself from the group in the cabin and goes forward.

Beyond the big, glassed-in cockpit the darkness is impenetrable. The instrument panels are reflected in the combat visors of the pilot and copilot. He thumbs a button on his comms helmet to select their channel and thrusts his head between them.

"How far off?"

"Almost on the beacon now, Captain," the copilot says. "Should get a visual on here any moment."

He points to the forward image intensifier display.

"What's our altitude?"

"Fifty feet, sir, we're flying on terrain-following radar. The village should be just beyond this plateau…"

His head jerks forward. "Holy…shit!"

The pilot slows forward progress still more. They gaze grimly at the screen. The ground is littered with bodies.

"Jesus."

Avery shakes his head in exasperation.

"Why the hell didn't they signal earlier if they needed backup?" he says. "That's what we're here for."

"Maybe somebody surprised them."

"It's their job not to be surprised. Take a look with infrared."

The copilot flicks a lever and the screen begins to alternate between visible wavelengths and infrared. He zooms in on each body in turn, looking for pale images alternating with the dark camo uniforms. There are none.

"Are you recording this?"

"Yes, Cap'n. Infrared and high-def video."

"Good, I want it all recorded. There's bound to be an enquiry and they'll need evidence." He clicks his tongue. "A crack covert team gone just like that. It's really going to hit the fan. How many so far?"

"I've counted nine. They're all dead, sir. Looks like the whole team's been wiped."

"There should be ten."

"Ah, hold on, there's one over there, away from the main group." The image glows white. "He's alive!"

Avery exhales. "Maybe he can tell us what went on here—no, ease back," as the pilot moves the craft in that direction. "I don't like it. Could be a trap."

"The beacon signal's genuine, sir."

"It could have been stolen."

"Electronic countermeasures are on."

"Good, keep them on. I'm going to talk to the squad back there."

He reaches up to the comms helmet again and switches channel.

"Okay, listen up. We've got a bad one here. Nine dead, one living. There could still be hostiles around. When we touch down, standard drill: secure the perimeter first. Medivacs?"

"Sir!"

"If there's no opposition, stretcher back the one who's still alive and keep him that way. Kumar, take the direction finder: locate the source of that emergency beacon signal.

Turner, Stokes, and Abadi: go down to the village. Just a quick reconnaissance. Go carefully, if there are hostiles around they'll have heard our engines so they'll be ready for you. If there aren't, they could have left booby traps. Use infrared and remote sniffers. No engagement. I don't want any more casualties. Understood?"

"Sir!"

"The rest of you: body bag duty. Any weapon with the body—put it in too. I want this place left clean. And move it, all of you: this is Serbian sovereign territory and air space; we're not even supposed to be here. All right, stand by, we're going in."

PART TWO

16

When I woke up I tried to open my eyes. The effort was too great. I just lay there, blood pulsing redly behind my eyelids.

I vaguely recalled surfacing earlier into a foggy awareness, groping around in a feeble attempt to remember who I was and, with nothing to hold onto, sliding back into nothingness. This time I seemed to have a slightly better grasp.

My face felt raw, and now and again the muscles twitched and convulsed. I lifted a hand to feel it, at least that's what I thought I was doing. I mustered the instructions in my head but nothing happened.

I was paralysed.

It washed through me like a wave of ice-cold water.

To stem the rising panic I tried to get some order into my thoughts.

Check functions. Sight first.

I managed to get my eyelids open long enough to bring my gaze to a focus on the ceiling. Okay, not blind. So far, so good.

Breathing?

I located my tongue and tried to move it. It rolled around like a dry leaf but it encountered no obstacles. I sniffed, then inhaled cool air into my open mouth. All right, no tubes in the nose or, it seemed, in the trachea. I must be breathing for myself. Another good sign.

What else? Swallowing?

It felt like ingesting a golf ball, but something was happening.

Head-turning?

No, that didn't work.

Arms, legs?

Nothing. It wasn't that I'd lost touch with my limbs, just that they weighed so much I hadn't the strength to move them.

My heart was banging.

Calm down. Remember your training. Take it one step at a time. Where are you?

I'm in a bed, in a brightly lit room...

I analysed it carefully, directing attention to each of my senses in turn. The ceiling was high and lined with white acoustic tiles. Set into it were fluorescent tube lights behind a diffuser panel—strictly institutional. Shifting my gaze I could see the sheets were pulled high and tightly tucked. They had a freshly laundered smell. Somewhere a phone rang. Then a door banged. Low voices and a metallic clatter—a trolley? It was a big room; I could tell from the way it soaked up the sound. A hospital ward—it had to be.

What in God's name am I doing here?

The effort was too great; I let my eyelids fall.

In my line of work you see a lot of buddies brought in injured: laser burns, ballistic weapons, stun grenades, blast damage, microwave beams—the lot. Some don't survive. Others survive but they can't remember what happened. Retrograde amnesia, the medics call it. The guy's mind is a blank for the whole attack and the minutes that led up to it, or the hours, or the days, or the weeks. That can be frustrating. You could be taking another squad to where he saw the action. You ask him, "Where did it happen? Did you spot the source of the incoming? Did you see the enemy? How many were there, how were they dressed, what were they carrying?" Chances are the poor bastard will say, "Leave me alone, I don't remember shit." You need an army psychiatrist to help you with the debriefing. He'll take him back, back to a time that he remembers, and slowly bring him forward to the point where he got hit.

That's what I needed to do: go back to something I could remember and work forward from there.

And I had to do it for myself.

17

Random images floated through my mind, nightmare images: Obadiah with black eye sockets, Gerry's shattered head, black smoke, a car on fire…

I snatched at the car.

We were pushed off the road. Sef was killed. I was knocked out. Was that it?

No, it had to be after that.

I struggled to hold the train of thought, but started to drift away again. I was like a man washed up on a beach, scrabbling to get a purchase on loose sand and sliding back with the pull of the tide. I made another effort, squeezed my eyelids tighter, got the image of the car into my head, the flames—

Two hit-men, looking for me. A black man with a strange forehead and an older man. I killed them, didn't I? There'd be trouble, lots of trouble. Harken wanted me out of the country.

Good, good, keep going!

A mission—he put me in charge of a mission.

That's right, it's coming back.

I flew to Prague, spoke to the Czech police. There was a girl—Lily? Lolita? Luljeta! All the kids in her village had been kidnapped by sex traffickers. And now it was happening in another village, and we got the call and flew out there…

I opened my eyes quickly. Above me was that high,

institutional ceiling with the clean, white acoustic tiles and the diffuse fluorescent lighting. But the air had moved.

It was no more than a faint stirring of the atmosphere but when you've been survival-trained you tune into the slightest thing. I knew someone was close by. And now I caught a hint of some dark oriental perfume—a woman.

My gaze drifted to one side. Something moved in the mist of my blurred vision. I pulled it into focus and the scene paled and sharpened. A flat, symmetrical face, olive skin. Black hair, disappearing into a white nurse's cap. Full, lavender lips. They moved.

"How are you feeling?"

I tried to say something, but all I could manage was a rattle. She picked it up.

"Water?" she asked. She didn't wait for an answer.

I felt the pressure of a straw against my lips. I concentrated, and with a tremendous effort sucked some into my mouth. The straw was withdrawn.

"That's enough," she said. "We don't want you choking."

I let the cool liquid sit in my mouth, allowing the dessicated tissues to soak it up. Then, with an almighty effort, I swallowed.

"More," I croaked.

She presented the straw again. I was beginning to revive. I had a thousand questions. I thought hard, trying to prioritise them because I knew speaking would be an effort.

"Where…?" I asked.

Her voice was soft. "State of Virginia. You're in an army hospital."

"Why…?"

She read my mind.

"They said you took a full stun charge. We gave you

neuromuscular blockers, otherwise you'd be in agony right now; every muscle in your body would be in spasm. It's beginning to wear off. If the cramps come back we'll have to dose you again until it settles."

As I let this sink in I glanced at her name badge. "J. Song".

I manoeuvred my newly hydrated tongue. It was beginning to feel more under my control.

"What's your name?" I asked.

The lavender lips pursed.

"Jenny," she said.

"Jenny," I said. "How are things in Manila?"

Her dark eyes widened, then narrowed and she looked at me askance.

Good, I'd analysed her accent correctly. At least something was working.

She put the straw to my mouth. As I drank some more she said:

"Now you're not going to give me any trouble, are you?"

I'd have laughed if I could. She was so small, so pretty, so clean and soft—the sort of girl who always made me feel big and clumsy and rough. I'd have been helpless in any circumstances, let alone these.

"I'll be a model patient," I assured her. The words were forming more easily now.

"I mean it: no getting out of bed."

"I have news for you, love. Right now I'm not going anywhere."

"I don't mean now, I mean when you get control of your muscles back. There aren't any restraints on the bed, but the windows are barred and there are armed guards in the corridor outside."

She must have registered the astonishment on my face.

"Look, soldier," she said. "As far as I'm concerned, you're just a patient who needs looking after. I don't know what you've done and I don't care. Just don't get any ideas, that's all."

"Jenny," I said slowly. "What, exactly, is the name of this hospital?"

"Newton Heights."

My heart sank. Newton Heights was the U.S. Army's high security prison hospital.

I was in big trouble.

And I didn't even know why.

18

My head was spinning and I realized I was over-breathing. What in hell's name had happened to put me in here? And what had happened to the others? Were they here, too? I couldn't see if there were any in the adjacent beds because my head wouldn't turn.

Now I was desperate to recall the events of that night. As soon as Jenny had gone I closed my eyes and tried to latch onto the previous train of thought. It was a struggle: I'd get a fleeting thought, but it would slip away before I could grasp it, worse than trying to catch the soap in a bath.

Then a scene came into my mind and stayed long enough to pin it down. It was an image in black and shades of green. It began to make sense. I was up on a plateau, reconnoitring a village through night vision binocs.

This must have been it. The last mission. To capture some kind of gang…

I made an almighty effort.

Sex traffickers! Led by a nasty piece of work called—Bogdan Zajc!

I felt a little surge of elation, and it wasn't just from making the link. It was as if I were there again, up on the plateau, anticipating an operation I could really be proud of. I started to recall features of the plan. We would split into two groups. One group would take care of the gang members. I'd take the other and go after Zajc.

Right then, we went down to the village. What happened after that?

Odd, I can't remember going down to the village. I can't remember any action at all. Did we take Zajc or not?

I was losing the struggle. A great weariness was drawing at the back of my eyes, pulling me down. I reached out of it once, a drowning man feeling for a hand, finding nothing, and sinking back into oblivion…

*

I jerked awake. I'd detected a slight stirring of the air, a hint of that perfume again. Jenny Song had come back.

"How are you feeling?" she asked.

I ran my tongue between my lips to unstick them. "Wonderful."

She gave me a dark look, lifted my wrist and took my pulse. "I'm just going to check your progress."

She took a cigar-shaped object out of her pocket. It had a couple of metal studs on the top and she pressed them to my elbow, then my wrist. I felt a thud, but if anything else happened it was outside my vision. She repeated it on my other arm, then drew back the bedclothes and did the same at the side of one knee and then the other. This time I thought I detected a movement. She replaced the bedclothes.

"Coming on nicely," she said. "Can you grip my fingers?"

She turned my hand and I felt the pressure of her fingers, smooth and cool. Incredibly I found I could close my hand over them, although I couldn't grip very hard.

"That's good. In a couple of hours you'll be almost back to normal. Look, this is a multifunction switch." She held up a switch on a lead, then placed it on my chest. "If you feel any spasms, press the big button and I'll come over."

"What are the other buttons for?"

"This one brings down the holovision screen—right now it's folded up in the ceiling above your head. And the others select different programs and menus. Try it out if you're feeling bored. You have enough movement in those fingers. The exercise will do them good."

"Okay. Thanks, Jenny."

Her smile was enigmatic, hardly more than a dimpling of the cheeks. She gave the bedclothes another little tuck, and went away.

I closed my eyes again. This time I simply let my mind wander. For some reason it ended up in that slack period before the Ubindi episode. At least it was slack for me—others were seeing some live action, going out and coming back in small groups and larger ones, but the assignments were secret: the rule was never to discuss them—before or after.

I'd devised ways of learning a little more. Harken made frequent visits to Washington. While he was away I'd go into the outer office and have a chat with Sergeant Bagley, his aide-de-camp.

Bagley was an inoffensive, weedy sort of chap, the kind who'd close his eyes at the last moment during bayonet practice. God only knows what made him join the army. Officially he wasn't SAF at all; I gathered he came with the baggage when Harken took command. He was good at clerical work, though. Must have been why Harken kept him on.

Try as he might, poor old Bagley couldn't look like a soldier. He had the regulation haircut, but his uniform always seemed too large for him, and he looked permanently sad, like a disappointed spaniel.

The others ignored him. If they had to see Harken they'd pass Bagley by like he wasn't there. His relationship with Harken didn't seem any better, usually limited to, "Yes, sir, no, sir." I think I was the only one who actually talked to him. It wasn't entirely out of charity: from time to time, he'd let something slip.

I'd go and sit on the edge of his desk and he'd heave a big sigh and hurriedly try to move things out of the way. A typical conversation would go:

"Hiya, Bags. How goes it?"

"Shouldn't you be defusing IEDs or something, Captain Forbes?"

"Come on, Bagsie, I know how much you love our little conversations."

"Oh yeah."

"Haven't seen Roy lately. He on a mission?"

And poor old Bags would say, "You know I'm not allowed to tell you that."

And then I'd know he was.

When eventually I stood up again, Bagley would pointedly rearrange the papers on his desk. It was a little game we played. There was no malice in it, and I suspect he enjoyed it as much as I did.

I shook my head—and it dawned on me that I actually could. I tried to turn enough to see the bed next door, but that was too much.

Why was it I could remember trivial stuff like my conversations with Bagley, yet I couldn't remember what happened to me in Serbia? Jenny had said I'd taken a big stun charge. Well, that would be reason enough. I was lucky to be alive, let alone remember what happened. I must have been evac'd just in time. There was a SEAL platoon involved, wasn't there? So who called them in?

It was no good. The wall was solid and I couldn't penetrate it.

Now that I'd drawn a blank on what really mattered there was nothing much else to do. I was bored. Then I caught sight of the switch Jenny had left on my chest. With an effort I brought my hand up and activated the screen. Holovision screens aren't quite as good as a full projection but the images are pretty realistic, just the same. I started to explore the channels. Some were just two-dimensional hospital information channels: visiting hours, dinner menus, that sort of thing. The cable channels were in stereo. Chat shows, contests, films—I couldn't be bothered with any of it. Then I hit the Science channel. They were discussing the Ryle space station now orbiting Mars with a crew on board, and the prospects for setting up a permanent scientific colony on the surface. I left it on; it was interesting. When that item was finished they turned to new developments in computing.

They spent quite a bit of time at Princeton, but soon the scene switched to the McDonnell Building, one of the more recent additions to the Massachusetts Institute of Technology. The camera tracked up an impressive flight of steps and followed the presenter through the entrance hall into a corridor. Then he was conducted through a series of high security checks: keypad, handprint and iris recognition. The place was like Fort Knox. Finally they were admitted to a large room full of equipment.

"This is the heart of the project," the presenter was saying, "and it's the brainchild of Professor David Hirsch. Professor Hirsch, as we've seen, this facility is protected by some pretty impressive security. What's the reason for that?"

The camera gave us a head-and-shoulders of the guy he was interviewing. The face was pale, very lined, but he had a full head of wavy brown hair, so it was hard to say how old he was. The voice was firm, with a slight American accent, but I knew immediately that he was English.

"You have to realize this will be no ordinary computer. What we are working towards is a machine that's capable of testing billions of combinations a second. You wouldn't want equipment like that to end up in the wrong hands."

"You mean it could be used by hackers, for example?"

"Yes, that's one risk category. Codes that would have taken years to decipher with conventional supercomputers would take only minutes with this one."

"So the military would be interested, presumably. Do you get funding from the Department of Defense?"

He laughed, and the skin around the eyes and in those hollow cheeks was wreathed in lines. "You wouldn't expect me to comment on that, now, would you?"

"Well, what can you tell us about this setup? Why is it so special?"

"Obviously I can't go into detail, but I can tell you in general terms what the principles are."

And he started to explain the basics of quantum computing. I found it pretty hard to follow, something about trapping particles that could be in any number of states at the same time, and switching them from one state to another. He was probably being lucid enough but I wasn't feeling that sharp, and my attention wandered to his curious lack of animation. As he was talking, the camera moved back and I saw the reason for it.

He was sitting in a wheelchair.

The contrast was almost overwhelming, and I felt a surge

of pity. Above the neck was a man talking about the most advanced computing concepts in the world; below the neck was a body like that of a ventriloquist's dummy. Where the trousers ended, the legs projected like a pair of sticks, disappearing into shoes that looked too big for him. The hands on the padded armrests of the wheelchair were shrivelled and distorted; only the fingertips moved.

They left the Professor, in his wheelchair, at the entrance to the building. The closing shot began with just him in frame, then zoomed slowly out, and kept zooming, so the field of view grew wider and wider, and this brilliant man shrank to just a small, lonely figure at the top of a flight of steps. That final image burned itself into my memory.

The credits rolled up and I switched off the screen and closed my eyes again.

I suppose I could empathise with him more than most, because right now I had just about the same amount of control over my body as he had. But I was going to recover, and he obviously wasn't.

How do you deal with something like that?

19

When I first came to M.I.T., ten years ago, I would fly up these steps. It's something I could never have imagined: that one day I'd be sitting here, at the entrance to the building, in a wheelchair.

When they finished filming I pressed the joystick on the armrest and motored back. Jack Speight, my regular physician, was waiting in my office. He introduced me to Dr. Norman Anderson, the neurosurgeon he'd brought with him. I couldn't shake hands, of course, so he just nodded, then settled into an armchair. Jack perched on the corner of my desk. He'd broached the subject with me last time so he got straight to the point.

"Let's be clear about this, Prof. You don't have to do it, but right now it's the only solution modern medicine can offer."

He always called me "Prof". I'd never got used to the first-name familiarity of the Americans and "Prof" was a suitable compromise. Normally they'd address a Full Professor as "Doctor" over here. But when I left Oxford I brought Andy Grierson, with me, and naturally he continued to call me "Prof", so after a while everyone else did. Poor Andy, he didn't realize just how much responsibility was going to settle on his shoulders.

It all seemed to have happened very fast. I'd discounted the feelings of numbness in my limbs. When I stumbled over those steps a few times I thought it was just tiredness. Then I realized I was having difficulty lifting my feet. That's when they started to run tests and I got the diagnosis.

I could manage with a stick for a while. Andy used to meet me at the entrance every day to help me up the steps. When that became too much of a struggle I was obliged to use the disabled entrance, out of consideration for him as much as anything else. I resisted the idea of a wheelchair, but in the end it made sense. It was designed to negotiate stairs, so paradoxically it made me more independent—for a while. But by now I'd read up the natural history of this disease and I knew its progress would be unrelenting.

And so it was. My legs no longer belonged to me. My arms had gone too, and even the small effort required to move the joystick with my fingers was becoming more and more of a challenge.

My nurse, Victoria, was standing somewhere at the back of the room. She was big and black and totally capable and I wouldn't have lasted a day without her. I knew she wasn't happy about this visit. I could sense her presence behind me like a great dark thundercloud.

"Who's going to pay for it, then, Jack?" I asked. As if I cared. I was only playing for time.

"Oh, it won't cost you a thing…" he stopped himself. But I'd noticed the way he flushed.

Without lifting my hand off the armrest, which I couldn't do, I pointed a forefinger at him.

"Aha. Who is it then? Who's been getting at you?"

He grimaced. "Okay, look it's not a secret. I was contacted by the Director of National Intelligence. He says the State will pay. He says the work you're doing is of incalculable value. It could avert wars, save thousands, maybe millions, of lives. He wants to preserve your genius for the sake of the nation."

"Bob Cressington, dear man. And he told you to persuade me."

"Yes, but that's neither here nor there. I'm your doctor, first and foremost. If I thought this wasn't in your interest, I wouldn't be suggesting it."

I sighed. "I know you mean well, Jack, but I'm tired. I've had enough."

"Your muscles are failing you— that's why you feel tired. If it wasn't for your body your brain would be as alert and lively as ever."

Victoria stepped forward with a brusque "Pardon me" and activated the electric motors that changed my posture and redistributed the pressure points. It was to prevent skin sores. You could set it to operate automatically but Victoria didn't like to leave my care to a machine. She looked after that just as she did every other aspect of my daily existence. Everything, that is, except the machine in the big lab. That was still exclusively my domain. Well, mine and Andy's, and a half a dozen trusted postdocs.

"And Norman here would do the operation?"

"That's right."

I looked at Norman Anderson properly for the first time. He was a big man with big hands, and I wouldn't have thought him capable of the delicacy required of a neurosurgeon, but Jack had told me he was one of the best in the country.

"In essence, Professor Hirsch," Anderson said, spreading those large hands, "it's just transplant surgery."

"So it's routine."

"No, I wouldn't go as far as that. You have to reconnect the brain stem and the cranial nerves and the major vessels.

It's a lengthy business, and it calls for a certain amount of surgical skill, but a number of people can tackle it now. I've done quite a few myself, and the results are very good."

This much I knew; I'd read it up after Jack mentioned the possibility a couple of weeks ago. I could recall almost verbatim the entry in the on-line dictionary I'd consulted first:

"Brain transplantation (abbreviation: Brain Tx) has been performed on a limited scale ever since the first successful operation in 2037. However, the technique had its origin many years earlier, in microsurgery for facial nerve paralysis. The outcome of that procedure was greatly improved by the use of a cocktail, derived from advances in regenerative medicine, consisting essentially of stem cells and nerve growth factors in a resorbable tissue adhesive. This led to the successful use of a similar approach in the repair of spinal cord injuries. Further refinement took these developments to their inevitable conclusion: the transfer of a whole brain into the body of a recipient."

"What about rejection?"

"That's not a problem. The brain is an immunologically privileged site."

"Well, how do you know that this—what I have—isn't going to happen all over again?"

"What you have is a rare peripheral neuropathy. The disease is in your spinal cord, and you'll be leaving that behind. The problem's unlikely to crop up again."

"So you transplant my brain into the body of a healthy donor. Who is this 'donor'? No one parts company with their body voluntarily. What are they—road accident victims?"

"Ah, no. Things start going downhill from the moment of death so we can't use accident victims. For maximum success the body has to be prepared at exactly the same time as your brain is removed."

"How do you arrange that?"

He paused and his mouth tightened slightly. "They're condemned criminals."

I was shocked. I just hadn't been prepared for it.

"You mean I have to benefit from the misfortune of a condemned man?"

Jack stepped in. I think he must have anticipated my reaction. "Prof, we're talking about mass murderers and serial killers. They've relinquished any right to be considered part of the human race. And capital punishment isn't new. Years ago these people would have been fried in an electric chair. In your own country, England, they'd have been hung by the neck; in Spain they'd have been garotted. Okay, people decided it was inhumane and they incarcerated them instead. So individuals who were a burden on society when they were on the outside became a financial burden on society inside. In any case, it wasn't a permanent solution: the prisons became overstuffed, so they started releasing these guys early, and many of them re-offended."

"What about lethal injection? That was practised in some states wasn't it? That's reasonably humane."

"Right, well this isn't so different. The subject goes to sleep and never wakes up. But instead of tossing his body into a hole in the ground or burning it in a crematorium, it's used to prolong the life of someone productive, someone who actually contributes to society. It becomes the receptacle for a brain, the brain of someone like yourself, who for no fault of their own finds their own body giving out on them."

I turned to the surgeon. "How do you square this with your Hippocratic Oath, Norman? You're supposed to save lives—aren't you?—not take them away."

"We're just a means to an end. And if the end is to prolong the life of a great man and give an outcast from society a final chance to make a positive contribution, that's no bad thing, in my view."

"Prof, there were extensive consultations when it was first proposed to use criminals as organ donors," Jack said. "They introduced all sorts of ethical safeguards. A whole generation of MDs has grown up with the system now— we don't question it any more. We take corneas, heart and lungs, liver, kidneys, bone marrow, blood—nothing is wasted. It's a completely logical progression from that to donation of a whole body, and the same legislation and safeguards apply. Of course, brain transplantation's a bit more sensitive so it's done quietly, otherwise the media would start to take an interest in whose brain went into whose body, and so on, and that would never do."

"What about me? Would I know whose body I'd be getting?"

"No," Norman said. "All records are anonymized. That was one of the conditions agreed with the ethicists when it was first debated."

Victoria stepped in again and set the motors whirring. I was glad of the distraction. Their arguments were persuasive, but it was an awful lot to take on board.

Norman waited patiently. I decided to shift the focus to practicalities.

"So when I come round I'm in someone else's body. How long before all the connections are properly re-established?"

"I'll be quite frank: there are no quick fixes. Even with the latest techniques it's going to take time. Six months is the best estimate. Nine at the outside. And extensive rehabilitation after that."

"And then life will begin again. With what sort of quality? Start with hearing. I like classical music."

"Hearing should be fine. In fact you'll hear better than you can now, and you won't go deaf for years."

"All right. Taste? I enjoy fine wines."

"Taste, yes. Smell—maybe not. You may get the donor's sense of smell."

"Smell is a big component of taste."

Jack intervened again. "Prof, let's get real, shall we? Look at your hands."

He picked one up. It sat high on his hand, the fingers extended at the first joint and flexed at the second, like a raptor's claws.

"Soon you'll lose the use of these altogether," he continued, "and then someone, like Victoria here, will have to feed you. It'll be pap because you won't be able to chew properly. Eventually you won't be able to swallow either, and we'll have to feed you through a stomach tube. Now just how good do you think wine will taste then?"

He must have seen my face sag.

"I'm sorry…"

"No, Jack, you're right to be straight with me."

I hadn't intended to be combative. These people were trying to help me; I had no business to project my own fears and moral qualms onto them.

There was so little quality of life left to me that in some ways it would be a relief to give up the struggle, to slip away into merciful oblivion. But could I refuse the operation? Jack might accept that decision, but Bob Cressington wouldn't. The truth of it was, I couldn't be allowed to die gracefully; my work was vital to the national interest. The potential for quantum computing was enormous. Soon we'd be able to monitor all the communications in the world, encrypted or otherwise. It would give the country a military edge and put us permanently ahead of organized crime and international terrorism. Even the major economies of India and China would come to us for intelligence. That wasn't a position the U.S. was prepared to relinquish. So they had to keep me alive.

Would that be so bad? I thought of the machine taking shape in the big lab. It would be the definitive version this time, incorporating everything we'd learned from the two prototypes, scaled up to make it even more effective. It would be the pinnacle of my academic career, the culmination of thirty years' research that had occupied my every waking moment. It would be worth living a little longer to see it completed.

"When could you do it?"

I saw Jack relax. "When do you think, Norman?"

"I'm told there's a possible candidate in the pipeline now." He addressed himself partly to me and partly to my nurse. "There's a narrow slot for this sort of thing. When it comes up we'll have to admit you fast so you'll need to be ready at a moment's notice. Can you bear that in mind, Victoria?"

"If it's what the Professor wants." Her voice was heavy with disapproval.

"All right," I said. "I hope you're right about this, Jack."

"It'll be for the best, Prof. You'll see."

20

"You okay there, Prof?"

The anaesthetist gave me a reassuring smile. Earlier on she'd come to the private room to take a complete history. That was before they wheeled me in here.

"A bit apprehensive."

"That's only natural. Don't worry, you'll be fine. I'm just going to check that everything is coordinating properly, then I'll come and give you your premed."

I lay there staring at the white ceiling tiles. Everything was so bright in here it was almost painful. I still had the fluttering feeling in my stomach.

It would be wonderful if this worked. It wasn't so much the physical agility I missed; it was the mental agility. I used to be able to cut through problems in an instant. Now it was as if the cogs of my mind were turning in some sort of thick goo. When we'd first discussed the operation, Jack had assured me it would change all that. I hung on to that prospect. I wasn't afraid to die, but I didn't want to make my exit as a feeble-minded old man. Not if it could be avoided.

*

Andy was shocked when I told him what I'd agreed to do. We'd worked together for more than twenty years, so it was understandable. He first joined me as a Research Fellow back in Oxford. He was a University Lecturer eight years later when they invited me to apply for the chair at M.I.T. I got him appointed as an Associate Professor, as part of my package. Now he more or less ran the lab. I couldn't manage without him.

"Are you sure, Prof?" he said. "It sounds terribly risky."

"It'll be worth it, Andy. Little by little, I'm going downhill. It's claimed my legs, my arms, my hands, and it's starting to claim my mind. I can feel the signs already; I know I'm not as sharp as I was. And it's all down to this tired, useless old body of mine."

He looked deeply troubled. "So you'll be coming back in someone else's body."

"Yes. Look, it'll call for a bit of mental adjustment, that's all. The 'me' that you know is up here." I'd intended to tap my temple but I couldn't lift my arm, of course, so I added, "in my head. My knowledge, my mathematical ability, the things that make me happy, the things that make me sad—all of them are in my brain. My body is only a vehicle for it, a sort of portable life support machine. Well, the life support machine needs to be swapped, that's all."

"You make it sound like a change of clothes."

"All right, it's a bit more than that. Externally, I'll look different. The only thing you're going to see of the original 'me' is my eyes."

"How's that?"

"I've been over it with the surgeon, and I've done some more reading myself. It seems my brain and my eyes can be treated as a subassembly. They prepare the recipient's skull by breaking out the thin bone at the back of the eye sockets. When they put my brain in, my eyes will fit in the new sockets. They reattach the eye muscles and then they replace the missing bone with a biomatrix." Andy looked a little pale. "Sorry, are you all right with this?"

He swallowed. "Yes, if you keep it in vaguely engineering terms and I don't have to think too hard about it."

"Okay. You see, doing it that way solves a lot of problems—for me as well as them. The olfactory lobes are part of the subassembly too, so I get five cranial nerves straight off."

"Cranial nerves?"

"Think of them as data busses, like the ones you use in the lab to connect the central processor to peripheral devices. What I'm saying is, I don't have to wait for I, II, III, IV and VI."

"What about V?"

"V is trigeminal. That has to regenerate with the other six, so I'll get it later. And I won't have any sense of smell until the olfactory lobes establish contact with the receptors in the nose. But I will get my sight back, and all of my eye movements, almost immediately."

"Will you be able to hear?"

"No, not for a while."

"How are we going to communicate, then?"

"That's what I wanted to discuss with you. First you need to be clear about the general scenario. My head will be inside a thing like a space helmet."

"My God. Why?"

"Two reasons. At this stage I won't have a blink reflex. That means my corneas could dry out or a mote of dust could scratch them and I wouldn't even know. So the air in the helmet will be filtered and humidified to protect my eyes."

"Okay. And the second reason?"

"It'll be a while before I can breathe for myself. The air in the helmet will be under intermittent positive pressure to inflate my lungs. You won't be aware of it. It'll just look as if I'm breathing normally."

He sighed. "It sounds horrendous, Prof. Are you really ready for all this?"

"Yes, I think so. You're right, it will be pretty horrendous for a while, but after a year or so it'll just seem like a bad dream—with a bit of luck."

"Luck? Does luck enter into it?"

"Well, Jack says the techniques are so good now there's a ninety-five per cent chance I'll come through it without any deficit. But I don't know how good their statistics are. Some people publish their best cases; they don't advertise their failures. That's why I want us to plan ahead. I want to be able to communicate during the recovery period when all I'll have is sight and eye movements. In the very worst case that's all I'll ever have, so what we decide now is important."

Andy sighed. "Okay. What do you propose?"

"I've talked about it with the rehab specialist. This space helmet thing will be fitted with an infrared system for detecting eye movements. You know the sort of thing, don't you?"

"Sure."

"Well, what they provide is a standard system: the display has choices and I move a cursor over them by moving my eyes to change the point of fixation."

"Right. Is this a holodisplay?"

"No, it's a standard virtual cube. If I look to any edge it rotates to the next face and shows me another display. One face will give me choices like turning down the lights, because initially I won't be able to close my eyes. Another one will have common words so I can spell out sentences. Basic stuff like that."

"You want to add to it, don't you?"

"Yes, I do. I want you to be able to tell me what's happening. That's straightforward: you'll speak normally and a voice detector will spell it out on the screen. And then I want to be able to switch to another display with choices, so I can respond."

"Like at the moment, when you say 'Good idea', or 'There's a better way of doing it.'"

"Exactly. And I want another display where I can do some programming for the project."

Andy's eyes were looking lively. I knew this kind of thing was exactly up his street. He was already writing the routines in his head.

"These systems you were talking about with the rehab specialist: can we get hold of them?"

"Yes, I've arranged to borrow one. It should be here this afternoon."

"Great! Well, it's simple, then. I can write the extra lines and I'll interface the system with the mainframe. I'll need to hack into their proprietory code. That shouldn't be a problem. I'll use QC-2."

QC-2 was the last complete prototype. In its own special field of application it was already running faster than any super cluster in existence. It could hack that code with ease.

"You know, my hearing must be going. I didn't hear you say that."

He grinned. Somehow he'd kept those chubby, youthful features, and his hair was still dark, but it was beginning to recede. His partner had suggested a stem cell implant, but he'd told her it wasn't important to him and it shouldn't be important to her. Sensible chap.

Something struck me. "You know, Andy," I said. "When

all this is over, I'm going to look younger than you."

He gave out a short laugh. "Something else to adjust to." He got up. "Anything you need before I go?"

"No, I'm fine. Victoria's not far away if I do need something. Sorry to saddle you with all this."

"It's not a problem. I'll come back to you when I've got something. Then we may want to try it out in case there's the odd glitch or things we want to add."

*

We didn't get the chance to try it out. The call came the following day, even sooner than expected, and now here I was.

The door swished and the anaesthetist appeared. She moved quickly, all business.

"Okay, Prof. Everything's lined up. I can give you the premed now. All right?"

She'd placed a line in the back of my hand earlier. She fitted a syringe to it, and a few moments later she straightened up.

"There you go. You'll feel a little drowsy soon. I'll be back in a few minutes. Think nice thoughts."

The door swished again and she was gone.

I tried to think nice thoughts, but my mind seemed to have its own agenda. It would fix on the least pleasant aspects of my situation, and return to them whenever I tried to steer it away.

I had no illusions. I was about to undergo a very radical procedure, and there was a chance I wouldn't come through it alive. I was resigned to that possibility, because the way I saw it, the alternative was even worse. But something else troubled me even more than that. It was the thought that somewhere, close by, there was somebody lying on another cot, waiting for his life to be terminated so that mine could continue. Whatever dreadful acts he'd been guilty of, I found that very hard to square with my conscience.

21

I lay there on the special cot, staring at the white-tiled, UV-irradiated ceiling. The air was cool, clean; no smell, except perhaps for the taint of cardboard coming from the disposable cellular blanket that someone had draped across my body. For my comfort. What a fucking laugh.

They'd left me alone for a few moments. There was no risk; I wasn't going anywhere, the restraints on my cot made sure of that: a wide metal band round each knee, one round my waist, one round each elbow, one round my neck.

Somewhere, not far away, someone else was waiting for this operation. Maybe they were giving him the premed now. He wouldn't be restrained. Not like this.

A sick feeling formed up inside of me; not just sadness, but hopelessness, frustration, futility. It coalesced into a tight little ball and it came up into my throat and forced tears into my eyes. SAF soldiers weren't supposed to cry.

Why not? I'm still human, aren't I? A thousand years ago criminals were hung in a metal cage until their bodies rotted or got picked clean by the crows. They say the most hardened villains wept when they were measured for their irons. So I'm allowed, aren't I?

I managed to blink back the tears.

*

I'd been hoping right up to the Court Martial that I'd get back my memory of the events that night. I didn't. It wasn't until they'd assigned my young Defense Counsel that I heard what had actually happened. When he told me the rest of my squad were dead, I didn't believe him at first. Chuck, Kit, Reza, Hermann, Dave, Gus, Eric, Tomaso, Reza, all dead? They were indestructible, they couldn't be dead!

He said they found the weapon that brought me down. The stun barrel was set to Level 10. That's full whack. I'm not surprised it clobbered me; the real surprise is that it didn't kill me—a charge like that generally paralyses your whole body, including your breathing. The medivacs must have done a fantastic job to keep me alive. Thanks to them I survived, but out of the ten-man squad I was the only one.

And then he told me I was to face a General Court Martial, accused of murdering my fellow soldiers. All of them.

Suddenly, a wave of stupid relief washed through me. For the moment it swept aside my grief. Was that why I was being arraigned? For killing a bunch of guys who were like brothers to me? It was so preposterous they'd never make it stick.

"Let's assemble our case," my Counsel said. "How do you explain what happened?"

"I told you before: I can't explain it because I can't remember anything about it. It's not exactly surprising, is it? Do you know what it's like to be hit by a Level 10 stun charge? Try driving into a brick wall, it'll give you some idea. I have no recall, none whatever. I get up to the moment we were ready to deploy and then it's a total blank."

He heaved a sigh. "All right, then, what witnesses can we call?"

For a moment I was speechless. "Witnesses? That's the

whole bloody point. There aren't any, are there? The only witnesses are a bunch of bandits and at this moment they're somewhere up in the hills laughing their fucking heads off."

"Now don't get excited, it won't help. What about character witnesses?"

I looked at him blankly. For some reason the first person to come to mind was Nurse Jenny Song. We'd struck up quite a rapport during the days I was in that hospital. But what was she going to say? That I was a big softie and I couldn't hurt a fly? No way; I'm a hard guy and it's my job to kill—for God's sake, that's what I was trained for. Prosecuting Counsel would take her to pieces. Who else?

Colonel Harken had visited me once in prison while I was awaiting trial. His main concern seemed to be what effect the case was having on the Force's reputation. Still, he was the only person I could think of.

*

I was led into a large, white-painted room. In front of me were the five officers who'd act as judge and jury. They sat in curious high-backed chairs behind a large oak table flanked by two flags, the Stars and Stripes on one side and the flag of the United States Army on the other. A portrait of the President hung on the wall behind them. Other than that, the room was bare of decoration.

My Counsel sat down with me at a small table. To our right was a similar table where Prosecuting Counsel was discussing something with his advisors. The witness stand was a lectern placed between them and the bench. After I'd taken my seat the court agreed to let me have the handcuffs removed. They weren't being generous; I'd seen the two armed M.P.s outside the door.

A clerk set a recorder going and I listened in a kind of daze as Prosecuting Counsel presented the case against me.

He called his witnesses: Captain Glen Avery, leader of the backup team who found us on the plateau; an army expert who analysed the video footage they'd taken; the Medical Examiner who performed the post mortems; an armaments expert…

It was very factual stuff. In most cases, my Counsel waived cross-examination.

For the defence we called Colonel Wendell Harken as a character witness.

"Colonel Harken," my Counsel said, "would you say Captain Forbes is a good soldier?"

"Objection, leading the witness."

"I'll rephrase the question. Would you like to give this court your opinion of Captain Forbes?"

"Certainly. He's a first class soldier. Excellent record. He's shown courage and initiative in difficult situations. Intelligent and resourceful. One of my best men."

"Colonel, in your opinion, is the Captain capable of the crime he stands accused of?"

"No."

"Your witness."

"Colonel Harken," the Prosecuting Counsel started. "How long have you known the accused?"

"A little over three years."

"But you're a busy man, Colonel, with responsibilities for running a large unit. In that time how much time have you actually spent with the accused?"

"Well, of course I monitor the progress of all my men closely…"

"No, Colonel, how much time have you actually spent with him, face to face?"

"We'd see each other in advance of missions. Ten times, I suppose, something like that."

"Have you ever fought alongside the accused in a theatre of war of any kind?"

"Well, no…"

"So on the basis of ten interviews with the accused, in a peacetime situation, you can be confident that he is not capable of what he is charged with?"

"Yes."

"Colonel, to your knowledge has the accused ever strayed outside the normal rules of engagement? For example, has he killed people who were not directly involved in the conflict?"

That was a hard one, because often you couldn't avoid collateral damage. There was a pause.

"Counsel, the missions undertaken by my people are dangerous. I can't always foresee what action might be required in the field. Those judgements have to be made very quickly and by the man on the spot. I'd say Captain Forbes always acted within the spirit of the instructions he was given. He undertook some very difficult missions. I don't believe any more casualties resulted than were expected."

Counsel turned his back on Harken, addressing his question to a point near the ceiling.

"Colonel, without discussing the details of the missions undertaken by Captain Forbes, would it be fair to say that he, and the men with him, would be operating in the equivalent of a war zone?"

"For the most part, you could say that, yes."

"And people can behave in unexpected ways in these circumstances, can they not? Showing extraordinary valour or selfless courage, for example?"

"Yes…"

He turned to Harken again and pointed. "On the other hand such conditions often arouse feelings of contempt for both enemy combatants and the local civilian population, do they not?"

"They can do."

"And unfortunately we know that stress, and sometimes sheer boredom, can translate that contempt into acts of brutality: torture, rape, and murder. We take pride in the high standards of our forces, but there will always be isolated elements who succumb to such behaviour."

Harken jutted out his chin. "The SAF has never—"

"Just a minute, Colonel. The difference between this country and so many others is that we do not tolerate crimes against humanity, and we will pursue the perpetrators and punish them whoever they are, and whenever and wherever they are found. The evidence suggests that they have been found here, and that is why this Court has been convened. Now, although you have attested to the character of the accused as you found him under normal, peacetime circumstances, it is quite possible, is it not, that under the pressures of this mission he behaved out of character?"

Harken frowned. "Counsel, all our men undergo a rigorous psychological screening before we even consider taking them on. During their training we put them through a variety of stressful situations, designed to exceed the worst conditions they're likely to meet in the field. What you're suggesting is highly unlikely."

"But it's possible, Colonel?"

Harken's lips tightened. He heaved a sigh. "Yes, it's possible."

"Thank you."

*

There wasn't anyone else to call in my defence. Before long I was facing the Prosecuting Counsel myself.

"For the benefit of the Court, the accused was part of an SAF team sent to the village of Raljevo to capture a group of criminals led by one Bogdan Zajc. Explain, Captain, if you will, what took place."

"The plan was to throw in a flashbang and then make a simultaneous entry through front and back doors and detain the target. The rest of the squad would be deployed down the street, ready to intercept his gang when they came running to the house."

"And what happened?"

"We got ready to move in. I can't remember anything after that."

"You can't remember anything after that. Well, what do you think happened?"

"We were ambushed, of course."

"I see. Did you land too close to the village?"

"No, we flew below the hilltops and landed five kilometres away."

"Were you noisy and careless when you approached?"

"No way."

"But nevertheless the gang was lying in wait, ready to ambush you. How did they manage that?"

"It's obvious, isn't it? Someone tipped them off that we were coming."

"I see. You're asking this court to believe that the SAF command, all of whom have been approved at the highest security level, tipped them off? Or the Czech police, who'd set up this operation, and who were as interested as anyone in its success?"

"Look, I don't know who was responsible."

"So who was responsible for ransacking the village, raping the women and cutting their throats, and murdering the rest of the inhabitants—men, women, and children?"

"Zajc and his people would have done that before we ever arrived. They'd already shipped out the youngsters they wanted for the sex trade."

"Ah yes, the deposition from the Czech police. It confirms that those children were kidnapped by the gang. But the children had no knowledge of any other atrocities being committed."

"Well, they may not have seen or heard anything, but it happened. The gang must have drugged them and used knives and silenced weapons. I gather that's what they usually do."

"Ah, but did they do it on this occasion? After all, Captain, you were found with your pack full of money and gold jewellery."

"So I'm told."

"And your comrades were dead, killed by rounds from your own weapon. Can you explain that?"

"No, I can't, because I wasn't conscious while all that was being done. Look, can't you see? Zajc and his gang had already massacred the villagers and they planted the jewellery and shot my comrades to make it look like I was responsible. It was a stitch-up from beginning to end. I fought with those guys in several theatres. We were like close family. No way would I ever do anything to harm them."

He turned his back on me and walked a short distance away, addressing the ceiling again.

"Captain, would you say the ten of you in that unit were

highly trained?"

"Of course. The SAF is an elite force."

"Yet you're asking us to believe that this gang of thugs, this Bogdan Zajc and his comrades, overpowered ten of you, without suffering a single casualty themselves?"

"I've thought about that. Your Medical Examiner said there were no wounds, other than the fatal ones. My team were wearing helmets and nanocarbon body armour. It would take something more than an ordinary munition to put them out of action. Zajc's people must have used a long-range stun mortar, fired from the village or thereabouts. Laser proximity detector, ranged to airburst at two metres—head height. A round like that would have knocked them cold without inflicting any obvious physical damage. It's the only explanation."

The Counsel turned to me, palms outstretched. "But we've considered this possibility already, and you heard Dr. Fairbrother, an acknowledged expert on the arms trade, testify that what you describe is an advanced weapon that has never been available on the international market, legitimately or otherwise."

"Well it was available to this lot."

He inclined his head, then moved nearer. "All right, let us suppose that such a weapon was in the hands of the people in that village. How do you explain the fact that it knocked out everyone except you?"

"What do you mean? I *was* knocked out by it. That's why I can't remember anything beyond that point."

"But you were found some distance from the others, brought down by a stun charge from your own comrade, Corporal David Cholmondley. It's no use denying it, Captain. His weapon had been discharged before it was dropped to the ground, still pointing at you."

"They must have dragged me there while I was still out. Dave would never have shot me."

"Not unless you'd betrayed him and all your other comrades."

His face was close to mine now. I stared back at him defiantly.

"I put it to you, Captain Forbes, that there is in fact an explanation for what happened. The gang had abandoned the village before you got there. You were going to be unsuccessful in your mission to capture Zajc, but you decided to make it look like one of his operations. So you and your comrades rampaged through that village, killed and raped the inhabitants, and stole any money or valuables you could lay your hands on."

I was breathing fast. "Never. I know my guys. We'd never do anything like that—"

He raised his voice, talking over me. "And when you'd finished, perhaps fearful that the others might betray you, or greedy for what they had, you took a fateful decision. It was you, Captain, who threw the grenade that stunned them, wasn't it?"

"No—!"

"Then you went to each one in turn, shooting them in the head or neck and taking what they had. And you would have got away with it, except that one of those men, Corporal David Cholmondley, although severely wounded in the throat, was still alive. He activated the beacon that brought in the backup team and managed to bring you down with a stun blast before he collapsed and died."

"It's not true. None of that's true."

He straightened up. "That, Captain, is for the Court to decide. Captain, is it not a fact that just before your hurried departure for Serbia you had murdered two civilians in

North Carolina?"

"Objection!" My Counsel was on his feet. "Prosecuting Counsel knows full well that this matter is sub judice."

The man smirked. "I withdraw the question."

*

Step by step, I'd watched my chances of liberty, and life itself, recede. Completing his summation, Prosecuting Counsel said:

"The massacre that took place in the village is not explicitly included in the indictment. Only a brief inspection was possible during the short reconnaissance conducted by Captain Avery's team, and no evidence was collected. It will, however, be quite sufficient to consider the evidence we have presented in respect of the calculated murder of nine serving soldiers of the Special Assignment Force, which is incontrovertible. The accused turned from a servant of the State into an enemy of the State. He has forfeited his right to live among the law-abiding people of this land and we urge this court to impose the maximum penalty."

Defense Counsel did his best.

"... a long-range stun mortar powerful enough to incapacitate the entire squad. The bandits then arranged matters so that it looked like the accused was responsible. I ask the court to take into account the character of Captain James Forbes, his impeccable record, and his courageous conduct in a number of previous missions in the service of this country. I ask them to consider whether a man such as this could be even remotely capable of the crimes of which he is accused."

The five officers withdrew to consider the verdict. It didn't take them long. They filed back in and I was told to stand.

"The verdict of this Court is that the accused is guilty of the murder of nine fellow soldiers. The sentence is that his conscious existence will be terminated, and his body will be used for the benefit of society in a manner to be determined."

22

The white tiles on the ceiling were beginning to burn into my retinas. I felt very tired. I could hear the surgeons talking as they scrubbed up in the anteroom. They didn't know they were being overheard, but then I've been trained to hear a footfall behind me, the snap of a twig two hundred metres away. It didn't help much in Serbia but I could listen in on these two all right.

"How's Marge?"

"In New York. She's meeting up with some old high school friends. One of these girlie things."

"Who's looking after the kids?"

"Me. I've got to pick them up after this one. Try not to overrun. Who's doing the main case?"

"Norman Andersen."

"Brought in the big guns, eh? Who's assisting?"

"Duke is. Theatre 3's prepared for them. Our recipient's in 2."

"Dominoes are always trickier. Where's Sue? She ought to be preparing the donor."

The voices faded.

What was that about dominoes?

The door swung open and shut. A woman had come in. I knew it was a woman before I could even see her; something delicate about the way she disturbed the air. Her face moved into view. Nice eyes. I always notice the eyes first. Large, despite the heavy eyelids and long lashes, a little bit tilted, big pupils, hazel irises, or were they green?

She gave me a little smile. Sympathy? Probably not. These people were civilians. Their manner was honed on ordinary patients, solid members of society, who needed a bit of reassurance. Not criminals.

"Sorry to keep you," she said.

As if I was in a hurry. Maybe I was. Maybe I did just want to get it over with.

"I'm your anaesthetist," she said.

"You mean my executioner."

She frowned, like I was a small child trying her patience.

"I have to check your identity," she said, looking at a sheet of paper. "Name?"

"John Doe."

"Date of birth?"

"Tenth of February, 2052." It was today's date.

She frowned again. "It really would be better if you could cooperate," she said.

"Better for who?"

"Please…"

"No, tell me. What are you going to do if I don't cooperate? Punish me?" I gave a derisive laugh.

She sighed and moved the blanket. All my details were on the leg tag. No one could tamper with that.

"Mr. James Forbes. Date of birth: seventeenth April, 2017," she read aloud, and ticked something off on her sheet. She moved out of my line of sight, then returned.

"Now, there'll be a slight prick."

I felt the sharp point of the needle as it penetrated the skin on the back of my hand. I couldn't see what she was doing, but I knew all the same. She'd slipped an intravenous catheter into a vein, and now she was taping it in place. I felt the tears welling up again. This time I couldn't hold them back. One rolled down the outside of my cheek. It felt cool and wet in my ear. One rolled down the other cheek.

She leaned forward. Her expression was different. She'd seen the tears. She tilted her head a little, wiped the tears away with her thumbs. Her skin was soft.

"Are you feeling sorry for what you did?" she asked gently.

That ball was still in my throat and the words wouldn't come. I swallowed hard and managed to unstick it.

"Let me tell you something, doc. I didn't kill my friends, any of them. Someone deliberately made it look that way. One day the truth will come out, and when that happens you'll know you killed an innocent man. I want you to remember that."

She straightened up, her lips pinched tightly together. "I'm not responsible for the judicial process, Mr. Forbes," she said stiffly. "I'm just doing my job."

She went out of my vision again, and then something caught the light. A syringe. She was holding it up to check the amount. My mouth went dry and I started to breathe fast through my nose.

"Now," she said. "I'm just going to give you something that'll make you feel a bit woozy."

I could feel the contact as she put the syringe into the hub of the catheter.

"There we are. All right, I have to leave you a little longer but I'll be back soon."

*

The ceiling had started to move, slipping down, then somehow back where it was and slipping down again. I was beginning to feel warm, almost comfortable. My eyelids felt heavy and I let them close.

My mind drifted. I saw myself in the high security prison, led out in shackles and handcuffs to consult with my lawyer across a glass partition.

"I don't see how they can do this to me. They have no evidence."

"They do have evidence, Jim, at least they believe they have. The bullets that killed your friends came from your rifle, it was in your hands and only your fingerprints were on it…"

"I know all that. I was cleverly set up, but they just can't seem to see it. Can't you appeal?"

"To appeal we need fresh evidence, something that wasn't available to the Court at the time of the original trial. Is there anything at all you can tell me?"

"You know there isn't. My mind's a complete blank from the point we were ready to go in. The next thing I knew I was waking up in hospital, paralysed."

He sucked in a deep breath. "Look, Jim, I believe you, but we're up against it. This was a bad business: a crack special forces team wiped out, evidence of civilian atrocities—"

"You know we had nothing to do with what went on in that village!"

"Yeah, I know, and you weren't on trial for it, but the prosecution made sure it was in everyone's mind, just the same. Those people want a culprit, someone they can point to, someone they can hold responsible. They think they have an open and shut case against you, so we can't expect a retrial from that direction. Keep turning it over in your mind. If you can recall the slightest detail that you couldn't remember before, let me know—I'll go for an appeal like a shot. But without that my hands are tied."

I shuffled back to my cell.

I lay on my bunk for hours, thinking of nothing, sometimes falling asleep. Each time I woke up I'd search that missing episode in my life, wondering if the blank, impenetrable fog in my memory had lifted, cursing to find it was still there.

I'm the sort of person who thrives on action. I'd been deprived of that possibility, and I settled into a state of numb resignation. I thought about my family, of course, but only fleetingly. I hadn't been in touch with them for quite a while. For some reason we'd never been close, and to contact them now would be pure self-indulgence. It would be painful and I couldn't see it would serve any useful purpose. Really it was better if they didn't know.

*

I heard the door, sensed a presence in the room again, and my eyelids flew open. She came into my field of view.

"Sorry about that," she said.

She had another syringe, holding it to the light.

I struggled against the drowsiness, my chest rising and falling, my heart thumping in my ears, my teeth beginning to chatter.

She bent to fit the syringe to the catheter. This was it.

"Remember me, doc," I said, looking at her, my voice shaking.

Nice eyes. Nice…

PART THREE

23

For all the reading I'd done, all the medical staff I'd spoken to, I was still totally unprepared. No one can tell you what it feels like to wake up with a living brain that isn't fully connected. I was unable to see, hear, smell, taste or feel anything. All I was aware of was a periodic coruscation, something like the cloud of sparks thrown up by a settling bonfire, each one brilliant but short-lived. Then I'd lapse back into a red, pulsating darkness, punctuated here and there by a stray spark, and I had the curious feeling of knowing I was aware but not knowing what I was aware of. After a while that state would fade to nothing. I don't know how long it went on for. I had no concept of time. When the scintillation was inside my head I was there for a while; when it disappeared, I was not.

*

The waking periods gradually acquired form; thoughts began to emerge, and memories returned. I recalled how Norman Anderson, a few days before the operation, had tried to tell me what to expect.

"Prof," he said, "when you wake up you won't have anything. You'll be in a body but you won't be able to operate it."

"Well, that's nothing new: I'm in a body now that I can't

operate."

He leaned towards me. "Right now you can blink, change your facial expression, chew, talk, breathe—you won't be able to do any of that. And you won't be receiving any information either. You won't have any special senses and you won't know where your limbs are—no input whatever."

"I'll have sight, won't I?"

"Well you'll have your eyes and all the connections, but initially you won't see because your brain will be in a kind of stunned condition. It'll wear off in a few days and then your sight will start to return."

"I suppose I can always sleep through it."

"The danger is, that's all you'll do. Normally the brain relies on input from the body to keep it awake. There won't be any, so we'll have to supply it for you. During the operation we'll implant some electrodes in your brain stem, in an area we call the reticular formation, to wake it up from time to time."

"How will you know if I'm asleep or awake?"

"That's easy: when you drift off, the alpha wave activity in your electroencephalogram will start to increase. Our instrumentation will pick that up and automatically shock you into consciousness again. We'll use these electrical alarm calls for about eight hours a day, to try to re-establish some sort of diurnal rhythm. We'll turn off the stimulation when we want you to sleep. It's all going to feel a bit strange."

A bit strange? He couldn't begin to imagine how strange.

*

Sight returned first. It was a huge relief. Sight is the biggest information highway of all the senses. It was important to regain that.

At the beginning, though, my vision was unstable. I was seeing double and I couldn't seem to marry up the right and left halves. Eventually it started to sort itself out and I realised that some of the remaining distortion was due to the curvature of the space helmet which was my constant companion. It must have been about then that the rehab specialist went to work on me. She would show me pictures, photographs of people I once knew, texts of my own papers and books. Of course I couldn't respond at that stage. Then my eye movements started to come back and that problem was solved; they set up the screen and I could move the cursor over letters and whole words just by shifting my gaze. She would ask questions like "Can you smell anything?" and I'd respond by seeking out the word "no". The answer was "no" pretty much all of the time, but at least they knew I was functioning. After a fashion.

It must have been a few weeks later when they let Andy in for the first time. He looked shocked, despite my warnings. I could see him speaking to the doctors and rehab specialists and glancing repeatedly in my direction. I guessed he was asking them if I was going to be like this permanently. They probably tried to reassure him, but how could they know?

He installed the new software and signalled me to shift the cursor to the edge of the screen to select the new displays. I could see right away he'd done a marvellous job. He used the voice-operated display to ask me a few questions about it, to which I answered "yes" and "no". Then he showed me some formulae to see if I could pick up my work where I left off. I recognised the symbols but it was very hard to maintain my concentration. It was like the drowsiness just before you fall asleep when a parade of images goes by and you can't grasp at any of them. After a while we both gave up. I needed to go further down the line of recovery before I'd be able to function at that level.

Unfortunately we'd neglected to include a cell with the message, "I feel tired", and I felt tired most of the time. Tired and useless. I was thinking then—if you could call it thinking—that I should have just let my body die. At least I could have withdrawn from life with some semblance of dignity.

At one point someone had the bright idea of showing me a calendar. Two months had passed since the operation. Two months? That seemed like slow progress to me.

Return of hearing was a mixed blessing, first because it only came back in one ear, and second because it connected up the organs of balance and my world started to turn upside down. I suppose my eyes were telling my brain one thing and my vestibular apparatus was telling it quite another, so vision became unstable again. The world spun around and if I used the display to darken the room it was even worse. I felt like I was going to vomit, although of course I had no control over any of the muscles you'd use to vomit. The spinning and the nausea went on and on, and I suffered horribly until one of the neurologists picked up the signs from my eye movements—he called it nystagmus—and popped in a drug to dampen everything down. It evidently worked because the vertigo subsided, although I never did recover the hearing in that other ear.

They worked hard on me every day, rolling me around on the ripple bed, massaging my skin, and testing various functions. Things were coming back, step by step. I could screw up my eyes and blink and make small jaw movements. Through the curved visor of the space helmet I could make out some sort of jerky motion under the bedclothes and I thought I was doing that, too, until I remembered: they'd be stimulating my limbs electrically to keep the muscles from wasting.

A doctor told me they were pleased with my progress. Cranial nerve X, the vagus, had come back and they could stop controlling my heart rate electronically. I was salivating, although it dribbled out of the corner of my mouth. That was encouraging because I could feel it trickling down the side of my chin, which meant I had some skin sensation. I could make a sort of noise in my larynx so there seemed to be a prospect of speech returning. I could move my tongue but it lolled aimlessly around. I worked on that with the rehab specialist, gradually getting it under control.

By four months I had all the special senses back—although smell and taste felt strangely foreign. From the neck down I was still paralysed, but I could turn my head a little to either side. When they realized I was making attempts to speak they removed the helmet for short periods, substituting electrical stimulation of my diaphragm and abdominal muscles to keep the breathing going. At last I could begin to communicate properly. The periods without the helmet became longer and, as I could swallow liquids by now, they removed the feeding tube they'd placed in my abdomen.

*

It took a long time to gain the use of my body. I say "gained" and not "regained" because, of course, it wasn't my body. It was a curious feeling, looking down on someone else's hands and trying to master a different set of limbs. Of course it was quite a while since I'd had any real contact with my own. If some miracle cure had materialized and my old body had been restored to me I dare say it would have felt equally unfamiliar.

I gather this one had belonged to a very fit young man. Well, it wasn't so fit now, not after six months of bed rest, despite the muscle stimulation. I felt floppy and uncoordinated. Not for the first time I wondered whether it had all been worth it. They put me on a prolonged course of exercise. Andy was trying to keep me up to date with what was going on in the lab but all that seemed very far away and unimportant. My physiotherapist had become the centre of my world.

She would attach me to a kind of robot, which bore my body weight while it gave me practice in standing and walking on a moving belt. Each day it transferred more and more of my weight to me. Eventually I could stand alone, although my physio had to be close by because my legs were still feeble and balance had only returned in one ear. Now that I could straighten up I found I was taller than I had been, which felt curiously gratifying. Then I started to walk unaided, very slowly, with my physiotherapist barking at me all the time "Heel strike first, now roll on to the toes". When I was too tired to continue, she handed me over to the occupational therapist, who sat me down to work on the myriad other motor skills I'd lost.

It was a full year before they sent me home and I could, at last, pick up my life once again. Victoria had another job by now, for which you couldn't blame her, but I didn't need a nurse any more: I needed a home help. Mrs. Alvarez was a motherly woman in her late forties, recently widowed. The arrangement suited both of us very well. She used a lot of chilli in her cooking, but that was all right because my sense of taste was a bit jaded. I also sold my small collection of fine wines. For some reason, I preferred beer to wine these days.

24

Initially it wasn't too bad, a feeling of drifting in some sort of limbo in an alien universe without sensation.

The only things I was aware of were the intermittent firework displays, like the moment after an anti-personnel shell-burst. I was a disembodied spirit floating through an unknown ether where all the departed souls of the world had gathered to lament the loss of their corporeal forms.

Well, if this was what it was like to be dead, it wasn't so bad.

I expected it to go on for ever, and I didn't mind that at all. But then things started to change. Each time those aerial munitions exploded the blackness would be replaced by a milky whiteness. Blurry shapes started to come and go in total silence. The images were never sharp, yet I was aware of reflections and distortion as you might get from looking out through curved glass. My thoughts whirled like a flock of starlings, congregating on one ghastly scenario after another. Eventually they settled on one, all-encompassing conviction. My spirit was not free after all. My brain had been dropped into some sort of glass tank, to be kept alive for some scientist to poke around in before it was finally trashed. And there wasn't a thing I could do about it.

I began to hear a hissing noise. This was accompanied by a chaotic, whirling sensation which made me feel violently sick. I couldn't relieve it by retching or vomiting so it just went on and on and on. Every waking moment was a nightmare of agony. I prayed that they would stop poking and probing, that they would just grind up my brain and flush it down the drain. But each time the darkness dissolved into light again I knew it hadn't happened, and more was waiting to be endured.

The noise became louder and started to sort itself into recognizable sounds. Sometimes I thought I could smell or taste something, but I put it down to memories of smell or taste that had been awakened in my tortured mind.

The dizziness receded, and my awareness extended to having the elements of a face and a tongue. It seemed that I was not just a brain in a glass tank: I had a head. It was strangely comforting. I couldn't exactly call the shots but at least my brain wasn't totally naked and defenceless.

Why did I have a head? I'd understood that my body would be used as a receptacle. Surely that meant the head as well? And what, if anything, was it mounted on? The little I could see suggested I'd woken up paralysed in a hospital bed again, but I knew that couldn't be. There was something down there, all right, and it made small movements, but it had nothing to do with me.

And yet the feeling grew that I possessed arms, and then legs. I knew about phantom limb sensation—when an amputee imagines his missing limb is still there—and I assumed it was something like that. Why it had taken so long for that sensation to come through, I had no idea, but how long was "long"? Time had no dimensions, no meaning. All this could have taken seconds or days or months or years.

Eventually I was forced to the conclusion that I had a body. I'd established full contact with my limbs. My vision was clear and I could hear and understand what people were saying. For increasing periods they would remove the glass helmet—the tank that had so cruelly deceived me earlier—so that I could breath for myself, strengthening my diaphragm and the muscles of my chest. Soon I could do without it entirely. One of the doctors withdrew a tube that I'd noticed sticking out of my abdomen. He said I didn't need it any more, now that I could chew and swallow. It was the closest to an explanation anyone had offered for what had been happening to me. At meal times, a male nurse would spoon pap into my mouth, but after a while, in a jerky and messy fashion, I began to feed myself. I spent some time each day in a wheelchair, although they had to use a gadget like a winch to transfer me from the bed. I was still very weak and uncoordinated.

When my nurse told me I was going to be moved I wanted to know more. The trouble was, I'd had no practice in speaking. Up to that point, no one had actually engaged me in conversation—they all seemed far too busy for that. They'd simply order me to nod or shake my head, and ask me questions with a yes-no answer like "Can you feel this?" or "Can you do this?" and then they were off somewhere else.

I tried to assemble the bundle of junk that made up my mouth and tongue and throat and said, "Where to?"

At least, that's what I intended to say. The mangled wail that came out of my mouth embarrassed both of us.

"Wei-oo?" I said. "Wei-oo?"

It was humiliating. His face registered a total blank. I tried again, a little more successfully, and stabbed with my forefinger for emphasis. Then I set my face into an attitude of expectancy so that he knew I was waiting for an answer. A light came on in his eyes.

"To a rehab-il-it-ation hospital," he said, enunciating it loudly and clearly as if he were talking to an idiot. You couldn't blame him. He didn't know what was going on inside my head. He'd probably nursed a lot of brain-damaged individuals, and I was just one of them.

It occurred to me then that this was the reaction I'd get at the rehab hospital, too. Wherever I went, I'd be treated as a basket case.

In the event, that concern was misplaced. The rehab people did their own thorough assessments, and they didn't seem to have any reservations about what I'd be able to achieve. I had a lot of one-on-one time in speech therapy, walking between parallel bars, swimming, all kinds of exercises, and games to improve my strength and coordination. Simple tasks like doing up a button and tying a shoelace were beyond me; they all had to be relearned. I saw little or nothing of the other patients. I interacted only with staff, and that revolved entirely around treatment.

Of course, as soon as I could communicate I was asking them all sorts of things. Where was I referred from? Why was I here? Who was paying for it? Mostly they just said they didn't know. I thought it was probably genuine. Whoever was responsible for this operation wanted to keep a tight lid on it, and the less these people were told about me the better. When I asked the name of the place I was in, they clammed up about that, too. They weren't allowed to discuss such things, they said.

There was one crucial question I thought I could get an answer to. I put it to my rehabilitationist.

"Doc, can I ask you something?"

There was a faint tensing of the body, a slight narrowing of the eyes; his guard was already up. Not surprising; this guy had stonewalled my questions before.

I pretended I hadn't noticed. "What's a domino operation?"

"Why ask me? I'm not a surgeon."

"Yeah, but I figured you'd know about these things."

His eyes narrowed some more. "What makes you ask?"

"Oh, I heard the expression somewhere. Just wondered what it meant."

He pursed his lips. "All right, it's a type of transplant operation. Here's an example. Patient has diseased lungs. He gets a heart and lung transplant because it's easier to do the two together. But his own heart was okay, so you don't waste it: you put it into someone else who needs just a heart. That's why it's called a domino operation: each patient affects the next, like a line of dominoes falling. Follow me?"

"Yeah, I follow you. Thanks, doc."

I waited until he'd gone and then I clenched my fist and muttered, "Yes!" He'd confirmed for me what I'd suspected all along. My body had been used for somebody else's brain, but for some reason my brain hadn't been junked; it had been transplanted on as well, into a different body.

What did that body look like? Up to this point I hadn't had a proper look at myself. I pestered them endlessly to let me have a mirror. I didn't need one for shaving, because they used a depilatory cream, which lasted for several days. I still preferred the old-fashioned razor, but I suppose they wouldn't allow me access to anything sharp. So in a way I could understand not having a mirror in my room or in the bathroom, but there didn't seem to be one in the entire building. It was policy, they explained: they dealt with all sorts of injuries and it could be demoralising if people saw themselves too soon. In the privacy of my room, I'd examine my hands and arms and legs and feet. They seemed unreal, like artificial limbs, yet I could feel them and move them as if they were mine. I spent minutes on end just running my fingers over them, trying to reconcile myself to the idea that these foreign-looking appendages belonged to me. And I still hadn't seen my face.

After a while they relented. One of the senior people led me to a room where there was a full-length mirror. At least, that was what they said it was. To start with, I couldn't believe they'd play such a lousy trick on me—it clearly wasn't a mirror at all, just a sheet of glass with someone else standing behind it. I was about to remonstrate when I noticed that my movements were being copied. I turned my head this way and that, and stuck out my tongue, and raised one eyebrow. It really was a mirror. I had been reborn into another body, and this was it.

In retrospect I shouldn't have been so shocked. After all, there was no reason why I should expect to see myself in that mirror. But I couldn't help it: my previous body image was still firmly cemented in my mind, and there'd been nothing to displace it. Looking at myself now, for the first time, I had to come to terms with a totally different appearance. I was a little taller, and whereas I'd been quite spare before, I was now heavier and deep-chested. It was a big frame, and whoever had it before was probably very strong, although the muscles had become slack and flabby from disuse. I leaned closer to the mirror. My hair had been brown and curly; now it was the colour of ripe straw, with just a slight wave. My lips had been thin; this mouth was more sensuous. There was a deep cleft in the chin. At least the eyes were mine, dark brown and familiar, although they looked a little strange surrounded by someone else's eyelids, the lashes thick and blond. It was quite a good-looking face, in an effeminate sort of way.

Panic gripped me. I hated this face, it didn't belong to me—nothing belonged to me. I'd been wiped off the planet and this—this artefact—had been put in my place. I saw it open its mouth to scream, but a strong hand took its arm, and led it back to its room.

After that I fell into a deep depression, and they added psychiatric counselling to my battery of treatments. Perhaps it worked. I only know that I was aware of a growing reservoir of anger and resentment. A sense of purpose emerged, which eventually coalesced into a firm resolve. I would find out who or what was behind all this, and I would get my revenge. To do that I needed to use the body I'd been lumbered with. All right. First, it was damn well going to get licked into shape.

Fitness had always been a big thing with me, so I knew what needed to be done. The staff were keen that I should recover my strength, but I don't think they were ready for the extent of my cooperation. I exercised on a treadmill and a stationary cycle and a rowing machine and worked out with weights, using every bit of apparatus in the gym. I'd follow this with a swim, doing more and more lengths, and then I'd start all over again. They were used to urging people on; with me, it was a question of holding me back. After a few months I was no basket case.

I started to entertain thoughts of escape. I was sure I could manage it; the security didn't seem to be to be high here. Even so, it wasn't a serious prospect because I had no identity and I hadn't a clue what I could do on the outside. I decided to wait things out.

I felt sure something was in store for me.

I just wondered what it was.

25

They took me from the rehab facility to some sort of training camp. Here there was a high double fence with razor wire and sentry boxes. I wasn't sure whether it was to keep me in or the rest of the world out. I just knew this wasn't a place where I could come and go.

There were no uniforms anywhere, the staff didn't wear name tags, and again it was clear I wasn't going to get any answers. Left to guess, I thought maybe it was a covert establishment that gave preliminary training to recruits for organizations like the CIA.

There were fifteen of us. The others kept themselves to themselves and that suited me fine. I wasn't feeling friendly, and in any case I didn't trust them or the staff. I don't know what I could have said anyway. I was all right when I was taxing my body to the limit. When it came to deciding who I was, I had plenty of problems.

I went around with a large chip on my shoulder. I didn't think it was entirely unreasonable. The best buddies I'd ever had were all dead, I'd been accused of killing nine of them myself, I'd lived through what I thought were my last moments on Earth, and then I'd been brought into a nightmare world which I endured for months without a clue as to what was going on. To cap it all, I'd been obliged to come to terms with a whole new body. Someone was going to pay dearly for all this: not just Bogdan Zajc, although he was at the top of my list, but whoever tipped him off, and whoever was behind the whole thing. If I was going to take that on, I needed to be ready, fit, and well trained. So when I found myself on a full-scale induction course for the third time in my life it wasn't unwelcome—in fact you couldn't hold me back.

We had no assault course this time, and no long runs in full kit—the emphasis here was on short, intense periods of activity rather than endurance. There was a lot of circuit training, which got progressively tougher. After each session we'd do uphill sprints, fully clothed. The sweat poured off us. The others bellyached— as I would have at one time— but I kept quiet. My new body was becoming trim, the muscles hard, and that's the way I wanted it. Whatever they threw at me, I took it and waited for more.

Combat training was close-quarters stuff, with pistols or assault rifles on the range, and knives or bare hands in the gym. The unarmed combat skills came back very quickly and even more effectively, because the arms and legs on this taller body gave me a longer reach. I didn't regard any of the others as mates, in fact I heavily resented them because they'd had it easy compared to what I'd been through. So I was as mean as hell, and pretty soon I was running out of people willing to take the mat with me. Then there were classes on survival skills and navigation; I'd done this sort of thing before, and again it came easily. Less familiar were poisons and antidotes, chemical warfare, techniques for breaking and entering, how to lay booby-traps and how to avoid them, and surveillance and counter-surveillance techniques, with the associated electronics. Finally they took us out to special courses where we could drive motorcycles, cars, and all-terrain vehicles through mud, over rocks, and around skid pans. There was a little flight training. I chose a VTOL simulator and "crashed" a number of times. The vertical take-offs and landings weren't too hard, but it took a long time to get the hang of hovering.

Whenever we left the camp it was in a covered truck. That confirmed my suspicion that the location of the facility was secret and they aimed to keep it that way. It had the additional advantage that no one got a good look at us.

In the evenings I went to bed early or watched holovision for a while. It was dominated by the forthcoming Presidential election. The parties held the various primaries and caucuses and the candidates and their running mates finally emerged. What interested me was that the Republican candidate, Senator Harrison Cawley, was ex-army. He made quite a lot of it, but the Democrat, Senator Harriet Nagel, seemed just as tough, and maybe a shade smarter. All the same it looked from the polls that Cawley had it sewn up. I didn't know what kind of President he'd make, but presumably he'd be good for the Department of Defense, and that meant the SAF.

The course continued to be physically demanding, and by the end of it two of the recruits had dropped out. I passed. Eighteen months after my brain was put into someone else's body I was summoned by the man who, if there'd been any clear ranking, I'd have called my CO.

He sat me down in his office. There was a large, sealed plastic bag on his desk. I glanced at it, then focused on him. I said nothing.

"Well," he said. "First of all, congratulations, Mr. Slater. You've passed this course with flying colours."

Hold on a minute.

They hadn't used names much in this place, and when

they had, they'd called me "Jim". This was the first time they'd used my surname, and that wasn't it.

"Forbes, sir," I corrected him. "My name's Jim Forbes."

His eyes locked into mine. He said slowly:

"Be assured, your name's Jim Slater."

I shrugged. What difference did it make? Jim Forbes was alive, but only inside my head.

He pushed the sealed bag across the desk to me. "Your personal belongings are in here. Be ready to leave at eleven hundred hours. The truck will be in the usual place. It'll drop you and the other graduates in a parking lot some distance away. You'll find your car there."

Car?

"Anything else?" he said.

"Only one thing, sir," I said, taking up the bag.

He waited, eyebrows slightly raised. I met his gaze.

"Why was I sent here?"

It was more a grimace than a smile. He sat back and interlaced his fingers.

"One thing I've learned about this job, Mr. Slater, is not to ask questions like that. My candidates come through certain prescribed routes. I don't know who they are, or where they go after they leave. I'd like to feel we've equipped them adequately, but I can't be sure of that either. No doubt someone would inform me if things weren't satisfactory. Why were you sent here? I don't know and I have no intention of finding out. In time your responsibilities may become clearer to you. They will never be revealed to me, and nor do I want them to be. All right? So-long, and good luck."

I stood up and gave him a cursory nod. "Sir."

His reply hadn't surprised me in the least. I felt like a piece on a gaming board, being pushed this way and that way by forces beyond my reach. All I knew was that they were lining me up for something and I still didn't know what it was.

Back in my room I couldn't wait to unseal the bag. I tipped it out onto the small table and poked the contents around.

The first thing that caught my eye was a United States passport. It was in the name of James Slater, and the photograph was clearly me—the new me. I wondered how they'd got it, but it would have been easy enough. Perhaps there was a camera built into that mirror; I wouldn't have noticed it—I was too busy studying the person on the other side. There was a wallet, which contained a bunch of credit tokens and a driver's licence, again with my picture in it. There was a proximity key for a car, with the licence plate on a tag, like a rental vehicle. There was a set of conventional keys that looked like they belonged to a house. I leafed through the documents. I had a bank account, a home address, a telephone and a broadband account—just about everything a citizen accumulates that makes him a fully fledged member of society. My occupation was given as "Journalist". There was even a Press pass, for some newspaper I'd never heard of. It was a totally manufactured identity, but at least it was an identity.

I looked up my home address on a map they'd thoughtfully provided. It was on the outskirts of Springfield, Massachusetts. It made sense to go there first.

26

"Andy? How's it going?"

"Oh, hi, Prof. Problems again."

He gestured behind him, where the insulated enclosure for the new computer dominated the big lab. Above it, the ceiling was a tangle of cables, and along the floor a grand highway of service pipework linked it with ancillary equipment. A similar, but smaller installation occupied the other side of the lab; this was the earlier prototype, QC-2, which was shut down at the moment.

"It's the superconducting bank," he went on. "Temperature management's all gone to hell. Took a while but we've tracked it down. There's a leak in the cooling plant."

"We were wondering why we were losing liquid helium," I said.

"Yep. Now we know."

I stood there with one hand cupped round the back of my neck, the elbow pointing forward. It flashed through my mind that I always used to adopt this posture when I was thinking; it was odd to discover that the habit was still there. Over Andy's shoulder I could see Paolo, Claude and Uri, huddled around a plan they'd unfolded over one of the large desks. Claude was tracing his finger along a line, but Paolo was pointing to something else. Their voices were too low for me to hear.

I looked back at Andy. "Typical, isn't it? You spend years

working up the electronics and the software, and then you get floored by a bit of plumbing. How hard will it be to fix?"

"Paolo reckons he can do it, but we'll have to close everything down first. It's going to delay the test."

"Can't be helped—we've got to get it right. Now, have you got a moment, Andy? Something I want to discuss with you."

"In your office?"

"Yes."

Andy shouted to one of the team who was standing near the enclosure. "Start shutting down, Russell. We'll have to bring it up to room temperature so Paolo can get in there."

"Okay."

We returned to my office. I took a chair at the desk and indicated another. I smiled at him. Like the others in the group, he seemed to have adjusted well to the Prof coming in with someone else's body and someone else's face. At least they were my eyes, and even if my voice sounded strange to them, they were my words coming out.

"Andy, you managed things really well while I was away. I just wanted to warn you that you may have to do it for a little longer."

He stiffened and a look of alarm crossed his face. "You're not going back into hospital, are you?"

"No, that's not the reason. I'm going on the campaign trail."

He flopped back. "Which party?"

I laughed. "Sorry, I'm not making myself clear. I'm not siding with either party. You know me and politics— I never had any time for it, and in one sense I still haven't. But there's a window of opportunity right now, and I don't want to miss it."

He looked troubled. I needed to reassure him.

"Don't worry, I'll explain. Andy, all those months I spent in hospital and rehab gave me a lot of time for reflection. I was about to re-enter the world, and I started to think about what sort of world I'd like it to be. My main worry is the loss of personal privacy—not just mine: everybody's. Everything you do these days is monitored. Everywhere you go, everything you spend, everyone you meet, gets recorded. The government says it's essential to national security, but it's got out of hand. I wondered how that had happened."

"Threats to national security are real enough, Prof."

"True, but I think there's a simpler reason." I leaned forward and tapped the desk. "Andy, they collect information because the technology lets them. People use the Internet and social media. Even when they don't, cameras and microphones are small, sensors are tiny and cheap—they're everywhere, even on the goods we buy. And molecular storage provides an unlimited capacity for squirrelling all this data away. In other words, it's you and me—or people like us—who enabled them to do it." I sat back. "We handed it to them on a plate."

"I suppose we did. So what? Technology progresses. You can't stop that. "

"No, we can't, but it was a mistake, all the same. We gave these people carte blanche to spy on us. Now they do it all they want, and it doesn't matter whether we're criminals, terrorists, or decent citizens."

He shrugged. "The genie's out of the bottle. You can't put it back."

I raised a finger. "Ah, but we don't have to sit on our hands, either. You see, there's a weakness, one we can exploit."

"What's that, then?"

"They have all these bits of information but they haven't a clue what to do with them. There's no way of processing all those parallel threads and comparing them in all possible combinations so as to pick out the patterns. At least there hasn't been up to now. You see where I'm going?"

His face fell. "Oh God, quantum computing. What we're working on could solve the problem for them."

"Exactly, and that's what I'm afraid of."

"But we need to cooperate with them. Fighting crime, detecting terrorist activity, getting intelligence on hostile military developments, all those are legitimate goals. That's what they fund us to do."

"Yes, but how do we ensure the same technology isn't used to spy on people's private lives?"

"We can't. Those are political decisions. We elect the people we feel are going to use the available technology in a responsible way."

I prodded a forefinger on the desk. "In theory, yes, but will they? Suppose they decide to license it out? What a money spinner that would be for the administration—better than taxation! Marketing organizations will have precise spending profiles for every citizen. Insurance companies will be able to calculate life expectancy from genomes, physical activity, and dietary and drinking habits. Media companies will adjust their expenditure to match the precise demographic for a holovision programme. The list is endless."

"But they can't let the technology out like that!"

"Who's going to stop them? We've given them the accelerator, Andy, but we haven't given them a brake."

He took a deep breath and expelled it slowly. "And you started to think about all this in hospital?"

"Well, I've had reservations for some time, but you know

how things were: I was so tired it was as much as I could do to keep up with the research. It's different now. I'm in a younger body, I have more energy. I feel I can do something about it."

"Like what?"

"Two things. First, I can generate public awareness of the problem. Right now the Joe in the street hasn't a clue what's going on. He needs to be told. What better time to do it than during a presidential campaign?"

"I still don't see how."

"You remember those science programmes I did before my operation?"

"Yes..."

"Well I pitched the idea to the same company. I promised them something contentious. They liked it. We ran a pilot on WGBX last Thursday and it went down a storm. I pushed the candidates hard on these issues and the debate got really lively. That's just what they wanted to see. The invitations have been flooding in. The channels are starting to address questions of privacy and personal freedom. Not that they're interested, but it makes for good holovision."

"And is it working?"

"Certainly. Up to then, audience ratings were dropping off. The public were bored stiff with anodyne political programmes. Now the two candidates are on their back feet, and everyone's watching. The companies are asking me for more of the same, and I'm ready to give it to them. It'll involve quite a bit of travel and preparation. That's why you'll have to manage without me for much of the time. It's only up to the election. There should be enough momentum, and enough commitment, by then. If not, I've failed. Either way, things will be back to normal here."

"That's all right, then. There's still a lot of routine preparation to do. We can cope for a while."

"Thanks, Andy."

"A moment ago you said there were two things you could do. What's the other one?"

"What I'm hoping to do is create such a head of pressure from the public that the politicians have to respond, have to make this a plank in their platform. I want to see a Committee of Civil Liberties set up. It'll control what information people are allowed to collect and what access others have to it. Organizations like law enforcement and the CIA won't have the automatic right to gather information on an individual or group of individuals; they'll have to present a case for it to the Committee. And sitting on that Committee will be members of the public who know about these things: human rights lawyers, representatives of the American Freedom Society, and so on. I've joined that Society, by the way. I'm very impressed with their agenda, but they've been getting nowhere with it. This is their chance."

"You're letting yourself in for a taxing time, Prof. Do you feel up to it? In yourself, I mean."

"Oh, I'll manage. It's good to get out of a wheelchair, and be independent again. These things aren't perfect, but I'll have to live with that."

"What do you mean 'they aren't perfect'? The operation was a success, wasn't it?"

"Yes, mostly. But I've lost my taste for fine wine. I can't listen to music—I have some sort of loudness intolerance. The foot drop on the right side is a nuisance, makes me trip over. And, oh well…"

"Yes…?"

I sighed.

"Andy, I have some numbness in the legs and feet, and I had some problems coming up the steps the other day. That's just the way it started last time. They didn't think the new body would be affected, but they could be wrong. After all I've been through, I may be on that same downward spiral yet again."

I saw the shock in his eyes. For a moment he said nothing. Then:

"Maybe it was just fatigue. Everyone experiences it from time to time. You're sensitized by previous experience. You could be reading too much into it."

"Maybe."

"So when does all this campaigning start?"

"Oh, it's well under way. I'm booked for several more programmes and there are some public meetings coming up. The candidates are frustrated as hell. It's forced a shift in their agenda. Cawley would prefer to talk about national security and preventing the spread of fundamentalism. Nagel wanted to talk about domestic and world poverty. But the only way they can get air time now is to accept the challenge, and address issues closer to home, ones that people feel are affecting them directly."

"Be careful, Prof. You're making yourself some powerful enemies."

"Seems to me I've been doing that all my life. One or two more can't make that much difference, can it?"

27

The parcel was delivered to my house in Springfield by a youngster on a motorcycle. He wanted a signature on his electronic pad. I hesitated for a moment, stylus poised. Then I scrawled "Jim Slater" and handed it over. I tried to grill him about where it had come from, but it was just a courier service and he had no idea.

I could hear him roaring off as I went back into the house. I'd been here for more than two weeks. It was minimally furnished, but it had everything I needed and the rent had been paid three months in advance. Once I'd stocked the fridge I was more or less self-sufficient.

I had no wish to interact with neighbours or anyone else. Out of sheer habit I familiarised myself with possible escape routes, both from the house and from the small garden at the back, and went for long runs, using the opportunity to reconnoitre every street in the district.

There was a computer and I spent a lot of time on the Internet. I wanted to understand, in much more detail, what had been done to me; that meant learning about the anatomy of the brain. It was hard going at first, because I'd never done anything like this before, but I persevered. I have a good three-dimensional sense, and things began to drop into place. In the course of these studies I developed a kind of clinical detachment and, despite myself, began to feel a grudging admiration for the skills involved in remaking all the connections and re-establishing the blood supply.

In the evenings I'd watch old movies or read. I'd lost interest in the Presidential election. The candidates were giving speeches in all the key states now, and the frantic flag-waving and tub-thumping only got me down.

I missed the comradeship of the old SAF base, but mainly I missed having any sort of structure to my life. In the many years I'd been in the army, not a day would pass without some sort of goal to achieve. Even in hospital and rehab I was working towards greater coordination and better fitness. Now I was just at a loose end, hoping vaguely for something to happen. The inactivity and the bitterness were having a corrosive effect on me. The parcel provided a much-needed diversion. I opened it eagerly.

Inside a lot of packing I found another box and a large manila envelope. I lifted out the box. It contained a plastic Glock 10 mm, a concealment holster with belt loops, a spare magazine, and a carton of the copolymer ammunition. I'd been given a sidearm that wouldn't show up on a metal detector. Was I expected to fly somewhere? I got the feel of the pistol, loaded it and unloaded it. It wouldn't be much use except at close quarters. I put it back in the box and opened the manila envelope.

The contents were strange. There was a transcript of a holovision debate on civil liberties and a flier advertising an upcoming meeting. I looked at the transcript. At first I wondered why it hadn't been handed to me on a memory tile. Then I saw the words at the top: READ, THEN BURN. It was good security. Electronic material could leave a trace, or be detected while you were playing it back. Once this document was burned no one would ever know it had been sent or that I'd seen it.

READ, THEN BURN
TRANSCRIPT OF DEBATE "THE MEANING OF LIBERTY"
ON GWBX-HV, 15 JULY 2053.
STUDIO 10, WGBX-HV, NEEDHAM, MASSACHUSETTS
MODERATOR: CLIVE HELLIGAN

(music, applause)

HELLIGAN

Ladies and gentleman, welcome to another edition of "Meet the candidates", the program in which we explore the position taken by the Presidential candidates on a variety of issues. And tonight the issue is "What is the meaning of liberty?" Let us welcome first the Democratic candidate for the President of the United States, Senator Harriet Nagel! Give her a big hand, everyone.
(applause)
And now, please welcome the Republican candidate for the President of the United States, Senator Brad Harrison Cawley! Give him...
(applause)

HELLIGAN

Thank you. And thank you to both of you for sparing time in a gruelling schedule to appear

with us tonight to debate the meaning of
freedom.

To help me in putting the issues to our two
candidates, our guest presenter this evening is a
man who you have come to know and respect
in recent months as a great champion of civil
liberties. He is one of the country's outstanding
intellects, Professor of Advanced Computer
Technology at M.I.T., ladies and gentlemen,
please welcome Professor David Hirsch!

I'd seen the candidates when I was watching the primaries back in the training camp. Professor David Hirsch was new to me, but the name struck a distant bell. I took the transcript over to an armchair. To start with, it was fairly innocuous stuff. The Professor made a statement, and the candidates responded with a lot of flabby rhetoric which didn't actually say anything at all. I think the Professor was getting a bit pissed off, because he cranked up the pressure and they started to smart under the onslaught. Cawley was the first to get an edge in his voice.

CAWLEY

Look, let me say this. It's all very well to
pontificate from inside an ivory tower, but out
here in the real world we have to be practical. I
think the people here, and the listeners out

there, know where I'm coming from. I've served this country in some of the most dangerous theaters of war that have ever been encountered. And, believe me, theory isn't much use when you're facing enemies like that. You have to take decisions, you have to act, because if you don't, you're dead. Now if I think there is the remotest chance that a terrorist is planning to bring down an aircraft or sabotage a data farm or release a bioweapon into the subway, or any one of the other miserable feats of cowardice that we've seen from these individuals, I am not going to stand by. I owe it to the American people to protect them, and, by God, that's what I'm going to do...
(applause. Senator continues more loudly)
...and I'll take whatever steps I have to.

HELLIGAN

What's your response to that, Professor?

HIRSCH

With respect, I think the Senator is missing the point. No one doubts the need to monitor suspected terrorist activity. But does that justify surveillance of ordinary, peace-loving members of the general public on the current scale? It's not just passports and driving licenses and social security I'm talking about. Right now every purchase or journey we make is registered on a database somewhere. Initially it was used by commercial organizations, in a piecemeal way, to assemble market profiles and monitor spending habits. God knows, that was bad enough, but now this information is passed to higher levels. We can't drive anywhere or walk anywhere without our movements being recorded. Our phone conversations are tapped, every destination we surf on the Internet is registered. In every facet of our lives we are being *watched*. Now, our lords and masters have got used to having access to all this information. What I'm saying is, just because we can, doesn't mean we should. It's an unwarranted infringement of the liberty of every law-abiding individual.

NAGEL

Maybe I can respond to that, Clive. First let me say that unlike my colleague over there I don't believe you need to have a military record to be able to take decisions. I've been taking decisions all my life, and if there is a suspected threat to the people of this country, make no mistake, I will not be lacking in resolution in rooting it out.

(applause)

But I think the Professor is underestimating the size of the problem we're dealing with. The perpetrators of these acts are not easy to detect. They don't wear a uniform or a lapel badge. Many of them were born here. They blend in with decent, law-abiding members of the public. Our job is to pick up their intentions and forestall them. What we're looking for are certain patterns of activity, patterns of communication. We can't say in advance what information is going to be useful and what isn't. Maybe if the Professor devoted his energies to devising software that could give us a more accurate profile of a potential terrorist threat we wouldn't be in the position of having to collect so much unnecessary data. That would be a helpful contribution to the problem. What is not helpful is stumping around the country telling everyone they're being watched.

HELLIGAN

Professor?

HIRSCH

What I'm saying is perhaps we should be turning that on its head. Let's determine what information is going to be useful and restrict ourselves to that, instead of putting it on record every time I take my trousers down in a public washroom.

(audience laughter)

No, you laugh, but there are cameras in those places, too!

CAWLEY

Well, public washrooms are an obvious target in view of the drug activity that goes on there. Maybe the Professor should take his trousers down somewhere else.

(audience laughter)

But seriously, Senator Nagel has drawn attention to the danger of this kind of bleating. The anti-government rioting we've seen in recent months shows us that places like LA and

Memphis are tinder boxes, an incendiary mix of people from different ethnic and religious groups and socioeconomic backgrounds. It doesn't take much to set these places off, and the enemies of this country know that. It's my belief that those riots were fomented by disaffected individuals who *feed* on the kind of message that *imported* academics like Professor Hirsch, and other namby-pamby commentators, are peddling. If the meaning of freedom is to give people like that license to spread panic, then perhaps freedom has gone too far.

(applause)

NAGEL

Well, it's not often I agree with the Senator, but I must say I share his view on this. And maybe the public interest is better served by professional politicians than part-time commentators from academic life.

HIRSCH

That sort of—

HELLIGAN

I'm sorry, Professor, that's all we have time for

now. We're going to have to leave it there. Our thanks to Senator Harriet Nagel, Senator Brad Cawley, and our guest presenter Professor David Hirsch. And to those of you out there: thank you for watching. If you have views on the meaning of liberty, don't forget to send them in on our chat line. Thank you, and good evening.

(applause, music)

END

I put the transcript aside and picked up the flier. It was for a meeting of the American Freedom Society, to be held in a couple of days' time at the Corby Memorial Hall. The Society had lined up four speakers, and second on the list was Professor David Hirsch. Clipped to the flier were two sheets, on which were the plans of both floors of the auditorium.

I went over to the computer and looked up the Corby Memorial Hall. It was primarily designed as a theatre, part of a big leisure complex on the edge of Rochester, New York State. They had an arena for baseball or football, gymnasia, cinemas and restaurants, a play and adventure zone for children, and various halls that could be used for staging tournaments of one kind and another. The Corby Memorial Hall was multipurpose, sometimes used as a concert hall, sometimes as a theatre, and sometimes for public meetings like this one.

By now it was crystal clear what the package meant. I was being instructed to kill Professor David Hirsch. He was considered to be a disruptive influence, a menace to public order, and a threat to the candidacy of—who? It seemed to me he'd become a thorn in the side of both candidates. So who'd ordered it? Of the two, Cawley seemed the more likely to seek a non-peaceful solution. Whichever one it was, they'd also be doing the other candidate a favour, which seemed a trifle odd.

So, in gratitude for the generous treatment I'd received over the last year and a half, I was expected to knock off Professor Hirsch. And what then? Another job, and another? Is that what I'd become: someone's personal assassin? How many jobs would I need to do to before they recovered their investment in me? Ten? More like hundreds. It wasn't feasible. There must be some other explanation.

There was only one way to find out. I had to go through with it.

And then I remembered where I'd heard that name before.

Professor David Hirsch. The man in the wheelchair at the top of the steps at M.I.T.

That's what I was expected to do. Kill a man in a wheelchair.

28

I parked the car, then tucked the plastic Glock into the concealment holster, which I was wearing inside my trousers behind my right hip. Then I flicked my jacket over it and got out. It was quite chilly, but I didn't want the encumbrance of an overcoat, and it was only a short walk to Corby Memorial Hall.

By the time I arrived, people were already filing in. There was no charge for admission: apparently the Society believed that no one should be excluded from attending on economic grounds. It was a noble sentiment, but the parking lot had been filling up fast, and I guessed that most of the attendees weren't in straitened circumstances. There were no ticket barriers, just a security arch with the usual metal detectors. I could see no sign of an explosive sniffer, but I was uncomfortably aware of the pistol as I passed through and tensed for the alarm. It didn't sound.

Moving with the crowd, I strolled through the foyer and up the red-carpeted staircase to the main auditorium. The seats were conventionally arranged in successive arcs centred on the stage. I paused, watching the people trickle down the aisles and into the rows, or parting left and right at a flat landing and descending to a second tier of seats closer to the stage. The stage itself was empty except for a lectern on the right. That told me how things would be organized. There would be no panel; the speakers would be invited to the podium one at a time.

It took only a moment to fit what I saw to the plans that were inside my head. Then I went down the aisle to the flat landing, and turned to the right. People were too busy finding their seats to notice the figure slip through the fire exit at the end.

I had thought the stairs would be untreated concrete, but they'd been lined with a pale brown composite that was non-slip and lightly cushioned underfoot. When I pushed through the fire door at the foot of the staircase I found the same material lining the corridor on the other side. This, I knew, led to the foyer in the front, but it also extended to the stage and the back of the building, where was an external fire escape—my planned exit route. Even more to the point, it was where I'd find the dressing rooms. My guess was that the speakers were in those rooms now, making their final preparations, the two women intensifying their makeup so that they wouldn't look like death under the bright stage lighting, the two men perhaps applying some powder over their five o'clock shadows. Professor David Hirsch would be in Dressing Room No. 6; I knew this because someone had helpfully scrawled an arrow and the initials "D.H." on the plan.

I followed the corridor to the rear, passed through a pair of swinging fire doors, and stopped as I saw the dressing rooms straight ahead. They were numbered with projecting signs, like the ones on the gates at an airport. I backed off quickly behind the swing doors. I would wait it out here. It was unlikely I'd be seen and if someone happened to come by I'd pretend to be checking the fire extinguisher that was handily placed on the wall.

The meeting was due to start. I could hear a faint noise from the auditorium, a hollow, fluctuating roar that reminded me of surf washing up on a beach. After a while it quietened down and someone started to speak. I couldn't make out the words, but it was clearly a welcoming speech and it would be followed by the introduction of the first speaker. There was a burst of applause and I checked my watch.

The voice that followed was female. Again I couldn't hear the words, but forty minutes later there was another burst of applause. The original voice returned to introduce the next speaker. I could almost make out the syllables: Pro-fess-or Dav-id Hirsch. More applause. I checked my watch again and pushed through the fire doors.

The corridor was deserted. I stopped at Dressing Room No. 6 and drew the Glock. It was time to be careful—whoever had wheeled him out onto the stage could have come back here. I opened the door quickly and stepped in.

The room was empty.

I looked around. It wasn't very big. There was a dressing table with a large mirror, a pot of makeup remover, and a powder puff sitting inside a drum of loose powder. A chair was pulled up to the table, and there was another chair to one side. On the opposite wall there was a double wardrobe. I opened the doors. It was full length, with a rail full of captive hangers. Two of these were occupied, one by a raincoat, another by a sports coat and trousers. Both were almost certainly his. I left the doors open and took the chair by the dressing table to listen and wait.

I'd have been bored if the adrenaline hadn't been running. Could I actually go through with this? I wasn't sure. I'd killed people before but usually they had a weapon in their hands and were looking at me in an unfriendly way. Shooting an unarmed academic in a wheelchair was a different bag altogether.

A voice inside me said, "What's so hard? You listen in case someone's pushing the wheelchair in. They'll probably leave him alone to change out of his suit. You step out of the wardrobe, and 'pop'. Of course, if he's too disabled to change himself, the carer will stay, and you'll have to drop both of them."

Just like that. Not hard at all. Except to live with for the rest of my life.

What if I decided not to do it? It wasn't really an option. Someone had gone to a lot of trouble and expense to get me transplanted, rehabilitated, retrained, and set up like this. If I wasn't useful to them I wouldn't last long, of that I was sure. Besides, I needed to get to the bottom of all this. I couldn't do that by walking away.

I glanced at my watch. He'd been speaking for thirty-five minutes. Then I heard the applause. It was time. I got up, pushed the chair in as I'd found it, got into the wardrobe and drew the doors shut.

A few minutes later, I heard the door to the dressing room open and close. There weren't any voices. It seemed like there was only one of them. I waited for a moment, then pushed the wardrobe door open a crack. A man was standing with his back to me, brushing vigorously at his face with a handkerchief. He wouldn't see any movement reflected in the dressing table mirror because he was directly in front of it. There was no wheelchair.

I was taken aback. Had I been given the wrong room? Perhaps they'd reassigned them at the last moment. Maybe he didn't need the wheelchair all the time. I had to take the chance. There were only two men on the list of speakers, so I had a fifty-per-cent chance of being right.

I stepped out, the pistol extended in front of me.

"Professor David Hirsch?" I asked.

He whirled round and I looked into my own face.

I saw the mouth moving but it may as well have been a million miles away because the sound wasn't reaching me. I'd gone rigid, the pistol frozen in my outstretched hands. Every clock in the world had stopped.

Again the mouth moved and this time something must have filtered through because suddenly the room was back and the chaotic jumble of thoughts bouncing around inside my head had congealed into a dazed incredulity.

I straightened up slowly and the plastic Glock sank down off target. When I managed to speak, my voice was little more than a low rasp.

"What... the fuck... are you doing in my body?"

28

The Professor and I stood there, staring at each other in silence.

I was still breathing fast. Shock had given way to an acute sense of loss and indignation. Somewhere deep down I knew he wasn't to blame for this outrage, but if I could have reached out and snatched back the body that had been stolen from me, I'd have done it in an instant.

His face was ashen. He glanced down at the pistol, now pointing at the floor, and the tension seemed to go out of him. He squinted at me.

"Your body?"

Again I seethed. That was my voice he was using.

I answered in the voice I'd been given. It rang even more strangely in my ears. "Yes, my body."

"Impossible."

I struggled to draw my scattered wits together. It was like gathering in a parachute after landing.

"You think I don't recognise myself? All right, check this out. Cheloid scar, left side, over the tenth rib. That was made by a knife. I was lucky; it didn't penetrate far, otherwise it might have nicked my spleen. Right shoulder, over the deltoid: long track from a bullet graze. I collected that one in Africa. Go on, take your shirt off. Have a look."

His mouth tightened. "I don't need to. I've seen both of those—and wondered about them. Great heavens. So, what are you doing here?"

"I was sent to kill you."

"Really?"

"Really."

Again he regarded me, head slightly to one side. "Well, if you're being paid to kill me you'd better get on with it."

I blinked at him. He'd not only recovered from the shock; he was cool. In a strange way it settled me, too.

"I'm not being paid."

"Then why are you doing it?"

"I've got my reasons."

"Sounds to me like someone is using you. Who is it?"

"I don't suppose I'd tell you if I knew. As it happens, I don't know."

"Would you like to know?"

I blinked again. "Yes, actually I would."

"All right, why don't you put that thing away and sit down."

He pulled out the spare chair.

I hesitated, then tucked the Glock into the front of my waistband, within easy reach. Who was I kidding? This was ridiculous. I knew I couldn't use that pistol. How could I shoot myself?

He sat down facing me in the other chair and crossed his legs. I was still amazed at how calm he was.

"So," he said. "Why do you think you were sent to kill me?"

"Let me hazard a guess. You're considered a danger and a general fucking pain in the ass. Particularly to two candidates for the Presidency."

He laughed. "Oh, I've irritated those two all right—but killing? It's a bit extreme, isn't it? Maybe there's another angle, Mr... what shall I call you?"

"You can call me 'X'. You're a mathematician, aren't you? It shouldn't be too hard."

He smiled, and I felt a growing respect for him. He was in the room with a potential assassin, yet he could smile.

"So you know something about me," he said.

"I know you're a prof at M.I.T. and you specialise in quantum computing."

"That's right. What we're doing could give this country supremacy in the intelligence gathering business, so perhaps you were sent by enemies of the state, or terrorists."

"I doubt it."

"Why?"

"Because of my previous history."

"I'd like to hear about that, but—look this isn't the time or place to be discussing these things. The speeches will be over in a minute and the organizers will be coming back here. They're planning to take all the speakers to dinner. Why don't we arrange to meet somewhere else?"

"So you can bring the cavalry with you next time?"

"All right, we'll go back to my office at M.I.T. together."

"And you hail the first gendarme we see."

"This isn't getting us anywhere. You're going to have to trust me."

"After what's been done to me? Not bloody likely. I don't trust anyone."

He gave me a sorrowful look. "Look, I accept you've been treated badly..."

"You don't know the half of it."

"Well, you'll have to decide one way or another. They'll be here any moment."

I thought for a moment. "How did you get here?" I asked.

"I flew to Rochester and they picked me up at the airport."

"No car, then."

"No. I can't drive any more. I haven't got enough control of my right foot."

"It was perfectly all right when I gave it to you." I said it bitterly.

He looked a bit blank.

"All right," I decided. "Here's what's going to happen. You're going to leave a note on your dressing table. Tell them you've been called away unexpectedly. Say you're sorry, and maybe you can do dinner another time. Then you and I are going to walk out of this place and over to the big parking lot where I left my car. It'll be crowded on the way out, because they'll all be pouring out of the Hall. Stay close to me and don't try anything. This," I pointed to the pistol before returning it to its holster, "won't be far away. And a copolymer round makes a big mess of your insides. Understood?"

He sighed. "Yes, of course."

I went over to the wardrobe, lifted out the raincoat and the sports jacket and trousers, and held them up.

"These yours?" I asked.

"Yes."

"All right. I'll carry them for you. Let's go."

Neither of us said anything on the way over to the car. I opened the door and he got in. I kept my eye on him all the way to the driver's side. I got in and locked the doors. Then I drew the Glock and placed it under one thigh where I could get at it quickly.

"Now what?" he asked.

"Well, you've missed out on your dinner so it seems only fair that I should buy you one. We'll stop somewhere on the way back. Then we can continue our little conversation."

"All right. Before we leave, can you tell me just one thing? I know I'm in someone else's body. What I don't understand is how it happens to be yours."

I took a deep breath.

"It was a domino transplant, Professor. Your brain went into my body, but my brain wasn't discarded. It was put into another body."

"That's not supposed to happen."

"I know."

"So whose body have you got?"

"I haven't the faintest idea."

*

We travelled in silence. Close to Albany I spotted a motel and restaurant complex and pulled in. I switched off the engine and turned to him.

"If you try any funny stuff…"

He held up a hand. "Let me show you something," he said. He dipped his hand into the inside pocket of his jacket.

"Slowly," I growled, my hand on the Glock.

What he pulled out was a small, white, squarish device with a switch and a prominent button. He held it out and I took it in my left hand.

"What's this?" I asked.

"It's a personal alarm. It sends out a powerful signal on the emergency wavelength, one that would be instantly recognised. You see, Mr X, some people may want me dead, but there are others who'd very much like to keep me alive. This was given to me for my personal protection. I could have activated it at any time while you were driving and you wouldn't have even known until it was too late."

"So why didn't you?"

"I'll tell you why. Whoever hired you is interfering seriously with freedom of expression in this country. Invasion of privacy is bad enough, but knocking off your political opponents is totally unacceptable. I'd like to know who tried to do it, and when I find out I'm going to expose them."

"Unless they get to you first."

"Yes, unless they get to me first." He looked at me squarely. "I'm not afraid of dying," he said. "By rights I should be dead already—I know that. I'm on borrowed time. I want to do something worthwhile with my extended life. And I'll take the risk."

I bit my lip. Then I gave him back the alarm and tucked the Glock into the holster at the back of my trousers.

"My name's Jim," I said.

29

We had pizzas with a side salad. I had a Michelob with mine; he had mineral water. We ate in silence. I noticed that we both handled a knife and fork the English way and I wondered how such a completely trivial thing had come to occupy my mind at this precise moment.

The conversation only restarted after the plates had been cleared and the coffee was in front of us.

"All right to talk now?" Prof asked.

I glanced around. I'd deliberately taken this table. From here I could view all exits and entrances, and neither of us could be seen from the outside. The other customers had taken the more popular window tables, and a holovision in one corner was making enough noise to cover our conversation.

"Sure," I said. "Go ahead."

"Jim," he said. "Who else knows about this domino transplant? Apart from the surgeons, I mean."

"My guess is, not many. Once I was transferred from the hospital I'm not sure anyone knew what had happened to me. As far as the rehab people were concerned I'd had a nasty climbing accident. I didn't bother to disabuse them of the notion."

He looked at me steadily. "If you don't mind my saying so, you don't sound like the average hoodlum."

"No, I'm kind of an exceptional hoodlum. I'm a soldier. And not all soldiers are dumbfucks, either. I went to university."

"While you were still in England."

"Yes. How do you know?"

"It takes one to know one. What did you read?"

"Geography. It gave me a taste for seeing the world. That's why I joined the army. I guess hanging out with soldiers has coarsened my vocabulary somewhat."

The professor nodded briefly. "Let's get back to the transplant. The rehab people didn't know what had happened to you. Anyone else?"

"Not that I know of. After rehab I was sent to some kind of camp and retrained for general combat and undercover work. No one there seemed the slightest bit interested in where I'd come from. At the end of the course the CO handed me a passport, driver's licence, car keys, house keys, and all the rest of it. Somebody had arranged a whole new identity for me."

"And that somebody is probably the only person who knows who you are. And since they ordered the domino transplant, we can be fairly certain they knew your body was destined for me."

"Presumably."

My head snapped round. Somebody had taken a table not far away. I looked carefully for an earpiece or any other sign that he was eavesdropping, but he seemed to be intent on his meal. I turned slowly back to the Prof and flicked my eyes in the direction of the customer.

He got the message, and lowered his voice further.

"Well, one thing's clear. These operations aren't cheap. Whoever's responsible for this has major resources behind them."

"That's for sure."

There was a long silence. I sipped my coffee, watching,

fascinated, as a different and more brilliant brain worked inside what I still regarded as my head.

Eventually he said, "Jim, it's been a long day and I'm tired. Were you planning to drive all the way back to Boston tonight?"

"Why, do you have an alternative suggestion?"

"This place doesn't look too bad. I was going to suggest we take a couple of rooms in the motel and start fresh in the morning. I've had a lot to take on board. It would help if I could sleep on it."

I looked at him, considering the idea.

What the hell.

I booked adjacent rooms and we wished each other good night.

*

When I was on missions I never needed an alarm. I'd tell myself "Reveille, 0400", sleep like a baby, and wake up on the dot. The others could do the same; it was almost part of our training. But when I woke up the following morning and picked up my watch I nearly leapt out of bed. It was eight-thirty.

I splashed my face and threw on my clothes, checked the Glock was in the holster, then charged to the next room and hammered on the door. No reply. I slapped my forehead with the palm of my hand. There were windows on the other side of the corridor and I looked out. I fully expected to see several hundred of New York's finest, with the National Guard thrown in for good measure, taking up positions on the perimeter, sniper rifles at the ready.

There was a guy mowing the grass.

Maybe they were still on their way. I ran down to the restaurant room and drew up short.

Prof was sitting calmly at the same table we'd occupied the evening before. He gave me a wave. I went over.

"I hope you don't mind my starting breakfast without you, Jim. Have a good night?"

"Yes, er, thanks," I said, getting my breathing under control. "Hang on, I'll grab myself some coffee." I pointed to his empty plate. "You want anything else?"

"No, I'm fine, thanks."

The buffet table was loaded. I didn't have much of an appetite, but out of sheer habit I took juice and a coffee, and picked up eggs and hash browns at the hot counter. On my way back I made a slight diversion to pass the windows, which overlooked the front. I was still wary, but the parking lot outside wasn't pulsating with red and blue lights. There were only a few people in the restaurant, all occupying tables on this side. The holovision was blaring.

He waited for me to sit down. Then he said:

"Jim, I've been thinking about this. The only way we're going to get to the bottom of it is if you tell me what's been happening to you."

"I thought I had."

"No, I mean before the transplant."

"Oh. You think that would be useful?"

"Absolutely. There's something unique about your role in this and I have to know what it is."

I hesitated. We weren't supposed to blab about operations. On the other hand, a lot of things weren't supposed to happen. I wasn't supposed to have had my brain transplanted into someone else's body. I wasn't supposed to be sent to assassinate a Professor.

He smiled indulgently. "Bear in mind that I have Top Secret security clearance. I need to have it for the kind of work I do."

I heaved a sigh. I had little enough reason to feel loyal to anyone—the SAF, Harken, U. S. of A., the whole damned shoot. I decided to chance it.

I told him about the Ubindi mission. There wasn't any point in covering my entire career, and I hadn't felt there was anything questionable about what we were asked to do before that. But that operation was different, and I was convinced there was something more behind it. Then I gave him an account of what happened in Serbia, up to the point where my mind had gone blank. The trial and its inevitable conclusion. The horror of waking up, thinking my brain was in a tank. The ghastly nature of the recovery. It was the first time I'd said anything to anyone about what I'd been through, and for some reason it felt good to get it off my chest.

He listened without a single interruption. When I'd finished he shook his head gently.

"Jim, you and I have been through a similar nightmare experience. But I was warned in advance what would happen to me. How you managed to come through an ordeal like that in total ignorance defies belief. I'm truly sorry."

We sat in silence for a moment.

After a while I said, "So do you think it helps, knowing all that stuff?"

"I'm sure it will. I haven't put it all together yet, but I'm beginning to. Tell me something, Jim. This business of assassinating me. If you were planning a caper like that for yourself, what kind of weapon would you choose?"

I wasn't expecting a question like that from him. I took a

mouthful of coffee and swallowed before I answered.

"Lightweight sniper rifle, Accuracy International or H & K, for preference. Suppressed weapon with subsonic rounds, to make it harder to localize. I could have done it from the gallery—I didn't see anyone else go up there. Or from the projection booth. From that distance I couldn't miss. I'd have had to find a way of getting in, but it could be managed."

"And that thing?" He pointed towards my belt, indicating the unseen pistol in the holster at the back of my trousers.

"The Glock's a short range weapon," I replied. "I could have popped you from one of the front rows with it. If I'd wanted to be mobbed instantly."

"They knew you wouldn't do that."

"Yes, what are you driving at?"

"Jim, the people who arranged the domino transplant are the only ones who know your identity. So they must be the people who sent you to assassinate me."

"That's right. I assumed it was some kind of quid pro quo."

"You know what I think? I think whoever gave you that weapon intended for you to meet me face-to-face. And they also knew perfectly well that you wouldn't pull the trigger."

"Hang on a bit…"

"Come on, now. They knew I was in your body, and you could hardly shoot yourself, could you?"

I looked at him. No wonder he'd been relaxed. He'd known that all along. Smart man.

"All right."

"Conclusion. You weren't sent to kill me at all."

I blinked several times. "But they made it blindingly obvious—"

"—because they knew how you'd respond. And they

wanted to be sure you'd make your move without anyone else knowing about it. They meant us to meet, Jim. Very discreetly."

"But why me? Why go to all that expense?"

"Look, someone's made at least three attempts to kill you: in the RotoFan, in the car crash with your friend, and in the Serbian operation. Actually I'm not sure why this man Bogdan Zajc didn't kill you with the others in that operation. Maybe he just took a malevolent delight in framing you and discrediting the unit. Anyway it resulted in a judicial death sentence so the net result was the same. Whatever this is about, somebody's prepared to commit murder—multiple murders—to keep it quiet. Right now, they think they've succeeded. What they don't know is that someone else has been taking a close interest. Thanks to them, you've survived—at least your brain has—and as a result the secret's survived with you."

I thought about that for a moment. "All right, that explains me, I suppose. Where do you come in?"

"I'm not sure. But my research gives me access to information at a very high security level. And even the prototype computers in our lab could decipher internal comms in government departments, if I was naughty enough to intercept them." He met my eyes in a conspiratorial look. Then he pushed his empty plate aside and rested his clasped hands on the table. "Jim, I have the feeling there's been a serious abuse of power in high places. Between us, we have to figure out what it is, and who's responsible."

"Prof, no offence, but I'm not into politics or civil liberties. There's only one thing I want to do. I want to nail that bastard Bogdan Zajc, and I want to nail whoever tipped him off and whoever was responsible for killing my best mates."

He spoke very quietly. "You won't find out on your own, Jim. We'll work together. That way you'll get what you want. And so will I."

31

After my conversation with Jim over breakfast he thought it best not to return to his house at Springfield. He had few possessions, he said, and there was nothing of any personal value at the rented house; he'd put everything he needed in the car when he set out for Rochester.

We drove to Boston and he dropped me at a subway. He said he was going to look for an inexpensive motel, but he was planning to move every few days anyway to make it hard for anyone to keep track of him. That included me, of course, so perhaps he was still wondering how far I could be trusted.

It would take a little time to get my inquiries under way. I gave him my office number so that he could call me after a few days. By then I thought I should have something worth reporting.

I'd opted for the subway because the T runs close to my home, and I wanted to hang up my suit and have a shower and shave. I got back to the department in the early afternoon and went straight to the lab.

Andy was up a ladder, watching someone, presumably Paolo, at work inside the cooling plant. Something like an electric screwdriver was whirring intermittently. He caught sight of me and came down the ladder.

"Hi Prof," he said. "Want any plumbing done? We're getting quite handy at it."

I glanced down at the sheaf of papers in his hand. They were full of diagrams, presumably the plans of the cooling circuit.

"Andy, this work on the cooling system. Does it affect QC-2?"

"No, the unit for QC-3 is totally independent. Why?"

"I'd like to use QC-2. Can you get it running for me?"

I noticed a flicker of curiosity in his eyes. It was unusual for me to be doing something like this on my own, but he was too tactful to ask questions.

"Sure," he said. "It'll take an hour or so for it to cool down to working temperature. Is that okay?"

"Yes, fine. Thanks, Andy." I jerked my head towards the new computer. "How's it going?"

"Not too bad. I think we're getting there."

A muffled shout came from inside the cooling plant. "Andy?"

He shouted back, "Coming, Paolo."

I lifted a hand. "I'll let you get on with it. See you later."

As I left the lab I heard the ladder creak under Andy's weight, and Paolo shout: "Which circuit are the red pipes on?"

The computer in my office provided a conventional front-end to QC-2, our last fully operational prototype. I logged in and a red "NO ENTRY" sign came up in the corner of the screen. It would remain there until the unit was down to operational temperature. I filled in the time by assembling the code for the searches.

An hour and a quarter passed. I'd pretty much finished writing the code when the "NO ENTRY" sign disappeared, to be replaced by "READY" in green letters. I was enjoying the irony of all this. The American government funded this work so they could spy more effectively on us. Now I was going to use it to spy on them.

I began to feed in the search routines.

*

Jim phoned three days later and we arranged to meet for lunch. I'd heard of the café; it was close to Harvard Yard, and popular with students. Normally I wouldn't go near these newer establishments, but I thought Jim could have his reasons, and didn't argue.

When I got there I hovered for a moment. Was I supposed to wait inside or outside? It didn't look that large, so I'd probably spot him if he was there already.

Jim appeared out of nowhere. He said nothing, just opened a palm towards the entrance, and we went in.

The interior was gloomy in the current fashion, all grey planes and satin chrome tubing. I knew it was dictated in part by the spill-repellent coating on all the horizontal surfaces; there's a limit to the decorative possibilities of carbon nanotubes. A diffuse white glow under the rims of some of the tables indicated which were available. We took one well away from the window, and the rim-lighting extinguished as we sat down.

Jim looked around, no doubt scanning the exits and taking stock of the people at neighbouring tables. He seemed satisfied, as I was. They were mostly students, and there was enough noise from their lively conversations, and a holovision somewhere out of sight, to cover anything we said.

"Did you take evasive manoeuvres on your way here?" he asked.

"Well, no... why?"

"If someone wants to keep an eye on us, you're the one they'll watch—they can't keep track of me. That's okay, I can always lose them afterwards. Iced water?"

"Thanks."

He filled two disposable cups from the dispenser in the centre of the table and pushed one towards me.

"We'd better order," he said, and lifted a small handset from the cradle near the dispenser. "Do you want to see the menu?"

"If they have a tuna salad, that'll do for me."

"Tuna salad…" he pressed to send the order to the kitchen. "And to drink?"

"Capuccino."

He pressed again. "Done. I'll have a sandwich… and a capuccino as well…"

He took out his cloudphone and passed it over the handset. When I began to remonstrate, he raised a hand.

"I'll stand you for this one." He looked at the screen. "It says, 'Order and payment accepted, estimated wait eight minutes. Thank you for eating at Mario's'."

"Gadgets," I commented.

"Speeds things up. And at least you know what you're getting."

"We'll see."

He let the handset retract, then put his hands together expectantly.

"So—any luck so far?"

I didn't like the idea of calling what I was doing "luck", but I passed over it.

"Some progress," I said. I looked around, then leaned forward. "I started with the Ubindi mission. I've felt all along there was something fishy about it. We both did."

"Go on."

"Your brief was to extract a hostage. That wasn't unusual."

"No."

"But you had to knock off the commander before you pulled out. And that was unusual."

"Not really. What was unusual was the way we did it. It was more like an assassination. Not something I ever thought the SAF would get involved in."

"But you're a good soldier, so you carried out your orders. Then this RotoFan gunship comes in and demolishes the entire camp. That sounds like two different operations, not one."

"Agreed. The gunship's not our style at all. And there were women and youngsters in that camp. It was a massacre."

"Right. Then we have Suzanne's reaction. As you said, Jim, not what you'd expect from a kidnap victim. More like the reaction of someone who expected to be rescued but didn't want to be."

"Yeah. Look, I know all this."

"Well, I tried to see where the authorization for this operation came from. I couldn't find any."

He shrugged. "And that surprises you? Our operations are supposed to be covert."

"Well it's true the detailed planning of your missions doesn't appear in the records, but the SAF isn't the CIA; I could usually find references to missions being discussed and authorized. Nothing about personnel—just the bare bones, the destination, the broad purpose. For Ubindi there's not even that much. So who authorized it?"

"Colonel Harken did. I don't know where he gets his orders from."

"Maybe we should ask him."

He laughed. "There's no reason in the world why he should even talk to us, let alone tell us that!"

"Tell me something. When you reported back to Harken did you tell him what you thought about the operation?"

"Sure I did. I was really pissed off. I didn't like what we'd been asked to do and I didn't think people had been up front about why we had to do it. It was a dirty business, and because of it I lost a damned fine soldier and a good friend. I said as much."

"And what was his reaction?"

"He warned me off. Something about getting into dangerous territory. More or less told me to carry out orders and not concern myself where they came from—or why."

"Interesting."

"Yeah, it made me think."

"And later your African friend—what was his name again?"

"Sef."

"That's right, Sef. He showed you the newspaper article about the RotoFan coming down. Did you discuss that with Colonel Harken?"

"I didn't, no."

"Did Sef?"

"He may have. I don't know."

"But you'd have been killed with the crew if you'd stuck to the plan. Who knew about that part?"

"Colonel Harken was aware of it, obviously. I don't know if details like that get passed to a higher level."

"And then you were run off the highway, and this time Sef was killed. What happened after that?"

"Harken shipped me straight out of the country as fast as he could."

"By sending you on an assignment where you were very nearly killed."

"Jesus. Look, I won't say I didn't have my suspicions about Harken. But later on, at the trial, he appeared for the defence, as a character witness. He supported me the best he could."

"Not quite enough, though. All right, that's enough about Harken. Let's talk about Obadiah."

"Yes, what about him?"

"Did you know he was in the SAF?"

32

I wasn't just surprised; I was gobsmacked. An image appeared in my mind of Obadiah, with his fat gut, trying to do the alligator crawl under the nets on the assault course. It was almost funny. Almost, but not quite.

"I don't believe it," I said eventually.

"It's true," Prof insisted. "Not recently, of course—this was nearly thirteen years ago. He was seconded to the SAF from Ubindi."

"How do you know that?"

"It wasn't hard. I started with a media search. There were three recorded interviews with him. In one of them he said he was a professional soldier, and that he'd served under the flags of Ubindi and the U.S.A. When the interviewer heard 'U.S.A.' he was curious. He asked which branch. Obadiah said he'd served with the United States Special Assignment Force for two years. So I looked up the Ubindian Army Records Office. That was easy, because it wasn't very secure. His CV was still there on file. It confirmed a secondment to detached duty from January 2041 to December, 2042. That's two years."

"It only shows he was seconded somewhere. It doesn't prove he was with the Force. He was a pretty big bullshitter. You're talking about a rebel leader. He could have said that to get American sentiment on his side."

"Quite right. So I thought it was time I dug a bit deeper

through SAF records. That wasn't so easy, but the QC-2 was up to it."

"QC-2?"

"It's a quantum computer. Not as powerful as the prototype we're about to test, but it still works very well. I broke the code and got a complete list of personnel, with dates. First Lieutenant Benjamin Obadiah was listed from January 2041 to December 2042."

I thought about it for a moment. "Well, that would explain why his troops were so disciplined. He'd have learned a lot during his induction. He must have trained them himself. What was he doing in the SAF?"

"He knows Africa, and he speaks four African languages plus a few dialects—that was on his CV, too, by the way. He was one of several Africans seconded to the SAF around that time. There were two from Nigeria, one from Uganda, one from Cameroon, and one from Ubindi—that was Obadiah."

"What for?"

"It had to do with the UN intervention in Nigeria. Know anything about that?"

"A bit." It was about five years after the UN forced the ceasefire in central Africa. As part of the negotiated peace, Rwanda, Uganda, and Zambia had to pull their militiamen out of the Congo. Unfortunately one of the larger militias moved north and linked up with the rebels in Nigeria. We were all hoping 1st Battalion would see some action out there. We never did. "The rebels took over offshore platforms, didn't they?" I said. "And started diverting oil to destinations in the Middle East in exchange for arms. I remember the West got very hot and bothered about it. I was never quite sure why. Oil hasn't been a major fuel for years."

"It's still important as a raw material—lubricants, coolants, paints, petrochemicals, plastics—all that sort of thing. And there's quite a bit of legacy equipment in the developing world that only runs on oil. That makes Nigeria strategically important. It has a pro-Western government and sub-Saharan Africa's largest oil industry."

"Who's for the tuna salad?"

I'd been so absorbed I hadn't noticed our waitress come up with a tray.

"Er, mine," Prof said.

She put the plate in front of him. I caught a glimpse of blood-red fingernails and a generous cleavage.

"And the sandwich," she said, setting the other plate in front of me. "And two capuccinos. Anything else for you folks?"

"No, that's it, thanks," I said.

She flashed a perfect set of teeth. "Enjoy," she chirped, and swayed off, swinging the tray. I watched her receding figure with interest, then turned back to Prof.

"I was expecting a robot," he remarked drily.

"I think she goes down better with the customers. If you want robots they have them at the self-service up the street."

"No thanks. I eat at restaurants, not production lines."

We busied ourselves unwinding cutlery from napkins. I added a little sugar to the capuccino and took a sip.

"Nigeria," I prompted.

"Yes," he said. "I've been giving myself a history lesson—there's plenty about it online."

He assembled some salad on his fork, put it in his mouth, and chewed for a few moments before continuing.

"The rebels were redirecting more than half a million barrels a day. That's a lot of oil. The U.S. wanted to send an international force to intervene but the UN opposed it."

I stopped in the middle of taking a bite out of a sandwich. "Oh? I thought a UN force did go in."

"That was later; they turned it down first time around. Not altogether surprising. The rebels' stated aim was to distribute oil revenues more fairly, so they had the support of Russia, China, Cuba, and Venezuela. Those countries are just as bad, of course, but it's politically correct for them to support a dirt poor population against oil magnates and corrupt politicians. So the vote went against it. Six months later there was another vote, and this time it went through."

"What happened to change their minds?"

"Atrocities. Holovids starting coming back from Nigeria. Horrific images of what the rebels were getting up to in the local villages. Men mutilated and beheaded, old people beaten to death, women and children hacked to pieces, young girls raped and slaughtered. The world media was full of it and there was a strong public reaction. Almost as soon as the votes had been cast, an international force went in with a large U.S. contingent. They retook the oil platforms and set up security cordons to protect the rigs, pipelines, and foreign nationals. Apart from occasional forays to attack rebel positions, it's been like that ever since."

He paused for several minutes, his attention apparently absorbed totally by the tuna salad. I had a few mouthfuls of sandwich and waited. Finally he pushed his plate aside, set his elbows on the table and interlaced his fingers, looking at me. A forefinger detached itself and pointed.

"So you see, the pivotal event in all this was the revelation that atrocities were being committed. Barely a month after the news hit the media, an international force was on its way. Within two months oil was flowing to the West again and the immediate crisis was over. Now those holovids started to arrive *before* the second vote. Officially there was no foreign military presence in Nigeria at that time. Could they have been shot by a civilian film crew?"

"No way, far too dangerous. Rebel soldiers were obviously operating in those areas. If they'd discovered a film crew transmitting that stuff to the outside world they'd have crucified them."

"That's what I thought. Could they have gone in with an SAF escort?"

"Yes. But it would be safer to leave civilians out of it altogether. What you're describing would be a standard reconnaissance mission in the Force. They could have handled the whole thing."

He took a sip of coffee.

"What about the international operation?" he continued. "Does that sound like the kind of thing SAF would be involved in?"

"Absolutely."

"And local knowledge would be valuable."

"Of course."

He opened his hands. "So now we understand the secondments from Africa."

"How're you folks doing here?"

The waitress was poised at the table with a jug of coffee. She must have spotted the empty plates.

"Get you anything else?"

Prof screwed up his face, then looked up at her. "I could fancy an ice cream."

"I used to love ice cream," I said.

"We have vanilla, strawberry, chocolate chip—"

We said it simultaneously. "Vanilla."

Then we looked at each other and laughed.

"Two vanillas, then?"

"Er no, just a refill for me," I said, pushing the coffee cup towards her. She poured the coffee, bent over the handset to add the ice cream, and went on her way.

Prof and I looked at each other and grinned. Then he said:

"Where were we?"

"Obadiah was in the SAF to help with an international operation in Nigeria. Actually, I don't see that gets us a whole lot further."

"It's the timing that's so interesting, Jim." He reached into his pocket and came out with a piece of paper on which there were a few scribbled notes. "Listen to this. December, 2040, the UN resolution to intervene in Nigeria is defeated. January, 2041, Obadiah is seconded to the SAF. March, an SAF mission is authorized to go out to Nigeria, 'to assess the strength of rebel forces in the area'. That was in the records, by the way—no personnel listing, of course. Late April, reports of atrocities start to appear in the media. June, a UN resolution to intervene in Nigeria is carried."

As he was putting the list back in his pocket the couple nearest to us got up. The light under their table turned red as it entered its self-cleaning cycle. There were several people at the door, and one came over almost immediately and sat down. I made a small movement of my hand to hold Prof back, and scanned the newcomer. He wasn't looking our way; he seemed to be engrossed in the handset. I couldn't see an earpiece.

I leaned forward. "Go on, but keep it down."

He nodded, then continued quietly. "Of the five Africans who took part in SAF operations, only one was seconded *before* the UN voted to send an international force, and that was Obadiah. Not weeks before, Jim: five months before. Why did they recruit him as early as that?"

"Maybe they were planning ahead, just in case the UN changed its mind. Or maybe they were planning to take unilateral action."

"Or maybe the first SAF unit to leave for Nigeria didn't go out to assess the strength of the rebel positions at all. Maybe their mission was to locate atrocities and film them to justify UN intervention. And that unit seconded Obadiah, trained him, and took him with them, because they needed someone who knew the territory and could speak the language."

"Well, that would fit with the timing all right. But you said yourself, they didn't specify who was on that mission, so you've got no way of proving it."

He tapped a finger on the table. "Aha, but I think I have!"

I shot a quick glance at the next table. The man was entering his order. I turned back to Prof, and he lowered his voice again.

"You see, I wanted to check that Obadiah was still with them the following year, as he'd claimed. I found him in the overall listing for 2042, but this time he was down as *Captain* Benjamin Obadiah. That's when it occurred to me that this mission had been incredibly successful, and it wasn't beyond the bounds of possibility that a grateful U.S. government had recommended promotions. So I looked to see who else had been promoted within the ranks of the SAF during 2041. There were three I thought you'd find especially interesting, and all three were in June. Are you ready for this?"

"Go on."

"One vanilla ice cream."

"Jesus Christ!"

The waitress looked puzzled. "I'm sorry…?"

I gave her a sickly smile. "It's, er, probably bigger than my friend expected. Thanks very much."

"You're welcome."

The response lacked a little warmth this time.

I watched her go. The man at the next table was looking at us.

I felt tense, but Prof was only just containing his amusement. After a pause he picked up the long ice cream spoon and pointed it at me.

"I've told you the first," he said. "First Lieutenant Benjamin Obadiah, promoted to Captain. Number two was Captain Wendell Harken, promoted to Major—"

"—Harken!"

"Yes, Harken. And number three was promoted from Lieutenant Colonel to Full Colonel, and awarded a Distinguished Service Medal. It was Brad Harrison Cawley."

33

I took a spoonful of ice cream and watched as Jim's eyes widened.

"Brad Harrison Cawley?" he repeated. "The Senator who…"

"That's right. The Republican candidate for the Presidency."

His eyes darted to either side. "Prof, we need to talk somewhere else."

I had another mouthful of ice cream, then put the spoon down and pushed it aside. Jim was right, there was altogether too much.

"We can go now, if you like."

I got up and started to head for the entrance, but Jim took my arm and guided me to an emergency exit.

Once out on the street he walked briskly, casting an occasional glance around. It was hard to keep up. I don't think he was being deliberately inconsiderate. The body he'd bequeathed to me was that of a fit young soldier; he'd probably forgotten that I have to swing my right foot out a bit to avoid catching the toes. After a dizzying series of left and right turns he slowed down and I had time to register that we'd entered the Harvard campus. I headed for a bench at the side of the path to recover my breath.

"I don't know how you navigate like that," I panted, dabbing a handkerchief to my forehead.

He sat down next to me and folded his arms. "Training."

"Like appearing from nowhere when I arrived?"

"Observing without being observed? Yeah. That, too."

I put the handkerchief away, took off my lightweight jacket, and folded it onto my lap. It was cooler here. Out on the street, the hard white light had reflected from every surface. In this square there was grass, and tall trees provided welcome shade from the autumn sun.

"Shall we resume?" he asked.

"Yes, go ahead."

"Obadiah, Harken, Cawley. How do we know they were on the same mission?"

"The international force wasn't sent to Nigeria until June. They had to have earned those commendations before the official start of hostilities. There was only one SAF mission during that time."

"So it connects all three," he breathed.

"Yes."

He continued to gaze across the square, seemingly focused on some distant point.

"You think Harken is still taking orders from Cawley?" he asked.

"Officially, no," I said. "Cawley's not in the chain of command. Unofficially? Well, Cawley sits on the Defense Appropriations Committee. That would hold the purse strings for all special forces, including the SAF."

He turned to face me, eyes alight. "Harken told me he was concerned about budgetary cuts! When he was briefing me he said the Ubindi mission would demonstrate our usefulness to those higher up."

"There you are, then. And if it wasn't officially sanctioned that would explain why it didn't appear in the records. It seems those two are in a position to do one another favours."

He chewed his lip thoughtfully. "But why knock off Obadiah?"

"Something happened during that mission, Jim, something that Brad Harrison Cawley wants to keep quiet. Obadiah knew about it, so he had him eliminated. It's the only explanation that makes any sense to me."

"What about Harken? *He's* still alive."

I shrugged. "Either Harken didn't know, or he was so heavily implicated himself he's equally anxious to keep it quiet."

"I still don't get it. Cawley could have ordered that hit years ago. Why now?"

"It must be the Presidential election," I said. "Cawley's been running on the ticket that he can bring security to this country because of his military record. If that record turned out to be tainted, his campaign would crash in flames. The moment he decided to seek the Republican nomination he became especially vulnerable; he simply couldn't take the risk any more."

"So he leaned on Harken. Made sure we'd knock off Obadiah while we were rescuing Ngozi's daughter."

"Yes. She's not even Ngozi's daughter, you know; she's his stepdaughter. She didn't adopt his family name, either—her name's Suzanne Mukewa."

Jim was thoughtful for a moment. "That doesn't bother me," he said. "You can be fond of a stepdaughter. But why go on to destroy the entire camp?"

"That's something I still don't understand. But if he wanted that covered up too, shooting down the RotoFan would a good way to do it."

"Seems to me Brad Harrison Cawley's got a lot to answer for. Including the death of my friend Gerry, those two air crew, and Sef."

"Jim—"

"And for all I know he could have been responsible for getting my whole unit ambushed and killed. Dammit he killed me, too."

"You're still alive," I pointed out.

"Well, was that his doing as well? Great idea! Keep me going as his personal hit man. Eliminate anyone who stands in the way of his grand design—you included."

"Jim, take it easy now. We don't have evidence for any of this. Nothing that would stand up in a court of law."

"My guys didn't have the benefit of a court of law."

"And is that a good reason for denying it to someone else?"

He grimaced, then heaved a sigh. "I guess not."

"Of course not. Now let's try not to leap to conclusions. The key thing we need to establish is whether something happened during that first SAF mission to Nigeria that wouldn't bear public scrutiny. Everything else hinges on that."

"Well, how are we going to find that out? Cawley won't tell us, and now Obadiah can't."

"I know."

He looked down. "Prof, I haven't said it, and I should. You did a brilliant job. Not just ferreting out the information but the way you put it together. I could never have done anything like that."

I inclined my head in acknowledgement. "Thanks, but we're not there yet. I have some more digging to do."

"While you're about it, do you think you could find something on Bogdan Zajc?"

"Zajc? Sure, I can try."

*

I did try. I didn't need to use the QC-2; I focused mainly on Press reports.

It's harder to get good quality information on an outlaw, because media sources aren't always reliable, and you've got to separate hard fact from pure speculation. All the same, a certain amount was clear.

Zajc had operated inside Albania, abducting young girls for the sex trade. There was a succession of articles about raids on villages, and then there was a gap in coverage. The last entry came from a Tirana newspaper, translated as "Sex trafficker flees country?" It featured lengthy quotes from the chief of police, saying that they'd closed the net on the criminal, but somehow he had escaped. He believed the gang had left the country.

The next time Zajc's name came up was in Africa, at a time when the newly reorganized Congolese government forces were still rounding up remnants of the militias. They'd descended on a group of mercenaries, led by Zajc, and jailed them in Kinshasa. There was quite a legal wrangle: the government wanted to put them on trial for war crimes, blaming them for atrocities in the region; Albania wanted them extradited to face charges at home.

And that was it. There was no record of any trial having taken place, either in the Congo or in Albania.

*

I met Jim again the following afternoon. This time he'd chosen the Arnold Arboretum. Following his instructions, I took the MBTA to Forest Hills, went in by the main entrance, and tried not to look as if I was expecting somebody else. He'd got the timing right; most of the visitors were coming out, and I knew he'd instantly spot anyone following me in.

Ten minutes later he fell into step beside me on Beech Path. He wasn't breathing hard. Again I wondered how he did it.

"All right?" he asked.

"Fine."

"You want to sit down?"

He seemed to have registered my awkward walk.

"I'm okay for a bit."

We walked in silence for a few minutes. The air was moist and still, fragrant with the vapours exhaled by hot foliage and decaying leaves. The rest of the world seemed a long way away.

"We can talk now," he prompted.

"All right." I told him what I'd found out about Zajc, ending with the trial that never happened.

"He must have escaped."

I shrugged. "Perhaps. I don't know how secure Congolese jails are."

"Pretty secure, from what I've heard."

"He could have bribed a guard, I suppose. Then it would be too embarrassing for them to say anything about it to the media."

"So," Jim mused, "the next time he surfaces, he's back in the Balkans, and crossing the borders frequently to wrong-foot the police."

"According to the reports, he's been popping up in Turkey, Bulgaria, Romania, and Albania."

"I wonder how he does it ? We know he has vans, painted

to look like legitimate traders; he uses them to transport his gang as well as the kids he abducts. But that's mountainous country. He could never manage long distances in those."

I spotted a bench and we wandered over to it.

"All right," Jim continued. "So that's as far as we can get with Zajc. How about the mission?"

I shook my head. "I couldn't come up with anything more. If something did happen, it's not on record."

"That's it, then. We've hit a brick wall."

"Maybe."

"What do you mean, 'maybe'?"

"There's one person left who might know something."

He sat forward.

"Who?"

"Suzanne Mukewa."

He recoiled as if he'd been stung.

"That sulky bitch? Why her?"

"Jim, think about it. She spent weeks in Obadiah's camp and there was no suggestion she'd been badly treated. The opposite, if anything. You said yourself it was as if she wanted to be there. Maybe they had something going."

"Her? With him? No way! Oh, he had a commanding presence, I'll grant you that. But he was overweight and he already had a wife, maybe more than one. She could do a whole lot better for herself, a handsome girl like that—what are you smiling at?"

"Just that it's the first complimentary thing I've heard you say about her."

"Yes. Well, all I mean is, she may have behaved like a spoilt brat but I won't say she wasn't good-looking. Surprising eyes—you'd expect dark eyes, but hers are a light ginger colour. I always notice the eyes. I always did…"

He tailed off. I looked closely at him.

"Jim, are you all right?"

He turned to me slowly, and there was a haunted quality in his gaze, as if he were coming back from somewhere.

"Yes. It's just that… "He cleared his throat. "No, I'm okay."

A family passed in the opposite direction, no doubt on their way out. The man was pushing a baby buggy in which a small child was fast asleep, rosebud lips parted; the woman was trying to hold the attention of a tired and fretful little girl. I waited until they passed.

"Jim? Sure you're all right?"

"Yes. What were you saying?"

I took a deep breath. "About Suzanne Mukewa. I looked her up. Graduated from University of Cape Town. MBA from Yale School of Management, Diploma in Political Studies from the London School of Economics. She's highly regarded. No wonder she's in Ngozi's cabinet—"

"She's a government minister?"

"Yes, you didn't know?"

He gave me a rueful look. "Just another thing no one thought to mention."

"She's Minister for External Affairs. Foreign relations are important. You need someone you can rely on not to put their foot in it. Mukewa's probably the most intelligent person Ngozi has."

"So she was on a diplomatic mission." He reached down to pick up a twig and twiddled it back and forth between his fingers. "Bit odd for Ngozi to send her into the camp of his sworn enemy, isn't it?"

"Yes. Odder still that she'd stay on there. They must have done a lot of talking."

"And you really think Obadiah may have said something to her during that time? About a mission that happened thirteen years ago?"

"The mission may be in the past, Jim, but Cawley's bid for the Presidency is here in the present. If it's relevant they could well have discussed it. I think you should find out."

"How?"

"Go there. Talk to her. She won't know you in your … as you are now."

"I can't just barge in there and talk to her. She's probably kept behind a security cordon."

"Go in as a journalist."

"What the hell do I know about…?"

He stopped, and I watched a slow smile spread across his face. He tossed the twig aside.

"Do you know?" he said quietly. "Actually I believe I could."

PART FOUR

34

To get to Ubindi I had to fly to Lumumbashi first. That leg of the trip was easy enough; the Dreamer is a comfortable hydrojet, fast and silent, like a floating city. The impression even continues on landing, when they deploy vectored thrust to take all the impact out of touchdown. That's when the problems usually start, because it's quite a challenge to handle the reception of nine hundred passengers; even so, the staff at Lumumbashi made a creditable job of it. A couple of hours later I was on a regional airline, headed for Kebe airport, and technologically it was like winding the clock back.

The last time I was in Ubindi I'd seen almost nothing of the country, so this trip was an eye-opener. For a state that was supposed to be a peaceful democracy, there were one hell of a lot of soldiers around. I expected a few at the airport, but on the coach ride to town the roads seemed to be full of army jeeps and lorries on the move, and there were plenty of khaki uniforms on the streets of the capital. I knew there were still a few militias in the countryside, but with Obadiah out of the way I hadn't expected such a high state of alert.

The roads were rough, but towards the centre of town they became wider and reasonably well paved. The buildings here were out of another era: I didn't see one modern edifice among them. The style dated back a century and a half, probably to the colonial era. It was a good thing they built to last in those days. Despite the cracking, dirty facades there was still an air of solidity about them.

There weren't many cars around, apart from rickety taxis and the ever-present army vehicles, but the streets teemed with people, bundles carried on their heads or loaded onto ancient bicycles. The soldiers wore boots, but the only other shoes I saw were flip-flop sandals worn by the motorcyclists. These were young men in grubby T-shirts and frayed shorts, who drove curious, thin-tyred motorbikes and weaved in and out between cars, pedestrians, and bicycles, usually with a passenger, often with an entire family. The congestion was so bad, and the driving so erratic, that the traffic looked denser than it actually was. Every street was hung with a pall of dust and exhaust fumes.

I booked into the Hotel Paradiso. Although some distance short of Paradise, it was tolerably comfortable, it had a large bar, and it was conveniently located near to the city centre and the administrative buildings. All the journalists stayed here. They had to. It wasn't exactly mandatory, but if they tried to book into other hotels, they'd discover a mysterious lack of vacancies.

That was one of the useful tips passed to me by an English correspondent, Logan Barrett. We found ourselves sitting together on the short leg from Lubumbashi, which wasn't a miracle because the flight was only half full, and most of the passengers were either diplomats or media men.

"How do they know if you're a journalist?" I asked him.

"I worked it out," he answered, his cherubic cheeks bulging into a grin. "When you go through Customs you're standing in front of a camera, right? The Customs Officer asks you if your visit is for business or pleasure, and you reply 'business', and he says 'What kind of business?', and you reply 'I'm a journalist on assignment'. After he's waved you through, he presses a button that sends your photo to all the hotels in the country. In this town, the only vacancy you'll find will be at the Paradiso. That way they can keep an eye on you."

Assuming a new identity as a journalist wasn't a problem, thanks to the documents they'd given me on my discharge from the training centre. Using the passport would make my movements easier to trace, but I had no real choice, and I planned to keep my eyes open anyway. As for the Press pass, it was going to come in handy after all. It made me wonder yet again who was behind my rebirth as Jim Slater, and how much of this they'd anticipated.

Posing as a journalist was one thing; looking like one was another. Before leaving the States I watched a lot of press conferences, with my eyes on the reporters rather than the person they were interviewing. I studied the way they dressed and behaved and asked questions. I noticed they nearly all used some sort of recorder. I asked Prof about it.

"It's a stenophone," he explained. "Microphone, solid state memory, microprocessor, voice recognition software, and network access, all rolled into one. You record what the spokesman is saying, add any commentary you want to make, and send it straight through the network to your media station as a text file. They do the necessary editing and layout. You can dictate your own articles and send them in the same way. I'm surprised you haven't noticed them before. They've been around for years."

I bought a model that looked pretty much identical to the ones I'd seen. But there was still a lot I had to learn about when and where press conferences would be held, and how to arrange my own interviews. Fortunately Logan was a friendly guy, and he seemed more than happy to give me the benefit of his experience.

We shared a taxi for the short ride from the coach terminal to the Paradiso. As we came in, a barefoot boy in a long cotton shirt was mopping the cracked marble vestibule of the hotel. He stood aside, head bowed, to allow us through. After the blinding light and sizzling temperatures in the street, the lobby was dark and somewhat cooler. We checked in and arranged to meet at the bar after we'd unpacked and had a shower.

The bar was on the ground floor, just beyond the entrance lobby. I insisted on buying, and we took a couple of beers through to the lounge. It was a large room with a lofty ceiling, the floor furnished with a dark red and blue carpet of indeterminate origin, shiny in some places, and threadbare along the well-trodden route to and from the bar. It stopped short of the walls, leaving a margin of stone flags. The air was heavy and faintly musty.

We sank into a couple of well-worn armchairs under a noisy television. Neither of us said anything about it, but I suspected the place was bugged, and I imagine Logan did, too. On the adjacent wall a louvred metal box emitted a periodic assortment of buzzes and rattles and a steady stream of warm air.

"So, what sort of media do you work in?" Logan asked. "Print? Broadcast? Internet?"

I showed him my Press pass.

"Never heard of them."

"I'm not surprised—it's a small provincial rag. But, what the hell, it's a steady income and they don't mind me doing a bit of freelance work on the side. I always wanted to do a piece on Africa, so they let me go, as long as I pay the bills. I thought I'd start in Ubindi, it being reasonably stable and friendly to the West."

Logan lowered his voice. "It's a friendly nation, Jim, but don't be deceived. Scratch the surface and there's a police state not far underneath." He jerked a thumb in the direction of the entrance. "Did you see the jeep parked across the street?"

"Yes, I did."

"They'll record all your comings and goings. Often as not, you'll find you're being followed. They don't even make a secret of it. I suppose the idea is, if you know they're watching you, you're less likely to step out of line. Saves everyone a lot of bother."

"Why are they so paranoid? What's there to hide?"

"Hide? Tut, tut, Jim. Didn't you know? Ubindi is a bastion of democracy and a bulwark against the spread of Islamic fundamentalism in Africa." He uttered a short, sardonic laugh. "Well, that's the way they present themselves. Your government in the U.S. seems to have swallowed it all right, hook, line, and sinker. They've been supplying them with arms for years."

Again I marvelled at how well informed Logan was.

"You think they've got it wrong?" I asked him.

He put down his glass and leaned forward.

"Jim, where exactly is this Islamist threat coming from? I do a lot of travel in this continent. Sure, there are some hot spots, but I have yet to see any serious signs of aggressive, military expansionism, religious or otherwise. General Obadiah's rebel army caused them some problems, but that's history now. There are a few militias left, but they're a disorganized bunch, and they aren't anywhere near the capital. No, I suspect all this activity is for some other reason, but what it is…" He opened his hands. "All I know is that for a dirt poor country there is a coterie of very rich people here. Where the money comes from, I have the good sense not to inquire." He sat back and drained his glass.

"Another?" I asked.

"Oh," he said, dragging clawed fingers through his thinning hair, "I should…"

"No, let me. Same again?"

"Thanks. Good man."

I walked over to the bar. What he'd said hadn't really surprised me. I probably have a simplistic view of these things, but I've travelled a bit, first with the paras, then the special forces. It seems to me that whenever you get a big military presence in a time of peace, it can mean only one thing: wealth and power are the preserve of a small minority, who are anxious to hold onto it at the expense of an impoverished and subdued majority.

By the time I'd returned with the beers, Logan's open-necked shirt, which had been fresh when we met up at the bar earlier on, was darkening under the armpits, and his forehead was glistening. I was coping reasonably well, but then my shirt disappeared straight down at the waistband of my trousers, whereas his had to deviate over the bulge of a remarkably spherical stomach.

To judge by our earlier conversations he'd covered virtually every country on the African continent. I wondered how long it had taken him to get familiar with their individual foibles. He looked to me like he was in his early forties. He'd probably been in this game all his life.

He filled his glass.

"Cheers," he said. "So, Jim, who are you hoping to see?"

"Suzanne Mukewa."

He compressed his lips and nodded. "Good choice. Smart woman. One of the few politicians I've come across in these parts who'll give you a straight answer. But you're out of luck, my friend. Just now she's out of the country."

I felt a stab of disappointment. I should have checked somehow.

"Ah. Any idea when she'll be back?"

"No. But she's not usually away for long. If you're lucky she'll give a press conference on her return."

"Probably worth hanging on for that, then." I took a sip of beer. "Think I'll be able to set up a personal interview with her?"

"Not a chance. Everywhere she goes, she's closely guarded. The nearest you'll get to her is if she gives a statement to the press."

My vague ideas about buttonholing Ms. Mukewa at a reception or after a press conference and arranging an appointment evaporated.

This whole thing was turning out to be more difficult than I thought.

35

It looked like I had some time to kill until Suzanne Mukewa got back, so I went to the Press Office and I said I'd like to see something of the country. They put me in touch with a tour agency that had a small fleet of off-roaders and we went out in groups. The other clients on these excursions seemed to be casual visitors. I stayed alone with my thoughts, saying very little, just in case there was a government observer amongst them. They seemed suitably thrilled, but truth to tell, there wasn't a whole lot to see. Most of the wild game on the plains had been hunted to extinction and the remaining reserves were small. Not like the Serengeti.

The Serengeti. That would have been about ten years ago. I was Jim Forbes then, and I'd just transferred from the paras to the SAS. We went there to sort out a particularly nasty poaching racket. Good mission, great place. Now that was rich in wild life. This doesn't bear comparison.

Our last stop, evidently regarded by the guide as the high point of the day, was a visit to the Jukwala, a sluggish, muddy brown river about thirty k's from Kebe. There were a few hippos floating languidly in the water, revealing little more than their ears and nostrils.

The guide pointed to the opposite mud bank and said, "You see crocodiles?" The tourists were all using their binoculars and making appreciative noises. The guide found a pair in the cubby of the off-roader and handed them to me. Now I could see them properly.

It's hard to love crocodiles, so I don't even try. The evil yellow slit eyes, the teeth—too long and too many to conceal decently inside the jaw—and, above all, the crooked grin that says, "I'll have you, mate". I can't help wishing they went the way of the rest of the dinosaurs.

One of the trips was laid on by the Press Office specifically for any interested journalists. The old hands, like Logan, gave it a wide birth, and afterwards I understood why. We went out to native villages about twenty k's west of Kebe. In each of these, we were told, the government had bored a well to give them a plentiful supply of clean water. Previously, it seemed, the women and children had a two-hour walk to and from the nearest source. The people in the village looked well housed and well fed, and all were remarkably cheerful. There wasn't the slightest question in my mind that these were showplaces, created for people like us.

The road passed through country not unlike the terrain we'd encountered during the SAF mission, and my mind kept wandering back to Gerry and Sef. It set up an ache inside me that lasted the rest of the day.

When I got back, the jeep was opposite the hotel as usual, the soldiers duly noting my arrival. It was a real intrusion into my privacy and it was starting to bug me.

In the evening I met up with Logan in the bar again and we had a few drinks. It had become a regular thing and I looked forward to it, because he was making use of his contacts during the day and he often came away with useful snippets of information, which he was willing to share. On this occasion he mentioned that there was a press conference with the Minister of Trade the following day. We arranged to go together.

*

I kept a low profile during the conference, being content to point my stenophone with the rest of them.

"The thing is," I said to Logan that evening, "he waffles on about the importance of international trade, but he doesn't say what they're exporting or how they pay for what they're importing. I can't see that tourism's a major industry. What is it they've got that other people want? Do they have anything in the way of natural resources?"

"Nothing whatever, so far as I know. That's no accident. When the central African states were reorganized the Congo ceded some territory, but it made quite sure it held onto its cobalt, copper, gold, uranium, and diamonds. Ubindi didn't get any of it."

He refilled his glass. We'd taken to buying several bottles at a time.

"That Minister gave a press conference last time I was here," he continued. "Someone asked him what they export. According to him they grow valuable cash crops in the north west. So I said we'd never seen any sign of them in Europe. He said they're African fruits and vegetables that don't suit European tastes, but they export them to the rest of Africa and some Asian countries. One of the other guys was interested and he asked if we could visit the region. He got fobbed off. 'You would be very welcome to, sir, but I'm afraid we are a poor country, and we don't have the resources to transport you there.'"

"I love the way they stand there in their beautiful suits, with the fashionably high collars, and tell you how poor their country is."

"They are poor, Jim. It's just that the poverty's unevenly

distributed."

I chuckled.

Logan went on:

"The chap said his company would pay. In that case, the Minister said, he may be able to charter the tourist helicopter that is kept at Kebe."

"A helicopter? Jesus! A fifty-year-old crate kept alive by Ubindian maintenance engineers? I don't think so."

"I know. We couldn't keep the grins off our faces. He didn't ask again."

"So what do you think? Do they have valuable cash crops in the north?"

"I doubt it. The whole country's very arid. In any case, there's only one crop I know that can support the economy of an entire nation."

"What's that?"

"*Papaver somniferum*, old chap. The opium poppy. And it's too damn hot to grow it here."

"Right. So you still don't know what's coming and going."

"No."

We sipped our beers in silence for a bit. Then I said:

"This is a landlocked country. Presumably stuff is imported and exported by air."

"That's right. Did you notice the cargo area at Kebe?"

"Yeah. I saw an old Airbus A400 parked there. Big four-engined job. Didn't the military use them at one time for transporting troops and tanks?"

I knew the answer, of course; I just said it so as not to appear too knowledgeable.

"A while ago, yes. Ubindi must have bought them to use as cargo carriers."

"I ought to take a look at that facility."

He winced.

"I'd advise against it, Jim. They don't allow photography at the airport, and they won't appreciate snooping either. You'd be in big trouble if you got caught."

*

That tempted me even more, of course, but I had to be sensible. I was here to interview Suzanne Mukewa, and if I got picked up trying to look where I shouldn't I'd wreck my chances of seeing her. Quite apart from which, I wasn't anxious to see the inside of a jail, least of all here. The lounge bar of the Hotel Paradiso was bad enough in this heat, and I could barely imagine what kind of shithole they'd put me in if I were arrested.

I paced around my hotel room, thinking about it. I could smell something going on here. If I could show Ngozi was mixed up in something unpleasant, it could mean the end of U.S. support, and his government would probably collapse. It seemed to me that in some way Ngozi was responsible for our mission, a mission that cost Gerry his life. I wouldn't mind taking a little trouble to unseat the bastard.

It would be best to go up there at night. I could get in and out, no problem, but what would I see? Fork-lift trucks offloading large crates from an A400M onto lorries? I wouldn't learn anything useful unless I went right in and jemmied a crate open, and that would be like leaving a calling card. Prof might be able to get access to satellite pictures, but that wouldn't tell us much more.

What about freight manifests? They could misrepresent what was in the crates but they'd still have to say where the cargo left from and where it was going to. It might give us some clues. All that stuff was stored electronically. Could Prof hack into it?

I decided to contact him. The stenophone could do it, but I'd had problems before now, taking untried gear into the field, and I never put all my faith in the reliability of one device, especially one as new as that. Instead I got my old cloudphone out.

I looked at it, then I put it away again. In many respects this country hadn't advanced at all in the last fifty years, but you could bet their comms were up to date, and they'd be eavesdropping on phone traffic for sure. I couldn't take the chance. The U.S. Embassy probably had a secure satellite link. I'd go down there the next day and see if they'd let me use it.

*

Because of the time difference I couldn't do anything until the afternoon, which meant the sun was well up. I put on my sunglasses and stepped out into the street. The heat met me like a wall and in spite of the sunglasses I had to pause to let my eyes adjust to the brightness. Across from the hotel, the jeep was parked in its usual place, taking advantage of a shady patch under a jacaranda tree. There were four soldiers lounging in the seats and the whole image shimmered in the waves of heat rising from the road. As they spotted me emerge from the foyer, one of them spoke into a throat mike. This time it really got to me. On impulse I went over to them.

There was an abrupt change in their manner. In an instant they were all on their feet, automatic rifles cocked and pointed in my direction. I lifted my hands.

"Relax, guys," I said.

They said nothing. One of the men in front had a sergeant's stripes on his sleeve. Under the pulled-down beret his eyes were black and bulging, and they were fixed on me with unwavering malevolence.

"Hi," I said, with a jaunty smile. "I've seen you guys over here every day, so I thought I'd make life a little easier and tell you where I'm going."

None of them so much as blinked.

"I'm going to go down to the taxi rank, and I'll take a taxi from there to the U.S. Embassy. I have a little paperwork to sort out. Then I'll come back here."

They continued to stare.

"Okay," I said, backing off. "Just thought you'd like to know. Have a nice day."

I walked away, feeling their eyes drilling holes into my back.

It was probably a stupid thing to do, but I felt good about it. And I'd discovered something interesting. What they were toting were M-35s. Those rifles are so antiquated I didn't think you could buy rounds for them anymore.

For years the U.S. had been equipping this army with up-to-the-minute weapons. So where were they?

36

Inside the Embassy it was as cold as a morgue. Coming in from the street, after a ride in a taxi with all the windows open, I was soon shivering. I wished I'd brought something to put on over my thin shirt.

The man on reception wasn't all that helpful. He looked at my U.S. passport and press pass.

"A journalist. Well, can't you call in your story in the usual way?"

"No, I can't. I'm an investigative journalist and there's a certain sensitivity about the information I'm sending back. I need a secure line back to the States."

"I'm sorry, I can't possibly allow you to use our encrypted connection."

"All right, but you have a secure satellite link here, don't you? And a Press Office? All I need is a little time on a phone. I'll be happy to pay for the call."

Reluctantly he directed me to the Press Office, where I had to explain my request all over again. The large, warmly dressed secretary didn't seem too surprised by it, and she led me to an empty office with a phone. I tried Prof's office. As I expected, he was already in.

I got down to business.

"Prof, can you access freight manifests?"

"Freight manifests? I don't know, I've never tried."

It was a typical, measured, academic answer, and it wasn't

what I wanted.

"Well, could you give it a go? I'm interested in cargo flights into and out of Kebe, what's in them, where they're coming from, and where they're going to."

"I can try. What company is it?"

"No idea. I've only seen one aircraft and I wasn't close enough to pick out any markings."

"Jim, does this have anything at all to do with the reason you're out there?"

"Yes, it could have a whole lot to do with it."

He sighed. "All right."

"How long do you think it'll take you?"

"Hard to say. Depends where and how the data's stored. It may take me a day or two."

"All right. I'll phone you the day after tomorrow, same time, to see how you've got on. Good luck."

"You too."

On the way out I asked the secretary if it would be okay to come back in a couple of days to do the same thing again.

She didn't look delighted, but she didn't say no.

Then I asked her if they had any material on Ubindi: history, geography, politics, that sort of thing. I explained I was a new arrival, and I realized I hadn't done my homework properly.

She went over to a counter and pulled out one document from each rack. Some were glossy, printed pamphlets, others were just computer print-outs. The wodge she finally handed me was as thick as a bible.

As I made my way to the foyer I leafed through the top few documents, and wondered why I hadn't thought of this before—and why old Logan hadn't suggested it.

*

I'd had enough of seeing the bits of Ubindi the government wanted me to see. I spent much of the next day and a half in my hotel room, reading the literature the Embassy had given me. I also bought half a dozen newspapers, Ubindian, American, and English, read them from front to back, and did the crosswords, or as much of them as I could manage. I was bored out of my skull, but all that was about to change.

My cloudphone rang.

"Jim, those cargos in and out of Ubindi. It's really interesting… "

A shock drilled right out along my veins.

"Stop right there, Prof. I'll phone you back in half an hour."

I clicked it off. Prof sounded very excited. Unfortunately I'd forgotten to tell him not to phone me on any account. You couldn't really blame him; he wasn't to know what kind of political system I was up against.

I stood there, looking at the incriminating instrument. I had a strong urge to chuck it into the back of the first passing vehicle, then use every counter-surveillance technique I knew to shake off my tail, and—

And that would be stupid. With or without the phone call, the moment they lose track of you they'll know they're not dealing with a journalist. You're on your own, with no place to go to ground and no way of getting out of the country—not once they've set up road blocks and alerted airport security. Your best bet is to bluff it out. Move fast but stay in character as long as you can.

I left immediately via the front entrance, gritting my teeth as the soldiers in the jeep opposite reported my movement. I took a taxi to the Embassy, and went straight to the Press Office. The same large secretary was there. Unfortunately someone was in the only empty office.

"Will they be long?" I asked. "This is urgent."

"I'm sorry, they're entitled to their privacy, Mr. Slater. I can't just barge in. Take a seat. I'm sure they'll be out soon."

I sat on a padded bench, my heels drumming a muted tattoo on the soft carpet, hands tapping out a counterpoint on my thighs. Whatever else was crap in this benighted country, you could bet their security was right on the ball, and they'd be giving priority to calls in a hotel that accommodated foreign journalists. I'd cut Prof off quickly, but it was still touch and go. I looked at my watch. Thirty-five minutes had already gone by since I terminated Prof's call. Two minutes later I looked at my watch again.

What's the matter with this guy? What's he doing in there, for fuck's sake?

It was fifteen minutes before a lanky chap emerged and ambled up to the desk. The secretary went over to him. I got up pointedly, and she nodded to me. He gave me a friendly look, and must have been surprised to get such a fierce glare in return.

I closed the door and put in the call.

"All right, Prof. We can talk now. What have you found?"

He was a little hesitant at first, perhaps puzzled that I'd cut his previous call short, but he became animated soon enough.

"You wouldn't believe how complicated it was, Jim! Different sectors, changes of plane, changes of carrier—there's no way I could have connected up all the different cargo manifests if it hadn't been for the quantum computer. I've got it sussed now, though."

"Go ahead, let's hear it."

"Right, this was just one incoming consignment. Ready? The cargo was identified as farm equipment, originating from Uzbekistan, dispatched at Nukus. First stop, Ghazni in Afghanistan. There, the cargo was transferred to another aircraft and flew to Bahkesir, in Turkey, for a refuelling stop."

"Afghanistan to Turkey, all right, go on."

"From there they flew to Mineciu, in Romania. That's only a few hundred miles. Then over the border to Stara Zagora, Bulgaria. From there to Kukes in Albania. Then a longer leg to Kaduna, Nigeria. And finally down to Kebe, Ubindi. So when the goods arrived at Ubindi their origin was listed as Nigeria."

"I see what you mean about complicated. Are they all like that?"

"Well, I've only traced one other consignment. There was some variation in the towns, but the sequence of countries was the same: Uzbekistan, Afghanistan, Turkey, Romania, Bulgaria, Albania, Nigeria, Ubindi."

"Okay, what about outgoing?"

"Outgoing, I've only had time to trace one, but it's interesting. Non-stop to Dakar, Senegal, in West Africa. After that it retraces some of the previous route—Albania, Bulgaria, Romania—but ends up at Rivne, in the Ukraine."

"All right, let me guess: drugs."

"Almost certainly. The farm machinery is just a cover. Afghanistan is the world's biggest producer of raw opium. One of the stops en route must be to offload raw opium, for processing locally. The origin of the flight may be significant, too. Nukus has a big chemical industry. It wouldn't surprise me if the cargo included barrels of acetic anhydride."

"What's that?"

"Well, drug traffickers prefer to work with heroin—it's more powerful so it's more marketable. You can convert opium into morphine easily enough, but if you're making heroin you need acetic anhydride for the next step. Uzbekistan isn't subject to international controls on chemicals like that."

"So many legs, and all that to-ing and fro-ing in the Balkans—what for? If it was just in one direction, I'd say they were delivering the refined drugs. But this is in both directions."

"I suppose it was to confuse anyone trying to track it. It certainly wasn't easy, even for me."

"What's the significance of Dakar?"

"Ah. Well, Dakar is the westernmost city in Africa. Transatlantic freighters leave from there for South America."

"I see. Onward distribution to the States?"

"Could be. The Drugs Enforcement Agency cracked down on the Colombian drug industry some time ago, but they never really rooted out the distribution network. All the drug barons needed was product. I think we've discovered one way they've been getting it."

"Okay, it's taking shape. During this sequence of flights, they offload raw opium and take on a load of pure opium or heroin that's already been processed. Final market is the U.S., probably distributed via Colombia."

"That's what it looks like. Of course, we still don't know exactly where the raw stuff was exchanged for refined, but there was time in each place to repack the cargo."

"And where does Ubindi fit in? To judge by the security it's not just one more country on a complicated route."

"That I don't know."

I glanced at my watch. "Okay, Prof, great job. There's just one problem. You've compromised me by phoning me at the hotel."

"Oh, Jim! I'm so sorry! I didn't think… you didn't say…"

"Look, there's no time for that. I have to call this off. Suzanne Mukewa isn't here at the moment anyway, and now I can't afford to hang around until she gets back. I'm going to get a taxi to the airport, and I'll take the next flight out of here, wherever it's heading."

"Good grief! Where are you at the moment?"

"The American Embassy. It's all right, this is a secure satellite link. But they've had nearly an hour to identify the other call and that's more than enough, so I've got to move. Now listen carefully. I'll phone you at your home first thing in the morning. That's morning here—sorry, it'll be in the small hours for you but it can't be helped. If you haven't heard from me by—" I did a quick calculation "—two o'clock in the morning, your time, start pushing every button and pulling every bloody lever you can. Otherwise you may not see me again."

"My God, is it that serious?"

"You'd better believe it. This is a police state with a wafer-thin veneer of democracy. Human rights don't mean a hell of a lot here."

"Okay, Jim, I'll do everything I can. But I hope you'll be all right. I'm so sorry…"

"'Bye, Prof."

I raced out, ran to the foyer, and went through the rotating door out into the street. After the refrigerated interior of the Embassy it was like being thrown into a volcano.

On the way here I'd noticed a big hotel just a couple of blocks away. The Embassy probably used it for people on temporary visits. There were a few taxis loitering outside. I'd take one straight to the airport. I wouldn't stop by the hotel; it was too risky. I had everything I needed in the security pocket in the waistband of my trousers: passport, credit tokens, Press pass, even the damned stenophone. I'd left the cloudphone in my room.

I turned left out of the Embassy and walked briskly. It would only attract attention if I ran.

They got me before I'd gone two hundred metres. I heard the jeep screaming up behind, and when I looked round there were two soldiers on the pavement and two in the jeep, all with rifles levelled. I looked to the front and there were two more. They must have stepped out of a doorway.

One of them barked, "Face down! On the ground! Arms out!"

The accent was thick but the motion with the rifle made it easier to understand. The M-40 may be an old weapon but they can still make a hell of a mess of you. I complied.

I felt my wrists being fastened together behind me. Then they lifted me roughly to my feet and bundled me into the jeep. One got in on either side, and they took off so fast my head jerked backwards. A few curious passers-by had stopped to watch the goings on, but it was all over in seconds.

It looked like I was going to see the inside of a Ubindian jail after all.

37

The punch caught me high on the cheek and slammed me back into the wall. I bounced off and fell forward, turning my face as I hit the floor, because my hands were still tied behind me. I knew I was set up for a kick so I rolled off to one side. The blur of a boot passed overhead.

"Who do you work for?" the man bellowed. He looked a lot like the sergeant with the bulgy eyes, the one I'd seen in the jeep, but I couldn't be sure.

He took another swipe with his boot, and this time he connected.

It was the third beating they'd given me. They seemed to be taking it in turns, but he was the most brutal.

It seemed to be going on forever. My legs were still free, and ordinarily I'd have flattened a slob like that, even without the use of my hands. But if I used those combat techniques I'd simply confirm his suspicions. It was hard, but I just had to keep taking what he was dishing out.

Just as well these people rely on the old interrogation techniques. I'm not sure I could stand up to some of the newer ones.

He lifted me by the collar and hit me again and I must have passed out.

*

I woke up to find myself lying on the stone floor. I didn't move my body, just my eyes, but it looked like I was alone. I crawled the few feet to the wall and managed to get myself into a sitting position.

In the gloom of the cell the air was wet, and thick with heat. I took short breaths through my open mouth, partly because my ribs hurt, and partly because my nose was full of blood. I considered the possibility of escape and dismissed it. I couldn't do anything with my wrists still tied behind me. Whatever they'd used was tight, and it was chafing them painfully. I became aware of a sweet, metallic taste in my mouth. I sought it out with my tongue, and found a rocking tooth, the gum bleeding where it had been loosened. My lips felt swollen and split. I craved water, but I knew they wouldn't give me any.

I shifted my position, trying to get more comfortable. It didn't help.

In spite of my discomfort I didn't feel any sense of violation. I was hurting all right, but I'd never felt this body belonged to me anyway, so it wasn't personal. It was a bit like having a crash in a rented car.

At least I knew now why they were so sensitive about what was coming through that cargo area. I wondered if the drugs were being processed here. I couldn't see why else the route should include a nowhere place like Ubindi. They'd make a lot of money by refining it and passing it on, but would it be enough to cover the purchase of the raw materials and the huge costs of transporting them in that elaborate way? I found it hard to believe the margins were so good they could keep a whole country afloat.

I didn't have any more time to contemplate the question. I heard boots tramping along the stone corridor towards my cell, and prepared myself for yet another beating. I slid off the wall and curled up on the floor.

Keys rattled in the lock, and the door clanged as it was flung open. Two pairs of army boots approached, and stopped, inches from my face. I felt my arms being gripped and I was hauled to my feet. Then they manhandled me out of the door.

I went limp, making out I was in worse shape than I was, trailing my feet so that they were obliged to carry me. All the same I was taking in every detail. We passed a duty desk. On the wall behind the chair were two rows of hooks, with large keys. They hauled me up a spiral staircase, through a door, and into a corridor on the right. We stopped at a lift. The doors opened and I glanced at the illuminated panel as we stumbled in. We were on the ground floor of the building. The prison was in the basement. This was no town jail.

One of the soldiers moved in front of the panel, the doors closed, and we began to ascend. I tried to count the floors; I thought it was five. Too high to jump. They bundled me out of the lift and along a carpeted corridor. There were windows on the right and as we passed I cocked an eye at the sky. It looked like evening, but it wasn't completely dark yet. It had been hard to keep track of time and this was my first clue. They'd picked me up late afternoon, but this wasn't the same day. I must have been in custody for over twenty-four hours.

We stopped outside a door. One of the soldiers knocked, and in response to a command from inside he turned the handle.

They hustled me into a large office. I took it in quickly, blinking in the bright artificial light. Thick carpet, walls full of bookshelves, a table and armchairs, louvred blinds on every window, all closed. A faint smell of aftershave.

The soldiers turned me to the left, shoved me into a chair, and stepped back.

I was looking across a leather topped desk at a large, immaculately dressed man. His forehead, black and shiny, extended back through a series of surprising bumps into crinkly black hair. The suit was dark, high-collared, well-tailored. His wrists were resting on the desk, and he was holding a gold pen between his fingers and turning it this way and that. He seemed to be in no hurry to begin.

"Mr. Slater," he said eventually, regarding me with a sardonic smile. The voice was quiet, yet it was more menacing than the shouts of the soldiers who'd beaten me up. "You seem to have sustained some injuries. It really was most unwise of you to resist arrest."

I looked hard at him, but said nothing.

He took a bag out of his desk drawer and tipped the contents onto his desk. I recognized the stenophone. The rest looked like my stuff, too.

"You say you are a journalist, Mr. Slater," he continued. "But you know and I know that you are not. Who do you work for, Mr. Slater?"

I moistened split lips and took a shallow breath. "I'm a staff journalist with the Roanoke Gazette."

He picked up the Press pass as if were contaminated, and dangled it distastefully.

"Yes, so this says." He flicked it onto the desk. "But Mr. Slater, we have looked for the Roanoke Gazette, and no such paper exists."

"It does exist, you haven't found it, that's all. It's a small, local paper."

"If it's a small, local paper, Mr. Slater, what are you doing in Africa?"

"I thought they were too parochial. I suggested a piece on Africa. They said I could do it, but I had to pay my own expenses. Ubindi's a friendly nation." I paused to make the point. "That's why I came here." I tried to wet my lips with my tongue. "Can I have some water?"

"In due course."

He shoved the stenophone at me. "Does this belong to you, Mr. Slater?"

"It might do. I had one like it."

"This instrument was taken from your clothing after you were arrested. The phone number of the Roanoke Gazette is not on it."

"I don't use it as a phone. It's for taking dictation."

"Is this your cloudphone, Mr. Slater? We found it in your hotel room."

"Then it probably is."

"The phone number is not on that either."

It was an oversight. But then, my occupation as a journalist was never designed for more than casual scrutiny.

"I don't know why," I said. "It ought to be there. Maybe someone erased it."

"I don't think so. It's not there because you are not a journalist, Mr. Slater. You are a spy."

"I'm not a spy."

"Then why are you taking such a close interest in the cargo area of our international airport?"

"Who says I am?"

That crooked smile had never left his face. "Are you going to deny that, too?"

"No need to, I am interested. Trade is part of a country's profile. I have to know something about it for the article. I made some inquiries, that's all."

He leaned back, still smiling. "You don't sound Russian, Mr. Slater, so who do you actually work for? The CIA? MI6?"

"I told you, I'm just a journalist."

He looked over my right shoulder, evidently addressing one of the soldiers standing behind me.

"This man is wasting my time," he said calmly. "Take him out and shoot him."

My guts lurched.

"Now just a minute. I'm a bone fide journalist and I'm a U.S. citizen. You're making an international incident of this. You'll lose any support you have from the West…"

Out of the corner of my eye I saw the soldier on the right draw his semiautomatic and swing back his arm. I winced, waiting for the pistol whipping I knew was coming.

The man behind the desk raised a hand, and the soldier stepped out my field of view.

"He's right. We do want to avoid an international incident, don't we?" The smile disappeared and his voice hardened. "First thing in the morning, take him down to the Jukwala, and feed him to the crocodiles." He turned back to me. "Visitors sometimes stray, Mr. Slater, and are never seen again. This is a wild country. We do everything possible to find them, but unfortunately they often disappear without trace." He looked up. "Take him away."

*

I sat on the stone floor with my back against the wall, trying to forget the way those uniformed thugs had thrown me into the cell, and their laughter, echoing down the corridor, as one of them shouted, "See you in the morning."

I was seething with anger and frustration. After all I'd

been through, to be sitting here, defenceless, waiting like a lamb for the slaughter... I had to get out, but how?

There was no way I could escape from this cell, even if my hands were free. Would I get a chance on the way to the river the following morning? They'd almost certainly keep the ties on my wrists. Would they shackle my ankles, too? Probably not. I could work with my feet.

I started going through the possible scenarios. How many of them would there be? Four, probably: two in the front, and one on either side of me in the back. It was about 30 k's. They couldn't keep an eye on me the whole time. What kind of vehicle would they use? If it was the jeep I might be able to lift my feet and kick the driver in the back of the head, send the thing off the road—and what then? If only one out of the four was functioning he could rake me to pieces with his M40. They probably wouldn't use a jeep, anyway. I'd been out that way with the tour, and there wasn't a scrap of shade until you got to the river. They'd use some sort of all-road vehicle with a roof, and that would have higher seat backs than the jeep.

What had Prof been doing? He didn't get a call from me, so at two o'clock this morning he should have gone into action. How long would he have? The soldiers would probably make an early start so they could get back before the worst heat of the day. Suppose they came to get me at 0600? That would give Prof just twenty-one hours to work some magic. He was well connected, but if he couldn't raise his Washington contacts until morning there'd be only fifteen hours. Diplomatic wheels grind more slowly than that.

It looked like I was going to end up in the river. I could see those sly, grinning reptiles shuffling forward and sliding off the bank, snapping at me, then twisting in the water, hear the gleeful shouts of the soldiers…

You couldn't really blame the crocs—they were just following blind instinct. But what kind of creatures would exult in seeing one of their number torn to pieces? And then I remembered the Ubindi mission, my misgivings about the way we killed Obadiah and his wife and obliterated the camp, and I began to wonder if I was any better. Without being fully aware of it, I must have spent my whole career speeding towards a conclusion like this. It had come sooner rather than later, that's all. And if Jim Forbes' brain had been washed down the sink it would have come even sooner. Maybe that would have been better…

Stop feeling sorry for yourself, soldier, and start thinking!

There had to be a way. Maybe I could I swim across, just using my legs. I guess it depended on how hungry the crocs were. Suppose I made it? Behind me there'd still be the four soldiers standing on the bank, laughing as they lifted their rifles to use me as target practice…

Questions circulated endlessly in my mind; questions, but no answers. I realised I was going over the same possibilities again and again yet I couldn't control it; my concentration was drifting. I'd had no food, no water, and I was weak and exhausted from the tension and the beatings. Adrenaline had kept me going briefly after the interview. Now that it had worn off it was hard to maintain focus. The anger receded, and the sickness in my stomach grew and spread through me in waves of lassitude. My vision swam, and I felt myself sliding sideways off the wall…

*

I awoke abruptly to the gritty sound of boots on the stone floor, the jangling of keys. Peering between half-closed lids, I saw the big guard with the bulgy eyes standing outside the cell door. He took his time, selecting a key from a big bunch. He placed it in the lock. He'd probably decided to come and give me a final pasting. I wondered how much more I could take. It wouldn't make much difference now whether I tried to retaliate or not, but I was in pretty poor shape to do anything effective.

A shadow moved in the cell on the other side of the corridor. There was a sizzling sound, followed by a sharp crack. I knew it so well: the sound of a stun charge travelling along a collimated plasma beam. The guard jerked up, eyes wide, mouth open, then folded to the ground.

The door to the cell opposite opened quietly and the shadow moved across the corridor. I heard the key turn in the lock and a creak as the door swung open. I got up cautiously, my back against the wall. A voice said quietly:

"What are you waiting for? Come over here."

As I moved forward the figure raised its head and in the dim light I caught a glimpse of delicately arched eyebrows and high cheekbones.

Suzanne Mukewa.

37

I didn't have time to be astonished. She produced a torch and shone it at me.

"Turn round," she commanded.

I did so. Something tugged painfully at the band around my wrists and I was free. I massaged my wrists, trying to restore some life without removing more of the chafed skin.

"Now," she said, "rub some dirt on your face, and put his clothes on. Take his weapon, too."

I complied without a word, putting on the sweaty camo shirt and trousers and fastening the belt with its holstered stun pistol. Then she said:

"Follow me."

I started down the corridor after her, then I said, "You go on, I forgot something."

I went back to the brutal guard and hacked him in the ribs two or three times as hard as I could. I paused for breath, then put in a stamp on one knee, jumping slightly to get plenty of weight on it, and followed up with a deft kick to the elbow. Now I felt better.

I rejoined Suzanne. With barely a pause in her stride she picked a beret off a hook by the duty desk and passed it over her shoulder to me. We went up the stairs and through the door, but this time we turned to the left and went out through an emergency exit into a courtyard.

She crossed over to an archway with a narrow, paved road

beyond it. Through the arch I could see a four-wheel drive standing there. She opened the rear hatch.

"Get in there," she said, picking up a blanket. "There's a security checkpoint on the way out. Stay quiet. It won't be for long. When we're out of town you can sit in the passenger seat."

I didn't argue, just climbed in and curled up on the floor. She threw the blanket over me and slammed the hatch. I heard the driver's door close, then the engine started and we drove smoothly away.

The blanket smelled faintly of petrol and it was hot and stuffy underneath. I rolled a little this way and that as the car took a series of turns. Then we slowed to a halt. I drew the stun weapon and held my breath, my pulse thudding in my temples. It was now or never. No way was I going back in that jail.

It seemed to be taking a long time. Footsteps crunched on the road. I braced myself for the rear hatch to open. If they lifted the blanket there'd be a moment of surprise, enough for me to get my shot in.

Silence. Then we started to move forward again. I let my breath go.

Again I felt the car negotiating the bends. I threw the blanket off and fidgeted, trying to shift my weight to avoid the bruises.

We slowed to a halt. Footsteps, then the hatch opened. Suzanne started when she saw the stun pistol pointing straight at her. I mumbled an apology and holstered the weapon. Somehow I managed to ease myself out and straighten up. It looked like we were on the edge of town. It was still dark, and the streets were deserted.

She closed the rear hatch with a quiet click and gestured

towards the passenger seat. I got in, she took the driver's seat, and we moved off again.

I tried to swallow, but my throat seemed to be sticking together. I parted it enough to croak:

"Where are we going?"

"It's better that you don't know," she replied calmly. "Just in case we hit a road block."

Once out of town she picked up speed. About thirty minutes later we pulled off the main road. The headlights swung round to throw black shadows into the ridges and potholes of a dirt track, but she continued at undiminished speed and I had to grab a handle to stop myself being thrown around. After a few k's, we came upon a small township, where she turned sharply into a shelter at the side of a house. As I got out, a cloud of dust, glowing red in the tail lights, caught up with the car and settled over the roof and rear screen and over me. She switched off the engine. I smacked the worst of the dust off my trousers and followed her into the house.

She switched on a light and moved ahead of me into a small room with a wooden floor, simply furnished with a table and chairs. I pulled out a chair and dropped into it.

"Coffee?" she said. "Tea? Something stronger?"

"Water first," I rasped. "Then something stronger. Thanks."

She disappeared into the next room, which I assumed was a kitchen. I heard running water and she came back with a jug and two glasses, which she placed on the table before leaving the room again. I knew I should take it slowly but I couldn't help myself; I filled and drank three glasses without pause. She returned with a bottle and two tumblers, put a generous shot of whisky into each, slid one over to me, and sat down. She watched me add a little water before taking a mouthful.

She smiled. "It's not a single malt."

I winced as the liquor stung my broken lip. "Force of habit," I said.

I took another gulp of whisky. It spread a soothing warmth inside me and I began to relax enough to take in my situation. In front of me was a confident, well-groomed young woman, immaculately attired in a pale grey trouser suit and high-necked blouse, her posture straight and commanding. I'd last seen her two years ago, when I was still Jim Forbes, and all I could remember from that time was a figure hunched morosely in the seat of the RotoFan like a withdrawn and sullen child. It was the same face, the high cheekbones, the arched eyebrows, the surprising ginger eyes, yet she could have been a different person.

"Look," I said, "it's time I said 'thanks'. They were about to feed me to the crocodiles."

"Yes, I rather thought they would."

"You're Ms. Mukewa, aren't you?"

"People normally address me as 'Minister'."

"Sorry. Minister—"

"You can call me Suzanne."

She smiled, revealing a perfect set of teeth. I'd never seen her smile before. It was like the sun had come out.

"You've taken a big chance for me, Suzanne. Why?"

"For the moment, let's just say that I'm anxious not to sour relations between our countries. Our people can be a bit heavy-handed."

I snorted. "That's putting it mildly. What are you doing here? I thought you were out of the country."

"I was, but we'd progressed more or less as far as we could

with the negotiations. I got a call from your State Department and left immediately. You have some powerful friends, Mr. Slater."

"Jim," I said.

I was thinking: Bless your heart, Prof. You really came up trumps.

I pointed vaguely at the room. "Are we safe here?" I asked.

"Safe enough. We won't be staying long. I can take you across the border into the Congo, and get you out on a diplomatic visa."

"What like this?"

I indicated the loose army clothes I'd taken from the sergeant. Apart from the way they looked I'd become uncomfortably aware of their pungent odour.

"No, not like that." She got up. "I put a change of clothes in the car. I'll get them now."

I followed her with my eyes as she went to the door. My previous impressions had melted away. There was an unselfconscious elegance about the way she carried herself. Her English was perfect, with a faint transatlantic burr that she must have picked up at Yale. She was cultivated and intelligent—and she'd just stunned a guard to rescue me. I shook my head.

I heard the hatchback door slam and she returned with a bundle over her arm and her fingers in a pair of shoes. I took them from her. There was a grey suit, a high tunic shirt, some underwear, a pair of socks, and the shoes. My eyes travelled from the clothing to her.

"I took them from my father's room. He has wardrobes filled with clothes—he'll never miss them. I hope they fit you all right. Should do—you're about his size. There's a bathroom through there. Have a shower, if you like. Make yourself comfortable—well, more comfortable, anyway."

"Thanks."

The shower was a very simple affair, operated by a single tap and emitting a fine spray of tepid water. I wasn't expecting even that much in a place like this. For a few moments I just closed my eyes and savoured the sensation of the water coursing over my skin, the tightness in my muscles letting go. Then I rinsed the dirt off my face and soaked away the dried blood, took the soap and washed my aching body, twitching every time I contacted another bruise or abrasion. When I'd finished I just towelled myself lightly and let the rest evaporate. The coolness anaesthetised the pain and I sighed with relief.

I put on the clothes Suzanne had brought me. Fifteen minutes or so later, I returned to the room, hung the jacket over a chair and put the bundled army uniform on the floor. The holster was wrapped in with the bundle; I put the stun pistol on the table.

"That was great. How do I look?"

She looked me over and nodded her approval.

"A bit banged about, but you'll pass muster. I may put a little powder on that cut under the eye just before we go through."

"You're doing such a lot for me, Suzanne. I wish I could repay you somehow."

"You'll find a way," she said. "Do you want to tell me how you ran into trouble with our security people?"

"Later, maybe. Actually I came to Ubindi to talk to you."

Her eyes widened. Again I noticed their remarkable colour.

"I give press conferences," she said. "You didn't have to get yourself clapped in jail to do that."

"The sort of things I want to know don't feature in press conferences."

"Such as?"

"Such as what happened during the time you spent with General Benjamin Obadiah."

She shrank back a little. Her voice acquired an edge.

"Just who the hell are you?"

38

"The journalist thing is just a front, Suzanne. I'm with the CIA."

She regarded me steadily. "You have some way of confirming that?"

"Afraid not. Those charmers who arrested me took everything. In any case we don't carry I.D. when we're on assignment, for obvious reasons. But I think I can establish my credentials. A little over two years ago I was given access to a report. A couple of operatives had just returned to the U.S. after extracting you from Obadiah's camp. Inside the camp they used some sort of air gun built into a camera tripod. They killed the guard outside your tent with it. You took his pistol, and a little later you shot another soldier in the crotch. That raised the alarm and you ran, but you were pinned down in a gully. The third member of the party was killed there before a RotoFan came in and picked you up. That craft also made a considerable mess of the camp. Have I said enough?"

"You don't have to be in Intelligence to get access to information like that."

"Oh yes you do—it was classified Top Secret. None of this was ever in the public domain—unless you yourself spoke about it?"

She stiffened. "I've never said a word about it."

"Not even to your father?"

"Especially not to my father."

"But he must have wanted to know what happened."

"He wanted to know only one thing. Was Obadiah dead? I told him no one could have survived an inferno like that gunship put down."

"That's true. But he was killed before that."

Her eyes ignited. "What?"

"Yes. He was assassinated by those operatives before they came looking for you. Sorry, I thought you knew."

Her voice was dull. "I'm not altogether surprised. My father badly wanted him dead."

"Yes, but those operatives were not employed by your father. They were Americans. And they weren't CIA. What I want to know is: who ordered the assassination?"

"How should I know?"

She'd said it a little too casually. I closed my eyes, then looked at her again. I decided to take a different tack.

"Let's go back a bit. We—I mean, the people who carried out that operation—were told you'd been abducted by Obadiah. Forgive me for saying this, but they were also told you were being held against your will, and abused with some regularity."

"That's not true!"

"Okay, do you want to tell me what actually happened?"

Instead of replying. Suzanne poured more whisky into my tumbler and refreshed her own. I waited.

"Ngozi sent me to negotiate peace terms with Obadiah," she said eventually.

"He sent you to the leader of a rebel army with a bad reputation. It doesn't sound like very fatherly behaviour to me."

"He's not my father." She said it with slow emphasis. "My

real father died when I was twelve."

"Even so, it's a curious thing to do."

She shrugged. "There was an ulterior motive. I wasn't aware of that when I was sent in."

"What happened when you got there?"

"The bad reputation wasn't deserved. Obadiah was a considerate host. He even put a guard on my tent, day and night, to make sure I was safe."

"So the man posted outside your tent was there for your protection?"

"Yes."

I took a deep breath. That was more or less what I thought.

"And your assessment of Obadiah?"

"A little bombastic at first, but that quickly subsided once you got to know him better. He's—he was—a cultured man, something of an idealist."

"What about the atrocities?"

"Atrocities?" she huffed. "Pure propaganda, put about by Ngozi to turn opinion against him. Look, if we're going to talk about this, you need a bit more background and you'll have to stop interrupting me."

"I'm sorry. Go ahead."

I took a sip of whisky, rolled it around my mouth, savouring the way it cauterized my bruised and bleeding lips and gums, and waited for her to resume.

She put long fingers together, evidently preparing her narrative in her own mind. Then she placed her hands in her lap.

"About thirteen years ago, there was armed rebellion in Nigeria. The U.S. wanted to intervene but it was blocked by the UN. As a precaution, several African countries were invited to recommend outstanding soldiers to be seconded to the American Special Forces. Obadiah was a First Lieutenant in the Ubindian army. His name was put forward and they selected him. After a couple of months' training his unit was posted to Africa as part of a special mission to Nigeria. Their brief was not to engage the rebels, but to report back about the position on the ground. They were there for about three months. Shortly afterwards a second UN resolution was passed, approving the deployment of an international force."

So far this accorded exactly with what Prof had told me.

"The unit went back to the States but Obadiah didn't go with them. He was asked to stay on in Nigeria, with the rank of Captain, to supervise training of the incoming troops. It made sense: he knew the language and the terrain, and he had first-hand knowledge of the conflict there. He told me he had mixed feelings about it, because his sympathies were more with the rebels than the government, but he was a soldier, and soldiers do what they're told."

That had a familiar ring to it.

"A Ubindian detachment joined the international force," she continued, "under the command of Lieutenant Colonel Jebediah Ngozi."

Now this was news to me. I hadn't realized Ngozi was involved in Nigerian operations at any stage.

"The two men got to know each other. They had long conversations about the situation in Ubindi, which was going from bad to worse. Have you heard of Joshua Bandajuku?" she asked.

"The name's vaguely familiar."

"He was a vicious, corrupt, self-serving dictator, and he'd been clinging to power here ever since Ubindi was created.

He was supported by the Americans—probably because he was rabidly anti-Marxist. There was charitable aid coming into the country as well, but the general population never saw any of it—Bandajuku and his cronies made sure of that. Obadiah and Ngozi began to trust each other enough to talk about overthrowing the government. Obadiah wanted to return power to the people, and he and Ngozi seemed to share the same platform."

I poured another shot of whisky and held out the bottle to her, but she declined it with a lift of her hand.

"The time came for the Ubindian detachment to return home, but first they had a surprise visit—from Colonel Brad Harrison Cawley. You may have heard of him."

"Of course. Senator Cawley is the Republican candidate for the Presidency."

"That's right. But at the time he was Advisor to the U.S. Department of Defense on African Affairs. He was on a fact-finding mission."

Prof hadn't said anything about Cawley returning to Africa, but this would have been outside the scope of his search.

"Ngozi raised the subject of U.S. support for Bandajuku, and told Cawley about corruption and human rights abuses in his country. They came to an agreement. The U.S. couldn't be party to an attempted coup, but if Ngozi could provide evidence for what he was saying, Cawley would use his influence. With that reassurance, Obadiah resigned from the Special Force and went back with Ngozi to work for a new order in Ubindi."

"It took two years," she continued, "but eventually the coup succeeded. Bandajuku was exiled, and Jebediah Ngozi became President. Obadiah held a senior appointment for a while, but the two of them quickly fell out. It was inevitable. If Ngozi had any democratic intentions to start with, he abandoned them almost as soon as he came to power. Obadiah's convictions, on the other hand, remained strong. So after a few years Obadiah left the government and set up an opposition party. It began to gather strength. Ngozi perceived that he had a dangerous rival and had him arrested on a trumped up charge of treason. Fortunately for Obadiah, he had plenty of friends. They helped him to escape and he set up a guerilla force. He'd amassed a big following by the time I met him."

"Oh? I had the impression that it was just a small force, using hit-and-run tactics."

"He could have mustered twenty times the troops at his disposal. He worked with small numbers so he could train them to a higher standard. And he only conducted operations with small groups—he believed in maximum mobility, you see. But wherever he went he was besieged by volunteers. You mustn't underestimate the extent of his support. In time, he'd have displaced my stepfather—if he'd lived."

Her eyes melted, and she swallowed hard.

"All this is what Obadiah told you?" I asked.

Her manner changed abruptly. "Yes, but I'm not completely naïve! His entire account agreed with everything I'd learned about that period—and believe me I've read a lot. He had a vision for this country, Jim. He had principles. He didn't care about himself, he wanted the best for the people. I shared that vision. That's why we got on so well. And that's why I stayed there as long as I could. I wanted to help him. I knew it was risky. I sent regular messages back to my father, to assure him the negotiations were progressing satisfactorily, that I was being treated well, that I just needed more time."

I thought of the distortions Harken had fed me prior to the mission—all that stuff about her being kept as Obadiah's personal sex slave. It made me angry to think how I'd been taken in.

"All right," I said slowly, "so Ngozi sent you to negotiate a settlement. But he didn't really want one, did he?"

"No."

"And I'm no nearer to understanding why he sent you, or who ordered the hit on Obadiah and his camp. So there's got to be more."

For some minutes we surveyed each other in silence. Then she said:

"There is."

"Well?"

She looked at me long and hard. "I'm sorry, Jim. I can't trust you."

I grimaced. "I understand."

I sat back, fingers resting lightly on the table. Outside in the darkness crickets buzzed in a continuous chorus. Curious how it hadn't penetrated my awareness until now.

She picked up her glass and studied it. There was a small puddle of whisky in the bottom. She drained it.

I said casually, "Did you know your country is propped up by the drugs trade?"

40

She spluttered, coughed, and put the glass firmly down on the table.

"No wonder they wanted to get rid of you! Do you have evidence?"

"Some. You didn't answer my question."

"I've suspected it for a long time, but I couldn't be sure. My stepfather doesn't take me into his confidence on things like that."

"It seems to me that a good deal of your internal security in this country is devoted to keeping it quiet."

She sighed. "It was inevitable, in a way. Ubindi was created out of the Congo peace process, but it drew the short straw: no oil, no gas, no minerals, poor agricultural land, and virtually no strategic significance. Drugs are just about all that's left. The best way to put a stop to it would be to make the country self-sufficient in some other way. Do you know what I was doing in Angola, Jim?"

"To be honest, I didn't even know that was where you were. Tell me."

"The Angolans are sitting on vast reservoirs of oil. They're already producing millions of barrels a day and they haven't begun to tap all their reserves. India and China are still heavily dependent on oil as a fuel and a raw material. I'm trying to negotiate the construction of a pipeline that would take oil across Africa, from the Angolan fields right to

Mombasa. It would cut the sea passage by at least five thousand miles, and it could supply other major African economies like Zambia, Tanzania, and Kenya en route. It would be funded by Angola, with support from the consumer nations." She paused, and her gaze was steady. "Jim, that pipeline would pass smack through Ubindi. The revenues, just from building it and having it cross our land, would keep this country afloat. With careful husbandry of our economy we could start to establish our own industries."

I felt a surge of admiration. "My God, you really do have a vision for Ubindi, don't you?"

She sighed. "Ben Obadiah was the visionary, but I could have made it happen. We would have been a good team."

I reflected bitterly that, as Jim Forbes, I'd killed her visionary leader. Not for the first time I was grateful to be here in a body that Suzanne didn't recognise.

"Suzanne, I think a lot of those drugs are destined for the States. If this gets exposed, the U.S. is certainly going to reconsider its support for this government. I think you should position yourself with that in mind."

She looked thoughtful. "Ngozi and his corrupt administration won't relinquish power easily."

"They may have to if an international court finds them guilty of drug trafficking. It wouldn't take much to track the cargo from the airport. A nicely timed swoop would expose the whole sordid trade. And people will fall over themselves to indict their superiors if it means they'll be treated more leniently. The government will collapse, and you'll be one of the few who won't be tainted with the scandal. What I'm saying is, you should prepare for that. You could be destined for even higher office."

She looked searchingly at me, and I could almost see her

mind working. Then:

"Why are you telling me this?"

I clasped my hands and leaned forward. Pains shot through my bruised back and ribs but I ignored them.

"Why? Because I want you to know that I'm on your side. Look, Suzanne. I think I should be up front with you about what I know and where I stand."

"Okay. I'm listening."

"From what you've told me, Ben Obadiah was a potential future President of this country. His assassination represents a gross interference with the affairs of a sovereign state. We can't bring him back to life, but we can bring those responsible to justice. All right?"

"Go on."

"You said he went to Nigeria on a mission with the Special Forces. You didn't say why, but you probably knew. Rebels were gaining the upper hand and jeopardizing oil supplies to the West. The mission was to find, and place on record, evidence of atrocities committed by rebel forces. The footage they sent back shocked the world. Up to that point the whole thing had been an internal problem. Not any longer. An international force went in, the rebels were driven back, and the flow of oil resumed. Suzanne, something happened during that mission, something that Obadiah knew about, and someone else wanted to cover up. I believe that was why he was killed.

"Now," I said quietly. "I've levelled with you. If you know what it was, I'd like you to tell me. You've saved my life, and there's no way I would ever betray your trust."

She blinked a couple of times. Then, to my surprise, she reached out and placed her hands around mine.

"Jim, if I tell you, will you promise me something?"

"What's that?"

"Promise me you won't divulge or use the information in any way. Not unless we do it together."

"Okay, that's a promise."

"All right."

She took a deep breath, pressed my hands lightly, and sat back. "I mentioned a visit from Colonel Cawley," she said. "But this wasn't the first time he'd been in Nigeria. That original mission was under his command, when he was a Lieutenant Colonel in Special Forces."

Here it was again: direct confirmation of Prof's brilliant detective work.

"The unit settled in quickly," she went on. "Then they started to go out on patrol every day. As I said before, they'd been told not to engage the rebels, but they went through the same territory. Whenever they entered the villages, Ben acted as interpreter. The people told him the rebels had come through and they'd given them food and shelter. There was no coercion; there didn't have to be. The rebels wanted oil wealth to be used for everyone's benefit, and the population supported them. Everywhere they went it was the same story. At no time was there even so much as a suggestion of atrocities.

"After two or three weeks of this, Cawley set up a secure camp and told the unit to stay put while he was away. He said he had some negotiations to attend to. A few days later he returned, and they went out on patrol again with Cawley leading the way. Three of the soldiers had been trained as film crew. They were carrying cameras, and Ben's squad was assigned the job of protecting them. They came upon a village that was still burning. The streets were littered with bodies. Old people and children had been hacked to pieces.

The young women were found in one large house at the end of the village—raped, then murdered in various gruesome ways. Ben had seen action, but he said it made even his stomach turn. Some of the film crew were physically sick."

A muscle in her jaw twitched. She reached for her whisky tumbler. I lifted the bottle, but she waved it away and filled the glass from the jug of water. She took a sip, then looked up again.

"After that, it became a regular occurrence. They would get together each morning, and Cawley would spread out a map. 'The latest intelligence,' he'd say, 'is that the rebels are active in this area. There's a village here. I think we should go take a look.' And they'd go, and find another village annihilated in the same manner, and film it. Cawley seemed to have an unerring ability to lead them to the right places."

A nasty feeling was starting to crawl under my skin. She went on:

"Ben became suspicious. He began to keep a closer eye on Cawley. One morning, just before dawn, Cawley left the camp and Ben tailed him. Before he joined the army, Ben was a skilled tracker—Cawley didn't suspect for one moment he was being followed. He met up with a man just outside a village. Ben couldn't hear the conversation but he watched them, staying out of sight. Moments later he heard the screams and shouts from the village. Later that day Cawley led them to the same village and they filmed the aftermath.

"That night Ben took a camera from the film crew's tent. When Cawley went out before dawn Ben followed him—with the camera. He got close and actually filmed the atrocities as they were taking place. Later he transferred the recordings to memory tiles, and wiped the store in the camera before quietly putting it back. The film crew hadn't even noticed it was missing."

She looked sadly into my eyes. "Jim, the atrocities were not committed by the rebels at all. They were committed by—or at least with the connivance of—your forces. That mission gave the U.S. administration just what it wanted—justification to use an international force—and the rebels were driven back."

My mouth tightened. This possibility had occurred to me some time ago, but I'd dismissed it. I simply couldn't bring myself to believe my former outfit was guilty of war crimes.

"Suzanne, with the greatest respect, this is only what Obadiah told you. Can you be sure of it?"

"Oh yes, I'm very sure of it. You see, I have the memory tiles."

41

My jaw sagged. "What?"

"Yes. I can also show you what's on them. It's not pretty, I'm afraid. Wait here."

She left me sitting at the table, motionless, my mind racing. A few minutes later she came back with a device similar in size to my old cloudphone but a bit thicker.

She held it up and said, "My little projector. I use it for presentations. Only two-dimensional, but that'll be quite sufficient."

She put it on the table and I brought the chairs around so that we could see what it projected on the wall. Then she opened her other hand, revealing two black squares: memory tiles. She inserted the first into the projector and I began to watch footage of the most sickening, unbridled violence I'd ever witnessed. At one point she paused the playback.

I looked up. Her expression was stony, her face a mask of self control. She pointed to the wall. A stocky, dark-complexioned man with a drooping moustache was being filmed coming down the street. Her voice was brittle.

"Ben said that's the man he saw Cawley with, the first time. He's sure he was the leader of the group that carried out the atrocities."

"Did he mention the name?"

"He did, but I've forgotten it. It was a strange name. Rather ugly, I thought."

"What's that he's carrying?"

She swallowed.

"It's a sort of contraption he always had with him. A collapsible wooden frame with leather straps. He…" The self control was slipping and she began to choke up. "He used it to tie the girls up in various positions… I'm sorry."

She turned away. I reached out to touch her gently, but she brushed my hand away, got up and walked away. For a while I heard her moving around in the kitchen. When she came back her face was set again.

"Suzanne," I said slowly. "Was that man's name Bogdan Zajc?"

Her eyes widened. "Yes, that was it! How do you know?"

It had all fallen into place for me.

"That frame is something of a trademark. Zajc led a criminal gang in Albania. They specialized in sex trafficking—they were quite capable of the sort of thing we've just been watching. When the police started to close in, he left the country and resurfaced in the Congo. He was active there for a while, but the Congolese army managed to round up the gang and they found themselves in jail. Before they could be brought to trial, they escaped—miraculously."

"Cawley…?" she breathed.

"Yes. He must have known about them, and what they could do. He sprung them from prison to recruit them into the scheme. He'd been unsuccessful in trying to uncover the sort of evidence people wanted back home, so he or one of his superiors got impatient and decided to make it happen. He probably bribed a guard at that Congolese jail to get them out. In return, Zajc and his nasty friends did their thing in Nigeria. All he had to know was where they were going to strike next. Does Cawley appear on this footage?"

"Yes, he's on both the tiles. Ben said initially he wasn't a party to the actual atrocities, but it seems he couldn't resist joining in. He's not shown killing anyone, but he… he did other things." The self control was slipping again. There was a pause, then she took a deep breath, straightened up, and added, in a matter-of-fact tone, "I'm sorry, I won't be able to watch any more with you."

"No, of course not. But I think I've got to sit through it, just in case there's anyone else I recognize. Suzanne, did Ben ever mention the name 'Harken' to you?"

"Harken? I don't think so. Why?"

"I think he was in this unit, but I don't know whether he was involved. That's one of the things I need to find out."

"All right. I'm going to leave you to it."

She left the room, and I restarted the projection.

At this stage I was still prepared to give Cawley the benefit of the doubt. After all, he could have been under orders to release Zajc and his gang, and to let them loose in this fashion. As I continued the playback, any such charitable thoughts vanished. At one stage Cawley was easily recognizable as he lifted the dress of a screaming girl, then signalled to members of the gang to hold her as he drew the wide army belt out of the waistband of his trousers…

No wonder Suzanne couldn't bear to watch. The man was a sadist and a rapist. And this was a candidate for the Presidency of the United States!

I sat through the material on the second memory tile with growing disgust, then shut down the projector. I'd seen no other SAF uniforms, nor any sign of Harken. That was a relief. Apart from Zajc and his gang, it looked like Cawley was acting on his own. If it hadn't been for Obadiah no one would ever have been the wiser.

As the ghastly images receded, my mind settled back into the plain surroundings of the room. I got up and went over to the window. The sky was suffused by a rosy glow, and the irregular outlines of the primitive dwellings outside had started to emerge in the pale light.

I heard movement behind me. Suzanne was standing there.

"You've finished."

"Yes." I went back to the table and handed the memory tiles to her with a slight grimace. "You'd better keep these in a safe place."

She took them from me. "This needs to be made public, Jim."

"I suppose that's why Obadiah gave you those tiles."

"He never said that. He knew he was in danger so he gave me the tiles for safekeeping. But how can you be in possession of something like this and not act on it?"

"You could have done that two years ago. Why didn't you?"

"I was afraid. Cawley's our chief advocate in the U.S. administration; without him, U.S. support for this country would dry up. If I revealed this, someone would certainly kill me: if not Cawley, my stepfather, or one of his lackeys. I thought of uploading it anonymously to the net, but material like that can be faked; it's worthless without the provenance. I tried to think of another way, but the opportunity never seemed to present itself."

"And now?" I said. "What's changed?"

"What's changed is that Cawley's running for President. I couldn't put it off any longer. I was wondering what to do when the State Department called. They said you were a fearless investigative journalist and had to be released. And I needed an ally. Suddenly the opportunity was there, so I grasped it." She looked at me, eyes narrowed slightly. "Are you going to help me?"

I didn't have to think. "I'll do every damned thing in my power."

She inclined her head. "Thank you." Then, holding up the memory tiles, "I'll put these away."

As she went out of the room she added, over her shoulder, "I was just preparing a snack. Do you want tea or coffee?"

I was so surprised it took me a moment to reply. "Er, either is fine."

"Stay here. I'll only be a moment."

I realised I was ravenously hungry.

A few minutes later, she returned with two plates and set one in front of me. On it was some sort of bread, stuffed with vegetables. I was stuck in before she came back with the coffee. I didn't know what it was and I didn't care.

We finished the snack in silence. I sat back with a sigh. "Thanks for that. It was a life saver."

"I take it they didn't feed you while you were in jail," she observed drily.

"No food, no water. Just regular beatings. I've known better accommodation."

My head jerked round as I heard some shouts from outside, but it was just children running into the street. The light from the window now cast a bright rectangle on the floor. Above it, as if awoken by the sun, motes of dust had begun a complex dance. The air in the room was thickening with the resinous tang of hot wood.

Around this time I'd have been shoved into a vehicle and taken out to the Jukwala for feeding time at the zoo. I wonder what they'll make of it when they go the jail to get me and find that fat bastard of a sergeant—

What had I been thinking of?

"Suzanne, when you helped me escape you knew exactly where to park and how to find your way out."

"That prison is in the basement of the Ministry for Security. It's part of the main government complex—my own Ministry is there."

"The person manning the security checkpoint—did he recognize you?"

"Of course. That's why he let me through."

I glanced at my watch but it wasn't there, of course. It was among the possessions they'd taken from me.

"When they find that sergeant lying on the floor in his underwear and discover I'm missing, they'll ask the sentry if anyone went out during the night. And he'll say 'Yes. Ms. Mukewa was here'. The timing will fit. They'll come looking for you. And if they find me with you, we are going to be in extraordinarily deep shit."

"They won't know this is where we came."

"All the same, I have a suggestion."

"Yes? What's that?"

"That we get the hell out of here."

She crossed calmly to the window and looked out. The slanting rays made a sculpture of her face. Again I realized how badly I'd misjudged her on first acquaintance.

"You're probably right," she said. "It's light enough now. We have a good lead on them, but it wouldn't hurt to start moving. I'll just clear these things up." I half rose, but she held up a hand. "No, you stay here."

She disappeared into the kitchen, and I heard sounds of running water. A few minutes later she returned.

"Ready?"

I put the jacket on and checked the safety on the stun

pistol before tucking it into my belt. Then I picked up the bundle of clothes from the sergeant.

"We can lose these somewhere en route."

She led the way out to the car. I noticed that she had a quick look up and down the street as we went out to the four-wheel drive, but there were just a few children playing. As they caught sight of us they started to run up, but Suzanne reversed briskly out of the shelter and drove off. Looking in the wing mirror I could just make out the children standing in the street, partially screened by the pursuing cloud of red dust.

42

In a few minutes we were driving through open savannah, with just the dirt road ahead of us.

"Was that your house we just left?" I asked.

"Yes. It belonged to my mother. She used it as a hideaway whenever she couldn't stand Ngozi's arrogance any longer. He never discovered where she went."

"Where's your mother now?"

"South of France. She wanted me to go with her but I decided to stay."

"Why? Because of your stepfather?"

"Not because of him—in spite of him. I love my country, Jim, and I still think I can do something for it. So mother gave me the house—she said I might need it from time to time. Someone in the village keeps an eye on it for me, cleans it, and makes sure there's something to eat if I visit unexpectedly."

I looked ahead and pointed. "That grove of trees, over there. May be a good place to hide the clothes."

She pulled up. I got the bundle out of the boot and hurried over. The sun was well up now and the ground was hot enough to feel through the soles of my shoes. The trees were all dead; bone white, with broken limbs scattered on the ground. I found what I was looking for—a shattered trunk with a deep hollow—and pushed the sergeant's clothes well down inside it.

It was far too hot for a jacket; when I returned to the car I took it off and put it in the boot. Then I climbed back in and she drove off.

After we'd travelled for an hour or so the grasses became lower and coarser and soon we were looking out over a semi-arid landscape, punctuated by stunted shrubs, all shivering in the heat. The road was unmade and by now the windows had a fine coating of dust. Suzanne was driving at speed, and the ridges and potholes jarred my aching body. I hung onto the grab handle and gritted my teeth. The last thing I wanted was for her to slow down.

For a long time we travelled in silence, but I was still on edge. I glanced behind me.

"This thing's putting up a plume of dust a mile long," I said. "It'd be dead easy to spot us from the air. Does the army have aerial capability?"

"No. The defence agreement was limited to equipping ground forces."

I should have realized that. The bureaucrats at the U.S. Department of Defense would want to limit their financial commitment. If they supplied aircraft, they'd have to train pilots to fly them and maintenance engineers to keep them in the air, and include fuel for operations in the budget. More important still, the U.S. stance was supposed to be non-interventionist. They could supply arms without attracting too much attention but if they created an air force there would be major objections from neighbouring countries—and their backers. Aircraft changed the balance of power, as the RotoFan had illustrated when it attacked Obadiah's camp. Still, if they were out looking for us, aerial reconnaissance would be by far the quickest way.

"What about the helicopter at Kebe airport?"

"What about it?"

"Have you ever used it?"

"Once. And once was enough."

"How big is it?"

"What do you mean, how big?"

"Well, is it a troop carrier or a small four-seater? Single rotor, or twin?"

"It's quite small. Single rotor. Four seats, as I remember."

That was reassuring. If the army wanted to use it, they'd have to employ the civilian pilot. They'd be aiming to bring us back, so that would occupy two more seats, leaving room for only one soldier. They wouldn't go for that. And if there was no way of shipping out troops other than in trucks, they couldn't set up road blocks ahead of us. It looked like we could make it to the border after all.

"All right, assuming we get out of Ubindi, then what? We can't stay in the Congo forever. Can your government close the Congo's borders? Or Angola's?"

"In theory, yes. In practice it's going to take them a little time."

"Why's that?"

"It comes under foreign relations. The Minister for Security has to liaise with the Minister for External Affairs. And I'm the Minister for External Affairs."

She gave me one of those wonderful smiles. I returned it with a broad grin. I began to relax.

We must have been driving for a couple of hours when I asked her if she'd like me to take over.

"Are you up to it?"

I passed a hand over my bruised ribs.

"I think so."

"All right."

She pulled up and we swapped seats.

I drove as fast as I dared. It was actually better than being a passenger: holding onto the steering wheel helped me to brace my body for the constant barrage of shocks sent up from the road. In places the way ahead degenerated into a pattern of deep ridges and I had to swerve to go around them. The seasonal rains probably turned this route into a river of mud, which was churned up by lorries and then baked hard in the sun. For a time I concentrated on what I was doing. Then my mind started going back over our conversation.

I glanced her way. She had her eyes closed, but I didn't think she was asleep.

"Okay to talk?" I asked gently.

"Go ahead," she mumbled, without opening her eyes.

"I'm thinking about Cawley. Once their job was done, he took that SAF unit back to the States."

"Yes, except for Ben. He stayed in Nigeria to help the international force."

"And that force included a detachment from Ubindi."

"Yes."

"And when that detachment is just about ready to go home, Cawley appears on the scene again, ostensibly on a 'fact-finding mission'. Is that really what it was?"

She straightened up. "Of course not. He knew Ngozi was taking the Ubindian detachment home. He wanted him to take some civilians with him. They were mercenaries, he said, but they'd been very helpful to the International Force. You can guess who they were."

"Zajc and his friends. They were still wanted in the Congo, and they weren't even supposed to be in Nigeria. He must have made a deal with them, told them he'd get them out."

"Yes. Ngozi saw his chance. He didn't have to accept orders from Cawley; if he was going to take these people he expected something in return. He told Cawley about the human rights abuses in Ubindi, and how he and Ben planned to replace Bandajuku. Cawley wasn't having any. The U.S. couldn't intervene in the affairs of a sovereign state, he said." She looked over at me. "As an agent of the CIA, I was expecting some hollow laughter from you."

I grinned at her. "But I thought you said Cawley agreed to support them."

"Shall we call it a 'change of heart'? Ben knew the coup wouldn't succeed unless they had the U.S. on side. He got Cawley on his own, told him what he knew about the Nigerian atrocities, and showed him the memory tiles and a few stills to give him a taste of what was on them."

"He blackmailed him?"

"Let's just say he didn't have to spell it out. Suddenly Cawley was remarkably cooperative. By the time Ben and Ngozi returned to Ubindi the coup was mapped out. The U.S. denounced the Bandajuku regime and withdrew their backing. They secretly supplied arms to the rebels, and recognized the new government when it came to power."

I'd narrowed my eyes against the waves of heat coming off the road but I saw the bad patch too late. The steering took on a life of its own as we bounced and jinked between ridges. It went on and on. How much of a battering could this vehicle take? Finally, to my relief, we emerged onto a smoother surface. Despite the air conditioning I was damp with sweat. I wiped my shirt cuff across my forehead and looked across at Suzanne.

"Do we have any water?"

She opened the cubby and took out a plastic bottle; then

she unscrewed the cap and passed it to me. I took a good mouthful and handed it back. Somewhat to my surprise she put it straight to her own lips and drank. As she screwed the cap back on she said:

"You don't suffer from any fatal diseases, do you?"

"Only curiosity."

She nodded. "In this country that can be fatal, all right."

Another set of ridges appeared ahead but I saw them in time and steered off to the right. We bounced over grassy hummocks before regaining the road and straightening up.

I prompted her to resume. "So that was the beginning of the special relationship."

"Yes. In the U.S., Cawley defended it with speeches about the threat of Islamic expansionism in Africa. Ben and I both laughed about that."

"Why?"

"It really isn't a local issue; it was something Cawley dreamed up to bolster his image as a defender of freedom and democracy. Ubindi does have a predominantly Islamic country on every border so theoretically, at least, you could say it was at risk. Anyway, it kept everyone happy."

"But then Obadiah became an outlaw."

"Initially I don't think Cawley was too worried about it. Then he started to campaign for the Republican nomination. His message to the party and the country was that a man with his outstanding military record knew how to take tough decisions, defend the American way of life, etcetera. Revelations like Ben's would have destroyed him—he just couldn't afford to take chances."

I sensed, rather than saw, her looking at me.

"I don't know how he managed it, Jim. All I know is that I was the bait in the trap. I helped to kill a man I admired, and who could have done a lot for my country."

"You mustn't blame yourself." If anyone was to blame, I thought, it was Jim Forbes for being fool enough to take it all on trust.

We drove on in silence for a bit. Then she said, "Would you like me to take over?"

I looked once again at my non-existent watch, then checked the clock on the fascia. I'd been driving for nearly two hours and my eyeballs felt red-hot from the bright light and the concentration.

"Thanks, I could do with a spell. You can probably go faster than me, too."

We swapped places again. Now that I could take my eyes off the road, I saw that the landscape had changed. There were still no trees, but there were more of the stunted bushes in amongst the coarse grass.

We'd only been driving for another ten minutes when a shiver ran through me. It was a while since I'd heard that noise, but it was unmistakable.

It was a helicopter.

43

I met Suzanne's eyes and knew she'd heard it too.

"Damn them," I said. "They must have rented that bloody thing, after all. They've been running up every route from the capital."

She bit her lip.

"Look," I said. "They're going to land on the road ahead of us, maybe slightly to the left or right. See that scrub up ahead?"

I pointed to a line of thorn bushes that encroached on the road from either side, perhaps the site of a watercourse in the rainy season.

"Yes?"

"Stop the car there. When he sets that thing down there'll be a lot of dust and it'll give me some cover. I'll make a break for whichever side looks best. I don't want them to find you with me on board. There's only room on board for one soldier. He'll probably want you to go back with him."

"No way, Jim! I don't know what they've seen or found. I could be taking your place in that dungeon."

"Don't worry, I'll make sure it doesn't happen. Stop up ahead."

"All right. Take my bag, will you? I don't want them going through my stuff."

"No problem."

I looped the strap of her bag over my head to carry it

diagonally, then shrank down as low as I could, so it would look as if Suzanne was alone in the vehicle. I drew the stun pistol out of my belt to check the charge level, and cursed lightly. There was only enough for a single discharge, level five.

I may need it later on. I won't use it unless I have to.

I returned it to my belt.

The helicopter chopped loudly over our heads just as we were reaching the line of scrub. I caught a glimpse through the windscreen as it passed. My recognition wasn't great for craft that old, but the lightweight construction suggested something from Aerospatiale. The tail and fuselage were just a spidery tubular steel framework, and it had a large plexiglass cockpit, the sort of thing they'd use for scenic tours—if there was any scenery worth touring.

Suzanne stopped the car and switched off the engine. I peered over the fascia to watch the helicopter hovering above the road. The tail swung round to the left and the craft began to settle, fanning up a great circle of dust. That was my cue.

I opened the door, jumped out, slammed the door behind me and ran for the line of bushes on the left. The note of the helicopter's turbine dropped slightly as the rotors slowed to an idle.

Individually, the bushes weren't as dense as they looked, but there were enough of them to hide my outline. I moved around so that I was directly behind the tail of the machine. The cabin door on the right swung open, and a soldier jumped down. He straightened up and flicked open the holster at his belt as he strode towards the car. He was massive.

Suzanne got out to meet him.

They shouted to make themselves heard over the noise of

the helicopter. I couldn't understand what they were saying, of course, but I could guess what was going on from the tone of voice.

Suzanne: initially puzzled.

Soldier: demanding, interrogative.

Suzanne: imperious.

Soldier: enraged.

I saw her turn round and he threw her up against the car. I clenched my fists. Then, as he gathered her hands behind her to fasten them together, I sprinted for the helicopter. It was only a few metres. I ducked under the tail and climbed onto the frame above the port skid, hiding behind the big cylindrical fuel tank. The exposed turbine was uncomfortably close to my ears and I could feel the draft as each rotor blade swept overhead. I crouched there, watching the ground on the other side.

Suzanne's feet came into view, moving slowly, then surging forward a few paces as if she'd been shoved from behind. One foot disappeared, then the other, as she climbed into the helicopter. The soldier's boots appeared. Close enough.

I dropped down, rolled under the craft, and drove my heel up into his crotch, doubling him over. Then I straightened up on the other side and sent in a kick to the head. His beret flew into the dust and he staggered back against the helicopter, mouth open. I hadn't done it hard enough. He fumbled for his pistol. I kicked again, but he managed to parry it with his arm. To my surprise he countered with a kick of his own, but it lacked speed. I blocked the ankle and grabbed the knee, pulling and turning, so that he dropped onto his face. As he got up I rammed the heels of my hands into the back of his head and banged it against the ground. He responded instantly, jerking his head up and catching me in the bridge of the nose. A blinding pain exploded across my eyes, and I didn't see the kick that sent me spinning face down in the dust. Before I could move he'd gathered me up from behind in a bear hug. In a moment of panic I realized what was happening: he was lifting my head into the rotors.

I could feel the swish of each blade, close enough to stir my hair. He was straining hard, trying to lift me that extra couple of inches. My arms were trapped but I used my heel, raking it down his knee and shin. He grunted with pain and loosened his grip just enough for me to free one arm and slam the elbow hard into his ear. He staggered backwards and I just had time to whip out the stun pistol and fire. He dropped and didn't come up again. I tossed my pistol away, took his, then leapt up into the cabin.

The astonished pilot had half risen to his feet. I levelled the pistol at him. I was gasping for breath and my hand wasn't all that steady.

"Out!" I commanded.

He began to protest, in a language I didn't understand. I said it again, jerking the pistol for emphasis, and he complied. Suzanne was sitting, wide-eyed, in the rear seat. I put a finger to my lips before I got down.

I had no doubt that this man spoke some English; he'd have to, as a pilot. I pointed at the unconscious soldier.

"If he stays here, he will die in the sun," I said. "Take him to the car."

The man looked at me, eyes dilated with fear. He waved his palms and began to gibber.

"Just do it!" I said.

He bent down, took the soldier's arms and tried to drag him but he was too heavy. I wasn't surprised; the guy was built like an ox. I tucked the pistol into my belt and took the feet. It was a struggle, but between us we managed to get him to the car and bundle him inside.

We straightened up, breathing hard.

I drew the pistol again and jerked the muzzle towards the helicopter. He went ahead of me as we ducked under the rotors and climbed into the cabin. He settled into the pilot seat.

"Keep still," I said, holding the pistol to his head. I turned to take a look at Suzanne's wrists. It was a standard plastic restraint.

"Give me your knife," I said to the pilot.

He licked his lips.

I held out my hand. "Give me your knife. I won't harm you."

He dipped into a pocket.

"Slowly!" I warned him.

He withdrew an old penknife and handed it over.

I opened it and sawed through the restraint on her wrists. A few hours ago she'd done the same for me, and I was pleased to return the favour, even if I was responsible for the problem.

I closed the knife and dropped it into my shirt pocket. It was a potential weapon, better in my hands than his.

I took the copilot's seat. My breathing was settling now. "What's your name?"

"Aaron," he said shakily. "Aaron Sapila."

"Okay, listen, Aaron," I said. "This woman is my hostage."

He gave me a very blank look. Perhaps aeronautical vocabulary didn't stretch that far. I looked over my shoulder at Suzanne and she shouted a couple of words at him. I thought she sounded suitably panic-stricken.

"I escaped from prison, and took her hostage. She drove me here because I was holding a gun to her head."

Again I looked over my shoulder and Suzanne translated.

"You tell that to your people when you get back," I finished.

She translated and he made a brief reply. It sounded like he'd got the message.

"Good. Now you are going to fly us across the border to the Congo."

He understood that, all right. He looked stunned, and held up his hands. "Not enough fuel!" he protested.

I looked at the control panel. I couldn't fly one of these things but I'd been in enough cockpits to read the instruments. His tank was three-quarters full. I sighed and thrust the muzzle of my pistol up his nose.

I spoke with great deliberation.

"Aaron, are you going to make me very, very angry?"

He shook his head the fraction that was allowed him by the pressure on his nose, never taking those wide, bloodshot eyes off me.

I withdrew the pistol. "Good. Set course for…" I barked at Suzanne. "You know this country. Tell him where to go."

She said something in her own language.

He swallowed and nodded.

"And if you want to live," I said, "don't try any tricks. "Aaron? Do you understand?"

He said something I didn't understand, but it sounded affirmative. He pulled his harness down and fastened it. Then he unhooked a headset, and pointed to me and to Suzanne to do the same, jerking at his harness to indicate we should fasten our own. When we'd both followed his example, he placed his feet on the pedals, took the cyclic in his right hand, and the collective in his left, and increased engine speed. Our view was obscured by a great cloud of dust, but that strange feeling of levitation told me we'd left the ground. In a few moments the dust was below us, and the road, much narrower now, came into view ahead. He tilted the craft forward and we gathered speed.

I took off Suzanne's bag, slid it back to her, and gave her a final, reassuring glance. It looked like we were on our way.

44

Now that we were airborne and heading for the border, the adrenaline subsided. At last I had a chance to settle back and think. Such a lot had come out of my conversations with Suzanne. Could I put the remaining pieces together?

I went back to my last trip to the American Embassy, and the hurried phone conversation with Prof just before the soldiers picked me up. Something Prof had said was nagging away at me, something about the route of those cargo flights. I went through the countries in my mind. From Uzbekistan to Afghanistan, Turkey, Romania, Bulgaria, Albania, Nigeria, and Ubindi. And out of Ubindi to Senegal, Albania, Bulgaria, Romania, ending up in the Ukraine. Why?

When it dawned on me I could scarcely believe I hadn't seen it before.

Turkey, Bulgaria, Romania, Albania. All places where Bogdan Zajc had surfaced, then disappeared! Put Zajc together with the cargo flights and the whole thing began to make sense. That was how he managed to transport his trucks and his personnel across so many borders, and get his kidnapped girls into the flesh markets of Asia and Eastern Europe. They could roll the trucks off in Afghanistan and drive them into Pakistan and India. And from the Ukraine they could cross into Slovakia, Poland, or Russia. With a series of flights like that he could transport drugs, move his own people, and traffic the girls, and the sheer complexity of the operation made it almost impossible for anyone to recognize what was going on.

Well, that explained most of the destinations, but how did Ubindi fit in? Ngozi had taken Zajc and his friends back there after the Nigerian business, and probably helped them get out of Africa altogether, but that wasn't a good enough reason to make Ubindi a link in the chain. A friendly little police state in which they could refine the drugs and keep it quiet? Possibly. Or was there something they had that Zajc wanted?

Again it was like a curtain had been lifted. Modern weapons, courtesy of the United States of America! They must be shipping the raw material for heroin manufacture to Ubindi in return for arms. Zajc would equip his own people and sell everything else in the countries they visited en route. He probably took orders from arms dealers in one direction and delivered to them in the other. Meanwhile, whatever Ubindi got from the sale of the refined drugs would be clear profit. No wonder the trade kept the country afloat!

Now I understood why Ngozi's soldiers were using those antiquated rifles; Ngozi was trading the up-to-date stuff before his army even had sight of it!

My mind was racing with excitement. Then, with a lurch, I realised there was something else I could explain: how Zajc's gang got their hands on a long-range stun mortar powerful enough to lay out my entire platoon in Serbia. The weapons expert at my trial said they weren't available on the black market. He wasn't aware of the cosy little arrangement Zajc had here in Ubindi.

It brought back all the frustration and despair I'd suffered at my trial. Well, with what I knew now, could I nail the bastard? I didn't have an answer to that yet, but some ideas were taking shape.

I looked over my shoulder again at Suzanne. Her expression hardly changed but her eyes shone as she returned my gaze. The tension inside me dissipated. I smothered a smile and turned back.

I felt a surge of warmth for her. She'd put her life on the line to get me out of that jail, give me food and shelter, a change of clothes—

Clothes! I looked down at my trousers. I'd left the jacket of Ngozi's suit in the boot of her car! My fabricated story about her being a hostage wasn't going to cut much ice now. She was a fugitive, too. And why? Because she believed in justice: justice for a dead rebel leader, justice for the people of her country, and another kind of justice for a man, currently running for President of the United States, who'd been responsible for unspeakable atrocities. For a woman—or any person—to make a sacrifice like that was remarkable; for a Minister of State it was almost unbelievable. You couldn't help but admire someone with such deep-seated principles.

Below us the shadow of the helicopter ran over the savannah, distorting briefly as it crossed grass and scrub and rose and fell through undulations in the landscape. Now that I was paying more attention I noticed there'd been a change in the vegetation: the grassland looked less arid, and it was dotted with low trees, both on their own and in small clumps. On the horizon, mountains were beginning to show through the heat haze and I guessed we weren't too far from the border. Soon the engine note rose and we began to gain altitude, following the sides of valleys to take advantage of ground effect. Aaron clearly knew the terrain.

Returning to my thoughts, I realized something new and

interesting was happening to me. When I emerged from the nightmare of the operation I had no identity; the bag of documents they'd given me on my discharge from the training camp was just a sham. I was the brain of Jim Forbes, disgraced soldier, transplanted into a body that now walked around with the name of Jim Slater. It was a curiously detached feeling: I had consciousness and memories, but they weren't part of my life. Even a secret agent, working under a false identity, knew who they really were; I didn't. The only thing that had given my existence any meaning at all was a determination to deal with the people responsible for my situation and for the deaths of Gerry and Sefu and the team in Serbia. Yet now, for the first time in this dark period, the different parts of me had started to coalesce and I'd begun to feel like a real person again. What had happened? Was it surviving the trauma of recent days? Was it something to do with Suzanne?

Right now I had no way of telling.

*

A small movement caught the corner of my eye. Aaron's hand had moved on the collective. Beyond the earphones I could hear a change in the engine note. I scanned the instrument panel. There was some fuel left in the tank, but not a lot. I looked at him. He pulled the microphone stalk closer to his mouth.

"We are crossing the border into the Congo," he said. "Soon we land. I must speak to ground control."

"Okay," I said. "Nice and easy, and you could still get home to your family tonight."

The exchanges were in English. I listened carefully, but

he seemed to be following normal procedure.

The airport came up ahead. It was a small affair. There was a cluster of terminal buildings, one with an antenna on the roof, and I could see five or six light planes on the apron but nothing bigger.

Ideal for our purposes. Good choice, Suzanne.

Minutes later we drifted in and slid sideways to settle on the pad.

Our first priority was to get shot of Aaron. Suzanne insisted on paying to refuel his helicopter.

"I must, Jim, or he'll never get back. The man is dirt poor. Did you see his shoes?"

"How are you going to pay for it?"

"It's all right. I can do it on a government account."

I grinned at her. I could imagine how delighted they'd be about that.

I watched her walk back to the pilot and speak to him. He listened attentively then began to bow deeply. I could imagine the man's relief, after flying virtually at gun point and landing his craft in another country with an empty tank, to know he was going home after all. I think he was about to get on his knees, but she restrained him with a hand on his arm, detached herself gently, and made for the terminal.

By now I was regretting the way I'd intimidated the poor guy. I walked over. The way he cowered made me wince, but I just reached into my shirt pocket and handed him back his old penknife. He looked in astonishment from the knife back to me. I laid a hand on his shoulder, muttered "Take care, pal," and turned back.

I was surprised to see Suzanne watching from a short distance away. No doubt she'd paused to see what I was up to. Her lips quirked.

I shrugged, a little embarrassed. "Didn't seem right to steal it from him."

She tilted her head, and the look she swept over me answered my earlier question. I felt whole again because of a sense of worth that emanated, in some undefinable way, from her.

A loud engine noise made me jerk round, but it was the fuel tender rolling out. I waited long enough to follow the operation, observing the way Aaron's lively demeanor reflected his growing spirits as the refuelling progressed. By the time the tender was on its way back he'd got in and started the engine. I watched the helicopter dwindle to a hazy speck, climbing then disappearing into the mountain range. The sound took a long time to fade.

When I looked round Suzanne had gone. I walked over to the terminal building and went inside.

Suzanne was engaged in a prolonged exchange with a less-than-interested border guard. She was clearly turning on the charm and this, together with some money that I spotted changing hands, secured the desired result. Again I saw why she'd opted for this remote airport; it might have been harder elsewhere.

We chartered one of the light planes to Lubumbashi and took a taxi from the airport straight to the Foreign Ministry. Apparently she'd been expected there the following week, to continue negotiations on the pipeline. She was hoping they could entertain an unscheduled visit.

I paced around for two hours before she emerged.

"All done," she announced. "We'd moved things on in Angola, so we could make some useful progress. At the end I mentioned the small problem of my car being broken into. Fortunately my own papers were with me, but both of my aides had theirs stolen. My friends here were most sympathetic. They've issued us with some diplomatic documents. I gave the names as Rebecca Mutabulu and James Hendricks."

"Who on earth…?"

"Come on, Jim! I'll be travelling as Rebecca Mutabulu. You'll be James Hendricks."

"Hendricks?"

"Yes, we'll pass you off as a South African working in the Congo. These are yours."

She handed the papers to me but I said, "You'd better look after them, Suzanne. My jacket's still in Ubindi."

A fleeting shadow crossed her face. She laid a hand on my arm. "Makes no difference, Jim. We're in this together."

I stood still, aware of the warmth of her hand through the thin shirt sleeve. Something unspoken hung in the air between us.

The moment passed. She took her hand away and tucked the papers into her bag. It was back to business.

"Anyway, these should be good enough to get us into France."

"France?"

"Yes. We're flying to Marseilles. I thought we'd look in on my mother."

45

I stood at the large picture window, admiring the intense blue of the Côte d'Azur. Next to me was Esther Mukewa. No one could doubt she was Suzanne's mother, with her light skin, high cheekbones and amazing eyes—a sort of hazel in Esther's case. She'd met us at the airport and driven us on the multiway out to Saint-Raphaël, where she had a nice flat with a sea view.

She followed my gaze, then looked up at me. "When you are livin' in a land-locked country for mos' of your life," she explained, "it's good to be near the sea."

"It's beautiful."

I meant it, too. After the last few days it was a joy to let the sheer tranquillity of the scene seep into me.

She turned away from the window. Suzanne was behind us.

"How long can you stay, children?"

"Two days?" Suzanne answered. "Maybe three."

"As long as you like. You can take the spare bedroom."

I met Suzanne's eyes. "The sofa will be fine for me," I said.

"What! Haven't you slept with my daughter yet?"

"Mama…"

"I don' know what's wrong with you young people," she complained. Then she wagged her finger at Suzanne. "This high-flyin' job you got is all ver' well, but you gotta listen to your basic drives, too! That's not politics, it's biology."

Suzanne and I grinned sheepishly at each other.

"Well, now. You two come all the way from Lubumbashi. You mus' be hungry."

"Jim certainly is," Suzanne said. "They didn't give him any food or water in prison."

Esther wagged her head in disapproval.

I felt a little embarrassed by the implied slight to her husband.

"I don't suppose the President knew what was going on…" I ventured.

"Don' you believe it!" she exclaimed. "That man knows ever'thin' that's going on. Well, let's see what we can put together."

She disappeared into the kitchen.

"Really, I can manage on the sofa," I whispered to Suzanne. "I slept on a stone floor in the prison."

She threw a glance in the direction of the kitchen, then moved close to me with a conspiratorial smile.

"It's a big bed," she said softly. "I'm sure we can manage."

Before I knew what I'd done, I'd kissed her. For a moment I just stood there awkwardly. Then she put her arms round my neck and we kissed properly. Her voice was low.

"I'd better see if Mama needs some help."

I remained by the window, the blood surging through me and pulsing in my loins. That part of my nervous system seemed to have connected up very successfully. I could hardly wait for bedtime.

The meal that Esther put on the table was not traditional Provençale fare. She served up chicken in a peanut sauce; okra, prepared with tomatoes, onions, green pepper and hot chili; mushrooms; and casava. There was also a basket of what she called "kwanga", a bread made from cassava flour.

It tasted vaguely of cheese.

"You wan' a beer with this?" Esther asked.

"That would be great."

Esther ate sparingly, but Suzanne and I were both ravenous and we needed no encouragement. When I'd finished, I sat back with a sigh.

"That's what I like to see," Esther remarked, as she collected my empty plate and the last of the dishes. "I hate food left over."

"No risk of that," I said. "It was delicious. How do you get all these ingredients here?"

"Down the market, in Saint-Raphaël," she called out on her way to the kitchen. "They got ever'thin'. You know it's a big African community here now." She came back and rejoined us at the table. "A lot of French people moved north to get away from the heat. They were short of labour, especially the farms and vineyards. The climate suits our people. That's why I came here when I couldn't stand President High-an'-Mighty Jebediah Ngozi no more." She looked at me, her head on one side. "He wasn't always like that, you know. Not back in Nigeria."

"Nigeria? What were you doing there?"

"I worked for the United Nations. They sent a delegation to see how the peacekeepin' force was doin'. I was an interpreter."

Suzanne added, "Mama speaks several African languages, including Yoruba. And English, of course."

"An' a bit of French, now," she laughed. "Jebediah was with the Ubindian army. His heart was full of the spirit of revolution. We all of us hated Bandajuku's guts, so naturally we came together. Suzanne's father had been dead a coupla years. I was lonely. I was a handsome woman, then."

"You still are," I put in immediately.

She gave me a playful shove and said loudly to Suzanne, "Where did you find this charmer?"

We laughed.

She looked at me, head tilted to one side, a gesture I'd seen echoed in Suzanne.

"Are you Irish?"

"I was born in England. There could be Irish ancestors—I don't know."

"My grandmother was Irish," she said. "She was an old lady by the time I knew her, but she still had lovely blue eyes."

That explained her colouring. And Suzanne's.

"Anyhow," she continued, "it's like I was saying. You got to look after your basic drives. So I married him. It was good for a while. But after the coup, he became President and that's when the rot set in. I tried to influence him but he tol' me to stay out of politics. I guess it's in the blood, though. Look at my daughter: Minister for External Affairs." She wagged her head proudly from side to side.

"Probably not any more, now, Mama. They tried to arrest me. You should have seen Jim in action."

"I wasn't having that," I said. "Not after she'd saved me from the crocodiles."

"It's good you helped each other," she said simply. "I'm glad you got outta that place."

She didn't seem to have a real grasp of what had happened, but I wasn't going to enlighten her any more than necessary. I was still wondering how long Ngozi's reach might be.

"Does Ngozi know where you live?" I asked.

"No. I didn't wan' him or his friends spyin' on me so I changed my name and moved a coupla times. You safe enough here. Let's go inside."

We moved into the front room. With the faux-wood floors, white ceilings and plain white walls this could have been just another anonymous modern apartment. In Esther's hands it had acquired a comfortable ambience permeated with her cultural identity. It wasn't the furniture, which was of contemporary European design; she'd achieved the effect with textiles: rugs, throws, and wall-hangings in bold, triangular patterns of pale green, bright blue, oranges, and browns. She took me by the hand to make sure I sat next to her on the sofa.

"It's nice you come to visit me," she said, lifting the hand and patting it. "You got some plans for yourselves the next day or two?"

"Not really." Suzanne settled into an armchair, smiling at the two of us. "We may have a wander around the market. Jim needs a jacket."

Esther gave my hand a final pat and relinquished it. "I better come with you. You have to bargain with those people or they rob you blind."

*

The evening neared its end and my anticipation, fuelled by frequent glances from Suzanne, was dampened by a growing sense of trepidation. As Jim Forbes I'd had a certain amount of experience, but not in this body. I felt as nervous and self-conscious as a teenage virgin. Would I be clumsy and inept? Would I be a disappointment to her? Would I ruin everything?

I needn't have worried. It was the most sublime night I could remember. If Suzanne and I hadn't been so dog tired from the escape and the journey, and so full of Esther's wonderful food, we'd have stayed awake longer, just to savour the pleasure of each other's bodies. As it was, both our complexions were high when we came into the kitchen the following morning.

Esther glanced up at us. Her eyebrows lifted, then settled approvingly. All she said was:

"What would you like for breakfast, children?"

*

On the second day Esther drove us inland. We walked round some pretty hill-top villages and had lunch in Les Arcs. While Suzanne and Esther were having coffee I excused myself for a few minutes. They assumed I was going for a comfort break. In fact I hadn't been able to talk to Prof since Suzanne got me out of jail and I thought it would be reasonably safe to phone from here.

I'd lost his contact details with everything else. I got the international operator to call M.I.T. and asked the switchboard there to put me through. There was no answer from his office, so I waited patiently while it relayed the call to the lab. Someone called Andy Grierson picked up, and asked if he could help me. I explained that I urgently needed to talk to Professor Hirsch. Was he there? No, he wasn't. Did he know when he'd be available? He didn't know. Of course he wouldn't give me his home number. He asked me if I'd like to leave a message, but there was no way I could do that. I took down the lab's number and the extension and said I'd try again later.

I wished Grierson had been less cagey. It made me wonder if something had happened.

I was on my own again. It wasn't a good position to be

in. I knew a fair amount now, about the drugs racket, the way Zajc moved his gang, the truth behind the Nigerian atrocities, and the way Obadiah's death had been organized. Prof knew some of it, but the rest would go with me to the grave if they killed me now, which was by no means a remote possibility.

In bed that night, I explained the situation to Suzanne.

"Ngozi's in Cawley's pocket. He's almost certainly told him that his stepdaughter's on the run with an escaped prisoner, believed to be an agent of some sort. He's probably sent pictures of both of us: he had plenty of you, and he has mine from the passport they stole."

"Why should Cawley care?"

"He'll guess something's up. If it wasn't really important you wouldn't have fled the country. He knows you were with Obadiah, and you were a witness to the attack on his camp, which is bad enough. If he suspects you have the memory tiles as well he'll be desperate. He'll try to get to us before we can cause him real damage."

"But he doesn't know where we are."

"That helicopter pilot—Aaron—will have told them where we crossed the border into the Congo. They've probably sent security men to Lubumbashi to see if we passed through. They may find out where we were headed."

"All right, it's not a problem, we won't go back to Marseilles."

"But we can't stay here for ever. How are we going to manage for money? They took all my credit tokens."

"They've probably closed my bank account in Ubindi, but I never kept much in there. I have one in Switzerland."

I kissed her on the forehead. "You're so smart. Where next, then?"

"The Hague. I want to go to the International Criminal Court. I know who we have to see."

"All right," I said slowly. "We'll take the train. Will Customs record our movements?"

"No, those European borders are all open."

"All right, and after the Hague…?"

"We can't do any more from Europe. We'll go to Amsterdam and fly to the States."

"Suzanne…"

"We'll be travelling under false names."

"Okay, that'll make it harder, but every airport has cameras recording biometrics. You can't disguise those."

"Jim, they won't have a clue when we're flying or where from or where to."

That was true. If they suspected we were making for the States they'd have to decode passenger manifests and compare multiple biometric parameters for hundreds of thousands of passengers a day flying to anywhere in North America from airports around the world. It was a mammoth computing task. We'd have landed long before they were even close to getting a match. But…

Before I could say anything more she'd kissed me. I hung on to my anxieties for just a moment longer. Then the lingering pressure of those soft, warm lips drew me down into a world where nothing else really mattered.

46

Quantum computing isn't easy; if it were, there'd be more labs like mine. Andy was coping pretty well with the hardware side of things. The problem was to serve up the data in a way the quantum computer could take on board. Just on its own, that required a high-density parallel processor. We'd built our own—we called it Gatekeeper—and it was housed in a separate room, adjacent to the main lab, because it required special cooling and ventilation. Programming Gatekeeper was my job. It was exciting and totally involving.

I was working at it when Andy put his head round the door.

"Phone for you, Prof."

"Damn. Who is it?"

"The Director of National Intelligence."

"Bob? Mmm, okay. I'll take it in my room."

It was unusual for Bob Cressington to be phoning me direct. I wondered what was up.

"Sorry to disturb you, Prof. You're required urgently for a meeting at the Department of Defense."

"What's all this about, Bob?"

"I can't tell you."

"Can't or won't?"

"Both."

"Well, do I need to prepare a presentation?"

"No, just come. My PA's booked your flight to Washington.

She has all the details. I'll pass you over to her now. See you tomorrow."

Fortunately I didn't have to cancel any speaking engagements. The public interest on civil liberties had waned, or so the holovision companies seemed to think. The focus was now on the candidates as they toured marginal states. I'd gone back to my work with a sense of relief. These public appearances had consumed a lot of time, and I wasn't sure any longer how much they really achieved. I hadn't given up the battle, but the voters would make their choice and after that I'd have to try to influence policy in other ways.

Before I left for Washington I considered what I could work on while I was there. I have a pretty good portable but it would struggle with the multi-tasking. In any case, it was bad security to be carrying the whole program around with me. I downloaded some largish subroutines that needed expanding.

Bob's PA had put me on an evening flight and booked me into a hotel so that I could be available for a meeting first thing next morning. I was less than thrilled to be stuck in Washington at this point. I tried to concentrate on the subroutines, but my mind kept wandering. What was so important that they'd call me away from my research at such a crucial stage?

*

When they showed me into the meeting room the following morning I found a long table with just two people sitting at it. One was Bob Cressington. The other was Senator Brad Harrison Cawley.

Bob looked distinctly uncomfortable. He tried to

introduce us, but Cawley waved it away.

"We've met before," he said. "Take a seat, Dr. Hirsch."

His manner was brusque. I recalled that the last time we'd met it had been in a live debate and he hadn't come out of it particularly well. He opened a folder, looked at it, then up at me.

"This research project of yours, Dr. Hirsch. It's costing us one hell of a lot."

My nerves began to tingle.

"It was fully budgeted at the time of application," I replied evenly. "Everyone knew the costs and the benefits before they committed to it."

"That's as may be. But the Department of Defense is reviewing its commitments. As chairman of the Procurements Committee I have a responsibility to ensure that we're allocating our resources in a sensible way. There's been a good deal of money ploughed into this research over the years. Including a fair piece spent on you personally."

So Cawley knew about my brain transplant! I wondered what else he knew.

Bob Cressington intervened. "The money for Dr. Hirsch's operation came from the National Intelligence budget, not the Department's, Brad, you know that. We considered he was essential to the project."

"Ah, but the question is, Bob: is the project essential to us? I have come to the conclusion that it is not. Enough is enough. We're going to pull the plug."

I had gone cold. Was he acting out of pique because I'd shown him up in a debate? Could he really play with the country's security in that way?

"Brad, with respect, that would be a very bad decision," Cressington said. "The research Dr. Hirsch is doing would give the country an edge in its dealings with hostile powers, and an incredibly powerful tool for fighting terrorism within our own shores. It would be crazy to relinquish our lead now."

"I've heard the rhetoric, Bob; I'm just not convinced by it. Look, I know you've had a big stake in this project—that's why I asked you to be here. But the major funding is not coming from you; it's coming from the Department. There are other calls on our resources, and after due consideration I have decided they'd be a better use for our money than a project that seems to be never-ending."

"Senator," I said. "It has taken a long time, I'll grant you that, but right now we're very close to success. In a matter of months you'll be able to capitalize on your investment."

"Dr. Hirsch, you say that at every review. We're always 'just around the corner'. But up to now we have not had the slightest indication that anything of *practical* value has come out of this research."

"You're saying you want some kind of demonstration?"

"All right, yes. I don't want to be unfair to you, Dr. Hirsch. A convincing demonstration would give me grounds to reconsider. For example, I understand there are a couple of escaped terrorists on the loose in Europe at the moment. They'll likely try to enter this country. Now I don't suppose that any existing computer could decode and search passenger manifests for every single flight arriving here or Canada and tell us the port of entry in time to intercept them. But if your supercomputer—or whatever it is—could do something like that—well, I confess I'd find that convincing."

You bastard. Now I see what you're up to.

My immediate reaction was disgust, but it contained an element of elation. There was only one person Cawley would want to get his hands on so badly that he'd go to these lengths. I hadn't heard from Jim since I'd asked the State Department to intervene urgently on his behalf. What Cawley had just said meant Jim had got out. But he'd said "a couple of terrorists". That set me wondering who Jim had brought with him.

Cawley was right about one thing. Other than Jim, no one outside the group knew what even the prototype, QC-2, was capable of. Bob himself had taken my word for it. The facility to hack into systems and databases could too easily be exploited for the wrong purposes and I was determined to keep it firmly under my control. Now Cawley wanted me to show him what the technology was capable of—by tracking down Jim.

What do I do? If I say yes, Jim's as good as dead. Cawley will be safe then—the little I have on him is far too circumstantial for a conviction. But if I say no, they'll cut off the funding. Thirty years I've worked on this project. I simply have to bring it to a successful conclusion: it's the culmination of my entire scientific career. And it's not just my reputation that'll suffer if they call a halt: it's everyone working on it. Andy, the postdocs—what I decide won't just affect me: it will affect all of them.

I looked at Bob Cressington. He tightened his lips as if to say, "I'm sorry, Prof. There's nothing more I can do."

"Well, Dr. Hirsch?" Cawley said. "Could your miraculous invention accomplish something like that?"

There was a heavy silence. I swallowed hard.

"Give me what you have on these two people," I said. "I'll see what I can do."

46

We left for Avignon early the next morning. Esther Mukewa dropped us off near the UGV station, but I asked her not to drive right up: there was a remote possibility that Ngozi's or Cawley's people were around, and I didn't want to put her at risk. We got out of the car and she embraced her daughter. Her eyes were glistening with tears and I took a tactful interest in the street. Finally she released Suzanne and I gave her a big hug and promised to visit her again. I felt a genuine affection for this remarkable woman. I'd arrived on her doorstep as a total stranger, yet she'd made me incredibly welcome and she'd brought Suzanne and me together in a way I could only have dreamed of.

We watched as she drove off, then walked towards the station.

"We should go in separately," I said. "If anyone's staking out the station they'll be looking for a white male with an African female."

"Jim, if they're watching stations they'll be at Marseilles, not here. That's why we came to Avignon—"

"I know, but it's best to be on the safe side. I'll go in first, then I can keep an eye on things. I'm a bit worried about leaving a trail of credit transactions, as well. Use your Swiss account for everything—they've probably got the most secure records in the world. When you're ready, I'll follow you to the platform."

"All right."

"Here we go, then. If there's trouble, make yourself scarce. Call the gendarmes if you can."

I walked confidently into the station, senses on top alert. There was a news stand on the other side of the concourse, so I went over and waited there, pretending to browse while I continued to scan the people passing through. After a few minutes Suzanne came in and joined the queue for one of the electronic ticket machines. I kept watch as the line in front of her got progressively shorter. Finally she came away. As she passed me she tapped discreetly on her watch.

I followed a short distance behind her, moving my eyes but not my head, feeling to the very edges of my peripheral vision.

Which was how I spotted the heavily built man who'd moved up on my right.

I whirled, dropping at the same time into a fighting stance—and found myself facing my reflection in a florist's window. Some passersby gave me curious looks. I scrabbled around on the floor, pretending I'd dropped something, then got to my feet, my face burning. Looking up, I could still see Suzanne, a little way ahead. Fortunately she hadn't noticed. I'd have a hard time explaining that, in my heightened state of awareness, I'd forgotten what I now looked like.

I walked a little faster to catch up, then waited on the platform with my back to a row of vending machines.

The train came in from Marseilles within minutes. I watched her board, hung back until just before the doors closed, then got into the next carriage. A few minutes later we were sitting together, watching the countryside flash by as the Ultra Grand Vitesse gathered speed. So far, so good.

We changed trains in Brussels and reached the Hague in

the early afternoon. As we walked out onto the pavement I detected an autumnal nip in the air, although there was plenty of clear blue sky between the clouds. I was glad of the jacket Suzanne had bought me in St. Raphael.

A taxi dropped us outside the new International Criminal Court. I got out first and surveyed the area. This wouldn't be an easy place to mount an ambush. The soaring building fronted on an open square with wide access roads and a large pool in the centre. You'd be able to see anyone coming a mile off. I glanced up. The solar-generating glass lent the entire facade a metallic blue sheen that seemed to make it vibrate.

I looked round to see Suzanne pass her credit token over the driver's pay terminal; he lifted a hand in acknowledgement and drove off. We crossed to the entrance.

Suzanne had arranged an appointment with one of the Deputy Prosecutors, Alfons Sulzmann. We reported at the front desk and the receptionist directed us to the twentieth floor. The lift was smooth and fast. We got out and walked silently along the thickly carpeted corridor to the suite at the end.

I let Suzanne handle Mr. Sulzmann's secretary.

"Please wait here. I will see if Mr. Sulzmann is free," the woman said.

We heard a knock and a brief conversation, and the secretary returned. "Mr. Sulzmann can see you now."

She led us down a short passage and through an open door into a large room. The windows, surprisingly transparent from the inside, afforded a stunning view of the city. Mr. Sulzmann got up from behind a large, leather-topped desk. He was a slim, mature man, with a fine head of silver hair. He greeted us courteously and indicated a pair of leather armchairs in front of the desk. Then he opened the jacket of his dark grey suit, sat down, and waited for us to open the conversation.

"Thank you for seeing us at short notice, Mr. Sulzmann," Suzanne started. "As I indicated, this is a matter of some urgency. We have reason to believe that a senior figure in the United States Senate is a war criminal."

He held up a hand. "May I stop you there? Would you have any objection to this conversation being recorded? It would save you the trouble of repeating your statement at a later stage."

She said, "No, I have no objection."

He took a small stenophone out of a drawer and activated it. Then he placed it on the desk and indicated with a gesture that she should proceed.

I eyed the device. It was similar to the one I'd used when I was posing as a journalist in Ubindi. That was just over a week ago. It felt like years.

Suzanne started. She gave an account of the atrocities in Nigeria, nearly thirteen years before. Then she told him of her diplomatic mission, the "rescue", and the complete destruction of Obadiah's camp. He listened patiently and impassively. At that point I took over, telling him about the assassination of Obadiah, and the ensuing cover-up: the unexplained crash of the RotoFan that had shot up the camp, and Sef's murder. I knew that my own role might emerge at some stage, but I wasn't prepared to reveal that part of it yet.

When we'd finished, the Prosecutor put his fingertips together and looked from one of us to the other. He stopped at Suzanne.

"These memory tiles you mentioned. You say they document the atrocities, and Mr. Cawley's involvement in them?"

"Yes."

"And they are in your possession?"

"Yes. In fact I have them here."

My head jerked towards her. I thought she'd left them in the hiding place, somewhere around her mother's old house in Ubindi. To my astonishment she opened her bag and withdrew a powder compact. She spread a clean tissue on the desk in front of us, opened the compact, and slid her fingernails under the loose powder to withdraw the two black squares. She tapped them off.

"I suggest you rinse these and dry them before you put them in the reader," she said.

Then she looked at me, her lips pressed together, suppressing a smile. I remembered her asking me to take the bag when the helicopter landed in front of us. I had no idea then what was in it.

Sulzmann took the tiles. "I think it would be helpful if you could allow me some time with these." He glanced at his watch. "Could you come back tomorrow morning, say at ten o'clock? By that time I will have viewed this material and copied it to a secure database. We'll also have print-outs of your statements for you to sign."

Suzanne hesitated, then inclined her head. "Very well," she said. "Until tomorrow."

We shook hands and left.

*

"Are you all right about letting him keeping the memory tiles?" I asked her, as we emerged onto the pavement.

"The Deputy Prosecutor in one of the most respected courts of justice in the world? Oh yes, I think so."

"When he returns them, how will you know whether you

have the originals or copies?"

She smiled. "I put a small irregular scratch on the edge of each one. I'll know."

Once again I could only be impressed by her foresight. "Good. There's technology for seeing whether recordings like that are the originals."

"That's why I did it."

Now we had to find somewhere to spend the night. We could look for a hotel, but even hotels recorded your biometrics these days. It was all searchable. I began to see why Prof had such a bee in his bonnet about civil liberties. I explained the problem to Suzanne.

"Jim," she said. "Don't you think you're being a tiny bit paranoid?"

"Possibly. But it's wise to assume that Cawley's pulling all the stops out. A scan of hotel registrations would be a huge job, even for someone with his resources, but I just don't want to take the chance. Let's find an old-fashioned bed-and-breakfast somewhere. We can have a nice dinner to make up for it. Come on, we've got a big day tomorrow."

48

The bed-and-breakfast was clean and comfortable but I was scarcely aware of it; a night with Suzanne was enough to fill my senses. During one interlude she lay in my arms, thoughtfully passing the heel of her hand across my chest. From the pressure I knew she was feeling the hardness of the muscles.

"I abhor violence, Jim. I know it's part of your training, but I hate it."

I held her close and kissed her hair. I was thinking how little she really knew about me.

"Sometimes it's necessary."

"Oh, I know—I had to stun that guard, and you had to deal with the soldier. But I still hate it." She batted my pec with her palm. "All this is very well, but the Jim I can admire is the one who gave the helicopter pilot back his penknife."

That damned penknife!

"It's not a question of one thing or the other," I said. "A man can be tender and loving to his children and still fight like a demon to defend them."

She shifted her position and I knew, even in the darkness, she was looking up at me.

"Man as provider and protector? It has a certain primitive charm, Jim, but modern society isn't like that. You need to ask yourself what the threat is—even whether it's real. Hawkish politicians have a habit of inventing threats—that's how they get to power. And once they're in, the military have a field day. You only have to see what's happened in my country."

I could sense conflict looming but I couldn't let her negate everything I stood for.

"That's different. In Ubindi they use the military to suppress individual freedom. In the States we have individual freedom; the military are there to make sure no one takes it away from us."

There was bitterness in her laugh. "You think people like Cawley will stop at that? He's a soldier, for God's sake! How peaceful do you think the world will be with him in the White House?"

I felt a flash of irritation. I still thought of myself as a soldier and I resented being put in the same bracket as a man like Cawley. I tried to muster a suitable response, something that wasn't too self-revealing, but I was afraid of what I might destroy and in the end the words stuck in my throat.

*

By ten o'clock we were in the Deputy Prosecutor's office.

"Let me start by returning these to you," he said, handing the memory tiles to Suzanne.

I noticed her glance at them. She replaced them carefully in the powder compact.

He put his fingertips together. "Intentionally directing attacks against civilian non-combatants is a war crime under Article Eight of the Rome Statute. Ordering or soliciting the commission of such a crime is covered by Article Twenty-Five. Of course, it's for the judges to determine, but in my opinion the alleged actions come within the Court's jurisdiction. To go further I will have to seek authorization from the Pre-Trial Chamber to open an investigation. I take it that is your wish?"

Suzanne said, "That's why we're here."

"Because it's only proper for me to warn you that these allegations are highly defamatory. If they can't be substantiated you could be laying yourself open to a serious suit. The damages could be very considerable."

I caught the look on Suzanne's face. "They'll be substantiated, all right."

He shrugged. "Very well. Now I have spoken to the Prosecutor. Typically the people we deal with have been associated—at least in the public eye—with a known crime or crimes. Whether or not they are guilty is another matter, but there is clearly a case to answer. This affair is very different— somewhat 'out of the blue', as one could say. And the person involved is a very senior figure, with a very high public profile."

I didn't like the sound of this. "No one is above the law, Mr. Sulzmann," I said.

"No, of course not," he replied quickly, "but we must be completely sure of our ground. This office will use all available sources to check the statements you have made, and the evidence will need to be scrutinized in considerable detail. If we conclude that there is a reasonable basis to proceed we will make the request to the Pre-Trial Chamber. They will then examine the request and decide whether to proceed with the investigation."

"You mean the trial?" Suzanne asked.

"No, no. First the person charged will be required to attend a hearing. The Prosecutor will present there the charges and a summary of the evidence, which may be challenged. Only if the charges are confirmed will we proceed to trial."

Suzanne sighed. "How long will all this take?"

"It's not easy to predict. Even a fairly straightforward case could take a year or more to prepare."

"A year!" Suzanne turned to me, aghast.

"Mr. Sulzmann," I said. "In six weeks' time the American people will be going to the polls to vote for their next President. One of the candidates is a sadist, a rapist and—at the very least—an accessory to murder. Miss Mukewa and I have risked our lives to bring you this evidence, because we believe that America—not just America, but the whole world—cannot afford to have a man like that as the head of state. If we're going to prevent it from happening, some action needs to be taken within the next few weeks."

He shook his head slowly. "Out of the question. We can't possibly achieve anything on that time scale."

"Not even to warn the voters that there's an ongoing case?"

"Certainly not. Justice means fair play for everyone, Mr. Slater, even someone accused of crimes as repugnant as these. This court would be brought into utter disrepute if we acted on insufficient information."

Suzanne and I looked at each other. Her mouth twisted in an expression of pained acquiescence.

We got up to go.

"Will you keep us informed?" she asked.

"Yes, that can be done. If you'd like to leave your contact details …"

"We'll send them on," I said. "Our movements are a bit fluid at the moment."

"As you wish. My secretary has your statements. If you're

happy with what has been recorded, perhaps you'd be good enough to sign and date them, and leave them with her. They'll form an important part of the dossier."

We shook hands and withdrew.

The secretary looked up as we came into her office.

"Ah," she said. She opened a drawer, withdrew two stapled sets of sheets, and handed them to us.

"Is it all right to read these in here?" Suzanne asked.

"Yes, of course," she said, pointing to a couple of chairs.

I sat down with my statement, but Suzanne hesitated, looking in her bag.

"Oh," she said. "I believe I've left my pen in Mr. Sulzmann's office. Would you mind...?"

The secretary got up and we heard a muffled conversation from the other room.

Suzanne stepped behind the desk, where there were racks of stationery and envelopes. She swiftly abstracted a couple of sheets, folded them in quarters, and slipped them into her bag.

"Suzanne!" I hissed. "What the hell are you doing?"

"I needed some scrap paper to take notes," she said.

The secretary returned with the pen. Suzanne thanked her and took a seat next to me. We read through the statements carefully. Mine was accurate and I signed and dated it. Suzanne sighed audibly and did the same with hers. I handed them to the secretary. Minutes later we were on our way out.

We stood on the pavement. Now that we'd opened a file on the case I had a sense of satisfaction. We'd taken the first step. All the same, we couldn't afford to relax. If ever Cawley was brought to trial we'd be key witnesses, and to be key witnesses you need to stay alive.

I glanced at my watch. "Coffee?"

"Something stronger."

"Okay."

I signalled a taxi from a waiting line.

We drove into town and stopped at the first wine bar we saw. It had a low ceiling, glass and chrome tables, and a tile floor. The hard furnishings echoed to the noise of conversation and the holovision sets in each corner.

I looked for a handset but this was clearly the more traditional type of establishment. After a couple of minutes a waitress came over. Suzanne ordered a glass of white wine. I ordered a coffee.

For a while we said nothing, alone with our thoughts. Then it gradually percolated into my consciousness that the holovision channel was covering the Republican Convention. Suzanne looked towards the screen. She'd registered it, too.

Cawley was about to announce his choice as candidate for the Vice Presidency.

"I stand for a strong economy, I stand for a strong America! And I have chosen someone who will stand by my side, someone who shares my vision for this great country."

There was an expectant roar from the audience.

"I have great pleasure in presenting to you my running mate, as Vice-President of the United States of America… June Masterson!"

There were more roars and applause as a young black woman moved out of the background and joined Cawley at the podium. He kissed her on the cheek, then turned to the audience and held her hand up high.

Louder applause.

"Ever heard of her?" I asked Suzanne.

"No, and I follow American politics."

"Probably a lightweight," I said. "A cheap attempt to secure black and female votes."

"Pretty girl, though." Then she added bitterly, "He seems to have a penchant for young African women."

I thought about it. "You could be right."

June Masterson was making a short, excited speech of acceptance. She finished predictably:

"It will be a privilege and an honour to serve with the next President of the United States of America!"

More roars, applause.

"We're too late," Suzanne said. "I should have done all this two years ago."

"The case is stronger now. He's dug himself a deeper hole by trying to cover his tracks."

"Yes, but it'll take too long! The polls say he's ahead of Harriet Nagel. He could be a year or more into the Presidency before anything happens. That's if anything ever does happen. The Commission has teeth but I'm not sure they're large enough to take a bite out of the U.S. top administration."

On the screen a band had started up and the camera switched to a correspondent, speaking over it in Dutch. They'd evidently been covering the Convention in world news.

I grimaced. "There has to be some way of stopping him."

"It's obvious, isn't it, Jim? Like I said, we have to go to the States. Then you can use your contacts in the CIA."

Something twisted inside me. Sooner or later she'd have to know I wasn't with the CIA, that I was once with the SAF but now I was working on my own, trying to find out who was responsible for killing my comrades and framing me. Should I tell her that now? Could I?

No, I couldn't. Some time, perhaps, but not now.

So we'd go to the U.S. With the identity I'd manufactured, that's what she expected me to do and I didn't have a rational argument to put up against it.

I said, "All right."

From one point of view it made a certain amount of sense: we'd exhausted the possibilities over here. It was a gamble, all the same. If Cawley did manage to track us we could hit trouble right at the port of entry. How could I minimize the risk?

The waitress arrived with the coffee and the wine. Suzanne looked at the mist forming on the cold glass.

"I don't know, maybe I should have ordered coffee," she said.

"Do you want mine?"

"No, I'll have this." She took a sip. "It's a Riesling," she said. "Nice."

"Good. It'll relax you." I stirred some brown sugar into the coffee. In the past I'd have had black coffee, no milk, no sugar. Ever since the operation I seemed to crave sweetness.

"So," she said. "Are we going to spend another night in The Hague?"

"No, if we're going, I think we should move now. We can take the train to Schipol and fly from there."

"Where to?"

"Doesn't much matter, does it? Boston, Philadelphia, Detroit, New York, Atlanta—anywhere like that. There are plenty of connecting flights within the States. It's just that…"

"What?"

"It's just that we'll be sitting ducks going back on a scheduled flight."

Her mouth twitched. "What do you suggest—swim?"

I smiled indulgently. I couldn't expect her to view things as seriously as I did.

"What I was wondering was, would your Swiss account run to a charter? We could fly a business jet transatlantic, no problem. There'll be plenty of small carriers at Schipol who could do it."

"Now I see what all this was leading up to," she said, prodding three fingers into my chest. "You just want to travel in full-out luxury."

I cupped my hand gently around the fingers. "Well?"

She sighed. "Oh yes, I can cover it. I'm not short of money, and God knows I've got nothing else to save it for."

"Thanks. That's what we'll do, then."

"If I'm paying, we can tell them where we want to fly to."

"Only up to a point. It depends where they've got landing slots, and what kind of flight plan they can file at short notice. I'm prepared to go with the flow."

I drained my coffee cup. She pushed her glass away, still half full, and got up. "I won't finish this."

"Stay there for the moment. I'll get us a taxi to the station."

Standing on the pavement, looking out for a taxi, I thought:

So we get back to the States. Then what?

I'll just have to take it one step at a time. If we can enter the country unscathed, I can enlist Prof's help. That's if I can get hold of him.

Where the hell is Prof, anyway?

49

After that fraught meeting with Cawley, Bob Cressington and I left together and stopped by his office, where his PA booked me on a flight back to Boston. I didn't have to leave for the airport immediately, so I returned to the hotel.

In my hand was an envelope containing the details of the two people Cawley said they needed to apprehend. I tossed it onto a table. My guts churned when I thought about what he wanted me to do.

With a heavy sigh I opened the envelope and spread the contents on the table.

I'd already given this stuff a cursory glance in Cawley's office. There was plenty on Jim: scans taken from his passport and driving licence, with photographs and biometrics, no doubt all sent to him by Ngozi. Cawley seemed to be unaware that Jim and I were acquainted so I was careful not to show any reaction. The only information he had on the person with Jim was a photograph, and I was surprised to see it was a woman. He said he wasn't sure what name she was operating under: international terrorists used a variety of them.

Now I had the chance to look more closely. It was a handsome, sculpted African face with high cheekbones and a smooth complexion, and the almond-shaped eyes were an unusual ginger colour...

I powered up my portable and started a search. It took me only a few minutes to locate the site for the Ubindian

Ministry of External Affairs, and there was a picture of Suzanne Mukewa, shaking hands with some visiting dignitary. It was as I'd suspected: the angle was different but the person on the screen looked very much like the one in the photograph.

My contact at the State Department had told me she was one of the few African politicians they could really trust. Unlike most of her colleagues, if she said she'd do something she would. Well, she'd got Jim out all right, but I didn't think she'd go on the run with him. Could I really be sure it was her?

There was a phone number on the web site. I glanced at my watch; it wasn't too late so I put the call through. The answer was recorded. A male voice said the Minister was not available until further notice. That clinched it. Presumably Cawley didn't want me to know I was tracking a government minister rather than a terrorist. He almost succeeded: if all I'd been looking for was a match between an incoming passenger and this photo I would never have made the connection.

*

I spent the whole flight thinking about how I was going to tackle the programming. It had become an intellectual challenge for me now.

The first thing to determine was whether they'd already entered the country. I would have to access Immigrations and Customs Enforcement. Had Cawley alerted them himself? Almost certainly not. He wouldn't want Jim and Suzanne detained on entry—they were as much a danger to him in custody as they were on the loose. No, he'd want them to come through freely to give his own people a chance to move in.

Would the two of them be travelling under their own names? Probably: they couldn't have had much time to equip themselves with false identities. Could Suzanne evade the normal checks by using her diplomatic status? That seemed unlikely. Ngozi and his cronies would want to make her movements as difficult as possible, so they would have withdrawn diplomatic privileges as quickly as they could.

I decided I'd run the program with their names, at least to start with. If it came up with a match, well and good. If it came up blank, I'd check again, using biometrics this time. I had that information for Jim; I could get hers from the Ubindian passport or driving licence registry. If there was still no match, it meant they hadn't entered the country yet. Then I'd need to find out which flight they were arriving on.

I heard the flaps roll out. We were on the approach to Logan. I looked out of the window but the cloud base was too low to see anything.

"...return your seats to the upright position..."

I shut out the familiar announcements and continued to focus on the programming.

Would Jim and Suzanne travel on a scheduled flight like this one? If they'd used a large transatlantic carrier they'd be less conspicuous among all those other passengers —and less vulnerable—when they came in. That would be helpful to me, too; the program would run much faster if I confined the search to major airlines operating out of European hubs like London, Paris, Amsterdam, Frankfurt. Of course, flight plans wouldn't be enough; if I wanted to match names I'd have to scan passenger manifests. The companies would place those in the system before take-off, so there should be adequate warning.

"..turn off all portable electronic equipment..."

I didn't need my computer; the lines of code were unrolling in my head. I had that sense of excitement I always got when I could see my way through to the end of a problem.

Fortunately all the airlines shared the same database; it was a necessity because of the need to access information on passengers who had to be rerouted. Once I'd hacked into it I'd simply search for Jim Slater and Suzanne Mukewa on the passenger manifests of flights entering the States. If that failed I'd use biometrics. The volume of data involved was enormous, so it would be an excellent test of QC-2's capabilities.

Now that the strategy was clear in my mind I couldn't wait to get on with it.

*

As soon as we'd disembarked I took a taxi straight to M.I.T. to start work. It was nearly four o'clock in the morning when I finished. I set the programs running and went off to make myself a cup of coffee. When I got back, the search on immigration records had come up blank, which meant they hadn't yet entered the country. We were into the second stage: searching passenger manifests.

At that point a thought occurred to me. Would they really come in on a regular, scheduled flight? Jim was on the run, and he'd surely want to enter as quietly as possible. Suzanne probably had funds; they could come on a private jet. That way they'd arrive at a remote terminal and the immigration formalities would be minimal. It was a distinct possibility. I aborted the run and modified the program to include all carriers, large and small. Then I set it going again, called for a taxi and went home to grab a few hours sleep.

The following morning I phoned Andy and told him exactly what I wanted him to do. Two hours later I was on a flight heading back to Washington.

*

We landed soon after midday and I spent the rest of the afternoon in my hotel room, trying to pick up the threads of my original task: the subroutines for QC-3. I even used room service for meals so that I could continue without interruption. There was no news from Boston. I was still short of sleep, so I went to bed early.

Next morning I was getting dressed when my phone sounded. It was Andy. The computer had found a match. In fact it had found two matches so it looked like Jim and Suzanne were together. The program had taken a while to run because they were travelling under false names and it had to match the biometrics. He read off the carrier, the flight number, the port of entry, and the estimated time of arrival. The time difference was in our favour: we had about seven hours in which to act.

I phoned the private number Cawley had given me.

"Cawley."

"Professor David Hirsch, here, Senator. I hope this will convince you of the capabilities we're developing. I have the information you requested. Our guests are arriving today, at 1705 hours."

"Where?"

"Atlanta."

I hung up before he could say anything more.

PART FIVE

50

The small aircraft climbed out of Amsterdam's Schipol Airport and didn't level off until we reached about fifty-five thousand feet, at which point it accelerated to supersonic speed. It was hard to draw my gaze away from the window. The sky was darker at this height and you could see the curvature of the Earth.

We'd had a two-and-half hour wait at Schipol, but that was okay; we were in no great hurry. Suzanne said she needed to check up on something and went off to find a cyber centre. I spotted a monitor screen with a twenty-four hour BBC World News service and sat in front of it while I was waiting for her. When the departure time approached, we made our way over to the desk and from then on it was VIP treatment all the way. In fact I was almost disappointed when the pilot announced we were on final approach.

Suzanne raised an eyebrow at me. "I trust the journey met with your expectations, sir."

I grinned at her. "I could get used to this sort of thing. Can we do it more often?"

"Certainly. Next time, you can pay."

We landed and taxied to a private terminal. A member of the cabin crew conducted us inside, where we faced an empty glass cubicle.

"If you could wait here just a moment, sir, I'll see what's happened to the Immigration Officer. They have to come in from the main airport… Ah, here he is now."

The officer climbed into the cubicle and held out his hand for our passports. I handed over the diplomatic documents.

"Where'd you get these?" he asked.

I used a South African accent. "Congolese Foreign Ministry. We had a bit o' truck with some local hoods. They took our begs. Our rigular papers were inside."

He took a long time, examining them closely, and tapping on the keyboard of his computer.

Then he said, "Normally you'd need a visa, but I'll accept your diplomatic status. These have limited validity, though. You going to apply for permanent passports?"

"As soon as ivver we can."

He nodded and handed the documents back. "Have a nice day."

We went through the exit together. If we'd had a limo waiting we could have left from there, but I needed to rent a car and unfortunately that meant going into the main terminal. My nerves were twanging like bowstrings.

The arrivals hall was swarming with people, coming, going, and brushing against us. I walked on the balls of my feet, poised for action. It was hard to know where to look first. At any moment I expected someone to turn and stick a knife in my ribs. I fervently wished I had a weapon tucked into my belt—at this point I'd have settled for Aaron's rusty old penknife. I saw a row of car rental agencies and steered Suzanne towards them, keeping as close to walls as I could to limit the field of attack.

To my mild surprise we got there without incident.

We joined the shortest queue and waited. I was restless, looking around all the time, and almost certainly transmitting my tension to Suzanne. Eventually we came to the front of the queue and Suzanne presented her Ubindian driving licence. The woman on the counter examined it from every angle and hummed and hawed while the people behind us in the queue sighed and looked at their watches. Finally Suzanne offered to pay a week's rental and the full damage excess up front. That clinched it. We took the proximity key and headed out to the car park to look for the vehicle.

It was even more dangerous here than inside, with fewer people around and a lot more places to hide. I moved along the lines of cars like a soldier patrolling the streets of a rebel-held village, scanning to the left and right, and turning every few paces to see if we were being followed.

Suzanne pointed. "It's over there."

I hurried her over to the car, we got in, and I locked the doors. I took a deep breath and blew it out. "We made it."

She looked at me calmly, as if to say "You see, there was nothing to worry about."

I started the engine and we moved off. As soon as we reached the superhighway I put the car into autodrive. That way I could pay more attention to what was going on in the rear-view mirror.

From time to time I wondered if the car behind was following us, but before long it would turn off or overtake and there'd be a different car there, and I figured it was just me being a little jumpy. It seemed like Cawley's people hadn't been monitoring passengers arriving in the U.S. after all. If they had, the task had evidently been beyond them.

"Where are we going, Jim?"

I'd given some thought to that. In the States even the smaller hotels and motels recorded biometrics and Cawley would locate us in no time.

"I have a small house at Springfield. It's a bit of a drive, I'm afraid."

"I don't mind, if you're all right driving. Let me know if you want me to take over for a spell."

Going to the house wasn't a soundly based decision, more of a feeling that whoever had gone to the trouble and expense of putting my brain in a new body, rehabilitating me, and setting me up with a new identity—including a rented home—wouldn't be high on the list of people who wanted to kill me on sight.

Of course, I could be wrong.

I turned off at the first service station and used Suzanne's phone to try to reach Prof. This time no one answered at all. I took a deep breath and drove back onto the highway.

We said little on the journey. I was trying to think what to do next. Suzanne had let me drag her halfway round the world in the clear expectation that I could help to take her case further. But to do that I needed contacts. I was relying on Prof for that, and I hadn't been able to raise him.

By the time we arrived, the light was fading. My house keys had been taken in Ubindi, of course, but I'd hidden a spare card under a tile in the back garden. I told Suzanne to stay in the car while I fetched it. I found it where I'd left it and went round to the front door.

I was poised to pass the card over the lock when a voice said:

"Hold it right there."

They just popped out—where from, I had no idea. One moment I was about to open the door, and the next moment there was a man on either side, pointing a semiautomatic at me. My eyes flicked left and right, but they were keeping their distance.

"All right, Mr. Slater, face down on the ground, wrists crossed behind you. Nice and easy now and no one will get hurt."

A quick look behind me revealed a third man by the car, pointing a pistol at Suzanne. I did as I was told. The sensation of a band being fastened around my wrists had become depressingly familiar. I clenched my fists to give me a bit of room for manoeuvre afterwards but he seemed to be wise to that and tied the band very tightly. Then he got me to my feet and escorted me back to the road. All the time the other one stood off, covering me with his pistol. They were well drilled, these guys.

As we were walking I looked over my shoulder to see what had happened to Suzanne. She'd evidently been taken out of our rental car because she was following us, the third man behind her, no doubt with his pistol aimed at her back. There was a large people carrier parked fifty metres away. They hustled us inside and I saw that her hands, too, were tied behind her back. It was the second time for her in less than a week and I imagine she was as pissed off as I was. One man got in on either side of us.

I didn't know where they were taking us or why, but our prospects were far from good. If I was going to make a move it had to be soon, but with my hands tied and a lot of hardware pointing at us, I couldn't see how to do it without endangering Suzanne as well as myself.

The interior light caught one of the semiautomatics, a SIG Sauer P420. That model could be loaded with small flexible baton rounds, non-penetrative but very painful if you happen to be on the receiving end. On the other hand it could also take lethal 8-mm caseless ammunition, seventeen rounds out of one magazine, plus the one in the chamber. I couldn't tell by looking which it was, and I had no desire to find out the hard way.

The third guy got in the front and took the wheel. The doors closed automatically, the light in the roof dimmed, and we moved off.

We drove for about three quarters of an hour, then slowed up and turned into an open area illuminated by arc lights. A deserted airfield. If they were going to pop us, it couldn't be a more ideal spot. I tensed, waiting for someone to make a move, any mistake I could exploit. Then the headlights swung round and illuminated a private jet. Apparently the journey wasn't over yet.

The doors opened and the man on my left got out, pointing the pistol at me.

"Out of the car," he said, adding, "please."

We walked to the aircraft. Heat was still rising from the concrete apron, which was blotted with overlapping dark stains, and there was a heady smell of oil and aviation fuel. A lot of private planes still used it. One of the men went ahead of us, up the steps into the aircraft, and we followed. I thought they'd release our hands for the flight, but they weren't taking any chances; we sat down as we were and they buckled us in. They took seats behind us. A crew member retracted the steps and closed the door. Minutes later the engines whined into life and we started to taxi to the runway.

It wasn't comfortable, sitting like that, and I was pretty sure it was against federal aviation regulations. Other than that, I felt a sense of relief. They hadn't killed us so far, and they'd had the perfect opportunity. That wasn't to say we were out of danger, but there was clearly some point in making this flight and something was going to happen. I found that reassuring in a strange sort of way. It was no longer down to me to take the next step.

I looked at Suzanne and gave her an encouraging wink. She answered with a rueful twist of the lips.

We flew for about an hour and a half before a change in the engine note indicated we were descending. I couldn't work out which direction we'd been travelling in. Mentally I constructed an arc and visualised a map with all the major cities we could have reached by now. Still, I needed more information to pin it down.

We landed and taxied to a halt. The copilot came out of the cockpit, opened the forward door, and lowered the stairs. I heard them rattle as someone came up. There was a conversation, presumably with the person who was standing just outside. I listened intently, not to the words, but to the accent.

One of the men unfastened our seat belts and ushered us out. The car waiting near the bottom of the steps was not unlike the one that had picked us up in Springfield. Again we had a man on either side; the third got into the seat behind us. There was a brief exchange with the driver. I noted that he spoke with the same accent.

I looked out of the window during the journey, but it was dark and there was little to see. Twenty minutes later we pulled up outside a long, low building. Again we got out of the car and they conducted us inside.

Our footsteps echoed along a tiled corridor. We waited as the man in front knocked on a door, then opened it. He gestured for us to go in.

Someone was there, sitting at a table. He rose as we came in.

I couldn't keep the contempt out of my voice.

"Harken!"

50

"You may be a civilian now, Jim, but it's still Colonel Harken to you."

There was such an easy familiarity about the way he addressed me that I could have been Captain Jim Forbes again, summoned for a briefing. It caught me off guard, and it was a moment before I fully absorbed what he'd said.

You may be a civilian now...

He knows who I am, and he knows who I was! Not even the rehab people had that information, so how the hell does Harken—?

Suzanne interrupted my thoughts. She spoke stiffly, addressing me without removing her gaze from Harken.

"Evidently you've come across this man before."

"His name is Colonel Wendell Harken. I served under his command earlier in my career, when I was with Special Forces. The Special Assignment Force to be precise."

I watched his face as I said it, but there wasn't a flicker of reaction. For him, this wasn't news. Suzanne didn't react either; I'd told her I was with the CIA but it wasn't unusual for them to recruit from the ranks of the military.

"What does he want with us?"

"I have no idea. Perhaps he'll tell you."

Suzanne drew herself up. "Colonel Harken! I am not accustomed to being manhandled in this outrageous way. I demand an explanation."

I regarded her with interest. It was like she'd become a completely different person.

Harken said, "I do apologise, Miss Mukewa. I know it's not the way to treat a visiting Minister—or even an ex-Minister. Unfortunately Jim, here, is a little unpredictable so it was a necessary precaution." Then, to one of the men, "You can release them now, Chris. You will behave yourself, won't you, Jim?"

I was too perplexed to say anything.

One of the men cut Suzanne's ties. Then he politely passed her bag back to her. I sensed the presence of another man behind me, and a moment later my hands were free.

Suzanne pointedly massaged her wrists. Meanwhile I was trying to take in our surroundings.

The stackable tables and plastic chairs were typical institutional furniture. There was a cupboard near one window with a pile of identical books on it. The brown carpet was a hard-wearing cord and the walls were painted in an institutional magnolia, grubby now and largely obscured by posters, primitive drawings, a map of North America, an electronic whiteboard, and several lists of names with ticks by them. A school room.

"Please have a seat," Harken said, indicating two of the plastic chairs which had been placed in front of the table.

Suzanne sat down opposite Harken; I took the one to her right.

"Where is this?" I asked, as I sat down.

"Oh, come now, Jim. Are you saying you've forgotten everything we taught you?"

Further confirmation—if any were needed.

I thought about our location, visualising the map again. The accent I'd heard earlier, on the steps of the aircraft and from the driver of the car, clinched it for me.

"All right, I'd say Washington, DC. Or thereabouts."

"Very good. Yes, we're on the outskirts of Washington."

I glanced sideways. Suzanne was looking at me, wide-eyed. I knew she was wondering how I did it.

"This is a school," Harken continued. "We've arranged to take it over for the evening."

"What for?"

"Sorry, Jim, you'll have to be patient."

It was all too smooth. I wondered if I could get him to reveal his hand by being provocative.

"Where did you rent the muscle, Harken?"

His jaw twitched, but his voice remained under icy control. "The muscle, as you put it, consists of esteemed members of the United States Secret Service."

I was taken aback. When I thought about it, I should have guessed. The dark suits, the perfect moves, and the SIG, which was standard issue. What the hell were they doing, getting involved in something like this?

At that moment there was a clatter, and the door to an adjoining room opened. Standing there with an armful of plastic chairs was the Colonel's aide, my old friend Sergeant Bagley. It had been a long time.

I stood up without thinking. "Hallo, Bags. You want a hand?"

He looked me up and down. "Who are you?"

The smile solidified on my face. Of course, I'd look a total stranger to Bagley. It brought me down to earth with a bang.

"The name's Jim Slater," I snapped. "Do you want a hand or not?"

"No thanks, I can manage."

I sat down abruptly and watched him go over to the stack of tables propped against one wall. He pulled three off and butted them up to the table in front of me, extending it to my right. Then he set out five chairs. He looked at the Colonel.

"Will that be enough, sir, or shall I get some more?"

"No, that's plenty."

"I'll be in the next room if you need me, sir."

I looked at the chairs.

Who's coming, and what do they want with us?

We settled down to wait. No one spoke, and the atmosphere was heavy.

I glanced around the room, using the opportunity to assess possible escape routes. The door we'd come through would have Secret Service men somewhere beyond it. There were a couple of windows on the left, with louvred blinds drawn shut. I could swing a table through one of them but they might be barred—I couldn't make that out when we approached in the darkness. The door Bagley had used would lead further into the building but there should be a couple of fire exits somewhere towards the back. That was the best bet.

Still, I wasn't in a hurry. If they were planning to torture us they wouldn't have done away with the wrist restraints. In any case this would be an odd place for them to choose. Why use a school?

Suzanne sighed noisily, making known her growing exasperation.

Then I heard movements outside, a familiar voice said, "Thank you, chaps", and in walked Prof.

We looked round and I half rose from my seat, covered in confusion.

"Prof! Where have you been? I've been trying to… what the hell are you doing here?"

"I'm sorry, Jim, there's no time for that. The others will be here very shortly." He nodded to Harken. "Colonel," he said, and took a seat further along on my side of the table.

Suddenly I felt terribly alone. Prof had been my friend, my partner. If he'd been deceiving me all along there must be something seriously wrong with my judgement. And then I remembered. Of course, it was Prof who'd blown my cover in Ubindi! I'd thought it was inadvertent but… Why? What did he have to gain by having me arrested and thrown to the crocodiles? And if it wasn't Prof who contacted the State Department on my behalf who was it?

Suzanne gripped my arm. "I'm sure I know that man," she said quietly, tilting her head towards Prof.

I realized she was seeing Jim Forbes, the soldier who'd pulled her out of Obadiah's camp.

"No," I said. "I don't think you've ever met him."

It was a half truth. I wondered if I could live it down.

One of the secret servicemen came in. "Excuse me, Colonel, but the others have arrived."

"Thanks, Ted. Please show them in."

Three men entered the room. I hadn't seen any of them before. Harken stood and made the introductions.

"Miss Mukewa, Mr. Slater, let me introduce Robert Cressington, Director of National Intelligence, Tony Sant'ana, Director of the FBI, and Don Machin, The Secretary of Homeland Security. Gentlemen, this is Miss Suzanne Mukewa, former Minister for External Affairs in the African nation of Ubindi, and Mr. Jim Slater, a former colleague of mine. Bob and Tony, you've already met Dr. David Hirsch but I don't believe Mr. Machin has."

Machin and Prof acknowledged each other. Then Harken indicated the chairs and we all sat down, spared the embarrassment of a prolonged shaking of hands.

So this is who we've been waiting for. For God's sake how high does this business go?

Machin sat at the head of the table, with Prof to his left and Cressington to his right. He was in his late fifties or early sixties, with a shock of white hair and a craggy, tanned face. He wore tinted glasses, which made his eye sockets appear hollow. Despite the expensive clothes there was a rumpled look about him.

"You better have a damned good reason for bringing me here, Bob," he grumbled. "I'm due to fly to San Diego first thing tomorrow morning."

"I think you'll find this interesting enough, Don," Cressington replied. "You may even want to reschedule that flight."

Machin sniffed.

Cressington was a little younger. His hair receded at the temples. He probably ran a couple of miles every lunch time—he had that sort of slim build. Sant'ana sat between Cressington and Harken, which placed him almost opposite me. His age was harder to judge, because he still had a full head of wavy black hair. His complexion was dark, the brown eyes were lively, and there was a kind of restless energy about him. He seemed young to be the Director of the FBI. Either it was a political move to appoint a Hispanic, or he was very bright, or both. I suspected both.

My spirits, already low, sank lower. If the FBI was implicated, there was little hope for us.

Machin grunted, "Let's get on with it."

Prof took the lead. "Very good. We've met here to present

to you, sir, evidence that we believe is deeply prejudicial to the security and reputation of this country. Colonel Harken. Perhaps you could start us off."

"Certainly," Harken said. "I should begin by saying that I was instrumental in introducing Dr. Hirsch to Jim Slater."

You were what? What are you talking about, man? I wasn't introduced to him; I damned nearly killed him!

"Why, or how it was managed, is something that needn't concern us immediately," he continued, "but we had a close interest in what would happen. Now a few days ago Dr. Hirsch was seen entering Senator Cawley's campaign headquarters in Washington. That wasn't in the script, so we arranged to have him followed. He returned to Boston, but inside twenty-four hours he was back here in Washington. This time he didn't go to Cawley's headquarters; he went to the headquarters of the FBI. When he came out we picked him up."

"What do you mean 'picked him up'?" Machin demanded.

Harken gave him a half smile. "I mean, sir, that I arranged for two men in dark suits to persuade him to accompany them to a car. They brought him to me and I asked him what the hell was going on." He gestured to Prof. "Do you want to take over?"

"I think it might be better coming from Bob."

The Director of National Intelligence took it up briskly. "You're familiar with Dr. Hirsch's research, Don?" he asked.

"I believe you've mentioned it before. Quantum computing, isn't it?"

"That's right. Vitally important, from a strategic standpoint, so most of the funding comes from the Department of Defense. The reason Dr. Hirsch was seen entering Senator Cawley's campaign headquarters was that he and I were asked to attend a private meeting there. Senator Cawley had a surprise for both of us: he was planning to withdraw support for the research. In the ensuing conversation it transpired that he would be open to persuasion if there was some clear demonstration of the capabilities of the new technology. Specifically, there were two terrorists at large in Europe who he believed would shortly be trying to enter the States. He wanted to know when and where they were going to arrive. After due consideration, Dr. Hirsch asked for the details. He then went back to M.I.T. to set up the search."

I sagged. How could Prof sell us out like that? I was bitterly tempted to say something, but managed to stay in control.

"Meanwhile I arranged for both of us to see Tony Sant'ana. It was a high-level issue and appropriate to involve the Director of the FBI. Tony?"

Sant'ana leaned forward. His arms rested on the table but his hands gestured in brief flicks, like a butterfly's wings.

"Thank you. Yes, they came to see me. You know, I was disturbed by what they told me. As far as I'm concerned a Senator is a member of the public. And if a member of the public has evidence that terrorists are entering the country the correct procedure is to pass it to law enforcement agencies."

Machin interrupted. "Maybe that's what he was planning to do. Once he had the demonstration he wanted he could pass specific arrival details to border officials."

"That's a reasonable assumption, Don. But what was very clear to us from the information Cawley provided was that these two people were not terrorists. They were, in fact, Miss Mukewa and Jim Slater, here. As we heard before, Miss Mukewa was, until quite recently, a high-ranking member of the government of Ubindi and, I may add, one of the most trusted and capable politicians in Africa. Dr. Hirsch knew Jim Slater personally, and he was prepared to vouch for him."

I sat there, my thoughts whirling, relieved only that I hadn't opened my mouth, and prepared at the moment to listen.

Sant'ana continued, "So we set up a little sting operation. Dr. Hirsch got the results of the computer search from his colleague at M.I.T. and told Senator Cawley when and where the two were arriving. We sent two of our own agents to the airport, a black female and a Caucasian male with a passing resemblance to the two who were expected. The moment they came through arrivals they were approached by three men and ordered to accompany them to a waiting car. What these men didn't know was that they were in the sights of three sharpshooters in the gallery. There were five more agents downstairs within striking distance. Our people waited until they were on the way to the car park before converging on the group and disarming the three men. They're currently in custody."

I frowned.

"We didn't see anything …"

"Ah no, I forgot to mention that this little drama was acted out at Atlanta." He flashed a mischievous grin at the others. "At about the same time you, Miss Mukewa, and you, Mr. Slater, were arriving—as Dr. Hirsch knew perfectly well you would—at Boston."

51

Everyone was smiling, except for Don Machin, who was scowling.

For me it was like emerging from a dark tunnel into brilliant sunshine. "So that's why we didn't encounter any trouble on arrival!"

"Yes," Sant'ana replied. "Not that you weren't being observed. We had people watching the airport and a succession of agents followed you. We needed to take you out of circulation as soon as possible."

"You took one hell of a risk, Prof," I said. "When Cawley finds out you double-crossed him—"

"I know," Prof replied. "Tony was kind enough to place me in protective custody until his men delivered me to this meeting tonight."

Bob was looking from Sant'ana to me and from me to Prof. He came back to Sant'ana.

"Did you find out who they were, the three you arrested in Atlanta?"

"We've taken their biometrics," Sant'ana replied, "and we're looking for matches. My guess is they're not FBI, CIA, or Secret Service. In all likelihood they're professional hit men. I'd like to emphasize that the only person who knew, or thought he knew, that Miss Mukewa and Jim Slater were arriving at Atlanta was Senator Cawley."

Don Machin placed both hands on the table in front of

him. They were large, powerful hands, the backs corrugated with veins, the fingers blunt. He leaned forward.

"If those men are professionals, like you say, they are not going to tell you one thing. You have no reason to suppose they were planning to commit murder. There's nothing here that would stand up in a court of law. If I may so, this smells strongly to me of a witch-hunt. Senator Cawley is a seasoned politician. He's served the Department of Defense and his country well. He deserves a shot at the Presidency. Really, an attack like this is unworthy of you, Bob."

Cressington's mouth tightened. "The point is, Don, why was Brad Cawley ready to go to such lengths to intercept these two people?"

"All right, why?"

"Colonel Harken, do you want to tell us?"

Harken was cool and imperturbable as usual. "A little over two years ago, Senator Cawley summoned me to Washington. They were reviewing the Defense budget, he said, and it looked like the SAF did not provide good value for money. Does this have a familiar ring, by the way?"

Cressington and Prof nodded.

Harken resumed. "They were planning to dismantle the Force and transfer its assets to the Navy and Army. He said this might be avoided if the Force undertook a mission that was seen to be politically useful. And it so happened that there was such an opportunity.

"He'd had a request for help from the President of Ubindi. President Ngozi, he said, was a friend of the West and a vigorous opponent of Islamic expansionism. His daughter, Suzanne," he indicated her with a gesture, "had been abducted by the leader of a local militia, General Obadiah, and was being kept—excuse me, Miss Mukewa, but this is what he said—as a sex slave. He also gave me some stills of atrocities he said were committed by Obadiah's army. The United States, Senator Cawley said, would like to see an end to Obadiah's activities, but there were namby-pamby individuals who would oppose such a move as interference in the affairs of a sovereign state. He wanted the SAF to undertake a black op."

It was interesting to hear this. I'd got it from Harken, not realizing it had emanated from Cawley.

Suzanne leaned towards me. "Black op?"

"Covert operation," I murmured. "Deniable. No official approval, no records kept."

Harken continued. "Their mission would be to rescue Miss Mukewa and assassinate Obadiah."

I heard Suzanne's intake of breath. Harken heard it, too. His face was grim. "Our people carried out their mission and we lost a good man in the course of it. And then the Roto-Fan sent in to extract them shot up the entire camp, with a heavy loss of life. It was a massacre. That part of the operation was not, repeat not, ordered by me."

I glanced around the table. They were watching Harken with rapt attention. Don Machin was frowning fiercely. Harken went on:

"What happened afterwards is especially interesting. The RotoFan crashed mysteriously on its way back to base, brought down, we understand, by a surface-to-air missile in an area not known for rebel activity. Some weeks later the two remaining members of the mission were attacked. One was murdered; the other escaped. What we have here, in other words, are all the signs of a cover-up."

Machin shook his head. I looked at him with interest. There was a certain weight about his presence that enabled him to wrest control from the speaker with the most minimal of gestures.

"I'm sorry to say all this is circumstantial, Harken. There's nothing on paper. It's just your word against his."

"And my word, Mr. Secretary."

All the heads jerked towards Suzanne, including mine.

"What Senator Cawley told Colonel Harken was a pack of lies. General Obadiah was leading a liberation army. He was challenging a corrupt dictatorship. He had enormous support in the countryside. The atrocities were a fiction."

Machin removed his glasses with one of those massive hands and stared at Suzanne. "Are you saying your father is a corrupt dictator?"

"He is my stepfather, and—yes—I repeat, the government he leads is a corrupt dictatorship. I should know: I was part of it, although the flow of money was always concealed from me."

"In a moment you will be telling me you weren't kidnapped either."

"No, I wasn't kidnapped. I was sent to broker peace negotiations. It was a plot. It revealed the location of Obadiah's camp, which Ngozi undoubtedly passed to Cawley. All they had to do was get me out and raze the camp to the ground. I now realize," she added, "that if they had not succeeded in extracting me I would have perished in that camp with the rest of them."

Machin clucked his tongue and replaced his glasses.

"While I was there, Obadiah explained to me his vision for the country. He was a hero and a future President. And he was cruelly murdered by your forces."

I swallowed. Would I ever be able to explain my part in this to Suzanne? Not to do so would put an unseen barrier between us. But if I made a clean breast of it, it would be the end of our relationship.

Suzanne became more strident. "And the reason why Obadiah was killed was that he knew what Cawley had done in Nigeria."

"Nigeria?" Machin said. The glasses came off again. "What the hell has all this got to do with Nigeria?"

It was Prof who answered. "We're talking about 2040, Mr. Machin, when the oil fields were being taken over by rebel militias. At that time Cawley was a Lieutenant Colonel in the SAF. He led a mission that filmed and reported back on atrocities. The furore that followed resulted in an international force being despatched to Nigeria. The rebels were driven back."

"I know all this," Machin said. "Everyone does."

"Yes," Suzanne said. "But what everyone does not know is that the atrocities were not committed by the rebels. They were committed by thugs employed by Cawley. He played a brutal part in them himself."

"Young lady!" Machin exclaimed. "With the greatest respect it sounds like you have fallen under the spell of this, this Obadiah. All we've heard here is a bunch of hearsay and innuendo. There's not one shred of evidence—"

"Oh, but there is, Mr. Machin," she said quietly.

She opened her bag, and once again the memory tiles came out of the powder compact.

Machin sat forward, peering intently at the two black squares as she tapped them lightly on the table.

"On these," she said, "you will find footage that Obadiah took in Nigeria. It clearly shows the part played by Cawley in those atrocities."

She spread them on the table and sat back, serene,

self-possessed, and apparently untouched by the babble of excitement her disclosure had aroused.

Harken was the first to recover. "I think we should see what's on those memory tiles, gentlemen, don't you?"

53

Harken went into the next room, and we heard him through the open door.

"Sergeant Bagley, do you think you could dig up a projector or a holovision screen to play these? This is a school. They should have something around. Thank you. As soon as you can." He came back. "This may take a few minutes to set up. May I suggest a short break? I can't lay on any refreshments, I'm afraid."

Chairs scraped as Machin and Cressington got up and went off to one side. Prof stayed seated, talking across the table with Sant'ana. I collared Harken.

"Can we have a word, sir?" I asked.

His mouth twisted sardonically at my newly respectful attitude. "All right, Jim. Let's take a walk, shall we?"

"Do you mind, Suzanne?" I said, turning to her. I wasn't really asking for her permission.

She shook her head distractedly and Harken led the way.

Outside, the area was brightly lit by a row of security lamps. At the door two secret service men straightened up. Three vehicles were parked at angles further down the entrance drive, and I could see more men strategically placed there. No way was anyone going to take this lot by surprise. Harken and I strolled out of earshot.

"Do you remember the last time we did this?" Harken asked.

"After you debriefed me on the Ubindian mission?"

"Yes. I told you at the time to keep out of politics. All the same, you set me thinking. A few days later, Sef showed me the article in his African newspaper. That RotoFan crash didn't sound like an accident to me, and you and Sef had been lucky not to be on board. Then Sef was murdered and that settled it. I sent you out on assignment as quickly as I could. There'd been two attempts on your life, and I didn't think they'd stop there. I'd lost Gerry and Sef; I wasn't going to lose you, too." He cleared his throat. "The Force had an investment in you," he added quickly.

I smiled to myself. The slip had provided a rare moment of self-revelation.

He continued:

"Then there was the debacle in Serbia. Another nine of my best soldiers gone. I never believed for one moment they had anything to do with what went on in that village. Zajc was clearly tipped off. We're a covert organization. How could we continue to operate with a gaping hole like that in our security?"

"Who knew about the Serbian operation?"

"Apart from me, only one person."

"Cawley."

"Yes, Cawley. Why did he do it? To eliminate you?"

"No, he simply tipped off Zajc and left the rest to him. If you remember, you were going to send Geoff Daniels on that mission; you substituted me at the last moment. It was a bonus for Cawley. He'd have been happy enough if I was killed with the others. Instead Zajc came up with an ingenious way of pinning the whole incident on me. The outcome was the same."

"The court case was a travesty of justice. It was a slur on

the honour of the unit and a personal insult to me."

"I felt pretty insulted, too, Colonel," I said heavily.

He grunted. "I'm sorry about what happened to you, Jim, I really am. It was disgusting the way you were scapegoated. Unfortunately I couldn't prevent it. Getting a domino transplant was the best I could do."

"So it was you who paid for the domino transplant?"

He laughed. "Not on a Colonel's salary, no. But I thought carefully about who else might have an interest. And someone did come to mind."

He stopped and turned to me. In the harsh overhead light from the security lamps his eye sockets were deep and black. "Strictly between us, Jim, understood?"

"Of course."

"Cawley's been playing the military card to good effect. He has a clear lead on Nagel in the opinion polls. War hero, hawkish politician, firm, decisive leader, zero tolerance on crime and terrorism—it's all gone down well with the public. Harriet Nagel and her team have spent billions on this campaign and they stand to lose it all. But suppose Cawley turned out to have a large skeleton in the closet? Do you see? It would turn the whole thing around."

So that was it. "Senator Harriet Nagel," I said.

"Your transplant operation and all the rehabilitation were costly but that was a very small item in her campaign ledger. And it would create the ideal operative for going after Cawley. You had the knowledge, the skills, and the motivation. And best of all," he laid a hand on my shoulder, "if you were caught, there was no way you could be traced."

"What do you mean? There were presumably biometrics on record for this—this body."

"As a dead man, your iris and retina patterns would no

longer be on file. In any case, they wouldn't tally with your body biometrics. A computer search would have reported no match."

"And if I broke under interrogation?"

"What could you tell them? Did you know who'd organized the transplant or who'd funded it?"

"No, of course not."

His hand was still on my shoulder and now he gave it a squeeze—something I'd never known him to do before. His voice dropped.

"I knew it was hard on you, Jim, but that's why I couldn't brief you about what was happening."

"Not in your wildest dreams can you imagine how hard it was." Then I let out a short sigh. "At least now I see why you did it that way."

"It's what convinced Senator Nagel: an excellent prospect of success, and no risk that it could ever be laid at her door. There are no medical records. She and I are the only ones who know that you... ah... lived on. But beyond the funding, she's had no involvement. She'll take full advantage of what comes out of it but she doesn't want it to taint her campaign. She wants to distance herself from the whole thing."

We turned and walked on in silence. Then I said:

"You knew where Suzanne and I were going tonight, didn't you?"

"I had a pretty good idea you'd return to the place I rented for you. Sant'ana's agents followed you from the airport, but they were instructed to back off once the destination was clear. The house in Springfield was staked out by secret service men."

"Part of Harriet Nagel's entourage?"

"Yes, they're assigned for the protection of a Presidential

candidate."

"Why use them?"

"It's a compliment, Jim. FBI men are good, but I didn't think they'd be a match for you. Those guys were hand-picked."

"Hah, thanks."

We were moving towards a separate building, out of the area illuminated by the security lights. I turned to go back, and Harken followed suit.

"You took one hell of a chance asking me to assassinate Prof. I might have done it."

He laughed. "Really? Could you have done that? Kill a man who was inhabiting your body?"

"Well, no, actually."

"Of course you couldn't—it would be like shooting yourself. But it set both of you thinking, didn't it? Being the target of an attempted assassination certainly got Prof's attention, and after that it was natural that he'd work with you. All right, it was a calculated risk, but it came off. We lost track of you, Jim—your countersurveillance was good. Prof was easier. We managed to follow him to one meeting you had, in a restaurant. It looked like things were going well."

"They did at first, but then we hit a dead end. We thought there was a faint hope I'd learn some more by going to Ubindi and seeking out Suzanne, so I did." I jerked my thumb towards the building. "In there you said you started to have doubts about Prof."

"Yes, about a month later. Harriet Nagel had people outside Cawley's campaign headquarters, watching who was coming and going—it's a routine way of collecting a little intelligence about what he was up to. They spotted Prof going in and reported it. She fed it back to me. We were both worried."

"You thought he'd gone over to the other side?"

"It seemed possible, and if he had, it could be bad for you. So her people picked him up and brought him to me. I asked him what the hell was going on, and he told me. We decided to protect him, but we couldn't do it for ever. The only sure way was to put Cawley behind bars. We had a good deal of circumstantial evidence. With the threats, and the sting he and Tony arranged at Atlanta airport, and whatever you and Suzanne Mukewa were bringing back from Ubindi, we thought we could put a case together."

"What made you think Suzanne and I were bringing back anything?"

"Why else would Cawley be so anxious to stop you?"

"True."

It all sounded convincing enough. All the same, I wasn't prepared to abandon all my prejudices about Harken. Suppose he was implicated in what happened in Nigeria? It would suit him to get all the blame heaped on Cawley. I tried a different tack.

"This Serbian gangster, Bogdan Zajc," I said. "Do you know what he looks like?"

He glanced my way. "No. I don't think the press ever had pictures of him. Why?"

"Oh, I thought you might have met him when you were in Nigeria."

"Zajc was in Nigeria?"

"You didn't know?"

"No. What was he doing there? I thought he operated in the Balkans."

"Things got too hot for him. He operated in the Congo

for a while, then he was caught. He escaped and turned up in Nigeria."

We walked a few steps in silence. Harken seemed to be buried in thought. Then he stopped abruptly and looked at me.

"Cawley went to the Congo! I remember that now. We'd been patrolling for a couple of weeks by then and he said he had to go to Kinshasa. He was gone for several days. You think Cawley helped him escape?"

"I think it's highly likely."

"But why?"

"You'll find out when you see what's on those memory tiles."

A gangly figure emerged from the front of the building, and stood there, silhouetted against the security lights. He seemed to be peering our way.

"Colonel? Is that you?"

"Yes, Bagley, what is it?"

"We're set up now, sir, if you'd like to come back in."

54

When Harken and I re-entered the room, the other four had already taken their seats. Bagley assumed, quite rightly, that Suzanne and I were already familiar with what was on the memory tiles when he'd set the equipment up. The others would get the full benefit of the projection.

It was probably unkind to do that to them. The material was hard enough to watch in two dimensions; it was all too realistic in three. I told Bagley he didn't need to show the whole lot. Instead I suggested we start about ten minutes into the second tile. I was right; it was quite enough for them.

At one point, Machin asked us to pause the recording. A man was standing there, unfastening his trousers. At his feet a naked girl was struggling in a contraption of wooden battens and leather straps. The man pointed and turned his head to speak to someone and Bagley paused the playback. There was no question about it: it was Cawley all right. He hadn't changed that much in thirteen years. We continued for a while, and things got more violent, and finally Bob Cressington said:

"For God's sake, turn the damned thing off. We've seen enough, surely?"

Bagley pressed the off button and turned up the room lights. Then he hurried from the room, making a low moaning noise.

For a full minute no one said anything. Bob ran a finger around his collar. They all looked shaken.

Bob said, "Was Cawley the only U.S. soldier involved in this?"

I responded. "I've viewed what's on both tiles. He was the only one I saw."

"Well who were these… these beasts with him?"

"A band of sex traffickers under the leadership of a man called Bogdan Zajc—he was the dark one with the droopy moustache. We believe Cawley released them from jail in Kinshasa specifically to carry out the atrocities."

"Zajc would be a key witness, then."

"Cawley knows that, too. The SAF nearly captured them two years ago, when the gang was occupying a small Serbian village called Raljevo. He tipped off Zajc, and instead of the gang it was the SAF team that got wiped out."

Suzanne removed the second memory tile from the projector and spoke as she returned both the little squares to her powder compact.

"Only Obadiah suspected Cawley's involvement in these atrocities, and he alone filmed them. For the others, Cawley was simply a brilliant tactician who was somehow able to lead his film unit into village after village where events like this took place. The pictures they sent back shocked the world. The second UN resolution was passed unopposed, the international force went in, oil continued to flow, and the revenues continued to line the pockets of a corrupt regime while their people went hungry. And all this because of a fiction, a cruel deception perpetrated by Cawley at the instigation of the United States Government—"

"Hold hard, there, Miss Mukewa!" Machin said. "Hold hard! You're assuming the United States Government was behind all this."

"Oh, but Mr. Secretary, isn't that exactly what the world will assume when it goes before the International Criminal Court?"

Machin's craggy jaw went loose. "International…?"

"Yes," Suzanne answered calmly. "These are the original files. Copies have been placed on file with the International Criminal Court in the Hague."

"Dear God!" His gaze switched to me. "Slater, were you involved in this?"

"Yes, I was."

"Are you aware of the consequences if this becomes public? What you've done is tantamount to treason."

"Treason, Mr. Secretary?" I felt the blood rising to my head. I swallowed, fighting to maintain self-control, and stabbed my finger at the space vacated by the holo image.

"We've been sitting here watching men, women, and children tortured and hacked to death. Who was responsible for that? Good Christ, you saw it with your own eyes! Cawley!"

They were watching me intently. I went on:

"A future head of state was assassinated. Who ordered that? Cawley!"

I was spluttering with indignation. My finger swept slowly round the table like a gun barrel.

"And who was responsible for the deaths of the two Rotofan pilots and my friends Gerry and Sef and the team that went to Serbia? Not to mention the one survivor of that mission, a soldier called Jim Forbes, who didn't kill his teammates but was sentenced to death for it anyway. For God's sake, don't these people deserve justice?" I took a deep breath and lowered my voice. "That's all we're asking for. Justice. Is that treason? If it is, then what... in hell's name... does this country stand for?"

There was a deathly hush. Machin buried his large head in his hands. "Jesus."

The silence thickened until you could reach out and touch it.

Slowly Machin's head came up. His elbows remained on the table, his hands clasped, his voice a low rumble.

"One thing needs to be made clear: this wasn't officially sanctioned. It was the work of an overambitious young man who badly wanted his mission to be successful."

I almost laughed. "You really believe that?"

He sighed. "Look, the administration that may have been responsible for it is no longer in power, and I wasn't a part of it. But I don't want to believe we'd order up something like this, and I don't want anyone else to believe it. The international reputation of this country would be dragged through the gutter. So I say Cawley was acting on his own."

"And when he's hauled up before the International Court that's what he'll tell them, is it? Not that he was simply a soldier obeying orders—oh no! The whole thing was his idea and his alone."

Machin winced at the sarcasm. "It won't come to that. They'd need rock solid evidence to pursue a case of this magnitude. Those memory tiles aren't enough. These things can be faked. Cawley's face could have been put in afterwards. How do we know the footage is genuine? There's no indication as to when these events occurred, or where. There are no eye witnesses—"

"No surviving eye witnesses," I said, with heavy emphasis.

"And surely that's the point, Don," Bob Cressington put in. "You have the fact that Obadiah was assassinated on

Cawley's orders, all those other deaths to cover it up, and now the attempted hit on Jim Slater and Miss Mukewa as they arrived in the States. If the Court takes all that into account, the evidence is deeply incriminating."

He pursed his lips. "Even so, I very much doubt whether they'll pursue it."

"There, Mr. Machin, I think you're mistaken."

Once again all eyes were on Suzanne. She opened her bag and withdrew a sheet of paper, which had been folded in quarters. Because I was sitting next to her, I could see it was the headed notepaper of the International Criminal Court.

"When we left the Court in the Hague," she said, "I asked them to keep me informed. They've been kind enough to do so."

She handed the sheet to Machin.

He scanned it up and down quickly, bushy eyebrows quivering. Then he looked over his glasses at the others round the table.

"This is from the Office of the Chief Prosecutor, International Criminal Court, The Hague. It appears to be a copy of a letter sent to Senator Cawley. I think I'd better read it to you.

"'Evidence has been deposited at this office concerning atrocities committed against unarmed civilians in Nigeria during April and May of 2041. It is alleged that these atrocities, which had been represented as the work of rebel militias, were in fact committed with the knowledge, and the participation, of a Special Forces mission under your command.

'Articles 8 and 25 of the Rome Statute grant the Court jurisdiction over such crimes. In order that the allegations may be investigated, the Pre-Trial Chamber requires that you attend a preliminary hearing to be held at the International Criminal Court, The Hague, on 29th September 2053.

'The Court recognizes the difficulties such allegations could represent to someone in your position. As an exceptional measure we are prepared to hold this hearing in camera, and information will not be released to the media. We can, of course, make no such guarantee about subsequent proceedings.

'We hope you will cooperate with the Court by presenting yourself voluntarily at the time and place indicated. This would avoid the need for the Pre-Trial Chamber to issue a warrant for your arrest under Article 58, and the adverse publicity that would inevitably result.'"

He looked up again. "It's signed by the Chief Prosecutor, with a copy to Miss S. Mukewa."

Prof and Sant'ana exchanged looks. Bob Cressington blew out a long breath.

Machin sat forward, looking at Suzanne. "You're saying that Senator Cawley has already received this letter?"

"He'll deny it, of course." She put out a hand for the paper.

"Could we make a copy of this?" he asked Harken, holding it up.

Harken grimaced. "There are probably facilities here, but we don't have passwords."

"All right, forget it."

He handed the sheet back to Suzanne, and remained hunched forward, his hands resting on the table in front of him, one cupped inside the other. There was a distant expression on his face.

The whole room was waiting. Sant'ana fidgeted.

Finally Machin sighed and straightened up in his chair,

his hands sliding back to grip the edge of the table. He spoke slowly, the vowels drawn out as if it took an effort to finish every word.

"I take no pleasure in what's been revealed to me tonight. But you were right to do so. I think we've got as far as we can for the moment. You had better leave this with me."

He placed his weight on his hands and rose and there was a rattle of furniture as everyone else got to their feet.

As they walked out Machin laid a hand on Bob Cressington's shoulder. I heard him say:

"All right, Bob, seems like I won't be making that trip to San Diego after all."

*

Cressington, Sant'ana, and Machin left to return to Washington. We watched them get into the car, saw the men in dark suits look all around before getting in after them.

Prof was to be taken to a secret destination. As he came out of the door he stumbled. I put out a hand, but he recovered his balance.

"You all right, Prof?" I asked.

He laughed off his embarrassment. "Yes, yes. Ground's a bit uneven, that's all. Goodnight."

After the car had gone I glanced down. Light from inside the doorway fell obliquely across the ground but I couldn't see anything he could have tripped over.

*

Harken came out. "You'll need to take care, Jim. By now Cawley knows you're in the country, and he knows he's been double-crossed. I could have arranged protective custody, but I thought you could probably look after yourself and Suzanne."

"Don't worry, I'll handle it."

We went over to the car that had brought us there. Before we got in I asked one of the secret service men to give me a weapon. He looked at Harken, and Harken nodded. I was hoping for a semi-automatic. What the man took out of the trunk of the car and handed to me was a semi-automatic all right: a Remington auto-shotgun.

Harken said, "Just in case you get unwanted visitors during the night, Jim."

"You want me to go in and out of motels carrying this?"

By way of reply, the U.S.S.S. man went back to the trunk and found the case, a leather-covered, anonymous-looking attaché case. Once he'd detached the barrel and the stock, it packed away very neatly.

Suzanne and I got in behind the driver and I rolled down the window. "There are still a few things I'd like to talk over with you, Colonel."

"I thought there might be. Phone me on this number when you're ready."

He scribbled something on a piece of paper and handed it through the window. Then he lifted a hand in farewell, and walked back to the school.

*

It had been one hell of a long day, so I got them to drop us off at a decent-sized hotel. There'd be some toiletries in the room and we could probably buy whatever else we needed in the morning before we checked out.

As soon as we were alone I said to Suzanne, "Where the hell did that letter come from? Sulzmann said it would take a year or more."

She smiled. "You remember I took the headed notepaper from the secretary's office?"

"Yes."

"And you remember that while we were waiting for the flight at Schipol, I went into a cyber centre?"

"You typed it there? Yourself?"

"It wasn't hard. I looked up the details I needed on the net."

"But suppose they check with the Court?"

"Do you think they will? I don't. We built the bonfire, Jim. The letter was only the match."

"You may well be right." I gave vent to a short laugh. "I have to say, there's a certain poetry about it. Cawley's been a master of disinformation. He hoodwinked the whole world into believing those Nigerian atrocities were the work of the rebels. He did the same when he lied to Harken about Obadiah, and the same again when he bullied Prof into finding out when and where we were going to arrive. Now you've worked the same tactics on him."

"He killed Ben Obadiah with his lies. Let him see how it feels to be on the receiving end."

"I still can't believe it. You must have been thinking way ahead."

"It was luck. I didn't know we were going to have this sort of confrontation. I did it as a sort of insurance policy. You were very jumpy about going back to the United States. I realized there was a good chance of us being detained or abducted on entry so I thought it would be a good thing to have around, something I could drop on the ground, or hand to someone. Anyone with their wits about them would see how important it was, and they'd probably take it to the media."

I shook my head. "You're a very clever girl, Suzanne Mukewa."

"I know."

I took her in my arms and pressed my cheek to her hair. "I won't let them get you."

55

Suzanne quickly tired of my security precautions. We were about to move again when she folded her arms and stood there defiantly.

"Is this really necessary, Jim? I'm fed up with being dragged around from place to place."

I took her gently by the shoulders.

"Suzanne, we can't afford to be a stationary target. That first hotel recorded our biometrics. Cawley almost certainly has access to the Intelligence Community database, and even their computers will have tracked us by now. They know we're in the Washington area, so that's narrowed the search. If we check into another motel late in the day we'll have just enough time to get a night's sleep. Then I'm afraid we'll have to move again. It's the only way we can stay ahead."

"It's information warfare!"

"Yup, that's exactly what it is. We're under surveillance and Cawley's using all the apparatus of government to do it."

She sighed. "I can't live like this. It's like being a vagrant—worse—vagrants aren't spied on all the time. How long is it going on for?"

"I don't know, it's up to Machin. They left it with him."

She grimaced. "Why Machin?"

"He was the senior man."

"I know, but he was defending Cawley until the very last moment."

That hadn't escaped my notice. I let my hands slide down to her elbows. "He was probably playing Devil's Advocate."

"Maybe. But can we trust him? Suppose he just sits on his hands?"

"No, he'll have to do something. Whether we like what he does is another matter. We'll just have to wait and see."

*

We didn't have to wait much longer. We were on our way to the third motel when I saw the headlines on an electronic hoarding.

PRESIDENTIAL CANDIDATE DEAD
SENATOR NAGEL PAYS TRIBUTE TO RIVAL

I told the taxi to stop and nipped out to buy news-chips for the Washington Post and the New York Times. As soon as we were installed in the new room, I plugged them into the reader and we sat down to view them.

A cleaner had found him slumped over his desk in the campaign headquarters. He'd blown his brains out with a pistol he normally kept in a drawer. There would be a thorough investigation, but police said they had no grounds to believe a third party was involved.

I glanced sideways at Suzanne. Her fingers were up at her mouth as she read. She took them away.

"Don Machin must have confronted him with what we had," she said. "Cawley saw the net tightening and decided to end it there and then."

"Somehow I don't think so."

"What do you mean?"

"Think about it. If Cawley went to trial, or if the media got hold of it, the whole story would have come out. Machin and the others couldn't afford to take that chance."

She stood abruptly. "You're saying they killed him and staged it as a suicide? How could they manage that?"

I got up, crossed to the reader and switched it off.

"How hard do you think it'd be? You've got Don Machin, Secretary of Homeland Security, which directs the United States Secret Service, and you've got Bob Cressington, Director of National Intelligence, who heads up the U.S. Intelligence Community, including the CIA. All they had to do was withdraw one of Brad Cawley's secret service minders and replace them with one of the CIA's professional assassins."

"Oh, my God. And that's what you think?"

"That's what I think."

She started to pace restlessly back and forth. "I didn't mean for it to happen this way. I wanted him brought before a court of law."

I felt a flash of annoyance. I was well satisfied to see Cawley dead.

"Well sure, he should have suffered for what he did: public humiliation and the rest of his life in prison—that's what he deserved. But that man would have shifted Heaven and Earth to stop us giving evidence at the International Criminal Court. You and I—and Prof, too—would have been in constant danger for years. You were fed up with running. Well, now we can stop running."

"But this... this can't be right. It's lynch law. Jim, I feel dirty."

It was too much. Anger surged up inside me. "You think I'm about to shed tears for that bastard, after what he did to me?"

I'd blurted it out before I knew it.

She stopped pacing and looked up abruptly, eyes narrowed. Her voice was slow and measured.

"What—exactly—did he do to you, Jim?"

This wasn't my Suzanne; this was the other Suzanne, the one with the commanding voice and the imperious manner.

I passed my tongue round my lips. I could try to bluff my way through it, maybe mention the friends I'd lost, but I knew it wouldn't convince her. It was time to come clean.

"Suzanne, when we all met at that school three days ago I talked about justice for a man called Jim Forbes. Jim was one of the three SAF soldiers who assassinated Obadiah and extracted you from his camp. Cawley managed to eliminate all the witnesses to what happened there, with two exceptions. One was you; the other was Forbes. To get Forbes out of harm's way, Colonel Harken gave him a new assignment. He led a team to the Balkans, tasked with capturing Bogdan Zajc and his gang."

"Zajc was in the Balkans again?"

"Yes. After Ngozi got him and his gang safely out of the country he must have gone back there and picked up where he'd left off, trafficking girls, plundering villages and massacring the inhabitants, just like before. The mission would have succeeded, except unfortunately Cawley's position in the command chain gave him access to the entire operational plan. He tipped off Zajc."

"Why would he do that?"

"If Zajc appeared in court, he might have spilled what he knew about Nigeria. Cawley had a choice. He could order up a hit on Zajc, but the man was a moving target and well protected. It was easier to tip him off. So Jim Forbes and his team walked into a trap. Zajc killed them—all except one. They left Jim Forbes unconscious and barely alive, with enough manufactured evidence to make it look like he was guilty of both the atrocities and the murder of his comrades. He was innocent, but the court found him guilty. Do you know what they do to common enemies of society like him?"

"No."

"They don't exactly kill them. They use their bodies as a receptacle for someone worthwhile, someone who's dying of an incurable disease. Just the body. The brain is discarded—mashed up and washed into the sewers."

She shuddered. "That's horrible!"

"In Jim's case, his body was used for a very worthwhile member of society: Dr. David Hirsch."

"Prof is in this man's body?"

"Yes. He had a terminal disease. It was the only way he could survive."

A light entered her eyes. "I knew I recognized him! It was hard to say, though: he looked and sounded different."

"Yes, he does. That's the effect of having Prof's brain in his body. I should know. I am Jim Forbes."

56

She fell back into a chair. Her mouth opened, but at first no sound came out. She blinked rapidly.

"I don't understand. How can you be two people at once?"

"Prof is in Jim's body. But Jim's brain wasn't mashed up at all; it was put into another body. It's called a domino transplant. Harken arranged it. He wanted to expose Cawley, and he knew I was the one to do it."

She was peering at me as if I was an exhibit at a freak show. It was very hard to bear.

"I can't get my head around this," she said. "Who am I looking at?"

My heart was hammering but I tried to sound casual. "You're looking at Jim Slater. It's not a bad body, as these things go; it does pretty much everything I want it to. But in my head, I'm Jim Forbes. I have his memory and abilities—and his hang-ups."

She leapt to her feet and ran her hands through her hair. "So which of you did I sleep with last night?"

I stood uncertainly. The violence of her reaction had taken me by surprise. I kept my voice low.

"Jim Slater made love to you, but it's Jim Forbes who loves you."

"This is grotesque! I don't want to be loved by Jim Forbes. Jim Forbes is a murderer."

"Not a murderer, just a soldier doing his job."

"You murdered Ben Obadiah," she said, shaking her head slowly from side to side. "You killed that wonderful man."

"Not personally, but I led the team. Yes, all right, I'm responsible. I'm not proud of it."

Tears welled up in her eyes. Her mouth was quivering.

"Suzanne…" I said.

I wanted to take her in my arms, but I knew she'd push me off and I couldn't face the rejection.

She turned her face away. "All this time! You lied to me, Jim. You deceived me."

"We were all deceived, Suzanne. Cawley sold us a bill of goods about Obadiah. We thought we were taking out a criminal, a butcher of his own people, not a potential statesman. And we thought you were being kept as a sex slave. You must understand—for God's sake, you were duped, too! Didn't you say yourself you were the bait in the trap?"

"That was different. I went there to negotiate a peace agreement. You went there to kill."

"I was following orders. It wasn't my idea of the sort of operation SAF should be involved in. Now I know why, but that's with hindsight. Everything was different at the time."

"You should have told me earlier."

"I couldn't, Suzanne. It was never the right moment."

"Rubbish. You concealed it from me. You were dishonest."

"I wasn't dishonest. Why do you say that? I'm still the person you thought I was. You wanted someone to help you get justice for Obadiah, and justice for your people. Well, I've done everything you expected of me. And as a result, Cawley's dead."

She threw her hands up in the air. "'Cawley's dead'—as if

that solves everything!" She breathed out through her teeth. "What a fool I've been," she said. "You're not a journalist. You're not CIA. You're not even a person. You're a construct, a chimera!"

I felt like I'd been stabbed. I swallowed hard. "That's uncalled for. It wasn't my fault that—"

"It's all over, Jim Whichever-you-are," she said. "It's finished."

I tried to reach out to her.

"Don't touch me!" she shouted. She backed away, hugging the wall, and skirted around me quickly to the door. "I'm leaving. Don't try to stop me, and don't ever come after me."

The door slammed behind her and I heard her sobs and the rapid tapping of her footsteps as she ran down the corridor. The sound faded.

I stood rigidly in the centre of the room, struggling to maintain my self-control. The pressure built and became too much. Slowly I lifted my fists to the air and my howl of anguish must have been audible two blocks away. I rampaged around like a bull elephant. I hurled bedclothes, kicked a chair into the corner, swung an armchair against the wall. It wasn't enough. I lifted the table and was on the point of throwing it through the window when a ludicrous thought entered my mind: I wouldn't be able to pay for the damage. I set it down. I wouldn't be able to pay for the room, either. I had no credit accounts and I was travelling on a set of diplomatic documents under a false name. Officially I didn't exist. None of that had mattered when I was with Suzanne—with her I had an identity. Now she'd gone. My body went limp.

I dropped onto the edge of the bed and buried my head in my hands. I felt crushed. I'd been insane to think it could have lasted. She was a woman of intelligence and sensitivity and I was—

She'd said it. I was a chimera, a misfit, neither one thing nor the other. I shouldn't have survived. They should have washed my lousy brain down the toilet like they were supposed to do.

Tears came, tears of misery and self-pity, and I gave into them, my body—my borrowed body—racked with sobs. I buried my head in my hands. I couldn't take any more. I'd had enough.

I've no idea how long I was like that. When eventually I looked around me, the room was dark.

I knew where to find it. My fingers sought out the catches on the attaché case and opened them. I felt the cool steel of the barrels, buttstock, and forearm as I took each one out. It clicked together effortlessly and I chambered a shell. It was soothing to go through the familiar routine. I sat there holding it, the barrel across my arm. A calm had settled on me. I ran my hands gently over the weapon, sensing its potency. It would be my escape; it would deliver me.

I placed the butt on the floor, closed my mouth over the muzzle, reached for the trigger and—

And then I remembered.

I straightened up, blinking rapidly and breathing fast. I'd almost forgotten, hadn't I? I'd almost forgotten the unfinished business.

My fingers closed tightly around the barrel of the shotgun and the old anger started to surge through my veins, energizing me. There'd be time enough for this.

I disassembled the shotgun and packed it away, then went to the bathroom and splashed my swollen eyes with water. I dried my face on the towel and stood there for a moment, looking at myself in the mirror.

The first goal had been achieved: Cawley was dead. I would have preferred to dispatch the bastard myself, but I had to be satisfied with that.

Now I had to deal with the second goal.

And that was even more important.

57

I phoned Harken and told him Suzanne had gone. He asked me where. I said I didn't know, but I thought she'd go back to France to stay with her mother. He was tactful enough not to ask any more questions.

As for the room, I wasn't to worry; he'd handle that. In any case everything had changed now. The time for motels was over; he'd already made arrangements for me to stay in guest accommodation run by the Department of Defense. He gave me an address in the centre of Washington. It was conveniently close to the Department.

He always seemed to be one step ahead of me.

*

"Have you been following the polls?" Harken asked.

We were on our own in a conference room at the DoD, sitting opposite each other at the end of a highly polished mahogany table that could have seated twenty. We were waiting for Bob Cressington.

"I gather Harriet Nagel is well in front."

"She's a shoo-in. June Masterson's taken over Cawley's campaign, but she doesn't have the stature."

I remembered Suzanne's reaction to Cawley's Vice-Presidential nominee. Harriet Nagel would wipe the floor with her.

The election didn't interest me anymore. Deep down it was anger that was driving me now, and I wanted action, not chit-chat. I changed the subject.

"Why did you arrange to meet here?"

"Bob isn't Director of National Intelligence any longer; he's been appointed Deputy Secretary of Defense—part of a government reshuffle prompted by Cawley's departure."

"Prof will be pleased," I said. "He's gets on well with Bob."

"So do we all. It's a good appointment. Bob's had his eye on it for some time, but Cawley was blocking him. He's a happy man."

I recalled it was Bob and Tony Sant'ana at the FBI who'd set up the sting at Atlanta airport. If my suspicions were correct he'd also had some involvement in Cawley's not-so-tragic demise. But even if his conduct hadn't been entirely disinterested, the fact remained that this was a guy who was quick on the uptake and not afraid to get things done. It would be useful to have him onside.

The door opened and we stood up as Bob came in. He hurried over and shook hands.

"Sorry, I'm running a bit late."

We sat down again, and he took the chair at the end of the table.

"Congratulations on your new appointment, Mr. Deputy Secretary," I said.

He smiled. "Bob will do." He crossed his hands on the table. "Seems we owe you a vote of thanks, Jim, exposing Cawley like that. To be frank, I never cared for the man but some of those things you showed us..." He shook his head. "Well, even I found it hard to believe."

"So did Senator Machin, apparently."

He shrugged. "Machin's a tough old bird. He had to be convinced, that's all—and in the end he was. I don't know what he said to Cawley but it was enough, it seems, to persuade him the situation was hopeless."

"You might almost say he held a gun to his head."

Our eyes met for several seconds.

"Yes," he said quietly. "You might almost say that."

There was an uncomfortable silence. Then Bob returned to his former brisk tone.

"Anyway, Cawley's gone. Harriet Nagel will make a fine President. You did us a big favour, Jim—not just me personally, the whole country."

"Well I'm glad you said that, because now I'd like to call in the favour."

His eyes narrowed slightly, then he sat back, propping his elbows on the armrest of his chair and placing his fingertips together.

"Go on. I'm listening."

I knew I'd have to be guarded about what I said to him. Only Harken and Harriet Nagel knew how I came to be Jim Slater. It had to stay that way.

"Bob, when we met at the school, Colonel Harken introduced me as a former colleague. That's true. Up to about two years ago I was in the SAF. I'd like to be reinstated."

He looked at Harken. "No problem about that, is there, Wendell?"

Harken hesitated. "Of course I'd be glad to have him back, Bob, but it could be tricky. There are procedures…"

"You can find your way round those, can't you?"

"All right, let's say 'yes', then what?"

I leaned forward and outlined my plan. They both listened intently.

Bob nodded thoughtfully. "I like it, Jim, but it's only going to work if it's properly resourced. Men, equipment, transport—"

"What size of force do you think this would take?" Harken asked.

"If we're going to have any chance of completing the whole mission we need three teams. I'd say at least six in each team—and that's the bare minimum."

Bob wagged a finger. "Let's not talk in those terms. Think about what you need to get the job done. Get it right. Pick good men and enough of them, and good officers to lead them."

Harken coughed. "Excuse me, Bob, but this is sizing up as a major operation. It could swallow our entire budget for about the next six months."

"Let me worry about that, Wendell. I'm the new boy on the block, so the first thing I did was look at the Department's finances. I've already discovered some contingency funds that Cawley never tapped into." He shot us a mischievous look. "This—I'd say—is just the type of contingency they were designed for."

I felt a sense of excitement. I'd expected obstacles; instead there was nothing in the way. It really was going to happen.

"When should I tell them to expect the consignment?" Bob asked me.

"I thought about six weeks."

"Why so long?"

"Well, we can be ready long before that, it's what happens at the other end. I want to give them plenty of time so they can put everything in place."

"I understand." Bob pushed his chair back. "Okay, let's go ahead with this. Arms consignments have gone to Ubindi many times in the past so my staff should know exactly what to do. I'll initiate the procedure this afternoon. The rest is up to you guys." He got to his feet. "Now you'll have to excuse me, I have another meeting to go to."

We stood up together. He gripped my hand and held it a fraction longer than he needed to.

"Good luck, Jim. Keep me posted."

PART SIX

58

We sat lined up along the sides of the cargo bay of the U.S.A.F. Leviathon, thirty crack soldiers of the SAF, all fully briefed and raring to go. Three teams, ten in each: Red Team under Major Fred Curtis, Green Team under Captain Colin McKenzie, and Blue Team under Captain Charles Lavergne. I'd met Fred Curtis before, although he didn't recognise me now, of course. The others were new to me, but I'd had plenty of time to get to know them during practise exercises.

As mission-leader I'd ended up in overall charge of a Major, two Captains, and twenty-six ORs. In recognition of that Harken got me reinstated at the rank of Lieutenant Colonel.

The engine note dropped and I heard a rumble from the flaps.

There was a brief crackle in my comms helmet. "Colonel Slater? We're on finals for Kebe."

"Copy that," I replied. "Any sign of an A400 down there?"

"Can't see it yet, there's some heat haze. I'll report back."

I'd made sure we had an air crew who'd done this run a couple of times before. They were Transport, Special Operations, and very professional. The pilot said that on two occasions he'd landed in Kebe and there'd been an old Airbus A400M in the cargo area. He drew me a picture of the layout and I briefed our teams accordingly. I wanted us to end up in exactly the same position, so our men would know what to expect when the doors opened.

I switched to the other channel and passed the word on. "We'll be landing in a few minutes. Keep it quiet."

They didn't say anything but I saw the rows of black-streaked faces nodding. I switched back to the cockpit channel.

The pilot came through again. "Got a visual on the cargo area, now, Colonel. Confirm sighting of an A400M in the usual bay. We'll taxi as we did last time."

"Carry on."

There were more rumbles as the flaps extended further and the undercarriage came down. From the way the floor was sloping I knew the craft was settled in for the approach, nose slightly high. A few moments later there was a bump as the wheels touched down; then the reverse thrust roared and faded and we were taxiing.

We stopped and the engines whined down.

I knew the sequence. The copilot would open the forward door and deploy the steps. Then a member of the ground crew would come up and inspect the documents. He'd take his copy, then give the all-clear and they'd get ready to unload. The copilot had been told to stand up there for a few moments longer to give us a better idea of what we were up against. That was what I was really waiting for.

Several minutes passed. With the engines off, the air conditioning had stopped running. Even in a cargo hold as large as this I could feel the temperature rising.

I toggled the switch to connect the two channels so that the whole force would hear what the copilot said. I spoke close to the mic.

"Signal if you're receiving."

I saw the thumbs go up. We waited.

A click in the comms helmet. At last. "Colonel? Ready to open cargo doors."

"Okay, who's coming out to us?"

"Two forklifts. About a dozen handlers."

"Weapons?"

"The handlers aren't armed. But there are soldiers in fatigues by the fence. Look like Ubindian army to me. They're carrying assault rifles—pretty beaten up M-40s if I'm right. And there's a bunch of guys lounging around by the warehouse. They're dark, but they're not Africans. A lot of them have beards. They're armed, but just small stuff; I don't think they're expecting trouble. Four camoed trucks by the warehouse. Can't see if there's anyone in them."

It looked like they'd taken the bait. They were expecting a large shipment of modern weapons from their generous American allies. Well, they were in for a surprise.

"Tell me when the forklifts and the handlers are waiting by the cargo door."

"Will do."

I spoke softly. "Visors down."

The quick-reacting solar visors would ensure that my men weren't blinded by the dazzling sunshine outside. It would give us a few moments of advantage before the handlers could see into the cargo bay.

"SGLs?"

The two soldiers on the end nearest the doors raised their hands. I could make out the big muzzles of the stun grenade launchers at chest level, the butts resting on the floor. I knew all the soldiers by name, of course, but in the gloom with their faces streaked it was impossible to identify them. I used their codes.

"Red Two, target the soldiers by the fence. Red Three, lob one into the warehouse. Then the rest deploy, as planned. Try and take prisoners, but if anyone shoots at you, drop them."

The helmet clicked. "They're waiting now, Colonel."

"All right. Open cargo doors."

The upper door opened quickly, the lower door a little more slowly, giving my SGLs another moment of cover. Then they leapt out and I heard the low thump of the launchers, then the large grenades, loud even with the noise-cancelling headset in my helmet. We all poured out.

I heard shots even before my feet hit the ground. Looking around quickly I saw a lot of scattered bodies where the stun grenade had landed near the fence. The hangar was similarly littered. But another bunch of soldiers had appeared at the side of the hangar. Red Team returned fire, and Red Five dropped to one knee to fire an airburst munition from a rifle cannon. It exploded right over them and the shooting stopped. More incoming fire, this time from a sentry box in the right-hand corner of the wire fence. Again Red Five shouldered his cannon and targeted the source. A big ball of flame expanded from the sentry box and it fell quiet. Boots scuffed on the concrete apron as Blue Team ran out to secure the perimeter. Green team separated: six soldiers rounded up the handlers, and four soldiers ran for the A400 with me. Then I heard one of the trucks start up. It was moving off even before my head whipped round.

"You go on," I yelled to the others, and pelted for the nearest truck. I opened the door, grabbed the driver by the collar and threw him out in one movement. Then I leapt into the driver's seat, started the engine and slammed it into gear. It lurched forward and I put my foot to the boards, the engine and the tyres screaming as I swung it round, the whole rig leaning dangerously. The gates were closed, but the other truck was racing at them. It was going to ram its way through.

I converged on the other truck just before the gates. I had an instant to brace myself, then I slammed into the side of it, just behind the front wheels. With a tremendous, jarring impact the bonnet buried itself in the other vehicle and drove it along sideways. It hit the gate-post with another crunch and rocked back. A cloud of steam spewed up, but through it I'd glimpsed a figure jump down from the opposite side and start to run along the perimeter fence.

I struggled to open the door but it was jammed. I slid across to the passenger side. It, too, was stuck. I kicked at it with both feet and it flew open. I dropped to the ground and raced off in pursuit. A quick glance over my shoulder showed me that Red Team soldiers were going for the other trucks.

For once I was glad of this long-limbed, muscular body. My feet flew over the concrete and I was gaining on him. Then I saw what he was up to. Above us, the smoking walls of the sentry box were hanging free, like torn wallpaper, but the platform was intact, and almost on a level with the fence. It was high, but if he could protect his hands from the razor-wire he could vault over to the other side of the fence. He looked round to see who was behind him and I saw a dark face with a drooping moustache. The face recorded on Suzanne's memory tiles.

The face of Bogdan Zajc.

59

Zajc had almost reached the ladder when I nailed him with a flying tackle. We hit the ground together. He lashed out with a boot and clipped me high up on the cheek but I was oblivious to the pain. He lashed out again, and this time I snatched the ankle and tried to apply a leg lock. He twisted away and we got up together, throwing punches left and right. I blocked his right hook and punched for his throat. He jerked back, giving me enough room to use my feet. No one had matched me on the mat and he was no match for me now. He doubled over to a good shot in the stomach and my follow-up to the side of the head sent him sprawling. I dived forward and landed on top of him, my hand round his throat, my knees pinning his arms.

He struggled but I had him firmly, my face up close to his.

"You don't know who I am, do you, Zajc? But I know who you fucking are."

His dark eyes flashed.

"You ambushed an SAF team at Raljevo. Killed them all, didn't you, Zajc? All except the leader, Captain Jim Forbes, and you pinned the murders on him." My grip on his throat tightened. "Thought you were clever, did you? Well, you lousy sonofabitch, meet Jim Forbes."

A different look entered his face. He rolled up under me and grabbed for something. Too late I saw the knife. With his upper arms pinioned he couldn't reach my body but he stabbed it into the back of my hand. I let out a howl and a curse and he launched himself backwards, straightening his legs under me. I went over his head, but extended the side of my hand, rolled over my shoulder in a break-fall, and rose in a fighting stance. He was already hurrying up the ladder, carrying the knife in one hand. I raced up after him and got a firm grip on one leg. He kicked viciously at my hand with his other foot, then there was a brief glint of steel as he lifted the knife by the blade. He threw it as I jumped back off the ladder, and a bolt of pain shot through my leg. I hit the ground, just managing to stay on my feet, and looked down. The blade was deeply embedded in my left thigh. I took a quick breath and drew the knife out, then flipped it at him. It hit the underside of the platform and stuck there, quivering. He'd already disappeared off the top of the ladder.

I lurched back to get a better view. Zajc was on the platform, taking his jacket off. I un-holstered my pistol and aimed carefully. It would take a clear shot if I was going to stop him without actually killing him.

The shot rang out—but it wasn't from my weapon. Zajc's arms flew out. He staggered, remained suspended for a moment on the edge of the platform, then dropped onto the wire. There was a long gurgling cry, then nothing.

I sank to my knees. Blood was gushing warm over my hand and down my leg. My head was swimming. A pair of boots appeared in my peripheral vision and I looked up to see the face of Major Fred Curtis. He put down the sniper rifle.

"Hang in there, Jim," he said gently, opening a pouch on his belt. "We'll get a dressing on those wounds for you."

I pointed a trembling finger at the figure on the wire.

"Forget it, he's gone," Curtis said.

"But it's Zajc."

"I know who it is."

He tore away my blood-soaked trouser leg, shook his head, reached into a pack, and tied a tourniquet around my upper thigh. Then he applied a medicated pressure dressing to the wound and removed the tourniquet.

"I wanted him to stand trial," I said.

"Is that why you didn't shoot at him before?"

"Of course."

"Sorry, Jim. My orders were that on no account was he to be taken alive."

He picked up my hand and bound it with another dressing.

I should have known. Zajc was the only one left who knew what had really gone on in Nigeria. The United States government couldn't risk him having his day in court. Now I understood why Bob Cressington was so keen on the mission. It tidied things up very nicely.

I got unsteadily to my feet. Curtis held onto my arm. "Easy now."

My mind was still racing but when I glanced around, I could see it was all over. Ground staff, handlers, and soldiers were being led, handcuffed, to the warehouse. More of our men were over at the fence, attending to the soldiers dropped by the stun grenade.

Looking up, I saw two of our guys trying to detach Zajc's body from the wire. What they eventually brought down was a slippery red mass. The razor wire had cut so deeply into his throat that his head was lolling almost clear of his shoulders. I limped over to them, Curtis still holding my arm.

They laid him on the ground at my feet. On an impulse, I reached out and brushed a thumb over the lobe of the left ear. Sure enough there, caked in congealing blood, was the diamond stud Luljeta had described, something the poor, violated girl would have seen at close quarters.

My gaze shifted to the gory features of the man who had brought death and misery to so many men, women, and children, who had killed my comrades, and who had—despite what I'd shouted at him—killed Jim Forbes.

And felt nothing.

Then the world started to rotate.

When I opened my eyes I was back in the Leviathon and Curtis was standing there. "Jim, you have a serious wound. You need medical attention. We're going to fly you to Nairobi."

I moistened my lips. "Our operation's nowhere near finished."

"It is as far as you're concerned."

60

At the hospital in Nairobi the emergency staff used a portable scanner to image the vessels in my thigh and locate the bleeding. Then they cleaned me up, changed the dressings, gave me some painkillers, and tucked me into a nice, clean bed. My hand and thigh throbbed a bit but otherwise I was pretty comfortable.

A nurse turned up at my bedside with a tray and started to unpeel sterile packs. She swabbed the back of my good hand and said:

"Now you'll feel a little scratch…"

I spotted the introducer. She was going to put a line in.

Suddenly I was back in that anteroom, my arms, legs, waist, and neck shackled, the bright lights and the white ceiling tiles drifting above my head…

I totally lost it. They must have heard my yells all over the hospital.

She fell back, mouth open. Then her expression hardened. "What a fuss to make, a great big fella like you!"

"Go away!" I yelled.

A man hurried over. "I'm Dr. Banda," he said to me. Then to the nurse, "What's the problem?"

Her mouth set. "He's refusing treatment," she said.

"I'm not refusing treatment!" I bellowed.

"I wanted to put the IV drip in. He won't have it."

"No needles!" I yelled.

Dr. Banda looked perplexed. He picked up my notes and started to read them.

"He's lost blood," the nurse went on. "He should have crystalloids."

Banda turned to me. "Colonel, you have to understan'. You been put in our care. If we cannot treat you and somethin' goes wrong, it's us what gets the blame."

I tried to control my voice. I was shivering and my teeth were chattering.

"I'll sign a waiver," I said. "You won't be held responsible. But no needles."

He cocked his head on one side. "From what I hear, you had a five-inch dagger flung into your thigh. This," he showed me the needle, "is not a five-inch dagger."

"It's a matter of association," I said. Then I added, because I couldn't think of any other explanation to give him, "It's a childhood experience."

He said, "Give me your hand a moment."

I withdrew it and put it under the bedclothes.

He said, "Come on, I'm not going to stick anythin' into it, man."

I offered it cautiously. He picked up the skin on the back of the hand and let it go. Then he shrugged and turned to the nurse.

"He's not so bad. Skip the IV drip." Then, to me, "You be nice to the nurse, now. She tryin' to help you."

I felt a bit sheepish, but I just hadn't been able to help myself.

*

They kept me in for several days. My hand was fine; it was the thigh wound. Dr. Banda showed me the scan: the knife had punctured an artery roughly two millimetres in diameter. It had stopped bleeding now but they were concerned that any movement might open it up again. On top of that I'd lost blood and he said it wouldn't hurt for me to gain some strength before I went back.

After the initial incident we got on rather well. On the second day, he sat on the edge of the bed and his ebony face split into a wide grin.

"I tell you, your leg muscles got a damn fine blood supply," he said. "It's all that trainin'. If you weren't so fit, it wouldn't have bled so much."

"It's my fault, then."

"Damn right. Well, that an' stoppin' a knife in your leg. Dat's never a good idea."

"If I hadn't jumped, I'd have got it in the throat or chest. That would have given you something to think about."

"Mmm, dat's true."

"How much longer do I have to be in here, doc?"

"A few days. We wanna be sure the bleedin's well an' truly stopped."

"Can't you do anything to speed things up?"

"You askin' me that, a man what can't stand needles?"

"Yeah, well something that doesn't involve needles."

"I don' recommend it. That vessel's big enough to bleed, but it's small enough to block if I try an' put in an artificial linin'. Any case, that involves needles. No, my frien', even with modern medicine sometimes it's best to leave things to mend theirselves. We'll jus' keep you from moving aroun' too soon, and stick to monitoring."

"My uniform's wrecked. Can you get another sent out to

me?"

"Sure, we can do that."

The next day he put me down for some light exercise under the supervision of a physiotherapist, but no weight bearing. I was bored to tears, but I managed to find an English channel on Kenyan holovision. To my astonishment the news was full of the mission.

"Bogdan Zajc, the man they called 'The Scourge of the Balkans', is dead."

The visual showed the face of the dead Zajc—suitably cleaned up, I noticed.

"He and his gang were responsible for murdering hundreds of innocent people, as well as trafficking young women. They were wanted in several countries, but he always managed to evade the law—until now. He was killed, and members of the gang were captured, in a daring operation by an American task force. The United States Deputy Secretary of State for Defense held a press conference earlier today."

The familiar figure of Bob Cressington appeared, standing behind a podium.

"You all have the press release. I'd just like to confirm that the operation was carried out by highly trained teams of the Special Assignment Force. I think we'd all wish to congratulate the men involved, and particularly their leader, Lieutenant Colonel James Slater, whose plan this was."

I was aghast.

Well that's blown me sky-high, hasn't it! What the fuck does he think he's doing, giving out that kind of detail?

My mind was racing. By the time I'd returned my attention to the newscast, Bob was already fielding questions. He pointed to a correspondent.

"Richard?"

"Where is Colonel Slater now?"

"During the operation he engaged Zajc in fierce hand-to-hand combat. That fight left the gangster dead, but the Colonel was wounded. Right now he's recovering in hospital. We'll be issuing further bulletins."

I blinked in disbelief.

"Charles?"

"The Press Release said this was an international operation. Presumably that meant crossing frontiers with an armed force. Did the countries involved have advance warning?"

"No, that wasn't possible—the success of this mission depended on absolute secrecy. This has been explained to the ambassadors of the countries involved and we've offered our apologies for the unauthorised incursions into their sovereign territories. The Foreign Ministers of Albania and Romania have already gone on record to express their thanks. We're grateful for their understanding."

He pointed again, this time to a woman. "Barbara?"

"Are you planning further operations of this type?"

"Obviously I can't comment specifically, but I can say this. Bogdan Zajc and his gang have been responsible for drug smuggling, sex trafficking, and atrocious acts of violence. All this has been going on for a number of years. What we've shown is that there can be no hiding place for international criminals like these. That's why I called this conference today. I want to make sure this message goes out loud and clear."

The newscast changed to another item and I switched off.

It crossed my mind to look at some other channels, but I thought better of it. The sort of detail I wanted wouldn't be there, and the rest would probably be garbled. In any case I felt too damned depressed.

I won't be much use for covert operations after this. What's behind it? Are they putting me out to pasture or sticking me behind a desk?

61

When the replacement uniform arrived I raised my eyes to the ceiling.

Shit! It's the wrong bloody rank!

I put it on for the flight home. I had no choice: there wasn't enough time to get another one.

To my surprise, Harken met me at the airport, right at the gate.

"Welcome back, Colonel," he said. He tilted his head to inspect the eagle on my collar.

I took it for sarcasm. Flushed with embarrassment, I said, "Sorry, sir, this is the uniform they sent."

"It wasn't a mistake, Jim, you were promoted in the field. You're a full colonel now."

I was about to stutter out something when he straightened up and I noticed the silver star on his collar. Brigadier General. He'd been promoted, too.

"Congratulations, General," I said, with a grin. "And, if I may say so, about time, too."

"Thank you, Jim. Now, do you have some dark glasses? There's a lot of press out there."

"Why?"

"Why? Because you're a war hero, that's why."

I wasn't ready for such a reception. The world turned white as I walked into a blitz of strobes, accompanied by a loud chorus of questions from the waiting journalists:

"How are you feeling, Colonel?"

"What are your plans now, Colonel?"

"How does it feel to be a hero, Colonel?"

Harken conducted me firmly through the crowd, saying, "Come on, guys, give the man some room."

I waved and mouthed "Thank you" and "I feel great".

We got into his car and the sudden silence made my ears rush.

Harken took the cap he'd been carrying under one arm and tossed it onto the back seat. As he did so I caught a glimpse of gold braid on the visor. He started the engine and we glided off.

"Well," he said. "I didn't actually ask. How are you?"

"I'm okay. They were just being super-cautious at the hospital."

"Not like you to get caught out. How did it happen?"

"I got a bit too excited. Zajc had a boot knife."

"Good thing it wasn't a pistol."

"Apparently he never carried. Must have been a way of asserting his authority: always got the others to do the shooting for him. I've been out of it ever since. What happened after that?"

"It went very well."

"Did we take any casualties?"

"Only you."

I breathed out. "Thank God for that."

He glanced in my direction and smiled.

"That does you credit, Jim. You think of your men before yourself. You're a born leader."

He joined the highway, accelerated, and flicked on the auto-drive.

I asked about the drugs.

"Right on the button. They found four large containers in that warehouse and each one was packed with heroin, obviously brought there by the trucks. It's like you said: the gang was expecting a large shipment of arms so they put the whole sequence into operation." He looked over at me. "How did you know Zajc would be with them?"

"He had to be there, didn't he? He knew the kind of scum he was dealing with; if he wasn't around to supervise the loading, they'd spirit half the stuff away. What about the refinery?"

"We identified the drivers and had them run Red Team out there. Our boys deployed and captured the whole installation. The Drugs Enforcement Agency's taken over now. I gather the personnel there are plea bargaining like crazy. If there are links with the government it's pretty certain they'll emerge, but Ngozi and his ministers haven't waited to find out, they've fled the country. The International Criminal Court will probably issue warrants for their arrest."

We drove in silence for a while. Then I asked:

"What about the rest of Zajc's gang?"

"We used the pilots of that A400M, as you suggested. Had them fly their complicated route back but with Blue and Green Teams in the cargo bay. Surprised them at every single stop. They took one or two casualties but we've pretty much rounded up the entire gang. Not to mention about two dozen terrified teenage girls they found in Kukes. They're getting physical and psychiatric help at the moment. Then we'll try to repatriate them but I'm doubtful if we'll find their families alive."

"Poor kids."

"Thanks to you, there won't be any more of those poor kids. So, Jim, total success, the whole mission. Bob Cressington's riding high. Everyone's riding high, for that matter."

Signs for the exit appeared ahead. He deselected auto-drive and we left the highway. I steered the conversation in the new direction.

"I wasn't expecting a media frenzy. Why did Bob go public? Whatever happened to covert operations?"

"Hah!" He glanced my way. "You want my take on it?"

"You bet I do."

"All right. This is the way I see it. Harriet Nagel will be sworn in next month. No doubt she's already putting together a fresh administration. Bob wants the DoD. He's a front runner: he has relevant experience, he gets on well with Nagel, and he played a good hand in the Cawley affair. But there's stiff competition."

"Go on."

"Well, he's clinched the appointment, hasn't he? He's seen to it that everyone who matters knows he authorized this operation. I'd be surprised if he told his senior colleagues about that Press conference ahead of hand—he'd want to make sure no one would steal his thunder. They can bellyache as much as they like now but they'll be doing it behind closed doors. Bob and the whole operation have a very high profile. If they criticize him openly they'll do so at their own peril."

He moved out to overtake a line of cars. "I must say," he added, "he timed it to perfection. The election's over, the investiture's next month, and in the meantime there's a news vacuum. A media release headed 'American Special Forces operation rids the world of international sex and drugs racket' was more than any of those news hounds dared to hope for. Of course it wouldn't have worked so well without a hero. That's where you come in. I'm afraid it's the price of success, my friend."

"Lovely. So to help Bob with his political manoeuvring my face gets plastered all over the media."

"You haven't done badly out of it, Jim. I don't know of anyone else who's gone from captain to bird colonel in little more than two years."

"Yeah, well I shouldn't think anyone else would like to try it my way."

He chuckled. "Possibly not."

We slowed up, turned into the base, and stopped at the checkpoint. The sentries looked in, saluted us, and opened the barrier.

"Incidentally," Harken said as we cruised up the short drive. "You've been recommended for a Distinguished Service Cross. I gather the award ceremony is next month."

I turned to look at him. "Was that Bob's doing as well?"

"Actually, no."

Our eyes met.

"Was it—?"

"Come on, Jim, you know better than to ask. I'll drop you here. Dinner's in the big hall tonight. Nineteen hundred hours. There's a special guest. Try to be on time, won't you?"

62

The long journey and the general excitement were beginning to take their toll, so back in my quarters I thought I'd put my feet up for a bit. I must have dozed off. When I woke up I yawned, opened my eyes wide, and tried to shake the cobwebs out of my head. Then I looked at my watch. It was already seven o'clock. I jumped to my feet, splashed my face and neck with water, ran a comb through my hair, and hurried over to the mess.

As I came in they all rose to their feet and clapped. Just about the entire camp was there. Someone took me by the arm.

"Over here, Colonel," he said as he led me to a seat at the top table, next to Harken. Then, as he left, he clapped me on the shoulder and murmured, "Fucking ace, man, fucking ace."

I noticed that the tables were crammed with cans of beer. Normally we didn't drink in the camp. Even now it hadn't registered. Still in a daze, I turned to Harken.

"Who's the special guest?"

"You haven't guessed? It's you."

My mouth dropped open, but before I could close it he'd got to his feet and banged on the table with a spoon.

"Gentlemen," he said, "as you know, we've come together to celebrate a well planned and well executed mission. Here's to the leader of that mission, Colonel Slater, and to the SAF!"

He raised his glass and everyone did the same. Then there was a lot of drumming of feet and cries of "Speech, speech!"

I stood reluctantly and looked around at a sea of expectant faces.

"I don't know what the fuss is about," I said. "I was lounging about in a hospital bed while you guys did the hard work."

There was a chorus of protests. I held up a hand and it died away.

"I'd just like to say this. In the past I've often felt this Force was underappreciated. We trained like stink, we put our lives on the line, and we lost some damned fine men." I paused, my mouth tightening at the memory. Those men included Gerry and Sef. If only they could have been here…

I realized the room had gone silent and continued quickly.

"Outside of this camp, no one knew, and no one gave a damn. Well, it seems to me those days are over!"

There were a lot of cheers and slapping of hands on the tables.

"Now we have the leadership we've always wanted—both here, and in Washington. So let's drink to those who couldn't be with us tonight—and to better times ahead!"

After dinner was over the evening continued in a riotous fashion. Looking around, I realized I'd never known morale to be so high and I felt good about that. I would have enjoyed it more except the high spirits only served to enlarge the void left in this gathering by my absent comrades.

Harken pushed his chair back. He didn't say anything and I assumed at first he'd gone to talk to someone, but then I saw him slip quietly out of the door. I realized that this was what the senior officers did, and it pained me to think of the way it would distance me from these guys from now on. I made my excuses and left the party in full swing.

*

The next four weeks passed in a blur. Initially there were press conferences to attend. As soon as the interest faded, as I knew it must, we had a fresh challenge on our hands. It was now general knowledge that the SAF was an elite outfit and the publicity brought in a huge wave of applications. Funds were limited, but Bob Cressington was willing to support a modest expansion in the Force. Because I was second-in-command I had to help Harken sift through them.

We had to be exacting in our standards and we rejected a lot of good men and women along the way. Finally we had a short list and conducted the interviews jointly. Just before the first candidate came in, Harken said to me, with his usual charm:

"Remember, we only want the cream, Jim. We're not scraping the barrel like we did when you were appointed."

"Thanks, Wendell," I said. "I'll bear that in mind."

With the interviews over and induction arranged for the successful applicants I hoped the administrative burden would slacken. It didn't. In keeping with his promotion, Harken had been put in charge of two other units and he had to divide his time between us, them, and Washington. He was still based at Fort Piper, but I had to run things when he was away—which was often—so I was too busy to think about much else. Almost before I realized it, the time came for me to leave for the award ceremony in Washington.

It took place on the Rose Lawn of the White House so that it could be covered by the media. I wasn't the only recipient, of course, but I looked pretty damned sharp in my dress blues, and I felt as well turned out as anyone there. The President made a short speech, then he pinned the medals on each of us in turn. When he came to me, there were a few words and a handshake and it was over.

What stuck in my mind wasn't the moment of the award at all; it was my meeting with Harriet Nagel at the reception afterwards.

She extended her hand and as I took it she engaged my eyes and said quietly:

"The nation recognises you as a hero, Colonel, but I'm aware of the personal courage you've needed to reach this point. If there was a medal for that, by God, I'd give it to you."

I was taken aback. I knew she'd wanted to distance herself from what had happened to me. Here she was, acknowledging it, at least in private.

"Thank you, Madam President," I said.

She smiled. "Senator for now, Colonel. You can call me that after the investiture next month."

"It will be an honour to serve you in either capacity, Senator," I said. I meant it, too. This woman had real charisma. She was going to be a worthy leader of the nation.

She spoke again, dropping her voice almost to a whisper:

"Tell me something, Colonel. When you're on the battlefield, do you like to have men behind you whom you can trust?"

It was a rhetorical question.

"Of course, ma'am."

She fixed me again with those electric eyes. "Politics is a battlefield, too, Colonel." She took my hand again. "Great things lie in store. Put the past behind you. Keep scanning the horizon. Goodbye."

I stared after her. Even at this moment of my triumph, it was as if she had seen the pain still inside me, reached out, and touched it.

*

At the time I was too staggered to think about it any further. Later on, I considered what she'd said. She wanted people behind her she could trust. Was that what it sounded like: an invitation to enter politics? The idea was absurd! I enjoyed being a soldier, relished the action. Yet when I thought about it, how much action was I going to get, stuck behind a desk? It set me wondering. Prof was trying to defend freedom in his way and I'd been trying to defend it in mine. Maybe I could combine the two at some stage.

Thinking about Prof made me wonder why he wasn't at the reception. I realized with a lurch that the last time I'd seen him was at the school, after Suzanne and I were picked up by the secret service men. That was nearly three months ago. He was probably as busy as I was, but that was no excuse. I decided to contact him right away. I couldn't get a reply from his numbers so I phoned the lab. Andy Grierson picked up. He was a lot friendlier this time and invited me to come over to M.I.T.

He met me at the top of the steps. I remembered the first time I saw that magnificent staircase. It was on a holovision screen above my head and I was Jim Forbes, a half-paralysed soldier lying in a prison hospital bed, looking at a small figure in a wheelchair. He must have been just about where we were standing now.

Andy led me to his office. When we sat down I saw the expression on his face and my face fell.

"What is it?"

"Jim, Prof's in hospital. I'm sorry, there's no easy way to tell you this. He's dying."

63

A cold shock ran through my body. My mouth worked, but all I could say was:

"Dying? Why?"

"It's that disease: the one he had before. They said it wouldn't recur, but it has. It started with numbness and the odd stumble, but it's progressed incredibly fast this time." His voice had become curiously high. He swallowed. "I'm afraid there's not much time left."

"Isn't there anything they can do for him?"

"They offered him another brain transplant. He says he's not prepared to go through that again. There's an experimental treatment, which could be very unpleasant and may or may not work. He's refused that, too."

I dropped my chin to my chest and took a deep breath. An enormous feeling of emptiness had opened up inside me. Andy waited quietly. I came back to him.

"Can I see him?"

"Of course. I'll take you there myself."

*

I sat at his bedside. His arms lay thin and limp on the crisply turned white sheets; his head was propped up on pillows, the eyes closed. It was disturbing to look into that face, a face I'd shaved in the mirror so many times. The features were familiar enough, yet now the eyes were sunken and the skin, grey and dry as parchment, was stretched tightly over the cheek bones. It was like watching myself age and die.

I waited patiently, reluctant to disturb him. A faintly stale smell hung in the air.

He opened his eyes and they registered my presence.

"Good to see you, Jim."

"Good to see you too, Prof."

He moistened lips that were strangely thin and drained of colour. The words came slowly, a little blurred.

"I heard what happened. Who's governing Ubindi now?"

His brain is as sharp as ever. It's his body that's letting him down. My body.

"The military have taken over. But the U.S. is putting pressure on them to hold early elections. We're promising aid if they return to democracy—only this time the aid will be food and medicines, not armaments. The generals will have to listen. The glory days of drugs and arms are over. They're presiding over a country with no source of income."

"And Suzanne?"

"My guess is, she'll return to Ubindi when they announce the elections. She's popular, and she wasn't tainted by the corruption. There's a good chance she'll become President and form a government. The U.S. won't intervene, but the Secretary of State's made no secret of his support. I think she'll do great things for her country."

"And the two of you…?"

"That's over, Prof. Her choice, not mine."

"I'm sorry."

He closed his eyes, and I thought he'd gone to sleep, but a moment later, without opening them, he said:

"You got Zajc, I hear."

"Yes. I'd hoped to bring him back alive but they made sure it didn't happen. Still, it's put a stop to the drugs and the arms and the sex trafficking. You had a big hand in that, Prof."

"You made it happen, Jim. But I'm glad I could help."

My throat constricted. I leaned forward.

"Prof, you must let the medics do something for you. You can't leave everything behind like this."

"I'm touched by your concern, Jim, but believe me, I'm quite happy. I want to make a dignified exit this time. Andy will carry on the work, and his success will be mine, too."

"You mustn't give up, Prof. I do have a say in this, you know: that's me you're inhabiting."

He opened his eyes and smiled. "No, Jim."

He took a deep breath and, with what seemed like a monumental effort, he lifted a hand and tapped the side of my head with a painfully clawed finger.

"You are up here."

*

A week later he died peacefully in his sleep.

The crematorium chapel was crowded. As I came in I spotted Bob Cressington, Don Machin, and Tony Sant'ana near the front. I took a place in the last row, aiming to be well away from anyone I knew. Behind me people were still arriving and standing at the back.

My eyes were drawn to the black-draped coffin in the central aisle. Inside was a body I remembered in its prime, a fit body, hardened by training, scarred in battle. It should have lasted another sixty years or more. What could Prof only have achieved in that time! What discoveries he could have made, what knowledge passed on!

I looked down, shaking my head.

This shouldn't be happening. It's such a waste. It's such a lousy, goddamned waste.

I noticed a printed programme on the shelf in front of me and picked it up. The proceedings would be completely secular, as I'd expected. There would be addresses by Bob Cressington on behalf of the U.S. government, and from the President of M.I.T. In between, there'd be readings of poems. Andy Grierson would give the main oration.

The committal was to be accompanied by Vaughan Williams' *Fantasia on a Theme by Thomas Tallis*. Apparently it was one of Prof's favourites. I suppose I could understand that better than most. It speaks of a pastoral England in centuries gone by, and at heart he was still a great Englishman.

Bob Cressington relayed a message of sympathy from President Harriet Nagel, who was abroad, and spoke on her behalf and that of the nation. Society owed Prof an untold debt, he said, for making the world a safer place to live in. He also registered his personal sorrow at the loss of a valued colleague.

When the time came for Andy to take the rostrum he had some difficulty controlling his voice. Reading from notes, he described Prof's early career, his brilliance, his pioneering work, but also his approachability.

"He tackled the greatest problems of the day, yet no problem was too small for him. Whether it was something that wouldn't work in the lab, or a personal difficulty, he was unfailingly supportive, generous with his time and with his wisdom and advice. Those attributes will be remembered with gratitude and affection by generations of students who passed through his lab.

"He believed implicitly in the value of what he was doing,

but he was also aware of the dangers and he had the courage to speak openly about them. I'd like to read you part of a transcript of a speech he made to the American Freedom Society. It could well serve as his epitaph. Here it is.

"'Every advance in the world of information technology is quickly exploited by the enemies of society. You have only to think of the Internet. Invented originally by physicists as a means of exchanging research data, it became the information highway of the world, a resource that served every area of communication and commerce. And in no time it also became the channel for computer viruses, for lies and propaganda, for sex traffickers, con men, perverts, and mass murderers. We are therefore in a constant race, to provide the new technology that enhances our lives while staying ahead of crime, terrorism, and threats to national security.

"'Somewhere, caught in the middle of this race, are decent law-abiding citizens, already being monitored in more ways than they can possibly realize. My friends, there is nothing new about systematic spying on the general population. It was practised routinely during the Roman Empire, the English Civil War, the French Revolution, and—a century ago—in Eastern Europe after the Second World War. It has reached new levels of sophistication in Georgia, South Ossetia, and Abkhazia since those territories were annexed by the Russian Union. But the technology that is currently emerging enables surveillance to be carried out on a scale, and with an efficiency, that previous regimes could only have dreamed of.

"'It would be a supreme irony—would it not?—if this great nation, which has so often defended the freedoms of other peoples, should deny those freedoms to the people within its own borders. We must vigorously oppose any such trend, not just because it is in our own interests but because if we let it happen here it will spread like a cancer.

"'We cannot declare an end to technological progress: that would be to abandon the race. But we must, as a society, place limits on the way the technology is used.

"'Those who govern will try to assure you that their responsibilities to you are recognized and taken seriously. But the art of politics, my friends, is to say one thing and to do quite another. We must ensure that their words are reflected in their actions, that processes are in place which will enable us to detect the guilty, yet protect the innocent.

"'What is at stake is our privacy, our liberty, and our freedom.'"

Andy looked up, his eyes swimming with tears.

"Goodbye, Prof, and thank you."

As he went back to his seat, hastily pulling a tissue from his pocket, the strains of the *Tallis Fantasia* floated out over the audience.

Suddenly the implications crashed in on me and I began to panic. That coffin contained Jim Forbes, and it was me sliding into the flames! My heart pounded, and sweat beaded my forehead. Over that serene music I could hear the faint roar of the furnace and it seemed to grow louder and louder in my ears. To keep myself from shouting I had to clench my fists so hard that the nails bit into my palms. I closed my eyes, told myself it was psychosomatic, a purely emotional reaction. Nothing helped. By the time the curtains had closed and the music had faded away I was drenched in sweat. Everyone sat down, and I dropped limply into my seat and didn't move.

After a while I heard a hesitant cough and looked up. The benches were empty. The staff, attired in black, were waiting patiently for me to leave so that they could bring in the next group. I muttered an apology, got to my feet, and hurried out.

I didn't want to see or speak to anybody so I cut off behind the building, where there was a cemetery set in an area of parkland. I headed into it, taking the path between the trees. Fallen leaves crisped under my feet and flew and tumbled across the grass to lodge, quivering, against the gravestones. I opened my tunic and the breeze searched my body with chill fingers.

As I walked, the grey, lichen-scarred slabs passed me in their serried ranks on either side. It was as if I'd been transported to a parallel universe, populated by silent sentinels, waiting quietly for me to join them.

I felt at peace and oddly liberated. Could that be right? I had just paid my final respects to a great man, someone I'd set out to assassinate, and who instead had become my friend. It was just as Andy had said in his address: he'd sat down, made my problem his problem, and helped me to solve it. Now he was dead. So why this lightness of spirit?

It took a while to sink in. So long as Jim Forbes's body existed it remained a permanent rebuke, a reminder of what I had been, what I could have been. Now Jim Forbes had gone forever. There was only one of me, not two. I was Jim Slater. I'd fought, and I'd come through it. I'd loved, and I'd lost, and I'd come through that. I'd been wounded and felt the pain and seen the blood flowing from my body, and I'd come through that, too. I didn't need a passport or a driving licence or a colleague or even a lover to tell me who I was. Not anymore.

I knew who I was.

I fastened my tunic, squared my shoulders, and turned back to re-enter my world.

ALSO BY STANLEY SALMONS, PUBLISHED BY FINGERPRESS:

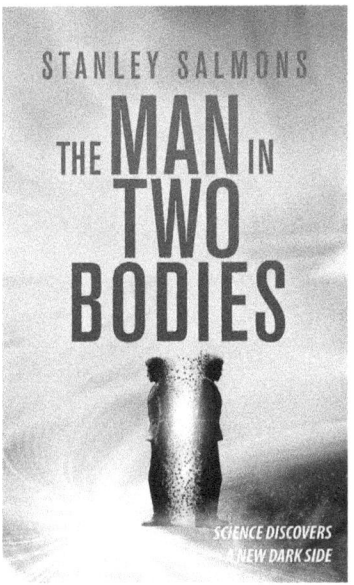

THE POWER TO BE IN TWO PLACES AT ONCE

Maverick scientist Rodge Dukas works in a damp basement surrounded by outlandish equipment. His discovery could propel humanity to a new Golden Age; but student friends Mike and Suzy have other ideas. Their increasingly reckless crime spree has the police baffled, but could only ever end in disaster.

"Because the author has a background in biomedical engineering, he makes the science parts of the book fascinating – and understandable"
- Jennifer Stewart, write101.com

ALSO AVAILABLE FROM FINGERPRESS:

A WORLD OF RESISTANCE,
BETRAYAL AND OPPRESSION

THE EVIL THAT MEN DO combines Fredrik Nath's trademark themes of love, betrayal, Nazi atrocities, suspense and an ending that will catch you off guard. This bleak-to-lavish war romance is a compelling tale of bravery in the face of evil.

inkflash.com/FredrikNath

Lightning Source UK Ltd.
Milton Keynes UK
UKHW010613121220
375051UK00001B/113